CHASM

CHASM

STEPHEN LAWS

PS Publishing Ltd / Grosvenor House /
1 New Road / Hornsea, HU18 1PG / England

editor@pspublishing.co.uk / www.pspublishing.co.uk

CONTENTS

CONTENTS

CONTENTS

CONTENTS

For my son, Jonathan.

ACKNOWLEDGMENTS

I'd like to thank Harry James of James Associates for allowing me to "assist" with the destruction of Killingworth town centre. Also, Mike Hunter of ScotDem Ltd, whose company had the demolition contract for the job, and whose horror stories about the dangers of dealing with pre-stressed cable encased in concrete have left me anxious about being in any building with four walls and a roof.

Once again, ADO Mike Reid, MIFireE, Emergency Planning/Hazardous Materials Officer, Tyne and Wear Metropolitan Fire Brigade, and Greg Holmes, Regional Health Emergency Planning Officer, Northumbria Ambulance Service (NHS Trust).

Pam Robinson, Sue Dick and Jacqueline Campbell for Managing The Monsters.

Steve Clarehugh and the members of Northumbrian Microlights.

'The evil that men do lives after them,
The good is oft interred with their bones.'

William Shakespeare, *Julius Caesar*

'Curtis thought about the stories he'd written over the years,
thought of the accidents and the murders and the tragedies.
For the first time, it seemed that he was aware of the true
nature of anguish and grief . . . and maybe even love. Were
those emotions real and tangible? Did they have solidity?
Had they been raging invisibly all around him at the scenes
of his reports, an expended flux of energy, invisible yet
somehow concrete? Real energy. Somehow, when expended
by the people who had created those energies, could they
become independent of the people who had created them?
And, once expended, could those forces really shape the
world? Unseen, and dismissed by the cynical and the weary
and the hopeless. But somehow the greatest forces in the
world.'

Antony Curtis,
Reporter for the *Independent Daily*
(*Somewhere South of Midnight*)

BOOK ONE | QUAKE

ONE YEAR LATER

J AY TOOK THE STREET CORNER AT SIXTY AND struggled to control the car as it slewed up onto its front and rear left-hand side wheels. He'd seen the stunt performed by experts on television a lifetime ago, couldn't believe that it was happening to him now . . . and yelled out loud in panic as he wrestled with the wheel. The car wobbled and swerved up onto the pavement, clipping the corner of a building and shearing away the trim in a welter of buzz-saw sparks. Jay wrenched at the wheel again to prevent the car from being flipped onto its back by the impact, and it slammed back down onto its suspension, cracking the rear window. And now the wheel was spinning madly in his hands as the car swerved all over the road, the headlights flashing over ruined and looted buildings.

He couldn't lose control now.

Not with the Vorla somewhere behind, hurtling through the night after him. He could feel it rushing after the car, could feel his skin crawling and knew how badly it wanted to get him.

"Jesus . . . "

A rubbish bin bounced onto the hood, disgorging crap all over the windscreen. Jay hit the wipers, cleared enough space through rotting vegetables and fruit to see that if he continued on down this street, it would take him straight to the edge of the Chasm. Pulling hard over to the right, he took the car around the corner of another burned-out building and finally got the vehicle on the straight. That's when he saw the Vorla in his rear-view mirror, exploding around that last street corner in its hunt for him. The tyres screeched. Hearing the sound, the Vorla gushed across the street in his direction. Jay slammed his foot down hard on the accelerator and took another corner at speed. He didn't know where the hell he was now. Could he swerve the car around, aim the headlights at the damned thing? But what then? His only hope was to put enough distance between him and it, abandon the car and try to make it on foot.

But it can smell you, Jay. It can smell the scent of your fear. It'll just keep on following that scent.

"Fuck it!"

The car screeched past the burned-out front of a grocery store, its valuable contents long since destroyed or looted—and then Jay cried out aloud again when he saw what was in the street before him.

He slammed on the brakes.

There were two—no, three—people in the middle of the street, frozen in the headlights. They had been hurrying across in the darkness, but had frozen when they'd heard the sounds of screeching tyres getting nearer and nearer. Unsure of which way to run, waiting in terror to see if the danger would pass them by, their fear had immobilised them. One of them was holding out his or her hands in an instinctive *"Stop!"* gesture as the car screeched and slid, with smoke rising from its tyres. Jay wrenched the wheel hard over and the car hit the pavement hard. His hands flew from the wheel to protect his face as the car exploded through the plate-glass windows of a fashion store. Bouncing and jerking with glass exploding on the roof and past the windows. The impact winded Jay; the seatbelt constricting his chest. He coughed and gagged for air.

One of the headlights had shattered, but the other still glared into the store. Suddenly, it seemed that the car was surrounded by human figures, all frozen in grotesque poses, their angular shadows all around him.

And there was a severed human arm on the hood of the car.

No, not a real human arm. It was the arm of a shop dummy, a department-store mannequin. At last, he realised that there were mannequins all around him, some of them smashed to pieces by the car as it came through the window.

Was the arm on the hood somehow smoking?

No, the smoke wasn't coming from the arm. It was coming from under the hood of the car. Something had ruptured there. Now smoke was rising in front of the cracked windscreen, and he could smell the petrol.

There was a blur of movement in the wing mirror and his door was suddenly yanked open—and now Jay could see the people that he had nearly run down. These were not people that he knew. These were other survivors: two men and a young woman, in rags and with a look of horror on their faces that he knew only too well. They were starved. The older man had pulled open his door while the other two clambered around to the other side of the car.

"You're one of *them*, aren't you?" snapped the older man, jabbing at him with a rusted iron railing. "One of those murdering bastards!"

"You've got . . ." Jay struggled to find his voice. "You've got . . . to get off the street!" Wincing at the pain in his whiplashed neck, he looked fearfully back out onto the street, knowing what could not be far behind. "It's coming after me . . ."

"We've been hiding here for a year," said the old man angrily, jabbing with the railing again. Up close, Jay could see that he wasn't old at all. The dirt and the scarring just made him look that way. "Hiding in these ruins for a whole bloody year, while you and your kind have hunted the others down like animals.

9

Now, we've got one of *you*, haven't we? Let's see how you like it, you bastard!"

"I'm not one of them," gasped Jay, slapping out at the iron railing. "And you've got to get off the street. *Now!*"

The woman had reached the passenger door. Did she believe him?

"You must have *something* to eat," she gasped. "It doesn't matter what. Anything. We've been hiding all this time. Please, you've got to . . ."

There was a sound from the street. A rumbling murmur, like the distant thunder of an approaching storm. The Vorla was coming.

"Get out of the street!" yelled Jay, finding his breath and startling the woman. "Hide!"

"We're *sick* of hiding!" yelled the younger man, suddenly yanking the passenger door open and clawing inside. Jay grabbed the shotgun lying on the passenger seat, raising it awkwardly in a one-handed grip.

"Back off!"

And then the older man lunged into the car, jabbing with the railing as the younger man tried to yank the shotgun out of his hands.

"We only want food!" screamed the woman.

Jay kicked out at the older man, tried to jam his elbow back into that blackened face as the younger man finally seized the shotgun barrel. Somewhere beyond, the young woman was screaming.

"You *idiots!*" yelled Jay.

His finger tightened involuntarily on the trigger. The explosive roar within the car was more than deafening. It stunned the senses of all three as the windscreen was blown out in an explosive spray of glass shards. The girl's screaming became hysterical, but Jay was the first to recover. The younger man had recoiled in shock as, with both hands on the recovered shotgun, Jay jabbed the stock viciously into the older man's face. He grunted and slithered away from the door as Jay scrambled quickly out of the car, kicking him out of the way. Banging the gun barrel down across the car roof, he pointed it directly at the younger man on the other side. He staggered away from the car, eyes wild, and held his hands up in sur-render. The woman sobbed uncontrollably, both hands clasped to her face and hopping from shredded foot to shredded foot on the broken glass that littered the destroyed storefront. Jay stood aside as the older man pulled himself up against the side of the car. Clutching his bloodied face he lurched hand over hand around the car to join the others. Now, the smell of petrol was overpowering, making Jay gag. They began heading back into the street.

"Not that way!" hissed Jay, rubbing at his neck. He looked around at the jumble of fashion dummies lying scattered over the store carpet. Their tangled limbs made it look like some bizarre, bloodless slaughter had taken place in here. "There must be another way out of here. Follow me . . ."

But when he turned back, his attackers had fled back into the street, out of sight.

He started after them.

And then he heard that familiar, sickening sound.

Like the sound of a crowd mumbling; or the underground rumbling of some poisonous river. The sound that was like a million whispering voices.

Moments later, the two men and their woman companion began to scream in terror and agony. High-pitched, whooping cries of torment.

Jay felt ill, as if he might vomit. Swallowing hard, he backed carefully away from the car, trying to avoid standing on glass and giving away his presence. The sounds continued, rising in agony. But the street outside was still empty. Whatever was happening was taking place just out of his range of vision, and for that he was grateful.

Something ignited under the hood of the car with a soft

whump! The hood jarred open an inch and smoke began to gush into the department store. Blue fire was surging and roaring in the engine. Jay saw drops of liquid blue fire dropping to the floor beneath the car, igniting a spreading lake of burning petrol.

Frantically, he looked around for a way out and could find none.

Should he run back out onto the street and take his chance there?

Jay heard the thousand-thousand whispering, hungry voices out there as the Vorla fed eagerly, taking its insane pleasure from the hideous torment that was being inflicted on its latest victims. The voices were still racked in agony, but somehow muted and further away—as if they had been lifted, and absorbed.

Christ, no! Not back out there!

Should he stay here in the store, take shelter, and hope that he wouldn't be burned alive?

Flames began to leap around the car as Jay sprinted across the store, leaping over the jumbled dummies. He whirled as the flames illuminated the interior. He could feel the pounding of his heart in his chest and his throat when he saw the Exit door sign on the other side of the store. Still clutching the shotgun, he ran to it.

Please God, after everything that's happened. Let that door be open. Let it be OPEN*!*

Part of him refused to believe it when that door did swing open.

Flames from behind illuminated the small alleyway beyond, his silhouette leaping gigantically ahead of him. There was only the sound of surging flame behind him now, the noises of feeding and torment drowned. He swung the door shut.

And in the same instant, the car exploded with a shuddering roar. Off to his left, a store window cascaded into the darkness around him, raining fire and a shower of broken glass.

12

Something beyond the store began to scream.

Something that was not human.

Jay ran down the alley as smoke began to drift behind him. There were double-gates ahead in the gloom, but he wouldn't have to climb them. The bolts were easily withdrawn and in the next moment, he was out onto a side street and running as fast as he could.

The sounds of screaming faded behind him.

The whispering, obscene voices were gone.

But as he ran, Jay knew that the danger was far from over.

He had to find somewhere to rest, somewhere to orientate himself. Somewhere he could work out in his mind the implications of everything that had happened since the nightmare of Day One, and just what the hell he was going to do to get away from the Vorla and back to the others.

He had no idea how far he'd run, knew that he could only go so far in any one direction before he reached the brink of the Chasm again. When he saw the unbroken shop frontage of an electricals shop, and could also see that the door was open, he knew that he could run no further. The poor bastards back there had probably ended up saving his life and buying him some time. Not to mention the burning car. He staggered through the doorway, only pausing to look back to make sure that the horde of voices and the darkness was not sweeping up the street after him. There was no relief in the desolate quiet of the empty street. It could come anytime, anywhere. Without warning.

Deep inside the shop, surrounded by shelves of silent televisions, DVD recorders and music centres, Jay slumped to the floor and dropped the shotgun at his side. He sat for a long time, just getting his ragged breathing back to normal again, feeling the blood pounding in his temples and his ears. Letting it all settle down.

But the deep, icy knot of anxiety would not go away.

And then he saw the dictation machines on the shelf beside him. Leaning over, he picked one up.

There were batteries inside, and a tape. When he looked more carefully, he could see other packets of batteries; other boxes of blank tapes.

He smiled grimly.

"Jay O'Connor," he said in a cracked voice. He looked at the dictation machine in his hand for a long time, weighing up. "This is Your Life."

He pressed the RECORD button.

And began to speak.

| CHAPTER ONE | THE JOURNAL OF JAY O'CONNOR: HOW IT HAPPENED |

I ALWAYS HATED MONDAYS AT SCHOOL.
Nothing unusual about that, I suppose. Lots of kids do. But when I waved goodbye to Burleigh High, I never thought that I'd be back there four years later, working as the school janitor. And just when I thought I couldn't hate Monday mornings any more than I did back then, I found that I hated them with a vengeance.

And it was my hatred which destroyed Burleigh High at exactly 12:30 p.m. on Monday, 22 April.

I knew that something bad was going to happen that day. Don't ask me how. I'd just had this feeling from the moment I got out of bed. There hadn't been any dreams. Normally, I dream a lot. But there hadn't been a thing that night. Maybe that means something; then again, maybe not. All I know is that from the moment I pulled back the quilt, slung my legs over the side and crouched with my head in my hands, I just *knew* deep down in a way that was impossible to describe. Even the air in the bedroom smelled different. I always slept with the window open, no matter what kind of weather, as if some special fresh breeze might come through that window to blow away the frustration and the anger, changing my life. Was today the day?

Something's going to happen, I thought, as I sat bent over on the end of the bed, waiting for the hangover clouds in my mind to clear. I remember asking myself aloud: "What?", rubbing my face hard to help wake me up.

Don't know. Something different. But not good. No doubt about it.

Just how different, I couldn't have guessed in a zillion years.

It was 6:17 a.m. with another six hours to go before my rage blew everything apart.

The taste of last night's lager was rank and foul in my mouth. When I ran my tongue around in there, I didn't seem to recognise the feel of my own teeth. I needed something to get rid of that taste. I'd had worse hangovers in my time, but today there was a throbbing dullness behind my eyes. Yawning, I staggered from the bedroom and across the landing to the bathroom. Once inside, I rinsed with mouthwash and attacked that stranger's mouth with a foaming toothbrush, looking at myself in the bathroom mirror. Short black hair. Eyes green. Like my mother's, I'd been told by the late sad bastard who had been my father. I'd never known her, but I knew that she'd killed something inside Dad when she'd left the area and moved south to live with her then brother-in-law. Messy business. But that's life, I suppose. That had been when I was . . . let's see . . . four years old. I can't really remember any time we spent together, but we had two or three photographs scattered about somewhere, and for the first time that morning, when I looked at myself, I could see that there was a real resemblance between us. There's a scar above my left eyebrow, and I guess you could call it a badge of honour. A kid had called my mother a whore when I was thirteen. One punch had put that kid in hospital and got me expelled. Later, a bunch of the same kid's friends had caught me in a back alley on this run-down housing estate. They'd thought it was going to be an easy punishment. But even though they left me lying in the overturned garbage from a rubbish bin, with two broken ribs, a split head, and the gash above my left eyebrow, I gave three of them reasons for a visit to Casualty. When I looked at the scar on the morning of Day One, it seemed like a lot of trouble to have taken for a woman who'd packed her bags and left us. I tried to control the rising anger again, but knowing what lay ahead of me that day, it was an impossible task.

The anger was still with me, simmering on a low burn, as I walked across the school playground towards the storage room. The sun was low, just rising above the surrounding rooftops, and the shadows of the school buildings lay deep around the cinder-block building. I'd gone to this school as a kid, had played in the very same yard; had thrown a rubber ball against the wall of that very storage building. The steel door had been painted since then. But that seemed to be the only change. I could never have dreamed then that I'd be stepping into the caretaker's old shoes four years after leaving Burleigh High School.

I hunted for the key in my pockets. My overalls were in there; the not-so-new uniform I'd been wearing these past four months since the court hearing. I turned the key in the lock and began to shoulder the door open.

And then, when the voice came from behind me, it seemed that I was catapulted back to those early days. Suddenly it was like I was a kid again.

"Late again, O'Connor?"

I turned, squinting into the sun as it rose over the school roof and silhouetted the stocky figure who had suddenly appeared from nowhere. I sidestepped out of the sun, shading my eyes.

It was the head teacher, Stafford. The man who'd tried to bully so-called sense into me when I was a less-than-model pupil at this school. Four years on, it seemed that I'd been brought back to this place so that Stafford could try and finish the job.

"Second time this week," he said, hands behind his back, rising up on his toes as if getting the extra height would somehow give him an edge. It made him look like an old-time copper on the beat.

"There's time," I said, still shading my eyes. "It's not seven yet."

Now I could see his face properly for the first time. Still the same white hair and white eyebrows. Still the same horn-rimmed glasses, magnifying his hooded eyes. The same tweed jacket and tobacco-stained teeth. Still the same old bastard.

"But work for you begins when you've signed the book in the main building. You haven't done that yet. And those are the rules."

"Look, I'm here, aren't I? I'm just getting the stuff I need, and then I'll sign the book when I get into the school."

"You never were any good at rules, O'Connor. That's why you've turned out the way you have, and why you're right back here where you started. Now, as to rules and procedures—do I have to remind you of the terms of your community service sentence?"

He smiled then, because I reckon he could hear me gritting my teeth. I could still remember that day in court vividly. My "friends" Sean and Forker had robbed a petrol station, while I was sitting in the back of the car. I thought they'd gone in there to buy cigarettes, hadn't known what they were going to do. There was a high-speed car chase when a cruising panda car was flagged down by the outraged owner. Sean and Forker got away, but I wasn't so lucky. Four years after I thought I'd waved goodbye to the place—and the person—I hated most in the world, I was standing in the dock before that very same person: Frederick Stafford. Not only a headmaster, it seemed, but also a local Justice of the Peace. I can't tell you how I felt when I saw him sitting there. You wouldn't have to use much imagination. At first I hoped that with so many kids passing through his hands he wouldn't remember me. But as soon as the power-mad bastard looked down on me, removing those horn-rimmed glasses, I knew that he not only remembered, but was getting a very real pleasure from seeing me there.

Surprise, surprise. I was found guilty.

Sean and Forker, my "friends," got off scot-free. Naturally, I lost my job at the car plant where I'd been working since leaving school.

Stafford sentenced me to a hundred hours of community service, feeling that "manual work of a socially responsible nature" would have more effect on me than a fine or a custodial sentence. And it just so happened that, since Stafford's school caretaker had recently been taken into hospital with appendicitis, I found myself carrying out those very duties until such time as he was fit for work again. My first reaction was to challenge the system. Surely Stafford was bending the rules? Was he *allowed* to do this? I would take on any other job. Digging trenches somewhere. Planting flowerbeds in old folks' homes. But not working for *him*. Wouldn't the caretakers trade union have something to say about it? And that was when I found out that Stafford also had a third role in life. He was a councillor for the local authority with a strong trades union connection. It seemed that every string that could be pulled was in Stafford's hands . . . so all I could do was bite the bullet; sweep the yard, clean the floors, the windows, and the toilets, and generally put up with every bit of crap that Stafford threw my way until my hundred hours were up. He was enjoying every minute. That's why he was there that morning at school, well before seven in the morning, when school didn't start until nine. Just trying to catch me out. Find some way to get me infringing the rules of that community service order, no matter how slight. He'd made it clear from the start that if I stepped out of line just once, then my sentence would be subject to review.

"I'm waiting for my answer, O'Connor," he said, rising up on the balls of his feet again.

"No, Mr. Stafford. You don't have to remind me of anything."

"Think you can get into the main building and sign the register before seven? Let's see. That's about . . . fifty seconds. Isn't it?"

I started towards the school, head down.

"Well, lock the storage room *door*, then! It was locked before you opened it, wasn't it?"

I halted, head still down. The anger had become fury. But there was nothing I could do about it. I turned back to the door, dragged it shut, and locked it. I could feel my face burning.

"Good. And that leaves . . . thirty seconds."

I started across the schoolyard again towards the main entrance.

"Only twenty-five, O'Connor. Better *run!*"

Aware of Stafford still standing and watching two hundred yards behind me, I let myself in through the front door of the school. On the table before me, already laid out neat and tidy, was what Stafford liked to call the "signing-in" book. I strode to it, and when I signed in the time, 7:01 a.m., the pen tore through the paper.

I walked back out into the schoolyard.

Stafford was nowhere to be seen.

Collecting up the bucket, mop, cans of cleaning fluid, and everything else I needed, I headed back indoors. Five minutes later, I was sweeping the mop across the assembly hall floor. That's when the other feeling came back; the first feeling I'd had when I woke up that morning. I knew—just *knew*—that something was going to happen. But now I felt that it was imminent, and was something to do with me. It's difficult to put this into words, but I could feel that something was going to happen *inside* me. Strange, but I felt cold inside now. Cold and waiting for that *something* bad to start happening. Any time now.

My face felt like stone as I continued "serving my community" that morning, before the kids arrived. I tried to put all of my frustrations into that simple task, using each stroke of the mop to get the frustrations out. By the time I'd finished, I felt a little better. The gnawing knot in my stomach hadn't exactly gone away, but I felt more in control. Still, the feeling of "something coming" was just as real as before.

If I'd only known what a short time I had to wait.

My last task was to make sure the toilets were clean before the school day began. It was the job I hated most. I caught sight of my own face in the communal mirror as I filled a bucket with water. I looked old this morning; my skin was white, my eyes bloodshot. Was it just the hangover, or was I getting a flash-forward view to what I'd be like in thirty or forty years' time? Now that I'd lost my job courtesy of my "friends," and got a criminal record in the process, would I still be cleaning out people's toilets then? I shuddered, cursing when the water began to overflow. I put everything into the work. Slowly, bit by bit, the anger would fade away altogether.

I was putting away the cleaning materials in the cinderblock storage building when the school bell rang, announcing lunch break. By the time I'd locked up again, kids were thundering down corridors and out across the yard.

"*O'Connor!*"

Stafford was standing directly ahead of me at the double doors leading into the main school block, in the same pose he'd adopted in the schoolyard. Hands clasped behind his back, raising himself up on tiptoes and down again, exerting his authority. This time he was angry—very angry.

"O'Connor," he repeated, this time trying to contain the anger.

I finally drew level, and fixed him in the eye, staring him out.

"Are you," he continued, closing his eyes as if this could help him from flying into a rage, "or are you not in charge of cleaning the urinals?"

"Apparently."

"Are you, or are you *not*, in charge of cleaning them, O'Connor?"

"Yes, that's one of my jobs."

"Yes, *Mister* Stafford."

"Yes, Mr. Stafford . . . I clean the toilets and do all of the other shitty jobs you feel I should be doing."

Stafford kept his eyes closed, one hand moving from behind so that he could stroke his temple with his forefinger, as if he were feeling for a "loss-of-control" button there.

"Follow me," he said, turning sharply to push through the double doors, holding one open without looking back to see whether I was following; pausing to snap at a couple of kids who were running towards him. The kids slowed to walk past. I grinned at them and winked. They were too frightened of the old bastard to acknowledge it. Stafford strode to the toilets. Now what? Reaching the door, he held it open. I stopped, waiting for an instruction. Stafford kept his head down, looking at the floor, and then indicated impatiently that I should walk on through. Fists clenched, I pushed past him into the main area. The door banged as Stafford came in behind. There was only one kid in there, looking over his shoulder as he stood at the urinal.

"Hurry up, boy!" snapped Stafford, and the kid zipped up quickly, grimacing and hurrying stiff-legged to the wash-basins when he realised that he hadn't been able to finish properly. Quickly wringing his hands under the tap, the boy dashed towards the door, wiping his hands on his jacket lapels. Without turning, I could see Stafford in the toilet mirrors. He was closing his eyes again to control his temper. I turned slowly. When I spoke, I tried to keep my voice calm.

"So . . . what?"

Stafford ran a hand through his hair and marched past me to one of the cubicles. He shoved open the door with his hand and pointed inside.

"What?" I asked again.

"Come and see for yourself, O'Connor."

"You're telling me that the toilet isn't clean enough. Is that it?"

"Come and see, boy."

"First of all, I'm not a boy. Secondly, I clean those toilets three times a day. First thing in the morning, again in the afternoon, and then when school's out. Probably one time too many, but I do it because you tell me to . . ."

"Come *here*, O'Connor!"

"So if the toilets get a little *unclean* in between times, then it's hardly my fault, is it? Mr. Stafford, sir? After all, that's what they're there for, isn't it? To put dirty stuff down."

"Do I have to enter insubordination and foul language into my report?"

I stalked across to Stafford, looking into the cubicle as he stood back.

Now I could see what had so upset my dear old headmaster. Someone had scrawled an obscenity on the tiled wall.

Stafford Sucks Shite.

I sighed, turning to look at him again. His eyes were closed once more, as if he couldn't bear to look at what was written there. When he spoke again, it was with great effort.

"It's your job"—he was forcing the words out—"to keep these toilets clean . . . and that . . . that . . . *filth* . . . is your . . . your . . ."

"My what? You're saying it's my responsibility?"

"Remove it. At once."

"You're saying that because one of the kids you've been bullying scrawls something on the wall, it's my fault?"

"It is your job to keep these cubicles clean."

"But it's my *fault*, is that right?"

"The culprit will be someone like yourself, O'Connor. Someone with absolutely no respect for authority."

"*Authority?* You want me to respect someone like you?" The

anger was out of control now. It was spiralling inside, rising to take me over.

"That's enough. Get that filth cleaned off at once."

"You've had a downer on me since the first day I walked into this school, Stafford. And it's not good enough that I managed to get through it all without you breaking me. You twisted all the rules and brought me back here as slave labour, just so you could have another go . . . "

"One more word and you'll be in severe trouble," said Stafford, marching past the cubicle and towards the main door. In the multiple mirror reflections, I could see that the colour had risen in both our faces.

"One word?" I snapped out as he passed. "How about two?"

Stafford paused as he pulled open the main door.

"Here they come, Stafford. *Fuck! Off!*"

And then he was gone, the door slapping behind him.

I stared at the door, feeling as if the anger in my eyes could burn a hole right through it, find Stafford on the other side and turn him into a ball of flames. Then, turning to the cubicle and seeing the graffiti again, I lunged forward to smack the palms of my hands against the tiled wall. The impact stung, but I didn't care. The pain was nothing compared to the spiralling hate inside. I leaned there, and suddenly I couldn't breathe. I hung my head, hands still braced against the wall; could feel and hear the blood singing in my ears. There was a lump in my gullet, and it was as if the hate had somehow become a blockage inside. More than that, it was growing and spreading; a physical thing, filling my insides. My eyes misted. I had kept the hate inside too long. It was somehow free now; free to spread and eat me alive unless I could find a way to let it out.

The graffiti was right before my eyes, on the tiled wall.

Stafford Sucks Shite.

My job in life. To clean off other people's toilet mess.

The anger exploded. Red mist speckled my vision.

I was out of control.

I began to punch the tiled wall. My knuckles were skinned. I was leaving blood smears on the cracked tiles, smudging the graffiti as I battered at the words. The sound and the feel of the tiles cracking killed any pain in my knuckles as I battered on and on. With each punch, each blow, the hate was streaming out of me and into the cubicle wall. As it left me, draining the great sickening knot inside, I could feel something else happening. I could feel the wall shaking, could hear a low grumbling as the hate streamed through the wall and on into the brickwork behind. Somehow, it was spreading to the entire school building. Now I could hear a shuddering, grumbling sound as the foundations of the school began to shake. But there was no way that I could stop now. I had to go on, had to keep punching at the wall, or those words, or that hate, was going to destroy me inside. Somewhere kids were wailing and shouting in fear. Above these sounds I heard a man's voice, shouting something I couldn't make out, as if he were trying to calm the kids but it wasn't working because he couldn't keep the terror out of his own voice. The commotion was drowned by a louder roar; as if a gigantic runaway express train were bearing down on the school, exploding through the classrooms, thundering in the corridors, crashing through the walls.

I collapsed to my knees, holding my bloodied hands before me in my lap. I gasped for breath. The hate was out of me now. Out of me and into the fabric of the building. I know that sounds crazy, but that was what was happening. In a moment, if I could just rest, I would be okay. The madness would go away, and then I could set about cleaning the wall and getting on with the rest of my community service sentence.

But why could I still hear the express train smashing through the school?

Why was the floor still shaking and shuddering where I knelt?

And as the throbbing of the blood in my ears dulled, why could I still hear the sounds of kids screaming?

This couldn't be happening.

I looked at the cubicle walls on either side of where I knelt. They were shaking. Somewhere beyond, there was a great shattering of glass. As if a mountain of it had been tipped into the schoolyard. It seemed then as if the screaming grew louder. And now the express train was the sound of a mountain avalanche, with tons of rock falling on the school roof and crashing through the toilet block walls. I clambered to my feet. Outright fear replaced my anger as I braced my hands on the cubicle walls, feeling them vibrate madly. I knew they'd suddenly collapse inwards and crush me. Something exploded above my head. When I looked, I could see a jagged crack in the plasterwork. The crack was still moving, still zigzagging away on all sides as chunks of plaster and white dust began to fall from the ceiling. I had a crazy image in my mind. There was a giant up there. He had brought his foot down on the roof. Now he was leaning all his weight on it, and the ceiling would cave in on top of me.

I yelled as the ceiling began to split and shift in mad, distorted patterns.

Beyond the cubicle, the mirrors shattered and fell apart.

There was a thundering roar of brickwork as another wall beyond the cubicle suddenly erupted inwards.

The giant's foot was coming down.

A chunk of plaster fell from directly ahead.

I lunged backwards, still yelling.

My hate was loose and destroying the school.

"I didn't mean it!" I screamed. "*I didn't mean it!*"

The plaster exploded before me on the toilet seat, shattering the enamel on either side and engulfing me in a choking white cloud.

Beneath me, the floor began to shift and grind and crack; just like the ceiling above.

"I DIDN'T MEAN IT!"

And then the ceiling came down on top of me.

There was no more screaming, no more sounds of destruction.

Just the darkness and the silence.

I died then.

CHAPTER TWO | ALEX AND CANDY STENMORE

IT WAS THE EMPTY WHISKY BOTTLE WHICH blew the Stenmores' lives apart.

Alex sat alone in his study, sipping the whisky that he'd poured an hour ago after arriving home from work early, only to find that Candy was not in the house. Candy contemptuously referred to the study as his "den." When she used the word, he knew what she meant, what she was thinking. Only lions had dens. In no way did she regard him as a "lion." After she'd been drinking, he knew that she was verbally gelding him when she called him a "pussy-cat."

He sat in his chair, behind the desk where he sometimes tried to write down his feelings, as if he could somehow rewrite his life and the way everything had gone. There were shelves on all sides of him. He must get around to reading some of the books there. Perhaps when he'd solved his problems. He drank, not used to it, hoping that the alcohol would dissolve the knot inside. Instead it made him shiver, cramping his stomach. He wondered if Candy ever got that feeling. His eyes began to fill with tears. It seemed that the study window was beckoning him. He didn't want to rise from his chair, didn't want to walk over there and look down into the garden. It was a nice view . . . wrong—it *should* be a nice view. But even though the swing had been removed from the bottom of the garden two years ago, he could still somehow see an after-image of where it had been. He had often wondered how things would have been if Ricky hadn't died. Would that gulf still have developed? Would Candy's drinking have started anyway? Sometimes he thought these things, but then felt guilty—as if he were blaming his own son for the way his parents' marriage had turned out. Sometimes he felt sure that the seeds of unhappiness had been sown a long time before Ricky had been born. His head was beginning to hurt now, just as it always hurt whenever he thought about that terrible autumn morning. He drank again, trying to drown the terrible images.

Candy, standing in the garden looking back at the house. Her face blank, somehow too white.

Himself, first walking towards her, then hurrying when he saw the terrible, vacant expression on her face.

And then, worst of all—worse than anything he'd ever seen in his life: the garden swing behind her, swaying gently in the wind, the chains squeaking against the metal pole. Remembering what he'd first thought when he saw Ricky apparently trying to climb up one of the chains of the swing, one hand clutched in it as he twirled slowly, his feet hanging high above the seat. Thinking: *What's he trying to do? Why is he so still?*

And Candy, still standing facing the house, not looking back at the swing as Ricky turned slowly so that Alex could see his face at last. A face that was purple and blotched. Eyes wide, puzzled. Tongue protruding. And then there were only the sounds of Alex's screaming.

He drank again, emptying his glass.

I will not weep again. I will NOT!

He spun in his swivel seat to face the door. But the window was still there behind him, still somehow beckoning him to leave his seat, walk over. Look down onto the garden. And remember.

No!

And then Alex heard the faint scratching from downstairs. The noise of a key in a lock. He sat and listened as the front door opened. There was some kind of fumbling commotion now.

Candy . . .

His first instinct was to call out; to tell her that he was here.

He was feeling really guilty now. He'd assumed that she'd gone out on one of her little jaunts again; assumed the worst because he'd come back to an empty house. She had every right to slip out for a little while, didn't she? She wasn't chained up inside the house. And now here she was, coming home again to get herself ready for their trip out that afternoon. But before he could say anything, Candy began to laugh. And something about her laughter made another part of him die inside. It wasn't the sound of someone laughing to herself. It was laughter for someone else.

Candy wasn't alone.

The door closed. Candy laughed again. But her laughter was suddenly cut off. There was a rustling sound from the hall. As if the laughter had been cut off by . . . what?

By a kiss.

Alex gripped the glass tight, feeling the anguish constricting his throat.

Candy laughed again, breathless. Now there was the murmuring of another voice. A male voice. Alex sat motionless, listening to the sounds of feet on the staircase, coming up. When they reached the landing, there was another silence while they paused. The sense of Candy's unseen intimacy was overwhelming. And this time it was too much for Alex to take. When he stood, his legs felt weak. He was trembling with an anger that seemed to rob him of all strength. When he reached for the handle of the study door, it somehow seemed miles away from him.

He saw them before they saw him.

Candy had been drinking; no doubt about that. She was

looking back down over her shoulder, her stance unsteady as she climbed the stairs, holding onto her guest's hand as she drew him up with her. She began to laugh again.

The man saw Alex before Candy realised he was there. He was youngish, perhaps twenty-two. Fashionably short hair and long sideburns; leather jacket, tan jeans. A smile that showed he knew he was on to a good thing. He stopped, his smile vanishing when he saw Alex. Candy seemed to think that he was having second thoughts about coming back home with her. She tugged harder at his hand, making a cooing noise of encouragement. She tottered on the step, grabbing at the handrail, apparently unable to understand his reluctance.

"What's wrong, Georgie?" Her voice was slurred. "You were keen enough in the pub. Getting nervous?"

Alex wanted to speak, but could not find his voice. All he could do was stand and look at the young man whom Candy was trying to drag upstairs to the bedroom—to *their* bedroom. Candy's visitor ran a hand through his hair and looked back down the stairs.

"I think . . . " he began. But there were no thoughts he could bring himself to utter.

"Awwww . . . " Candy tried to pull him up again. She paused then, and Alex saw her cock her head to study her companion's face, trying to understand why he'd had a change of mind. Suddenly Alex knew, just *knew*, that she had become aware of his presence. There was no further movement from her, just a certain kind of stillness. She gave a low laugh. No humour in it, just the low mocking sound she often made these days. She let go of the young man's hands. As he started back down the stairs, mumbling inaudible apologies for the fact that he couldn't stay, Candy turned slowly and deliberately. When she was facing him, Alex could see that her eyes were closed. She opened them as the front door closed. The young man was gone.

"Well, what have we here?" she asked.

Alex tried to say something. Nothing seemed adequate.

"Came home early, didn't you?" she went on. "And tried to catch me out."

"No . . ." Alex's voice sounded weak and pathetic in his own ears. A small boy's voice coming from a man's mouth. He looked down into his whisky glass and saw that it was empty.

"But you did, didn't you?"

"Why the hell do you do it, Candy? What the hell is the matter with you?"

"It's you, Alex. Just you. That's what's the matter with me."

"We were going out this afternoon . . ."

"That's what you think."

"We agreed. Last night. After our talk . . ."

"*Talk!* That wasn't a talk, darling. If you recall, you did all the talking. I never said a word."

"This can't go on, Candy. We've got to sort it out."

"I've told you before! Don't call me Candy! My name is Catherine."

It was her ultimate insult. She'd always made a point of letting everyone know that only her friends called her Candy. The guest list of close acquaintanceship no longer included Alex. Somewhere along the way, the fact that no one ever called her Catherine seemed to have been lost.

Candy stormed up the stairs, looking over her shoulder only once to yell back down to the front door: "Wimp!" She pushed past Alex, walked up to the next landing . . . then realised that she was heading in the wrong direction. Angrily, she turned unsteadily on one foot and pushed past him again, heading downstairs. This time Alex followed.

"We've got to talk, Candy."

"Piss off, Alex. I need a drink."

"You *don't* need a drink."

"Says you. The man with an empty glass in his hand. How much have you put away while I've been out?"

"Just the one."

"Right. That's just what I need. Just the one. A large one."

Alex followed her into the living room. Candy made her way straight to the corner bar. She grabbed the empty whisky bottle, raised it to her face and was suddenly still. He knew what was coming next. She slammed the bottle back down on the bar and turned, bracing her hands on the counter. Alex watched her rage build as she tensed her hands on the bar, as if she might launch herself from it, straight at him, with fingernails raking at his eyes.

"Where is it?"

Alex stood up, looking at her. Again, he didn't know what to say. This wasn't the right time. He hadn't planned it to happen this way. He'd wanted to come home early and talk to her while she was still sober. He became aware that his mouth was open. "Catching flies", Candy called it, always with that put-down laugh.

"Where *is* it?"

"There isn't any more."

"You *what?*"

"Candy, there was a three-quarters-full bottle there when I went to work this morning. When I came in, there was a half-inch in the bottom. I drank that. Just the one, because I needed it."

"Because you needed it. I see. Well, I need it, too. A damn sight more than you do."

"Maybe you've had . . . "

"Don't you *dare*, say it. You mealy-mouthed bastard. Don't you *dare* say that I've had enough. Living with you, I never have enough."

Candy pushed herself away from the bar. Alex stepped quickly out of her way as she lunged past him and headed for the kitchen.

"We were going out," he said, following behind. "We were going to talk."

"You're always fucking talking."

33

In the kitchen, Candy flung open the cupboard doors above the sink unit and began rummaging through the tins of food. Cans began to fall to the floor around her, bouncing and rolling on the linoleum.

"You won't find it in there," said Alex from the kitchen doorway.

Candy paused.

"What?"

"I said you won't find it in there. I threw it away."

"*What?*"

"The half-bottle of Scotch. I threw it out yesterday."

Candy turned her head slowly to look at him, eyes glaring pure hate.

"And you won't find the vodka bottle in the upstairs wardrobe. Or the other one in the bookcase."

"Conspiracy," Candy said, and grimaced as the word came out all wrong. She closed her eyes as if dealing indulgently with a naughty child. She tried again, and almost got it right. "Conspiracy. You've been hatching a little plot, haven't you, darling?"

"No, Candy. I've never stopped you drinking. There's always been drink in the bar. But I don't see why you have to hide it all around the house."

"You think I'm ashamed of myself, don't you? *Don't you?* You think that's why I've got my little hidey-holes."

"No, I don't. I just think you want to disguise how much you're drinking. Not only a bottle a day at the bar, but all that other stuff to keep you topped up."

"You think I'm frightened of you. That's what it is."

Candy slammed the cupboard doors, the impact dislodging more cans and packets of instant soup from the shelves. As they cascaded to the floor, she started slowly towards Alex.

"I'll show you how frightened I am, Alex. I'll fucking well show you just how frightened I really am."

And this time she *did* launch herself at him.

34

"Candy! *Don't!*"

Alex tried to step back out of the kitchen and into the hall without taking his eyes off her. His heel caught the edge of the carpet and he stumbled. In the brief moment when he fought to regain his balance, Candy was suddenly on him. One hand raked his face, fingernails drawing blood from his cheek. The other grabbed his hair. "*Candy!*" She clung tight to his hair, dragging his head down while kicking hard at his shins and beating at him with her free hand. The force of her fury whirled Alex around, and this time he did lose his balance, falling hard against the wall. His hand was trapped between the wall and his side, the whisky tumbler splintering. He pushed away from the wall, shoving Candy to one side. This time, as he tried to rise, she brought her leg up to kick him again. Accidentally, her knee connected with his chin. His jaw clicked shut, his head snapping back. The next moment he was lying on the floor of the hallway, looking up and wondering what the hell he was doing down there. There was a patch up there, above the kitchen door, that he'd missed when he'd been redecorating. Very curious. Candy suddenly came into view, leaning against the wall and sobbing for breath. She pressed both hands to her mouth now as the grief came out of her. Still dazed and winded, Alex could not understand what was happening. There seemed to be movement beneath him now. A strange, shuddering feeling. Surely he couldn't be lying on the floor after all? Was this a dream? Because now it seemed that there was a rumbling noise; faint at first but getting louder and nearer. He tried to get up, but couldn't move. It took all his strength to raise his hand in front of his face. He was clutching a handful of glass shards. The shattered glass had cut his palm, and blood was leaking from his fist and down his forearm. How could that possibly happen? He couldn't remember anything about hurting his hand. When he looked back at Candy, he could see that she had stopped sobbing. She too had heard the rumbling noise, and Alex watched curiously as she stood back from the wall, as if there were something inside there that had moved. The rumbling sound was louder now, like a waterfall. The ground beneath him was shivering, and his vision was blurring.

"What's happening, Alex?" gasped Candy, her voice muted by the sounds of the gigantic approaching waterfall. "Oh Christ, what's *happening*—?"

Glass crashed nearby, making Candy flinch. Alex saw something moving overhead and looked up to see that the light hanging from the ceiling was swaying wildly backwards and forwards. Something cracked up above and a thin cloud of plaster dust began to fall from the ceiling. He still couldn't rise. He tried to brush the dust from his eyes and smeared blood all over his face.

"Alex, what *is* it?"

Something groaned and stretched and splintered, very close by. Candy dropped to her knees, leaning over Alex and looking wildly around as the sounds of the waterfall engulfed them. There was another crashing of glass, and then something detonated like a bomb. Candy shrieked, throwing herself across Alex's body and knocking the breath from his lungs. He tried to touch her, tried to tell her that everything was all right, and that it was just a bad dream. But then the floor that was not a floor any longer shivered . . . and tilted. In the next instant, both he and Candy were falling into darkness.

CHAPTER THREE | THE JOURNAL OF JAY O'CONNOR: DEAD AND BURIED

MY EYES WERE OPEN, BUT I COULDN'T SEE a thing.

I was lying face down, and ice water was pooling around my face. The shock of it made me catch my breath and I tried to sit up. For some reason I could only raise my face out of the cold water, but I couldn't roll over or sit up. My entire body seemed to be in pain. My arms, my legs, the small of my back. I waited for the darkness to lighten. It didn't. Something was wrong with my eyes. I fumbled at my face, just to make sure that they were open. I was still somehow unable to sit up, so I had to pull my arms around to the side before they reached my face. I groped at my eyes. They were open. But the darkness remained. Oh Christ. Was I blind?

Then I became aware of a great weight on my back, pinning me down.

I panicked then, thrashing and squirming to pull myself out from under whatever had trapped me. I couldn't remember what I was doing here, or where in hell I was. Something bad had happened, and I had to get free and into the light. There was a crack, a rustle and patter of loose stones or gravel, and suddenly I was able to move. I began to pull myself forward. Whatever was on my back seemed to be made of wood, but it wasn't heavy enough to keep me pinned down anymore. Was it a door? I slid from underneath it, and it seemed that every sound I made was muffled, as if I were underground. Was that the reason why everything was so dark? What the hell was happening? In the process of freeing myself I realised that there was rubble all around me. A building site? In the middle of the night? There was a hissing sound nearby, and when I finally managed to rise stiffly to my haunches, crouching on the rubble, I realised that it was the sound of running water, as if from a burst pipe.

Now that I was almost upright, the headache began. But this was worse than any headache I'd ever suffered before. It began in my temples and then seemed to creep around to the base of my neck. From there it stabbed into my brain. Moaning, I clutched at my temples and felt something tacky there. I knew that it was dried blood. The pain in my head suddenly became too much, and I sprawled forward to empty my stomach. It made me feel a little better, but as I crouched there, drawing in breath, the air appeared to be getting thinner. I'd been frightened before, but this was really bad. Once, when I was a kid, I was playing hide-and-seek and got locked in my aunt's wardrobe. I'd been in there for perhaps fifteen minutes, screaming and kicking, before someone came to let me out. That memory had haunted my nightmares. It was back now, worse than it had ever been. I had to get out of this darkness. I still couldn't remember what had happened or where I was, but something seemed to whisper in my ear, telling me that although I wasn't a kid anymore, I was back in that wardrobe and I was going to stay there forever, or until I suffocated. In panic, I clawed at the rubble around me, trying to find some light, trying to find a way out. The sounds of my fear—the moans, the sobbing—all came back to me amplified, bouncing off the walls of the wardrobe, making my fear all the worse.

"Jesus Christ, what's *happening* . . . ?"

I scrabbled across the wooden board or door that had been

pinning me down. In the darkness it seemed to me that it was lying at an angle. I clambered upward, hearing the rubble slip and slide all around me. There was new terror now. It sounded as if everything were sliding down on top of me to fill up this hole that I'd found myself in. I grabbed the rim of the wooden board and hauled myself over the edge.

The slipping, sliding sound had become an avalanche, a gathering roar and rumble of sound. I kept scrambling upward, cleared the top of the mound of rubble—and the next moment I was over and falling. There was a sheer drop on the other side. I clawed and flailed at the rubble as I fell, crying out loud. It was sliding with me, down into some bottomless, pitch-black pit.

Water engulfed me, shooting into my mouth and jetting into my nostrils. I reacted instinctively, gasping for air where there was none—and filling my lungs with dirty water in one great sucking intake. The rubble was piling down all around me. It would push me down to the bottom of this water-filled pit, bury me and drown me. My legs thrashed and squirmed as I desperately tried to find something solid beneath my feet.

And then I was standing in the hole, clawing at its side and vomiting out the water that had filled my lungs. It was waist deep, and there was an unbearable and unmistakable stench down here too. Suddenly I remembered what had happened to me that day. Stafford, and the writing on the wall in the toilets. My overwhelming anger. And then the whole world somehow falling apart and collapsing into darkness.

Darkness?

There was a smear of light down here; just ahead of me, seeping under ragged brickwork. Still coughing and gagging, I clawed at the sides of the cesspool into which I'd fallen, trying to pull myself out. The shattered brickwork beneath my pistoning legs and clawing hands slid and crumbled as I ran on the spot, like some terrified animal in a caged exercise wheel. I was certain that my frenzy to pull myself out of the pit would make the sides cave in all around me, first trapping my legs and then dragging me down into the filthy water.

Something happened to me then.

Something was going wrong inside. I'd always known how to handle myself. I'd had to learn how to handle myself "on the street." But I'd never known terror like this. I don't know how to describe this properly—but in a crazy sort of way, it was like I was . . . catapulted out of my mind for a moment. Even though it was pitch dark down there; I was suddenly somehow up in the air, above myself and looking down. And despite the darkness, I could see where I was. In a rubble-filled pit, and the mad, clawing, thrashing thing beneath me was more like an animal than a human being. From that detached distance, I could see my desperate efforts to crawl out of the hell hole. And from up there I knew—just *knew*—that the fear was doing something to my mind, something bad deep inside.

Suddenly, it seemed that the figure beneath me was able to brace its foot on the rubble beneath it. When it lunged this time, it was able to crawl out of the water-filled pit. In that moment I was catapulted back into the figure. Now I was that thrashing, clawing animal again. The edges of the pit were crumbling even as I got one knee over the rim. Sobbing, I clambered up and over the broken rubble towards the ragged line of light. Behind me, I could hear rubble sliding into the water, could feel and hear debris falling from overhead. I was out of the water pit, but my optimism was short-lived; because now I knew that this underground place was going to cave in on top of me and bury me alive.

I clawed towards the light, pulling broken brick and crumbling plaster away.

It was working. More light was flooding into this dark place.

My fingers were bleeding, my palms torn by the ragged debris.

Something hit me hard between the shoulder blades, knocking the breath from my lungs. The "ceiling" was coming down on top of me. I was going to be buried a second time in this living hell.

I was going to die a second time.

CHAPTER FOUR | GORDON TRANWELL

GORDON TRANWELL FLINCHED WHEN THE pebble cracked against his windowpane.

He resisted the urge to jump up from the edge of his bed and run to the window; it only ever made things worse if he showed his face. If they knew they were getting a rise out of him, it just made them more insistent. Instead he remained sitting there, with his eyes screwed shut; hunched over his guitar, the last incomplete chord still hanging in the air as the music from the CD system he had been playing along with kept on going. From somewhere in the street below he heard the sounds of jeering. He clenched his teeth, leaning over to switch off the music, and then regretted that he'd been goaded into even doing that. When the laughter came again, it was because they knew they'd gotten a reaction out of him after all. He should just have let the music keep on playing, and to hell with them.

Below, one of the girls began to sing the old Beatles song: "Nowhere Man." The lyrics were meant for him. He gritted his teeth again when another pebble skittered across the window, leaving a scratch. More laughter, fading away. And again, Gordon could feel the bitterness inside. He was close to tears. He screwed his eyes shut, then leaned over to rewind the tape.

Pressing "Play," he carefully placed both hands in position for the opening chord. He had played this piece of music so often, had memorised its chord sequences so well that he even knew by heart the pop and crackle on the tape, taken from an old LP years ago. It didn't bother him. There were only a few recordings available by the maestro, and he treasured every one of them.

The music began again. That first melancholy phrase that he now knew to be a minor chord. Gordon had never studied music, could not read it. But he could play by ear now, his love for this particular music style filling all the heart-breaking gaps in the rest of his life. There were no disappointments with his music. This track, for example. It had everything of loss and regret and loneliness . . . it seemed to mirror his life. But then the music changed . . . it surged ahead into a major chord sequence, changing the sorrow and the melancholy into something else. It had a yearning quality that he strove to emulate in his own playing. Sometimes he managed to get it, at other times it seemed that his fingers' awkwardness in finding the chord brought it out too "flat." Now the resolution, as the emerging melody cast off all the bad memories, finally bursting into that last wonderfully melodic phrasing. It was like finding light in dark cloud cover, soaring for it, bursting through the rain-clouds and finding the sun. It was ecstatic then, and it made Gordon ecstatic, too. At his best, copying the maestro, he could finally express things inside himself that he'd struggled all his life to express.

Gordon was eighteen, but could barely speak. His stammering had been treated in the early stages, when his mother and father had taken him to the consultant. But six months into the programme, when Gordon was eight years old and progress was being made, his mother and father had been killed in a car accident. It seemed to him now that he could remember very little of those days. There was a darkness; a chasm inside that seemed to blot it all out. But one thing had come out of it. It had cured his stammering, in a manner of speaking. Quite literally.

Cured it in the sense that he just didn't talk anymore. It was so easy, really. Don't try to talk and you won't stammer. His aunt and uncle, the ones who had taken on responsibility for him with an attitude approaching resentment, could not afford to continue with his special treatment, and there had been no insurance cover for the death of Gordon's parents to enable the treatment to continue. So he had been transferred back to the "normal" education system; a school where he knew no one, where teachers were given the barest of instructions about his problems with communication, and children who felt that someone who didn't talk was only behaving that way because he didn't want to talk to *them*. As a result, Gordon was ostracised from the beginning. In desperation and fury and grief, Gordon had learned another thing. He had learned that he *could* speak, after all. If he tried hard enough—and was angry enough. When something happened that really hurt, or when he was really angry at his inability to speak—he could muster up the anger inside and spit out one word.

One word. Maybe two. Sometimes three.

Always spoken with anger.

Just confirming what the other kids thought: that he didn't like them, that he didn't want to talk to them. That he considered himself different.

The jeering continued in the schoolyard. The beatings continued. His uncle died, and his aunt became more withdrawn.

And the overworked, overburdened teachers in a stressed-out system somehow managed to avoid the problem.

At fourteen, he had discovered an old guitar at the back of a cupboard. His cousin, now grown up and moved to another country, had bought it. Knowing his uncle as he did, he wasn't surprised that his own son had put a sea between them. His aunt had forgotten that the guitar was there, didn't notice when he took it. She never questioned him when she heard him trying to tune it, plucking absently at the strings. Over the months, and then the years, Gordon had got used to the feel of the instrument. He had learned where the notes were, the chord combinations. He'd heard a story once; about how if you put a monkey at a typewriter and left it there for eternity, with the animal just pounding at the keys, eventually it would turn out the works of Shakespeare. Ruefully, he wondered if he was like that. Instead of a typewriter, he had a guitar.

And then one day, on the radio, he heard an instrumental piece of music. Something that sounded foreign; maybe Italian, or Spanish. He wasn't into that kind of thing at all, but something about it made him turn up the volume. That first time he missed who had composed and performed it. But there was a special quality that haunted him, made him keep on tuning into the same station in case they played it again. They did. A week later. It was called "Come un uragano"—"Like a Hurricane." An instrumental theme composed by a Spanish guitarist called Nicola Spagnole, who'd had some success on the Continent with a small orchestral group. Someone on the radio termed it "rock flamenco," with something that sounded like a smirk. It was a minor hit, staying in the charts for three or four weeks, never reaching the top twenty. But something about that music had lit a fuse in Gordon. For weeks, months, after the music had vanished from the airwaves, he continued to practise on his battered old guitar.

The Monkey and the Typewriter.

Eventually, he discovered how to play the lead guitar part. That understanding gave him his first knowledge of the musical scale, gave him an understanding of the basics. From there, he had sought out other music by the same man, discovering with real disappointment that Spagnole had died shortly after "Come un uragano" had been released on the Continent. He had been young—thirty-six—dying of a congenital heart condition, leaving behind a mere three CDs and a handful of singles.

Unable to communicate, unable to make friends, and with the normal avenues of expression denied to him, Gordon found in Spagnole's music and his cousin's battered guitar a way to bring out the feelings inside. Even if he couldn't share them, even if his loneliness continued, he could still make that beautiful music himself, could practise and practise until he had learned each track, each chord combination. Sadness, joy, melancholy and anger. All of them coming from his fingertips, purging the frustration inside. Soon he was also learning to play the harmonica and had moved to keyboards.

But to the kids at school, the kids who threw rocks at his windows as they passed (because only a fucking weirdo would listen to that crap over and over again, and never come out of there to show his face), Gordon remained as distant and strange a lunatic as he had always been.

The window rattled again, and Gordon missed a chord. The discordance made the anger flare inside again. Now the track was fading, and he'd cocked up the beautiful final phrasing. Once more, the window rattled. But this time it sounded different. Not like a pebble or a rock being thrown; more like a heavy goods vehicle passing by outside, making the foundations of the house shudder, making the windowpanes tremble. Except that couldn't happen here. There were weight restrictions on this road, with a major water main running down the centre. Again, the shuddering. Angrily, Gordon turned from the window, rolled over the mattress and grabbed his headphones from the bedside table. Jamming them over his head, he rolled again and plugged the lead into his CD player. Stabbing at "Track 1," he rolled for a third time and swept up his guitar. Refusing to look at the windowpanes, refusing to give in to the goading from the street below, he prepared for the first chord yet again. When it came, he was on cue, and the music had distanced him from what was happening beyond the windows on the street below.

When the track finished, with its final flourish, Gordon

46

felt that he'd never played better; knew that even though he couldn't hear how he was performing because of the headphones, he hadn't made a single mistake. Defiantly, he looked back at the windowpanes.

To see that something was happening there. Something strange.

They were . . . *blurring*.

Each pane still reflected the light from his bedside lamp, but the light was somehow shifting and flashing. The second track began, but Gordon leaned over to switch the CD player off, and as he did so, two things happened simultaneously.

First, he felt the bed shift, as if one of the legs had broken. And then he heard the noise. As if a piece of fluff had caught somewhere on the CD, causing it to make a ragged, roaring sound. Gordon snatched the headphones from his head, but the noise was even louder now. A grinding and roaring that seemed to be coming from outside. Now anger was overcoming his fear. He tore the headphones from around his neck and flung them across the bed, kicking himself clear of the mattress to stand in the middle of the room.

And instantly became aware that the noise was both outside *and* inside his bedroom. In fact, it was filling the room; had been filling the room for some minutes, but until now, he had not been able to hear because of the headphones.

It was the sound of thunder.

Not outside, not in the sky. But here, right now, in *this* room. It was shaking the walls, making the bed rattle.

When he looked back in alarm at the scratched windowpanes, he could see them trembling and reflecting light from the bedroom lamp in even wilder patterns. The thunder was in the floor now, juddering into his feet and legs. In fear, he stooped and grabbed both thighs, trying to steady himself. Was he somehow imagining all this? Above him, there was a rending crack. Suddenly the air was filled with talcum powder; a great drifting cloud of it from above, falling like thin snow all over his bedroom. Instinctively, he dropped to his knees and sheltered his head with his hands, watching the talcum powder float and drift in the air. When he looked up he could see that the plaster in the ceiling had cracked. Even as he watched, there was another shifting, grinding sound—and then the crack spread on both sides, racing to the corner beside the window and right across the room to the door frame. Gordon lunged back to his feet and felt the floor tilt. The movement shifted his balance and he reeled across the carpet to clutch at the windowsill. He looked outside into the day.

Someone was running down the alley on the other side of the street. Now there were three, four . . . and a young girl. Were they the kids who had been jeering and throwing stones up at his window? He didn't recognise the silhouettes as they ran, but there was something—something *wrong*—about the way they were running. Something wrong about the way they were holding their arms. They were lurching from side to side, their arms thrown out as if they couldn't keep their balance. They looked like sailors in a ship's corridor, when there was a high sea and the vessel was pitching from side to side. Gordon felt a great shuddering in the windowsill, and the next moment the entire facing wall of the building opposite cracked, split and burst apart in a chaos of bricks and mortar and an erupting cloud of dust. Gordon flinched away from the window in shock as the running figures disappeared from sight in the dust cloud. An avalanche of masonry crashed across the street towards Gordon's home. It stopped halfway, the sound of thunder now intensified and the erupting dust cloud billowing up across the windows to obscure everything from sight. Suddenly Gordon was across his bedroom and yanking at the door. There was no lock, no way to jam it shut. But somehow the door *was* jammed shut.

Gordon panicked.

His world was falling apart, and he couldn't understand what was happening.

Overhead the ceiling cracked again, and a chunk of plaster was dislodged. It exploded into a white spray of debris on the floor behind him. And now he had torn the door open, the hinges screeching. Did something want to keep him in the room when the ceiling collapsed? On the landing he steadied himself against the wall as another tremor shook the house. Was that someone in the distance, screaming?

Gordon tried to call for his aunt.

He opened his mouth. But nothing would come out. In anger and fear, he screwed his eyes shut, tried to form the words *Aunt Sheila*.

But he could only gag.

Gordon threw himself down the stairs, clutching at the handrail when something exploded somewhere—something that sounded like another house collapsing, shaking the foundations of his own home. He almost fell at the bottom step, but clung to the rail and twisted down the hallway. From his bedroom came the sound of another screeching roar, and another great shuddering convulsion shunted the staircase supports out of the wall in a rattling spray of plaster. Had the bedroom ceiling finally caved in? Still yelling his aunt's name, he flung himself down the passage to the kitchen door. Would that too be somehow locked or jammed? This was a dream. It *must* be a dream. How else could he be moving so slowly when everything around him was shaking itself to pieces and his world was falling apart? He could see his hand, impossibly large, reaching for the door handle as the very ground beneath him vibrated and juddered. With his aunt's name still locked between his teeth, he forced his hand onward. His grip on the handle felt unreal, hardly solid.

And then the kitchen door was open.

Aunt Sheila was there, standing beside the gas cooker and looking at him as if she could hardly understand his rude entrance. She was holding a pan of boiling milk in one hand, and even from here Gordon could see the blue glow of the gas ring on the cooker. Overhead, the ceiling shuddered and another cloud of plaster dust cascaded around her in a talcum-powder shroud. She brushed at it with a ridiculously calm gesture, as if there were a bothersome fly somewhere around her head, and now he knew for sure that this must all be a dream. Why else did she seem so unconcerned? When the ceiling gave another crack, just like the sound in Gordon's room, he suddenly remembered that his own bedroom was directly above the kitchen. If the ceiling had come down, then it must mean that the kitchen ceiling was also in danger of collapsing. The roaring sound was suddenly louder and nearer, and with a brittle snap the kitchen window suddenly crazed into a jagged glass cobweb. The sound of it seemed to bring the dream into focus a little more clearly, make the danger more real than it ever had been until this moment. Gordon braced himself in the doorway and tried to yell at his aunt that they should get out of the house straight away, that something very bad was happening.

"Gordon?" admonished his aunt, putting the pan carefully back onto the gas ring even though the entire kitchen was now shaking so much that she had to brace one hand on the wall beside her. Gordon struggled to yell her name, but still could find no words. In a moment he would emerge from this bad dream and everything would be okay.

And then the ceiling came down on top of his aunt with a deafening roar.

Something slammed into him at the same moment, throwing him backwards through the doorframe and into the passage. Instinctively he covered his head and face with his forearms as he hit the carpeted floor. The impact jerked the breath out of his lungs and whiplashed his neck. Somehow the violent blow had loosened his jaws.

"*Aunt SHEILA!*"

The two words were ejected with his breath—a cry of terror. Gasping for air, moaning in pain, Gordon scrabbled away from the doorway as rubble began to fall towards him. On his feet again, pain and fear seemed to be one enveloping spasm as he clutched at the splintered stair rail and tried to wave the gushing clouds of plaster and concrete dust from his vision.

"*Aunt . . .*"

The dust choked him. Coughing and gagging, he became aware that the thunderous roar was now somehow muted. Could it be that the rattling vibrations he could feel beneath his feet and in his grip on the staircase were fading? Yes, even now, the shattering roar had become the distant rumbling of a passing thunderstorm, the vibrations now no more than might be caused by a vehicle passing on the street outside. But the passage was still filled with the whirling dust storm as Gordon began to stumble back over the littered carpet to the kitchen doorway.

"Aunt . . . Sheila! Are you . . ."

Gordon refused to recognise the last moment, the look of bemusement on his aunt's face as her figure was suddenly obliterated by a tumbling mass of plaster and concrete. He stumbled on the debris underfoot, called her name again . . . and this time fell forward, clawing at the rubble that now filled the passage. The dust cloud swept past him and began to subside. Gordon could hardly believe what he was looking at, less than three feet from his nose.

The kitchen doorway was filled with compacted, shattered rubble—from floor to ceiling, in a great wedge of devastated masonry. It had spilled out perhaps six feet into the passage, and he realised now that if he had not been thrown clear he would most certainly have been buried—crushed to death beneath the accumulated devastation that had been the roof, his bedroom floor and the kitchen ceiling.

Gordon clawed at the unyielding wall before him. He tried to call his aunt's name once more, but his voice had locked. There was a wild fluttering feeling in his throat, as if every last moment of his daily grief and anger and fear had suddenly come down upon him with this avalanche of masonry. Gordon clawed again, breaking his nails, bloodying his fingers. She was still alive in there, trapped on the other side perhaps. But he was never going to reach her from here. Pushing himself away from the rubble, he twisted back along the corridor to the front door. He tried to yell: "I'm coming. Hold on, I'm coming!" But nothing would come out of his mouth. When he tore open the door and hurtled out into the front garden, he was aware that something wasn't right out there. There were changes. Frightening changes. Somehow the garden had been ploughed; great chunks of soil and grass had been churned up in the centre of his aunt's treasured lawn. The garden wall wasn't there anymore. Burglar alarms were sounding from all over the council estate. A great cloud of dust was billowing on his left. But Gordon refused to look at these things, barely took them in as he hurtled around the side of the house towards the back garden. His aunt would probably be out there by now, staggering around to meet him. Gordon grabbed at the brickwork in his flight, swung around . . .

. . . and fell over the pile of rubble that had once been the back wall of the house. He sobbed as pain stabbed in his knees, scrambled back to his feet and swayed there, looking at the devastation.

Rooted in shock, he couldn't take in what he was looking at.

It was as if some giant knife had cut through the middle of the house. He could see a cross-section of the property, open to the air. He could see the loft, and below that his own bedroom, from which he had fled not a minute ago. There was his bed, the headphones still lying on the quilt. It rested on the last remaining section of floor, somehow looking like a bed in a doll's house. Below the flooring, the upper wall of the kitchen, and then . . . only rubble. The entire upper half of the house had come down in a sloping avalanche on top of the kitchen, the rubble spilling out across the back garden. The kitchen simply didn't exist anymore. And no one could be alive under that devastation.

Gordon made no conscious decision. The next moment he was scrambling forward over the rubble; clawing at the bricks, throwing handfuls of debris over his head and behind him.

"*Aunt Sheila!*"

He had no idea how long he had been clawing at the debris, was uncaring about the blood that streamed from his ragged fingertips, before he realised that he must be standing on top of his aunt's body. Still sobbing, Gordon staggered back from the heap of masonry and collapsed to his knees on the one bare patch of grass in the back garden that hadn't been covered with masonry. Now, as well as the banshee wailing of all the burglar alarms, Gordon became aware of the other sounds—sounds that until now had been drowned out by his own sobbing.

The sounds of other people somewhere out there. Wailing and crying.

Climbing to his feet, dazed, Gordon stumbled over the rubble and around the side of the house to the street. Smoke was billowing from around a corner, and the dust cloud seemed to fill the sky all around him. But he could see no sign of those others who were also giving vent to their grief. When he reached the front of the house, he became aware of the rain on his face and arms. He looked up, but the dust cloud blotted out the sky. As he moved on down the fractured garden path, he could see where the rain was coming from. A gaping fissure had appeared in the main road. Somewhere below, the water main had burst and a geyser of water was rising in a fountain from the crevasse. Pavements on either side of the road had been uprooted and shattered, now glistening in the falling rain.

Gordon leaned against the garden gate and let the water fall on him.

Someone would come.

The devastated street remained empty. There were only the

swirling dust clouds, the smoke and the hissing of the fractured water main. And somewhere out there the sounds of multiple distant voices, weeping and calling out the names of the dead and dying.

Someone would come and make things right.

Someone . . .

CHAPTER FIVE | **THE JOURNAL OF JAY O'CONNOR: DAMON, WAYNE AND THE CRYING KID**

I WASN'T BURIED.

But that didn't stop the terror being any less real. The second shuddering, the second rumbling and crashing in this black hellhole, I was later to discover had been a second tremor. I lay there, face down, hands over my head, and I think I began to pray or something. When I heard the voices, I thought maybe my prayers had been answered.

The ragged light was gone again; everything was pitch black once more. But the voices were definitely there. When I listened more closely, I realised that they weren't angels sent to pull me out of this place. They weren't firemen or rescuers shouting encouragement. These were the voices of people who were just as terrified as I was. There were two, maybe three of them, weeping and wailing, and one of them crying for her mother.

I crawled over the rubble, half-expecting the stuff to shift again under me and slide me back into another watery shit-pit. The smell was still bad, but let's face it, that was the least of my problems. I didn't know in which direction I was heading. Up, I think. But I couldn't make any sense of anything down there. Suddenly I heard one of the invisible snuffling voices say:

"*Listen!* Someone's coming."

"Oh, thank *Christ!*" said another. "We're over HERE!"

The third voice just kept snuffling and weeping.

"Don't!" hissed the first voice. "Don't shout, or you'll bring the roof down."

"Get us out of here!" The second person didn't seem to care whether the roof came down or not. "Please, HELP US!"

"Where are you . . . ?" I seemed to have reached the top of the mound I was on. There was still no light, but the voices seemed very close now, down on the other side.

"Oh, thank you, thank you . . . "

"Don't thank me for anything," I groaned. "I'm not here to save you. I'm stuck down here as well."

"Don't joke. I mean, whoever you are, don't fucking . . . "

"Where are you?"

"Where are *you?*"

I clambered over this new ragged barrier of broken masonry and some of it began to slide down the other side. That's when the third person began to scream at the top of her voice. Maybe she thought that the movement of the rubble was the roof coming down again, after all. The two others began to yell at her too. Suddenly, the whole of this cramped, underground no-place was filled with screaming. The sound was too much and, yes, I knew that it might make the place fall apart on top of us, but I couldn't help screaming at them to shut up. We all went mad in there for a while.

I slid down the other side, and suddenly someone was clawing at my legs, grabbing at me, as if just getting some kind of grip on me would make everything all right again. I couldn't tell whether they were the hands of a man or a woman. I slapped them away. When I came to rest, there was just the blackness and the sobbing, panting sounds of four people in despair.

"You're not a fireman or a policeman," said a dull, flat voice at last.

"No."

"You haven't come to rescue us, to get us out of here?"

"No."

"Oh God, we're all going to die." The girl began to weep again.

"What happened?" asked the first voice. "Do you know what happened?"

I thought back, and everything seemed crystal clear at last. The toilet cubicles. Stafford. The writing on the wall. Everything coming together, focused, as if I were looking down through a magnifying glass and seeing myself pounding all my anger out into the wall. How could I tell them that I had destroyed the school?

"It was an earthquake, wasn't it?" said the second voice.

"We don't have earthquakes in this country," said the first.

"Wait a minute," I interrupted. "Since we can't even see each other down here, we may as well know who the hell we're talking to."

"Damon. Damon Briggs."

"Wayne Shaughnessy."

I waited for the girl to stop weeping, or for one of the others to tell me her name.

"Who's the girl?" I asked at last.

The other two laughed. It was a desperate sound.

"Hear that, Paulie?" said the voice called Wayne. "He thinks you're a girl."

"Well, he can bugger off, then, can't he?" said the weeping voice.

"His name's Paul," said Damon. "He's only twelve."

"I'm Jay O'Connor . . ."

"We're going to die," said Paul, and began to weep again. "We're never going to get out of this place."

"We're not going to die," I said. "Is anybody badly hurt . . . ?"

"You didn't see what I saw," said Paul in his quavery voice. "If you did, you'd *know*."

"What's he talking about?" I asked.

"We were outside, in the schoolyard," began Damon. "When it happened."

"What happened?"

"The ground. It began to . . . well, it began to shake. Not shake, exactly. More like . . . "

"More like it just wasn't solid anymore," continued Wayne. "Like when you're trying to walk over a trampoline. Everyone just stopped and looked. All the kids in the schoolyard. Like they were painted into a fucking picture or something. Things got, like, blurred. Everything was shaking, and everything was blurry. The windows in the school building started to crack and fall out. That's when people started to scream and run. Christ, I saw Jenny Rogers and Philippa standing by the main glass doors when they fell out on top of them. Jesus, there was blood . . . "

"And then I thought I saw the main roof cave in," Damon went on. "I don't know if that's what happened. That's what it sounded like. There was this big *roaring* sound, like the sea or something.

"The school bell, the one in the tower. That started to clang like hell, and I thought maybe someone was ringing it for a . . . well, for a danger signal or something. But then I looked up at the tower, and I saw the whole thing . . . the tower, I mean . . . the whole thing just, like, fall apart. Didn't topple over or nothing, the way you see it on the telly. It just sort of went to pieces. That big fucking bell clanging all the way down.

"Wayne grabbed my arm then and pulled me to the . . . "

"Side entrance. The fire exit. But . . . "

"I started screaming at him not to be stupid. We had to get *away* from the building if everything was collapsing, not run *into* it, but then . . . "

"The schoolyard," said Paul in his cracked voice. Each word was like a sob. "It . . . just . . . cracked open. Pulled apart. Like an earthquake. Big crack. Right . . . in the middle. It pulled open and kept opening and all the kids were running, but it just got bigger and wider and I could see the tarmac stuff all crumbling and falling into this great big hole and they were running but they couldn't get away and they . . . they . . . *fell*."

He started to sob then, crying for his mother. The other two rounded on him, not because they were any braver than he was; maybe because they felt if he kept it up they were going to start bawling as well. Truth to tell, I was pretty close to blubbing myself.

"Shut up, Paulie! You great big fucking *baby*!"

"You pathetic little shit! Stop it, or I'll kick the living . . . "

"Leave him alone!" I snapped. "Come on, we're getting out of here."

"But which way?" moaned Damon. "We can't see a thing down here."

I began clawing at the rubble in front of me. I didn't know which way to go, but we couldn't stay down there. I'd seen light before, so there must be a way out somewhere. We were in another "dip" between piles of rubble. I began to climb the pile on the far side, moving by touch. It was firmer, and didn't slide underneath me like before. At the top, I could feel air on my face and see a thin, ragged crack of light; just like before. Dim and hazy, but light nonetheless. The sight gave me extra energy. There was a rattling slide of rubble as I heaved myself over the rim and began to slide down on the other side. Behind me, the others were frantically following. They couldn't have tried to get out earlier, or they would have seen that light before I arrived. I kept my eyes locked on the light, and the next thing I knew I was falling into stinking water again. Terror took over once more. Was I going to be trapped in another rubble-filled pit? The water came up to my waist, but there was solid ground beneath me—and the next moment I catapulted myself out of it, clawing towards the hazy light; yelling back to the others, warning them about the water. Things became a little hazy after that. I remember scrambling through the broken bricks, tearing them away and letting more of the grey light into that stinking place. There was blood on my hands, I remember that. I must have shredded my fingertips as I clawed out of the rubble. There was another rumbling sound, but by then I wasn't even thinking about what might happen if my frenzy brought the "roof" down. I could hear animal noises. Maybe it was the kids somewhere behind me, trying to catch up. Maybe it was me.

Fresh air on my face. Cool and clean.

A space hardly big enough for my head to go through.

But now I was pushing on through it, my shoulders widening the gap, my legs kicking and thrashing behind me as I squirmed out and up. I could hear the others right behind me. It didn't matter if I broke my arms and legs getting through the hole. I had found a way out. That was all that mattered.

For a while, I didn't have the strength to look around me. I just scrabbled away from the ragged hole, across the mound of rubble, leaving a space for the others to follow. Dust swirled all around me, making me gag and cough. I sat with my head in my hands, clearing my lungs as the dust began to settle.

The first thing that hit me was the quiet.

No sounds of crying or people calling out for help.

No wailing sirens from fire engines or ambulances or police cars.

Just the sounds of me hawking and spitting and getting my breathing under control.

When the dust had cleared, I looked up.

I can still hardly believe what I saw when I looked around.

| **ANNIE
AND LISA**

I N   T H E   T H R E E   Y E A R S   S I N C E   FEMMES
Hardware started in business, there had only been three
telephone calls from would-be customers assuming that it
was a leather-fetish fashion company for lesbian bikers. More
often than not, most of Annie and Lisa's customers were local,
or visited after word-of-mouth recommendation. The potential novelty value of two women in their early to mid-forties
opening a hardware shop in the middle of town had long since
worn off.

And in the three years since the opening of their store, no
one had openly challenged them on the sexual implications of
their thriving little business. Lisa felt that it was an in-joke;
Annie was more open in her stance that it was a Big Statement.

They had been together now for five years. Annie had never
married; had always known where she was coming from, and
had had only two lovers prior to meeting Lisa. Lisa had found
her true self six years into an abusive marriage. There were
two children—both boys—whom she never saw after her ex-
husband had successfully used her new-found relationship
with Annie to convince the anti-gay judge at the court pro-
ceedings that raising two boys in that kind of relationship was
unhealthy and didn't provide adequate role models. Somehow

the loss of the boys was something that neither woman discussed anymore. There had been a lot of pain.

On Monday, 22 April, at 12:15 p.m., the hardware store suddenly came alive.

Annie had been in the back room, making coffee. Trade was slow but average for this time of day. Lisa was taking stock and trying to work out where the hell she'd put the brass doorknobs. At first it seemed that the rumbling noise was being caused by a heavy lorry passing outside. Lisa absently looked up through the shop window, but nothing passed, so she returned to her search.

The rumbling continued.

And then the shelves began to shake.

Lisa watched in astonishment as the jars standing on the shelf before her started to rattle and judder. The cardboard packets of screws and nails began to dance crazily on their hangers. From all over the store came the sounds of jangling and clattering. When she turned in bewilderment to look, it seemed that the entire contents of the store had suddenly acquired life.

"Lisa?" Annie came through the rattling plastic-bead curtain, with two cups of coffee steaming in her hand. Their eyes locked, still not understanding.

And then the front window of the store cracked, making them both cry out aloud in fright. The two cups fell from Annie's hands and shattered on the floor. She hopped and skipped as the hot coffee burned her feet. Another crack. And Lisa suddenly had a vivid childhood memory. Winter, in the park behind her grandmother's house. An icy Sunday morning, walking over the frozen puddles on the tarmac playing area. Listening to the ice crack and craze under her feet. Now, as she and Annie held each other close in a frightened embrace, she saw jagged, frozen lightning streak from bottom left to top right of the window. The building was still shaking and juddering, the tins and the bottles and the cans still clattering in a mad dance on their shelves. Yet another crack. And this time the entire window disintegrated, falling out of its frame into the street beyond with a great crash. Now the ceiling was juddering and shaking.

Annie suddenly had a vision: an aeroplane, crashing out of the sky. It was almost directly above them, and it was no use trying to hide beneath one of the tables, because even if it didn't plough straight into their store, she knew that its gas tanks would rupture, just like they had at Lockerbie, and they would be engulfed in a fiery hell. They had to get out of the store and run. Grabbing Lisa's arm, she ran for the front door.

The door was jammed in its frame. No matter how hard she yanked and tugged, it would not open. There was only one way out before the entire store collapsed. Through the shattered front window. Lisa was already stepping over the jagged rim and holding back her hand for Annie. The ground was alive beneath their feet, shards of glass skittering and dancing around their ankles. Behind them something fell from overhead, and just before she clambered out onto the littered street with Lisa, Annie looked back to see that the strip light was swaying wildly and chunks of plaster were crashing from the ceiling.

"Come on!"

Hand in hand, they ran from the storefront into the street.

Someone screamed, and as they turned in alarm they realised that it was not only their store that was being affected. A young couple were tottering along the pavement opposite, moving hand over hand along a tottering brick wall as if they were blind. Other people had dashed out of their homes, and from the grocery store further down the road; were staggering into the middle of the street, just as Annie and Lisa had done. It was a surreal sight; people milling about, looking back at the houses or the store from which they'd just staggered. As if they'd been ejected by the buildings themselves.

"This isn't happening . . ." said Lisa, in a voice that was

too low for Annie to hear, buried by the enveloping sounds of grumbling and shuddering. Glass seemed to be breaking inside every building on the street. Even as Annie turned to look, the grocery store window split and showered its on-street customers in a glittering spray. Instinctively, she started forward to help—and then the ground seemed to wobble beneath her feet, as if all solidity had been lost in the concrete and tile tarmac; as if she were suddenly standing on a trampoline. She staggered, grabbing at Lisa.

And from the far end of the street came a grinding detonation. As if lightning had suddenly struck the tarmac. But there was no zigzag lightning in the sky, no thunderous rolling in the clouds. The detonation became a steady roar—a tearing assault on the ears. The sound grew louder and nearer.

And neither Lisa nor Annie could believe their eyes when the road surface at the far end of the street began to *open*. There was no gradual disintegration, no warning of what was about to happen. The very fabric of the road was suddenly split apart, right down the middle, in a crack that widened as it moved with terrifying speed towards them. Concrete crumbled and fell into the ten-foot-wide crevasse that raced down the centre of the street in their direction. Water sprayed from broken mains underground, steam gushing from the ground as it was torn open. Pipework squealed, shrieked and erupted from tarmac. And now the shrieking was the sound of human voices as two elderly ladies, unable to believe what was even now bearing down upon them, were unable to get out of the way. Their attempt to avoid falling was horrifying in its very ordinariness. They didn't flail at the lip of the crumbling ravine, didn't try to run. Unbelieving, they stooped and held out their hands as if this were something they could stop with a casual and loving gesture, as if they were trying to gently subdue grandchildren rampaging too loudly in a suburban living room. The split widened; they tottered on the disintegrating tarmac, and were gone. The pavement on the far side of the street tilted and fell, taking fifteen people with it, almost too fast to register. There one moment; suddenly, with no ground beneath their feet, gone from sight without a sound into the roaring abyss that had been the town's main street.

The tarmac and concrete buckled and crumpled not ten feet from where Annie and Lisa stood, arms around each other. Terror immobilised them. They could only watch the approaching fissure. But suddenly the rumbling and tearing ceased; now there was only the sound of faraway thunder, like a storm vanishing over the horizon or an express train on its way into the distance. The crevasse had stopped. Steam hissed and rose from the depths. A drizzle of rain from fractured pipes began to soak them as they stood there, staring into the fissure.

Beyond the ragged edge, they could see layers of soil and clay in the crevasse before all details were lost in the murky chasm below. Like the layers of some gigantic, surreal cake.

Something shrieked on the street behind them, shattering their inertia.

Annie pulled Lisa back from the ragged edge, towards their crumbling storefront.

And then a car came around the corner, tyres shrieking as it hurtled down the street towards them. Lisa had sight of a white and terrified face behind the driver's wheel; whether male or female she couldn't tell in that one split second. The car accelerated down the street, engine roaring.

It was heading directly towards the fissure in the middle of the road.

"Oh God . . . " Lisa could only mumble. "It's not going to stop."

"STOP!" yelled Annie, staggering over the fractured pavement and waving her arms.

Behind the wheel, the shocked face saw the figure waving and stumbling towards the car. There was no reason, no real sanity in that face now. Terror had descended, and perhaps the driver thought that it was all to do with the waving figure. Lisa saw the driver tug the wheel, winced as the car swerved in the street, as if to avoid her—and kept straight on for the fissure.

"NO!"

The front and rear wheels on the right side of the car slewed into the crevasse, the entire frame tilting and wedging itself into the fissure. But the impetus of the car's flight carried it on down the street in that position, wedged sideways into the gaping crack. Sparks flew from the bodywork as it scraped and slithered ahead, the roof crumpling and ripping under the strain. The car was too wide, even at that angle, to fall into the abyss. At most, the crevasse was four feet across there, before widening to the ten-foot gap where they had seen the people fall. But the power of the engine rammed it on ahead, and down. Lisa shrank back as the rear left wheel spun crazily in the air, not twenty feet from where she stood. There was a horrifying inevitability about the way the car was forcing itself into that great crack, as if the vehicle had fallen or been pushed into a working junkyard compressor.

No one seemed inclined to go near the car when it finally shuddered to a halt, wedged in the crevasse; smoke and steam rising around the crumpled bodywork. People on the far side of the street milled in confusion; looking first at the car then at the sky and back at the buildings from which they'd escaped, as if waiting for the next development.

"Someone must come . . ." began Lisa. "I mean, it's all over. Someone will come . . ."

"Telephone for the police!" shouted Annie to the people on the other side, as she edged along the fractured pavement nearer to the car. "Go on! Someone! Find a phone!"

Lisa reluctantly moved forward with her, their attention fixed on the car.

And then, only feet from the rear of the vehicle, both women suddenly recoiled in alarm as two spectral white hands suddenly slapped against the interior of the rear window. A young boy's face suddenly appeared in the cracked glass; eyes wide in shock and fear, hair straggling over his forehead. He began to yell, hammering the flats of his hands against the window, looking back over his shoulder in the direction of the front seat, and then turning to yell in greater distress at what he could see there. But whatever he was yelling, his voice was muffled inside the car. Lisa hurried to the rear window, leaning down to try to make eye contact with the young boy. He was perhaps eight or nine years old.

"It's all right, honey," she said, aware that she was lying and didn't know what to do. "Just stay calm. We'll get you out . . . "

And then the car juddered again, emitting a squeal of metal.

The boy fell from sight.

The car pitched sideways, the bodywork sliding further down into the crevasse.

"Oh no!"

The boy reappeared in the rear window, screaming in terror, smacking his hands desperately against the glass. The car continued to slide into the crevasse, inch by inch. Soon it would keel over completely on its side and drop into the yawning pit.

Lisa staggered around the side of the car, bent down and seized the passenger door handle. She began to yank at it. It opened, but the door was wedged tight against the top rim of the crevasse. There was only a couple of inches' space. Suddenly the boy's fingers were touching her own as he scrabbled at the gap, trying to push his hands through. Now she could hear his agonised pleas:

"Please! *Please* get us out! My mam and dad are hurt! *Please*!"

"Watch your fingers, love! Sit back . . . oh *Christ*!"

The car lurched again, and the boy was gone once more; flung back down across the seat as the entire vehicle groaned and resumed its slide.

"Watch out, Lisa!"

Lisa pulled away from the door, and saw that Annie was wielding something over one shoulder as she ran towards the back of the car. In an instant she understood what Annie had done. While she had been trying to open the door, Annie had scrambled back through the shattered store window and grabbed a pair of heavy-duty wire-cutters. They were the first thing she'd been able to lay her hands on, and now she was wielding this four-foot-long metal tool, bringing it down heavily against the rear window. The entire pane disintegrated like frosted sugar. Discarding the wire-cutters, she lunged across the glittering boot and thrust both hands through the shattered window.

"Come on, son! Take my hands!"

Further shocked by the violence of Annie's sudden action, Lisa rallied and hurried around to her companion, bracing one hand on the boot and hooking a hand through Annie's belt in an attempt to stop her falling forward. The car juddered and squealed again. Lisa cried out, the downward twist of motion throwing her off-balance. But she hung on tight to the belt as she fell on the edge of the crevasse.

Screeching, the car turned completely sideways.

Like a living thing in tortured agony, it dropped away from sight; down into the smoking depths of the abyss. Straight to hell.

"Oh no, Annie! No, no, no . . ."

"Shut *up*, woman, and help me!"

Lisa twisted to see that Annie was still hanging over the edge of the crevasse, was even now struggling to pull herself back from the edge. Lisa clung tight to the belt, felt something tear and knew that Annie was wrongly balanced and would surely follow the car down. But now Annie was heaving herself back, and as Lisa lurched forward to grab her shoulders, she could see why she was having so much difficulty retrieving herself.

She was hanging onto the boy with one hand.

Just below the edge of the chasm, the boy had both of his hands fastened on her fist. Her other hand braced on the crumbling edge, Annie was trying to haul him up.

Quickly, Lisa thrust herself forward, reached down over the edge and seized the boy's collar to ease the strain on Annie's arm. His shirt began to tear, but she kept on hauling, praying aloud as the edge of the crevasse continued to crumble beneath them.

"We've got you," she sobbed, in a voice that knew he must fall.

"Pull hard, Lisa!" shouted Annie. "For God's sake, we're going to *lose* him."

And suddenly, impossibly, they were back on the splintered pavement.

Both women breathing heavily and lying flat on their backs; the boy crumpled between them, curled up like a foetus and with both hands clasped over his face as if he wanted everything to go away and everything to be better again.

The nightmare was far from over.

Suddenly the ground beneath them began to shudder. There was a great subterranean roar, as if something deep below was reacting in rage to the intrusion of the shattered car which had dropped into its depths. Both women rolled over instinctively, grabbing at the ground, hugging it tight. Lisa put an arm across the boy, grabbing Annie's shoulder. She began to pray then; convinced that the fissure edge would crumble, that the abyss would suddenly yawn wider and that they would all slide down into Hell. As the roaring thundered on, she looked back over her shoulder, to the other side of the street.

The buildings over there were shuddering. The remaining windows were exploding and cascading down into the fractured street, on top of the figures who screamed and ran in confusion; terrified of the fissure before them, but equally terrified of running back into the buildings which were, even now, shaking themselves apart. Plaster dust and debris exploded through the frontages as if bombs had gone off behind them. Lisa cried out when she saw a knot of terrified people, maybe five or six, huddling together at the rim of the crevasse. The edge crumbled, their arms pin-wheeled. She could see the look of terror on their faces as they seemed to hang in midair. And then they were gone, tumbling into the darkness like dolls, vanishing from sight.

When she saw what happened next, she could not utter a sound; could not give vent to the utter terror that had overcome her.

It was just like one of those horrible newsreel shots she'd seen as a child. The shots of the first atomic explosion sites, where houses and stores had been built close to the test site and cameras set up to observe the effects of the blast. She remembered all too vividly the sight of those houses first swaying on their foundations, as reeds and water plants might sway underwater in the current. And then, with a second ripple, the houses blew apart, disintegrated instantly and were blown away in gigantic clouds of debris.

It happened now.

The houses, the greengrocer's store, the car franchise. Everything within sight on the other side of the road beyond the crevasse suddenly rocked as the great roaring continued. And then, before her eyes, the entire street imploded, disintegrating into fragments as if a great wind had suddenly descended on it. But somehow—impossibly—there was no wind. Lisa, Annie, and the boy were not sucked into the yawning ravine. They lay there in terror as a great cloud of black dust erupted from the crevasse, sucked itself back, and then surged upward with renewed ferocity to obliterate the utter destruction that had been wreaked on the other side of the street.

Annie felt the boy moan in terror and put an arm over his shoulders. Her hand connected with Lisa's, and they held each other tight over the boy.

Both women wept, and waited for the end to come.

| CHAPTER SEVEN | THE JOURNAL OF JAY O'CONNOR: FRYING PAN AND FIRE |

THE SCHOOL HAD CEASED TO EXIST.

I was sitting on a pile of rubble; all around me, more piles of rubble. It was like . . . well, I was in a different place altogether. As if I'd been buried alive, crawled underground for miles, then managed to come out through a hole in some different world. Smoke was rising from some of the rubble. Then I saw something that made me realise I was still in the same place. About a hundred feet away was the blockhouse the school cleaning gear was stored in. It had been untouched. Running behind it, and around the rubble piles, was the iron school fence. Parts of it had been twisted and torn where rubble and masonry had fallen over it and scattered in the street. I recognised the houses and buildings over there. Most of the roofs had caved in, and the streets were cracked and filled with more rubble.

I couldn't get my head around it all. It didn't seem real.

Then I saw a couple of kids lying a little way off, half-buried in broken bricks. They were holding hands, heads together; as if they were playing some kind of game. Maybe blindman's-buff. They were lying like that, face down, covering their eyes and counting while all the other kids in the school were hiding. There was a big, dark stain around their heads that stopped me from calling out or going down to them. I turned away.

And that's when I knew that all this couldn't be happening. What I was seeing now wasn't real.

Not ten yards from where I sat was a great wall of spinning dust. It was a gigantic, spinning, twisting whirlwind. All gushing and turning in on itself, like when you see clouds on the television, clouds that've been speeded up. Imagine that, all black and brown and reaching up so high you couldn't see the sky. But that wasn't the worst of it.

The worst of it was—there was no noise.

The way that dust cloud was moving about there should have been a noise like a whirlwind. But there was no noise, no rushing wind, no storm sounds. Just dead, dead quiet. When I looked again properly, things just became more unreal.

The dust cloud was all around me.

I followed the great cloud down to the street, where the school fence vanished into it. There was parkland just beyond the blockhouse, where kids used to play football. Just grass and a few straggling bushes. It was going to be developed as a factory, someone had told me. But about five hundred yards out in the middle of that "field" the dust cloud had formed a great barrier all the way round, curving in towards the housing estate. Following the line of this impossible swirling cloud, I could see about eight or nine hundred yards of council houses; maybe three streets. Some of the roofs had caved in, but all of the windows were blown out. There were people down there in the streets, but I couldn't see what they were doing. The cloud barrier seemed to go right along Irskine Street—you couldn't see anything beyond, except the gigantic wall of black-brown stuff. Then the dust cloud swirled up into the shopping complex. I could only see half of the shopping centre. It seemed as if there were buildings missing. Great big spaces between offices and shops that weren't there before. But I couldn't be sure.

Crazy, but I reckoned that the cloud, the silent whirlwind—whatever—had hemmed us in a quarter-mile all around; so that I couldn't see anything beyond it.

At first, when I tried to stand, my legs just wouldn't do what I wanted. Shock, maybe. I stood still for a minute, and then began to pick my way through the rubble, waiting for my strength to come back. Then I saw what was half-buried just before me, and I froze.

It was half a body, the lower half of an adult.

I guessed that it was one of the teachers, but I had no idea who it might have been. I supposed it was a man—anyway, it was wearing trousers. But the upper half was buried under rubble. Whoever he was, he was very, very dead. I dry-heaved, but I felt as if I'd swallowed a large stone. I started to move down past the body, trying not to look. Rubble and dust began to slide under my feet, and for a moment it seemed I might lose my balance. I dug in my heels, clouds of dust rising around me, and the cracked brickwork that had been covering the upper half of the body—and its face—fell away.

That's when I was sick, bending at the waist and retching, trying not to see what I'd already seen.

It was Stafford—what was left of him.

His smashed spectacles were still on his face, his eyes wide and staring, his mouth open as if he were in the middle of delivering another lecture. The back of his head . . . well, the hell with telling you that. You know what I mean. I had cause to hate him, but he didn't deserve what had happened to him.

Moaning, I hurried on past him, trying to give the body a wide berth. Then I heard someone calling my name.

"Jay! Jay O'Connor!"

For a moment I froze. Was it *him*? Calling me back, telling me what else I'd done wrong? Then I realised it was a younger voice and looked back to see that Damon, Wayne and Paulie had managed to scramble out of the same hole as me. They'd started a mini-landslide of rubble down towards me. I yelled at them, but I was glad when some of the debris covered the corpse and hid it from sight.

"Follow me," I called, as I turned and headed out across the fractured remains of the schoolyard. About fifty feet away was the huge cloud of whirling dust. I remembered what one of the kids had said about the schoolyard just opening up, realising that the cloud must be coming out of the big crack they said had appeared there. It was almost hypnotic, watching the twirling, churning smoke. It wasn't *real*. The fact that it was all around, like some kind of cage. It made me feel small, and when I looked up into it I felt as if everything was upside down and I might fall. Fall right up into the sky.

"What are we going to do?" asked a voice to my rear. When I turned, I saw that Damon and Wayne were right behind me. Their clothes were torn, their faces dirty. I guess I didn't look too much of a picture myself. The boy called Paulie was a little way behind them. His head hung like a kid getting a telling-off. As I watched, he just slumped into a cross-legged squat. Like a naughty boy, waiting to be told what to do.

"What's *happened*?" Damon gestured hopelessly back at the mounds of rubble and shattered brickwork.

"An earthquake, judging by the looks of those other houses down there," I said flatly.

"So what do we do?" asked Wayne.

"Find the emergency services," I said. "Get help for anyone else trapped in there."

"Why . . . Why hasn't someone come?" asked Damon. "Where's the fire brigade, and the ambulances? Christ, the place fell apart and we were left in there . . . and no one *came*!"

He was right. There was an eerie silence out there. Where were the sounds of fire klaxons and ambulance sirens?

Paulie made a noise behind us—a noise like he'd been hit over the head with something. Then he made a high-pitched sort of keening noise and began to sob. The two other kids turned on him, yelling abuse. I didn't like the noise he was making. It was too distressed.

"Leave him alone!" I snapped.

Damon and Wayne kept on yelling at him to stop. Now they were picking up stones and throwing them at him.

"I said leave him alone!"

I moved forward to stop them, but suddenly I couldn't walk straight. My legs felt strange. Like I was floating. Suddenly Wayne, Damon and the crying kid were no longer there. I had to get away, back to the real world. I was reeling. The school gate was right in front of me. When I reached for the bars, I felt sure they'd feel as if they were made out of rubber. But they were cold and hard, and when I took my hands away, they were covered with red rust.

That's not rust, said a little voice inside. *That's dried blood.*

I dry-heaved then. Folded up double on the shattered concrete, hugged my guts and tried to get the nightmare out of me. Nothing would come, because there was nothing inside. But my eyes felt as if they might swell and pop out of their sockets with every convulsion. Next thing I remember, I was staggering down the main street away from the school. The ground beneath me was cracked and rutted, just like a ploughed field. Somewhere behind me, I could hear Damon and Wayne yelling at Paulie.

Then I was falling.

At the last, just before everything went black, I felt sure that I'd run straight off the edge of the world. Straight into one of those bloody great cracks in the ground.

I was falling forever.

Third time dead?

This time I didn't seem to care.

| **THE COMMUNITY CENTRE**

"ALL RIGHT, EVERYBODY!" SHOUTED THE MAN in the paramedic gear.

The crowd in the community hall were in no mood to listen. Someone, somewhere, began to weep, and that set the half-dozen kids crying too.

The paramedic climbed up onto one of the plastic tables. It wobbled beneath him and he did a tightrope walker imitation with his arms at either side before it settled.

"Everybody!" he yelled again. "*Listen!*"

This time the hubbub began to quieten. Now there were only the muffled sounds of weeping.

"When the hell are they *coming*?" shouted a man from the back of the room. His remark set everyone off again; all hundred and fifty packed into this room, all frightened, all traumatised. The paramedic began waving his arms and yelling for quiet once more.

Alex Stenmore ran both hands through his hair, remembering his fight with Candy at home, just before the ceiling fell in and their lives fell even further apart than he'd believed possible. He looked down to where she half-sat, half-crouched against the community hall wall. She was staring at her hands, chewing her bottom lip. The sight of her stirred something inside, and he moved to touch her. But he knew what her reaction would be; could see in his mind's eye how she would slap his approach away. He knew that she was suffering; knew that she needed a drink. He couldn't get close enough to her to discover whether she was suffering withdrawal, or whether she was still in a state of shock. She had said very little since they'd staggered out of their collapsing house and into the main street. From a safe distance, they'd watched it fall apart. First, the front wall caved in, blowing the garage doors out across the street. When the dust had cleared, the ceiling had gone, all of the windows had been shattered. There were other people in the street, all milling in confusion and staring at the devastation. No matter how hard Alex thought back to it, he couldn't remember how they'd got out of the house. Everything had been blurred by the nightmare. Trapped in that milling throng, they had also got caught up in a stampede through the smoke-filled streets when the gas main under the house across the road had ruptured and exploded, engulfing the windows in a gigantic fireball. Later, in shock and drained of strength, they had sat at the side of a fractured pavement with a crowd of others, waiting for help to come.

But there had been no wailing of sirens, no police cars or reassuring blue uniforms telling them where to go or what to do. Eventually, hours later, only two paramedics in a battered ambulance, both with expressions of shock and bewilderment; the vehicle filled with the broken and the bleeding and the dying as it crawled and bumped along the ruptured street with its blue light slowly blinking in silence. The paramedic hanging out of the back doors had told those on the street to follow behind. Some had tried to climb up into the ambulance, others had tried to drag the paramedic out as anger overcame them when he refused to jump down and help their injured loved ones. The man had lashed out with his feet, hanging in the doorway, barring anyone else from climbing in, yelling at them to follow and bring the injured with them if they could.

If not, to leave them. They'd be back for them in a while. But the ambulance hadn't led them to a hospital or an army station or a clinic. It had led them to this community centre.

Just an ordinary redbrick building that had somehow survived the tremor. The roof was intact, the walls hadn't caved in. The only damage had been to one of the three large windows, which had cracked and splintered. Someone had managed to nail hardboard covers on it and had swept away the glass. Inside, the building looked more like a school gym. There was a serving area of sorts at one end where a bar was set up for local dances. Bare-board floors. Strip lights. Notices of forthcoming events.

When Gordon Tranwell had shuffled in with the others, his guitar slung over his shoulder, a woman with a bandage across her forehead and the beginnings of two spectacular black eyes had asked him for his name and address. He had seen her taking names from the people in front of him and knew what was going to happen. When it came to his turn, he tried to speak but knew that nothing would come out.

"Name and address, please?" asked the woman in a flat monotone.

Gordon waved at his throat and shook his head.

The woman looked up from her clipboard. Gordon repeated the action.

"Can't you tell me?"

Gordon shook his head again.

"I know it's been a shock for you. For everyone. It's terrible. But we have to know who we have here."

Gordon tried to push past, head down.

"Please. Can't you . . . ?"

Anger, shock and plain resentment flooded Gordon. It was the necessary fuel he needed.

"Tranwell! Gordon! Got it?"

The woman flinched as Gordon pushed ahead into the main area. He didn't look back. His face was burning. Now he hated

78

himself and struggled to control tears. His aunt was dead, buried beneath the falling rubble in her own kitchen . . . and he couldn't even tell anyone about it. He elbowed through the crowd and found a place against a wall. Bracing his back against it, he sank to his knees, slinging his guitar across them and listening as the paramedic on the wobbling table tried to get some attention. People had been laid out in the middle of the floor, on makeshift mattresses. There were a couple of IV drips set up on makeshift cradles. But there was something wrong here. Why were people being brought *here*? Why hadn't they gone to the hospital? Where were all the doctors and nurses?

Gordon looked across at the two middle-aged women and the white-faced little boy. They were trying to catch the attention of a woman with a pile of what seemed to be gauze bandages and medical supplies in her hands.

"It's the boy," said Annie, to the woman. She tried to push past, but Lisa caught her arm and made her stop. "Something's wrong with him," Annie went on. "He won't talk, won't do anything but stare. I think it's shock, and he needs to be seen. His parents . . ."

"I'm sorry," said the woman, and now they could see the look of distress on her own face. Hair straggled down over her red-rimmed eyes. She could barely speak. "I'm not . . . not a nurse. I don't know what to do or where everyone's sup-posed to be. My husband, you see. And my little girl . . ." The woman pushed off through the crowded room, taking her anguish with her, and was lost from sight.

"Will you be quiet and *listen*!" yelled the paramedic from his insecure perch on the plastic table. It was not so much the sound of his voice which did the trick as the fact that, as one of the few authority figures in the room, his tone betrayed a sudden loss of control. And with so few here in control, with so few authority figures, the sense of shock was palpable as the room quieted, apart from the wailing of one baby and the sniffling of a child. The paramedic pulled himself together, loosening a collar beneath a suddenly purple face. He wiped one hand over that face, breathing deeply, before continuing.

"That's better. Better. Now . . . I know you have lots of questions, but if you'll just . . ."

"Where . . . ?" began a man from the other side of the room.

"*Just* . . . " The paramedic caught himself again, regaining control. "Just . . . wait a moment. Now, look, I know everyone's frightened, and there are people here who are hurt. But there's only me and Sean over there in the corner at the moment, and the stuff we've got in the ambulance outside."

"When can we get out of here?" wailed a woman. "When can you take us to a proper hospital? My husband needs a *hospital*."

"The radio in the ambulance still isn't working. We don't know why, because it wasn't damaged. But at the moment there's just static. We're still trying to get through . . . "

"Why don't you just take us to a *hospital*?"

"Because," said the paramedic, fighting to keep control, "you know and I know that something isn't right here. Something isn't right about that dust cloud that's got us all hemmed in. We daren't risk driving into it. Have to wait until it clears."

"Why doesn't somebody come? Where're the police, for Christ's sake?"

"Look, we just have to hold out and wait. Give the emergency services a chance to organise."

"You know more than you're letting on, don't you? You're deliberately keeping us here . . . "

Alex turned away from where the paramedic tried to maintain order. Everything was too confusing. The aura of fear in this room was very real, and despite the fact that the man on the table was trying to act in a rational, caring manner, anyone could see just by looking in his eyes that he was terrified, too.

"Alex."

He looked down to where Candy sat, cross-legged. For a long time she had been staring down at the floor.

"Yes, love?" he asked.

"I've got to have a drink."

"There's a water cooler over there, I think . . . "

"You are such a stupid fucking bastard, Alex. I'm talking about a *drink*."

Alex was overwhelmed by conflicting emotions. Distress, helplessness and seething anger. "Can't you . . . ?" He gritted his teeth, not wanting to lose control. "Can't you just wait? I mean, until everything's sorted out here."

"I need a drink now. I'm not wanting an argument about it. I want one. I need one."

"Where am I going to find alcohol right now, Candy?"

"Don't call me Candy."

Alex looked back at the paramedic, straining to hear what he was saying, needing to tune out of this conversation.

"It's not smoke, no," said the paramedic. "There are no fires. We've checked everything out in these two blocks. There've been no electrical shorts. No problems with gas mains after the first explosions. Nothing like that. The stuff we're seeing all around us is . . . well, it's dust."

"But dust doesn't act like that," said an elderly man, head swathed in bandages. "It's all around us, and it just keeps . . . just keeps . . . swirling and moving. Dust is supposed to settle after a while, isn't it? That's smoke, it's got to be."

"It's not. I've been right around the periphery. We're in a half-mile-square area here. Bounded by Wady Street on the west. Part of the shopping precinct to the north, although most of that has been destroyed. The A19 on the east. And Main Street to the south."

"Why don't you tell us what's really happening?" asked someone else. "You know, don't you?"

"I'm as much in the dark as anyone else. Look, we just have

to sit tight and wait for the emergency services. Whatever's happened, it won't take them long."

"Twelve hours is long enough! Why isn't there anyone here? Why aren't you taking us *out of* here?"

"That's all there is to say!" snapped the paramedic. Steadying himself, he jumped down from the table, asking himself the same question he had been fielding since the quake.

"*Why doesn't anyone COME?*"

CHAPTER NINE | LOOTING

WHEN ALEX LOOKED AWAY FROM THE clearly distressed paramedic, trying to maintain calm, Candy was no longer there. He spun around, not believing that she could have left without him seeing her. But she was nowhere to be seen in the packed community hall.

I need a drink.

"Oh no . . ."

He pushed past the two ladies and their little boy, straining to look through the crowd towards the exit. He felt sure that he saw a flash of auburn hair and the sleeve of a pink blouse. Yes, it must be her.

"Excuse me!"

Alex hurried through the crowd, almost stumbling over a man lying on the floor with a broken leg. For a moment, it looked as if the man's wife would physically attack him. But he quickly stepped over the prostrate form and pushed ahead. No one tried to stop him.

Outside, the street was littered with broken glass and debris. Ahead, the shattered fascia of a row of terraced houses. Rising above the roofs, the omnipresent swirling cloud of dust stretching far away to left and right. The light was fading now. There was a stillness that unnerved Alex. When he moved out into the street, the sound of his feet crunching on the broken glass seemed unnaturally loud. It felt as if this entire area were somehow a film set, built to depict this disaster.

"Candy?" His voice sounded lost and forlorn.

Somewhere off to his right, he heard the tinkling of glass. He couldn't see any movement, but he headed in that direction, taking care not to snag his legs on any of the debris or fragments of broken windowpane.

"Candy?"

At the end of the street, Alex paused to look at the swirling dust cloud about thirty yards away down a side street. Like a living curtain, it rose to the sky; blurring and fading as it ascended. Impossibly alive and churning. Now he knew that the paramedic was right. This cloud that hemmed them in on all sides couldn't be caused by fires. Because if there was a fire, there would be the *sound* of fire. Crackling and roaring. But there was only silence as the clouds churned and twisted, self-regenerating and deeply unsettling to look at. Then Alex saw the storefront down the side street. Like most of the other buildings, its windows had been shattered; a glittering lake of shards lay in the street before it. He could see the sign from here: Off-Licence.

I need a drink, Alex.

"Candy?"

Alex hurried down the side street, aware that he was drawing close to the dust cloud. He felt as if it were somehow alive; as if it were waiting for him to come close, so that it could suddenly swell and billow out in his direction, swallowing him, plucking him up from the street to suck him screaming into its churning depths. There was another tinkle of glass from within the store, and it gave him an added surge of courage. Gritting his teeth, he reached the front door and peered through the shattered pane into the darkness.

"Candy, love? Are you in there?"

More glass tinkled.

Alex shoved the door. It shuddered open, jamming on the littered floor. He squeezed in and stood for a while, until his eyes were accustomed to the dark.

"Come to stop me?" said Candy's voice from the darkness. "Or come to look *after* me?"

"Jesus, Candy. We've got to get back to the others. This building might not be safe."

"Safe?" And suddenly Candy stepped out of the darkness. She'd found an unbroken bottle from one of the shelves. It looked like vodka. She drank—an extravagant and defiant gesture, as if she were rehearsing for the part of a drunk. "Nothing's safe, lover boy. Look at me. I never have any luck, do I?"

"Candy, please . . ."

"I mean, if I was lucky, then the ceiling would come down on top of us. Then we wouldn't have to suffer each other anymore."

"Candy! Come away from here! If the rescue services come and we're not at the community centre . . ."

"Let them come. I've got a home from home here."

Alex pushed past the jammed door, angrily striding towards Candy's shadow.

"Don't you . . ." she began, but Alex had dashed the bottle from her hand to the floor. She swung hard at him, hitting him on the side of the face and making him stagger back. "Big man! Big fucking man!" Whirling away from him, she seized another unbroken bottle from the shelf next to her. Without even looking at the brand, she smashed the neck of the bottle against the shelf and poured it straight into her mouth.

And then there was a sound in the darkness behind her.

Candy turned in alarm as another shadow emerged slowly from behind the main serving counter. It seemed as if the figure had been lying on the floor and was pulling itself to its feet. Now it rose slowly. Bracing both hands on the bench, it stood there silently, looking at them.

"You going to pay for that?" asked a man's guttural voice.

"What?" asked Candy, backing off.

"I said are you going to pay for those bottles?"

"Well . . . yes . . . Alex, pay him."

"Otherwise you're looting. You know that, don't you?"

"Look," said Alex, taking Candy's arm and pulling her away. She refused to let go of the bottle. "No trouble. We didn't think anyone was in here. After what happened." He strained to get a better sight of the man. It was impossible in the gloom. He was just a hunched silhouette, standing beside the cash register. He seemed to sway for a moment, putting a hand on the register to regain his balance. "Are you all right? Are you hurt . . . ?"

"There's punishment for looting in a national emergency," continued the figure. "Did you know that?"

"I'm not looting!" snapped Candy. "I needed a drink, that's all."

"Very serious consequences," said the silhouette.

"Pay him, Alex, and get me the hell out of here."

"I don't have any money . . ."

"You see?" continued the figure. "No money to pay. So that's looting. Isn't it, Candy?"

Candy paused, defiantly drinking from the bottle again. "Do I know you? Is this your store?"

"Oh, I know you, Candy. And your husband. I know you both very well."

"What's he talking about, Alex? I've never been in this store in my life. You know this character?"

"There's a darkness in you both that will destroy you," said the shadow. "Not the drinking. That's a symptom. No, the real problem lies deep, deep down."

"Who the hell *is* he, Alex?"

"I don't know," said Alex uneasily. "I've never been in this place either. Who *are* you?"

"Alex, your wife thinks that you killed your son. And Candy, you think that Alex is responsible. That's why you hate your husband so much. But don't you know, Alex? No matter how much forbearance you show, you hate her just as much as she hates you. That's the darkness. Now, do you want to know the real truth . . . ?"

"Who the hell are you?" shouted Alex, pushing past Candy. The shadow remained unmoved, its voice just as cold and balanced as before.

"The real truth is very simple. You see, you *both* killed your son. You're both to blame."

"Let me see your face." Alex bunched his fists.

The man laughed.

"I said, let me see *your face*!"

"Do you want to know something else?" asked the silhouette, moving slowly around the edge of the serving counter. "Something about little Ricky? Shall I tell you? All right, I will. Little Ricky damns your names in hell. He hates *both* of you, just as much as you hate each other."

Alex stepped forward just as the man moved into the faint light spilling down from a ragged hole in the ceiling.

And then Alex stopped when he saw the man's face.

Candy saw him at the same time, and stifled a scream as the vodka bottle fell from her hand.

The man was perhaps in his late fifties, and wearing an apron with the motif *Best Booze in Town*. His shirtsleeves were rolled up, since he'd been helping out in the cellar when the quake hit Edmonville. When the ceiling began to shudder and shed clouds of plaster dust, he had clambered quickly up the cellar stairs in time to see and hear several hundred bottles of assorted liquor falling from their shelves and shattering. He had clutched at the doorframe as the front window fell out and the ceiling came down. But he had no time to question what was happening, because the splintered wooden beam from the ceiling had split raggedly and plummeted from overhead. A fifteen-inch splinter from the beam had stabbed into his right eye like a wooden dart, erupting from the back of his skull to splatter the red jelly that had been his brain down the back of his shirt and his trousers. He had died instantly, and had lain there for thirteen hours behind the serving counter.

Until Alex and Candy had come in.

"Not pretty, is it?" asked the walking corpse with the wooden shard protruding from its face and a black-red stain all over its previously pristine white apron. "Being dead, I mean. Tell you what's worse . . . "

"For Christ's sake, keep away from me." Alex backed off, flinching in terror when Candy grabbed his arm with both hands.

"What's really, really worse . . . "

Candy backed into the jammed door, making it shiver on its hinges. Neither she nor Alex could really believe what they were seeing or what they had heard, but both were filled with an undeniable terror. Now it seemed as if the world really had ceased to exist. There were only two of them, and the nightmare man-who-should-be-dead-but-wasn't.

The man stopped and cocked his head, giving them a ghastly smile.

"Watch and see."

"You're . . . hurt . . . " began Alex, knowing that it was a ridiculous thing to say. "You need help. There are some people back at the community centre . . . they can help."

"No one can help," said the man-who-should-be-dead. "Not me . . . or them. Now, come on. Watch."

He was leaning towards them now. Not coming on any further, but leaning forward at the waist, and thrusting his mutilated head forward. There was something leering in his hideously destroyed visage, but worse than that was a palpable feeling in the very air that *something* was going to happen. Something so terrible that it should have them both clawing around the edge of the door and running out into the littered street before they could witness it. But for some reason they held back. There had been so much unreality, so much nightmare. Perhaps here and now there was a very real confirmation provided by this living-dead man that everything they'd experienced was some kind of fantasy. If they stayed and watched, maybe nothing would happen . . . and maybe then they'd wake up. Or maybe something impossible would happen, and that in turn would wake them from the nightmare and catapult them both back into the real world—even if it was, for them, such an unhappy world.

But then it started to happen.

And they weren't waking up.

The store-owner's face was still thrust forward in that leering pose, and something was moving there; moving where the ugly, splintered shard of wood had embedded itself into his eye socket. Now it seemed that the man was straining, his already half-destroyed face grimacing with effort. Impossibly—so bizarre, and yet so obscene in the context of this nightmare—it was as if the man were straining to pass a bowel movement. Even now, he was letting out an explosive breath with the effort. Holding his breath now, and squeezing again . . . and they could see that it was the shard of wood itself, in his face, that was moving. Inch by inch, it was squeezing itself slowly but surely out of the ruptured eye socket. If there had been three inches of shard to begin with, now there were four. Now five . . . Now six.

Alex recoiled, Candy clawing at his back, when the bloodied wood suddenly popped out of the eye socket. With a liquid hissing, as if fuelled by compressed gas, it shot across the store and embedded itself like a dart in the wall not one foot from where Alex had been standing. The man laughed at their terror; a sharp bark of derision. But both Alex and Candy were still frozen, unable to comprehend. And in sheer glee at their fear, the man arched his back, throwing back his head as peals of manic laughter filled the store. The noise of his laughter was somehow wrong. Now it seemed as if there were more than one voice laughing, even though there was no one else in the store. It was as if a dozen men and women were somehow sharing in this hideous joke, the sounds of their deranged laughter erupting from the wide, wide mouth of the store-owner. When he looked directly at them again, the torrent of noise was still erupting from his mouth—a howling, shrieking horde of mad revellers.

The sound galvanised Alex. Shoving Candy back, he dragged the door open and pushed her out onto the street. Lashing with his foot, he kicked the door back into place and saw the man still standing in the same position, staring at him.

"Oh Christ," he said then. "Oh Christ . . . Candy . . . *RUN!*"

As the shriek of laughter reached an insane crescendo, it suddenly became the sound of a rushing, howling wind. And in that moment, Alex saw something even more impossible than everything they had so far witnessed.

A black torrent, like an explosion of tar or oil or black water, exploded out of the dead man's ruined eye socket. Instantaneously, it gushed out of his wide-open mouth, out of his ears—exploded from between his legs. Alex saw the man's remaining eye fly out of his head as another black jet of liquid erupted from the socket. In a moment, it seemed that an exploding black geyser had burst forth from every orifice of the storeowner—gathered and launched itself in a boiling, churning black fury at the shattered door.

Hand in hand, Alex and Candy fled back the way they'd come, down the side street and towards the main road. Candy knew that Alex had seen something else back there, and twisted to look back in shock when the front door of the store exploded out onto the side street. A black tidal wave gushed out of the doorway and the shattered window frontage, crashing in a great black wave against the cracked fascia of the buildings opposite before churning angrily back upon itself. The tidal wave filled the street, and with the tumultuous sounds of a roaring storm changed direction and hurtled after them both as they ran. As the black torrent surged and splashed against the walls on either side of the street, clouds of sprayed droplets beaded and flew in the air like black mercury, splattering the brickwork but quickly speeding back into the main black mass, behaving like no liquid on earth; as if each drop were a sentient, living part of the whole.

The sight served to slow Candy, her legs weakening. Alex knew that if he turned to look, whatever was happening back there would also rob him of strength. He could not see the black wave hurtling down upon them, but he could hear the howling of the tempest.

"Candy, *come* ON!"

He yanked at her hard, and Candy whirled away from the terrifying sight as they reached the main street. The community centre was perhaps three hundred yards away. Would they find safety there? Candy was weeping now as they ran, her fingernails biting into Alex's palm as they clung to each other.

The tidal wave exploded into the main street, crashing against the buildings on the far side; boiling and churning and erupting. Again, it seemed to gather itself, waiting to build up bulk and weight and power.

"Alex!" screamed Candy. "Alex, make it go *away!*" And then the black torrent surged down the street, filling its entire width as it bore down upon them.

| CHAPTER TEN | **THE JOURNAL OF JAY O'CONNOR: PANIC** |

A T FIRST, I THOUGHT I MUST STILL BE LYING in the street. Because the first thing I saw was Wayne and Damon standing above me, arguing. Wayne had a sticking plaster on his forehead, a big one. Then someone stepped between them to look down at me; a middle-aged guy wearing a blue, official-looking shirt and a worried expression. Now I could see, and hear, that Damon and Wayne weren't arguing with each other; they were arguing with this new fella.

"You all right, son?" asked the stranger. Then I could see a ceiling above him, and realised that I wasn't still in the street, after all. I tried to speak, but my mouth didn't belong to me anymore.

"All right," said the man when he saw me struggling to reply. "Don't answer me. Just take it easy and . . . "

"No one came!" shouted Damon, grabbing the man's shoulder. The man slapped the hand away, still looking at me. "We were stuck under all that fucking rubble, and no one came. Had to dig ourselves out! Where *were* you?"

"You've had a crack on the head," the blue-shirt went on, still talking to me and ignoring Damon. "Don't think it's a fracture or anything. But you might be a little concussed. Just rest."

"We could have died!" snapped Wayne.

"Yeah, well, you didn't," said the blue-shirt tightly, as he turned from me to look up at them. Now I could hear the hubbub of other voices and turned my head to see that the room we were in was full of people. Some of them were lying on the floor like me; others were bandaged and hobbling about. Kids were crying, people were arguing with each other. There was fear here. I could see it and taste it. There was a sign just above what looked like a restaurant serving hatch: Edmonville Community Hall. I realised that I'd been here a few times, once for a friend's wedding party, another time for a disco.

"Well," the blue-shirt asked Wayne, "are you going to tell me what this lad's name is, or what? We need all the names for the rescue services."

"You keep talking about the rescue services," replied Wayne. "But they should be here already, shouldn't they?"

"They're coming. Don't worry." His face was far from reassuring. "Now what's this lad's name, please . . . ?"

And that's when I heard the commotion. A door slammed close by, and a woman yelled something like: "*Christ, help us. It's behind us . . . and it's COMING!*"

I twisted to see what was going on, but suddenly the yell had let loose all the fear that I could sense among everyone in the community hall. Maybe everyone had just been waiting for something even worse to happen, and here it came. The room was suddenly full of people jostling each other and trying to get out. Someone collided with the blue-shirt and he all but fell across me. Another blue-shirt was shouldering his way angrily through the crowd to where the commotion was taking place, yelling for people to be calm, but he might as well have saved his breath because now some other guy was yelling: "*It's right behind us. A tidal wave. Water or oil or sewage or . . . SOMETHING!*"

Then I saw this man and woman, both of them wild-eyed

and looking terrified out of their wits, pushing through the people who were surging towards the front door. The paramedic caught the man by the arm and tried to haul him around, shouting something. I suppose he was trying to find out what it was that had scared these two so much before they'd burst in through the front doors. But he could get no sense out of them and there was no way anyone was going to stop the people in this room from getting out into the street. Even if the worst thing in the world was right behind those two and headed this way, the crowd in here weren't just going to stay and wait for it to arrive. Wayne and Damon tried to shove through and join them, but now they'd both been snagged between the paramedic and the wild-eyed man. In a knotted tangle, the whole lot fell across me. I covered my head as feet came down on top of me. My head was hurting bad as I squirmed my way on elbows and knees through the tangled bodies and thrashing legs. After everything I'd been through, it seemed like I was going to be buried alive *again* under a clawing mass of bodies.

Suddenly I was clear. Lights were spangling in my eyes and I felt as if I might throw up at any moment. But if I was right about having been in this place before, I knew that there was another way out that no one else seemed to know about, or had forgotten about in the mad rush to get away. When I looked up, I could see the fire exit double doors in the back wall with the security bar across them. If they were locked . . . well, there wasn't time to think about that. Someone fell across my legs. The pain and the anger seemed to dissolve the lights and the next moment I was staggering to my feet and heading fast towards the fire exit. Right next to it was a young guy with a guitar. He was just sitting there, guitar cradled across his lap, gawping in sheer amazement at what was happening. Two middle-aged women were dragging a kid with a white face away from the panic. When the man and the woman who'd burst in here and caused the panic stumbled in front of me, I yelled at them to get the hell out of my way and yanked the woman aside. The guy tried to fist me, but I shoved him back hard and then I'd hit the security bar with both hands and the doors slapped open hard into the night.

There was an open grassed space behind the community centre, terraced houses stretching away on either side. I had a brief glimpse of the smoke-fog wall, or whatever the hell it was, and then I was on my knees again, looking back at the community centre. The people I'd seen when I broke away from the crowd had followed me. The guy and his wife, the kid with the guitar, and the two women and their white-faced kid. Even as I looked, Wayne and Damon suddenly came sprinting out of the doorway. Just as they cleared it, I saw something happen inside the community centre that shocked me rigid.

In one brief moment, I could see the people still crowding away, clawing over each other towards the main door. A bloody great twisted knot of arms and legs. No one seemed to have looked back to see that a back entrance was open. Then the white-faced kid started to scream right next to me, one of the women pinned him down and tried to hush him up, I tried to yell back at the people inside . . . and then . . . and then . . .

And then just before the faint light in the community hall was snuffed out, I saw the windows beside the front door, and the one I could see on the left-hand side suddenly implode like a bomb had gone off out there and blown in the glass. There was a roaring sound, not exactly like a bomb, more like . . . well, more like some animal roaring . . . or a tornado suddenly exploding inside, or maybe a dam bursting open. Something came in through the windows then, with the broken glass. It was just a split second, but it looked like . . . well, it looked like gushing black water, or maybe oil the way it was glistening black.

Then there was only darkness. And the brief sounds of screaming beneath that roaring, thundering noise. But there was something wrong about what was happening. I mean, it sounded like people were being drowned or torn apart or

95

something inside the building. When I rolled and flinched and looked back, I knew that it couldn't be a tidal wave, or water, or oil. Because the back entrance doors were wide open, and nothing was coming out. There should have been a great gushing black wave or something foaming out of the fire exit towards us. But there was only complete blackness, and the sounds of the thundering that had almost, but not quite, drowned out the screaming.

I looked at the woman who was trying to quiet the kid. He was silent now; eyes closed, lips quivering like he had pneumonia or something. She was looking back at the community centre, and I saw her mouth "Oh my God" . . . when the next really bad thing happened . . .

| CHAPTER ELEVEN | **INFERNO** |

THE CALOR GAS HEATER IN THE BASEMENT of the cellar had been placed there only two days previously. The first tremor had tipped it on its side, and it had rolled sharply against the nearest concrete wall. The impact there had hurled it to the other wall, where the container had been fractured. The second tremor had repeated the manoeuvre, making for a slow leak. And then, when the windows imploded and the Darkness came in, the temperature in the community centre dropped by 120 degrees in three seconds. Enough to penetrate instantly through the wooden floor to the basement, where the Calor gas container still rocked gently from side to side. The canister ruptured and a jet of flame erupted in the basement, igniting the slow leaks in the gas mains that had also been caused by the second tremor. Although severed to east and west by the fog-mist barrier, and with the gas trapped in that section of the mains in ways that would never be known, the pipe exploded like a bomb, blasting up through the floor. Just as the windows had imploded to admit the Darkness, orange-yellow flames exploded through the same shattered windows, the front door and the exit, turning the community centre into a huge fireball. The fireball erupted through the roof, throwing burning debris high into the air with a shuddering roar. Lisa and Annie sheltered the boy, now quietened, his eyes wide and staring at the fire-filled sky. As Damon and Wayne rolled and scrabbled towards the others, the roaring subsided, but it seemed that the screaming had returned.

But this surely could not be the screaming of the people inside.

This was more like some gigantic animal, suddenly trapped inside a furnace. The hideous shrieking filled the air as sparks and burning splinters fell around them. Jay slapped at a smouldering piece of fabric which almost fell directly on his head, kicked it away and finally began to retch.

Candy clutched her hands to her ears to deafen the hideous screaming sound. Alex could only look at the raging furnace that had once been a community hall. There were . . . *shapes* in there. No longer moving—burning, huddled bundles wreathed in intense flame. Stunned, he looked away, falling to his knees when he realised that only seconds ago he and Candy had been caught up in there, in the mad crush. First the thundering tidal wave that had never arrived, and now this hideous fire. Alex bent double to control his nausea, slapped his hands on his thighs angrily, hoping that he would wake up. When he looked back at Candy, she had taken her hands from her ears. Wide-eyed, she was staring at the fire and at the sparks flying in the night. Then she stared at Alex, as if he should have all the answers to what had happened and what was happening. But there were no answers for that hideous black tidal wave. No answers for how a dead man could walk and talk and somehow see right into their souls. No answers for how he could give birth to that terrifying black flood. No answers for how an entire city could somehow fall apart and be hemmed in by this impossible wall of smoke. No answers for this horrifying explosion and the death of all inside.

"Alex," said Candy, turning to look back at the burning community centre. He looked at her for a long time before she spoke again. "I want to wake up now."

He could find nothing to say. Instead, he turned to look at the others.

They were all staring into the fire, and saying nothing.

CHAPTER TWELVE | THE EDGE

THEY SPENT THE NIGHT WHERE THEY WERE, beside the blazing pyre of the community centre. Despite the horror of what had happened close by and the knowledge that forty or fifty people had burned to death in there (or had they been dead *before* the fire erupted?); despite knowing that those bodies were still burning somewhere within that inferno, they remained at a safe distance throughout the long night. It was an instinctive refusal to leave the fire: a primal instinct that told them that perhaps the flames were keeping the terror that had descended on the city at bay. Drawn to the flames of the community centre by their primal need for protection, they were simultaneously repelled by what those hellish flames had done—*were* still doing. When sleep came, it was the sleep of utter exhaustion, an aftermath of the shock that each had endured. For each, it was a troubled sleep, filled with stark playback nightmares. When the roof of the community centre finally collapsed in a roaring cloud of sparks, each of the survivors woke in alarm, but quickly returned to their fear-drugged sleep.

Lisa woke to find the boy cradled in her arms. The sloping bank on which they lay was grassed and relatively comfortable, but her joints ached badly. Her neck was cricked, but—worse—there was a wretched hollowness inside that gave her no false comfort that everything might have resolved itself during the night and that everything they'd experienced was no more than a bad dream. She shifted, sitting upright. The boy moaned and clung tight. Not far away, she could see the sole survivors of last night's horror, also lying on the grass and still sleeping: a young man with a guitar gripped tightly across his waist, just as protectively as Lisa was holding the boy. Behind and above him, a man and a woman, lying—curiously—back to back. Down below, two teenagers, perhaps sixteen or seventeen years old; one of them curled up in a foetal position. And the young man who had broken open the rear exit and saved them all.

The community centre had all but burned to the ground. Now there was only a pile of black-and-white timbers, almost burned to nothing but still with glowing orange embers; a skeletal tangle in mounds of grey ash and fused debris. Clouds of grey-black smoke plumed up from the wreckage. Lisa followed the smoke up into the immensity of a blank grey sky.

And then she realised that the undulating cloud barrier that had hemmed them in was gone.

She snapped alert, the boy moaning again and clinging tighter. When she looked around, she could see the terraced houses ahead with their cracked walls and shattered windows, great patches of slate missing from the roofs of houses that were still standing. On either side, a ragged outline of buildings and tilted trees. But no smoke barrier, if smoke was what it had been. Could this mean that the nightmare was over? Even now, were ambulances and fire crew on their way at last? She turned to Annie . . . and saw that she wasn't lying at her side, as she'd imagined.

"Annie . . ."

Fear stabbed in her stomach. The boy must have felt it, because he started to wake, groaning but keeping his face buried against her chest. Had something happened to Annie in the night? The sound of Lisa's anxious voice was waking the others now. But when she twisted around to look behind her, she saw with vast relief that Annie was still alive. She was about fifty feet away, walking slowly back towards them, head down. Had she woken and gone for a walk? Strange that she hadn't woken her. And now the relief was tinged with anxiety again. There was something about the way Annie was walking. Too slow, head down as if preoccupied with bad thoughts.

"Annie!"

This time when she called the others were well awake. But Annie still didn't look up as she walked on. When she was still ten feet away, she lifted her head.

"What is it, Annie? What's wrong?"

"I think . . . " Annie looked slowly behind her, as if still trying to work something out in her mind. Something that was troubling her badly. "I think everyone had better come and see for themselves."

"The smoke," said Candy, standing up and looking around. "The clouds, the smoke. Whatever it was. It's gone."

"Thank Christ," said Alex.

"I wouldn't thank anyone for anything," said Annie. "Until you've seen what I've seen."

Lisa stood up creakily. The boy clung tight to her hand, and when they walked up to Annie he also took Annie's hand when she proffered it.

"So what's the big mystery?" shouted Wayne.

Annie didn't answer.

"*What?*"

She turned back to look at Wayne and Damon, seemed about to say something; but it was as if she couldn't find the words.

"Just come," she said simply. "You'll see."

Candy and Alex were already following. Gordon slung the guitar over his shoulder but seemed unsure.

"If that smoke-thing's gone," said Wayne, "then it means we can get home again. My folks'll be going spare."

"And mine," said Damon. "Look . . . I'm getting back. I've got to see if they're all right. My sister and her kids . . . "

Annie didn't turn back.

Wayne and Damon turned and headed in the opposite direction. They gave the smouldering ruin of the community centre a wide berth as they made their way through an alley between the crumbling terraced houses that led back to the main street.

Gordon tried to say: "My aunt. The ceiling came down. I've got to find out if she's all right . . . " But nothing would come out of his mouth. Even as he struggled to find the words, he knew that he was only fooling himself. He had clawed through those ruins before giving up hopelessly. His aunt could never have survived that fall of rubble. But he had nowhere else to go. It wasn't right that her body should be buried under there, and no one knew about it. Someone had to come and dig her out. He watched Damon and Wayne heading off, and took a step in their direction. Then he saw that the other guy was standing up at last and dusting himself down. They exchanged a look, and then Jay began to follow Annie and the others.

"My . . . " Only one word would come. Enough to make Jay look back at him. But when nothing else came out, he ignored him and followed the others across the parkland. Gordon hung his head, fury and grief smouldering inside. And then he realised what seemed so strange about this new morning. Not that the sky was a dull grey with no sign of clouds, not the smouldering ruins. But surely someone else would be out on the streets this morning? Now that the smoke barrier had gone, surely the emergency services should already be there. Where were the people from the surrounding houses? Were they all really still crouched inside their ruined homes, too frightened to come out? Where were the siren sounds of fire engines and ambulances? It seemed as if they were the only people left in this part of the city. He looked again at the smouldering ruins of the community centre and seemed to see something like a ribcage underneath a smoking timber. Quickly, he looked away . . . and then strode angrily after the others. When he looked back for the two other youths, they were gone.

They'd covered about half of the grassed parkland when Jay suddenly stopped. The others ahead of him kept walking. When Gordon drew level with him, he stopped and saw the look of puzzlement on Jay's face.

"There's something wrong," said Jay, without turning to look at him. "I know this park. Played here lots of times when I was a kid. Walked here every other weekend when I wanted to get my head together. Place hasn't changed in years."

"*What?*" Gordon wanted to say, but could only grunt.

Jay looked at him, trying to weigh him up, then said: "Don't you live round here, then? Haven't you *been* to this park before?"

Gordon looked around and saw nothing out of place.

"Up ahead," said Jay, pointing. "Where they're all going."

Gordon looked at the group.

"The park should be *bigger* than this."

And now Gordon knew what Jay meant, wondered why he hadn't noticed it for himself.

The others were walking towards the place where the smoke barrier had once been. There was a mound there now. A churned-up ridge of soil, stretching right across the park as far as he could see. The ragged barrier went right up to the corner of a crumbled pub on the left, cut right across the park's playing field in an erratic gash to disappear into trees to the right. Some of the trees had toppled and were hanging at weird angles over the edge of the gash. It was as if an army of bulldozers and earth-moving machines had been at work, ploughing up the ground just ahead on all sides and ramming the earth up into this irregular barrier. But there was no man-made straightness of line here. The mound of soil and grass was jagged and cracked on all sides.

"That pile of soil and stuff," continued Jay. "It cuts across the midpoint of the field. But it's like . . . like there's nothing beyond that ridge. There were houses there. Kinwright Street, and the Hotspur bar at the end. You should be able to see them all from here. That ridge isn't big enough to hide them. Christ, don't tell me *everything's* been flattened past that point. You should be able to see for miles and miles . . . "

Jay continued on, Gordon close behind. He began to run to catch the others, and Gordon began to trot along too. There was only one thought in Jay's mind now.

What has that woman seen beyond the ridge? What's over there that's so bad?

Then Jay saw a familiar sight that slowed him down. When he saw it, he breathed out an almighty sigh of relief, then bent to put his hands on his thighs and suck in good air. Gordon drew level again, and waited.

"It's okay," said Jay. "Okay. Thought I was freaking out there for a minute. But it's all right now."

"What?" asked Gordon, and was surprised at how easily the word had slipped out this time. Sometimes it happened like that.

"See that?" Jay pointed to the church spire which had suddenly appeared over the mound. "That's St. Michael's. My mate got married there. Me and my pals stood in the back row and coughed when the vicar asked the usual question, '*If* anyone knows why these two shouldn't be joined together.' Church is still there, though. Means everything's still where it's supposed to be." Jay laughed. "The vicar must have put a word in with God. Everything else has fallen to bits, but the church is still in one piece." He carried on. Following behind, Gordon watched more details of the church spire reveal themselves as they drew nearer to the mound. It began to rise before them like a rocket heading for the heavens in slow motion. The effect was heightened by the absence of clouds. Just that dense, grey backdrop of the sky, with that great black needle rising before them.

Annie had forged on ahead but now paused before reaching the mound, turning to wait until the others caught up. Even from a distance, Jay could see the look of confusion on her face. Clearly there was something over there that made her anxious. She began to speak while they were still drawing near.

"I don't know why I went for . . . a walk," she said hesitantly. "When I woke up, I mean. I had a dream. Nothing that'll make sense to you. Just that something was . . . different. I had to go and see what it was, before I woke you up, Lisa. When I saw the smoke barrier was gone, I nearly woke you. But I didn't feel *right*. I wanted to make sure that what I was seeing was really there. Or rather, *not* there."

"Annie?" Lisa was concerned. She had never seen her reacting like this before. She touched her arm and Annie continued.

"I came here. I don't know why. The dream, you see."

"Look, I'm sorry," said Alex. "But you're not making any sense. Why have you brought us out here? What is it?"

"Look for yourself," said Annie, stepping cautiously up the mound. "But be careful."

Jay pushed past and climbed the mound.

"Be careful!" warned Annie again.

Jay reached the top of the mound, and could see St. Michael's church a hundred yards away.

But there was nothing else between him and the church.

Nothing.

Just a yawning gap, with the church apparently sitting on a crag of rock, only slightly wider than the building itself. A cliff face dropped away from the church on all sides, into nothingness. Jay stumbled on the mound, arms waving, and saw a mind-reeling drop of sheer rock faces and impenetrable darkness below. His mind reeled before the immense depths. He staggered, then felt something grab him from behind.

Stumbling, he realised that the kid with the guitar had pulled him back.

"You see?" said Annie. "You see what I mean?" She sounded as if she wanted to hear him say: *No, you're wrong. You're seeing things. That's all.*

Uttering a sound of exasperation, Alex pushed on past them all to the mound and peered over the rim. What he saw left him speechless.

"What is it?" Candy was spooked, but didn't want the others to see how much. When Alex motioned to her without turning from the rim of the mound, she nervously began to climb. The others followed, carefully reaching the raised edge to look on their new world.

No one spoke. No one *could* speak.

The playing field had been severed by the quake at its midpoint.

The raised mound was cracked earth pushed back by the immense collapse of land, to form the ragged cliff edge on which they stood. Different colours of soil and clay were revealed in descending layers in the facing side of the pinnacle. It was like a cross-section view of some surreal geologist's underground survey from what had once been ground level to the unfathomable depths below, testimony to the passing of the ages. Behind the church on its stone pedestal and off to the right was another pillar of clay, soil and stone. This was larger, perhaps four hundred yards square in ragged dimensions. There were four ruined houses there, and the remains of a road vanished over the edge of its precipice.

To the left were several more of these impossible towers. There was nothing on them but meaningless rubble, but on one was a solitary tree. Where the cliff edge mound curled away to their left past a row of crumbled terraced houses practically perched on the edge, there had once been a bus depot. That too had been replaced by another stone tower, this one perhaps bigger than the others, although it was impossible to see around the bend of the cliff edge. But most of the nearside of the depot had fallen away into the Chasm. There was a double-decker bus parked on the ragged edge of the tower, its left front wheel in space. At any moment, it seemed, the vehicle must topple over the edge. To the right of the church, perhaps two hundred feet lower, was another stone tower with a flattened top, like a miniature plateau. Whatever had previously been at ground level, which would have brought this tower up to the same height as the church, had shattered and collapsed, leaving only this lower crag of ragged soil and stone, like a flattened building site. Behind the church and the shorn-away tower on the right stretched another cliff edge, on which were perched the remains of a collapsed frozen-food factory and other industrial buildings.

Even more bizarre, beyond the peaks and crags which were all that was apparently left of this part of Edmonville—was *nothing*. There was only a blank expanse of greyness that must somehow be an all-enveloping mist or fog, hiding what lay beyond from sight. But surely even mist had "substance"? It was possible to feel, even sense, the moist dense barrier of a real mist or fog. So why were there no wisping curls, no shifting cloud banks? Why only this utter, blank greyness?

They all felt it then, when they looked out into the void; the unnerving sense that they were looking past these surreal towers and crags of crumbling stone into an awful and empty *nothingness*. It was as if the world beyond, and on either side of the cliff edge on which they stood, had simply ceased to exist.

"You see," said Annie at last, and she had to clear her throat before she was able to continue. "At first, I thought that I was seeing things. It can't really be like that, can it? I mean, not like *that*. It's just not possible. Is it?"

"Come back from the edge!" shouted Candy, and everyone reeled back to see that she had quietly scrambled back from the awesome sight. She began to shake her head, staring at her feet, as if by simply refusing to look, everything would return to the way it was before. "Alex! Come back from the edge. We'll fall. If we get too close, we'll fall."

"We should do what those other two did," said Alex, scrambling back to her. "Go find help."

"But where is everybody?" asked Lisa. "It's like . . . like we're the only ones left. Do you think . . . " She stopped then when the boy crushed hard against her, burying his face once more.

"What?" asked Jay. "Go on . . . say it."

"What if the only ones left were those in the community centre? I mean, those two men in the ambulance had gone around looking for survivors and were bringing them back there. What if everyone else was . . . burned up . . . in there?"

"In a whole city?" said Alex. "No, there'll be help. I'm going back."

"What about the man?" said Candy. She was still looking at her feet. "What about the man in the off-licence shop? And the . . . black water?"

"What are you talking about?" asked Jay.

He remembered the strange darkness that had erupted through the windows of the community centre. Something that might have been black water, or oil, but couldn't possibly have been either—not when the entire community centre had burst into flame only moments later.

"Nothing," replied Alex. He reached for Candy's hand as he moved off. "It was nothing. Come on, Candy . . . " Candy pulled away from him, but also moved off.

"Wait a minute," said Jay. "You were running away from something back there at the community centre. It was you . . . and the woman . . . who came pelting back into the place, just before . . . before the place blew apart. What the hell was after you?"

"Leave us alone," said Alex. "We're going for help."

"What the hell *was* it?"

"You want some aggro, sonny?" Alex whirled around, fists bunched. Candy shied away from him, and walked on past, head down. "'Cause I've just about had it!" His eyes were wild now, the pressure of everything he had seen and experienced, and the horrifying and inexplicable events after the encounter with the Dead Man, coming to bear at last. Jay stopped himself moving forward to meet him; the old instincts again, anger flaring in any confrontation. The man was perhaps twenty years his senior, but looked in bad shape. And even if Jay's head was still swimming, even if he still felt weak from his ordeal in the school ruins, he reckoned he could take him on if he had to. But he held himself in check as the wild grimace faded from the man's face. Now Alex looked like he was going to apologise for his outburst. Instead, shaking his head, he turned and marched after his wife.

"What do we do now?" began Lisa. "I suppose that man's right. We'll have to . . . "

"Wait," said Gordon, forcing the word out. When they all looked at him, he knew he wouldn't be able to get the rest of it out. Instead, he pointed ahead, past Alex and Candy—and what they hadn't yet seen as they plodded on, heads down.

Two figures were running across the park towards them.

It was Wayne and Damon.

At last, Candy and Alex saw them coming. Candy shied away again from their headlong dash. Alex stood his ground, as if this time he really was ready for a fight, with whoever or whatever. But both kids staggered to a halt before they reached him, gasping for breath and trying to speak, now pointing back the way they'd come.

"Oh Christ," said Annie, as if she knew.

"Back there . . ." Wayne managed to get out at last. "There's . . . God . . . there's . . . "

"What?" yelled Alex, unprepared for more confusion. He wanted this nightmare to be over.

"Just past the school!" gasped Damon. "Down Davion Street and up to the shopping centre. Where the smoke and stuff was. Where they said no one could get through . . . "

"What?" yelled Jay.

"It's all gone!" continued Damon. "Oh Christ, it's all fallen away into a great fucking *hole* or something. There's just . . . like . . . a big cliff edge. Everything past that has fallen into this big . . . deep . . . " He couldn't find the words to describe it, but with sickness in their souls, everyone knew what he was talking about. "My folks," babbled Damon. "My brother and his wife. The street where they lived. It's just . . . *gone!*"

"There's bits and pieces of houses and buildings and factories and things," Wayne cut in. "All balanced on these big, thin mountains . . . or something. They go down so deep, you can't see what's at the bottom . . . "

We're cut off, Gordon tried to say. *It's the same all around us. Behind, ahead. And on both sides, where those houses are over on the left. And where the trees are on the right. It's a half-square mile of land, stranded and separated from the rest.* But when he looked at everyone else's shocked and white faces, he knew that they were all thinking the same thing.

The earthquake had done more than demolish their city.

It had changed their world.

Forever.

From behind, beyond the cliff edge, came the sounds of a distant and grumbling thunder. They turned in alarm as the sound changed, becoming a crackling and shivering that filled the air with ratcheting echoes.

"Oh God," said Lisa. "Look . . . "

The church spire was disintegrating.

Slowly, far too slowly, it seemed, the tower fell apart before their eyes. As if it had somehow been detonated at the base like a redundant factory tower. The lower half disappeared in a gushing cloud of dust and whirling bricks, the spire coming apart like some massive brick jigsaw as it toppled and began to fall out across the Chasm. The bell in the tower clanged. It was a hollow, booming death knell. Wayne moaned and sank to his knees, hugging himself. It was just like the bell in the school tower, and the horror of the similarity overwhelmed him. The disintegrating spire vanished in its roaring shroud of dust, an avalanche of shattered brick, cement and stone vanishing into the depths of the Chasm.

Candy shrank back when the bus balanced precariously on the crag of rock that had once been a bus station suddenly juddered forward as if it were alive; pushing forward until both wheels were over the edge, as if watching the church spire vanish into the darkness. And then the tarmac edge crumbled and the bus lurched forward over the rim.

"Christ . . ." said Annie.

The bus showed its undercarriage and suspension as it turned over lazily in the air. There was nothing for the vehicle to hit on its way down. Silently, looking like a toy in that immense gulf, it fell . . . and fell . . . and fell . . . until it was gone into the darkness below. There was no sound of impact. Just the muted hush of the vanished church spire as its disintegrating rain of brick and stone swept down the jagged, sheer face of the stone tower on which it had stood. Only a faint whispering of dying echoes from the Chasm below, like the waves of some vast and bottomless underground sea.

They stood and listened, until there was nothing else to hear.

CHAPTER THIRTEEN | **THE JOURNAL OF JAY O'CONNOR: AFTERMATH**

I DON'T THINK ANYONE WAS IN THEIR RIGHT mind then. Not me, that's for sure. I was still feeling like hell and my vision was blurry. And it seemed that what had just happened—the church spire falling and the bus going over after it—was like some kind of warning. Like we were all being told that it wasn't over yet.

Wayne and Damon just slumped down there on the grass as if all the wind had been kicked out of them. Wayne was grabbing handfuls of turf; as if he was afraid that the ground might suddenly give way beneath him. I didn't blame him for that. Everyone was spooked. It was the guy called Alex who first suggested we find out who we all were. The two women were called Annie and Lisa, and they owned a hardware store. Although I thought that the kid with them must be a son of one of them, I was wrong on that count. They'd saved him when the quake hit or the bomb dropped, or whatever the hell had happened. But his parents had been killed. The kid with the guitar didn't seem to want to talk to anyone. When we pressed him for his name, he only spat out one word: "Gordon." Whether it was his first or his last name, no one knew at that stage. I supposed he was in shock like everyone else. Something funny happened when the guy called Alex introduced his wife. He said that her friends called her Candy, and I could tell by the way they looked at each other then that something was up. It didn't have anything to do with whatever had hit Edmonville; it had to do with the fact that they hated each other's guts.

But it was bloody peculiar, the way everyone was sitting and standing around, telling everyone their names—like we were at some kind of group therapy session or something. Like, if we all did the sensible thing, started to act as if nothing had happened, then everything would sort itself out. Afterwards, Alex said:

"We've got to have a proper look around. Check out the . . . entire area. Just to make sure."

He was right—we couldn't be sure that it was the same cliff edge and the same destruction all around us. Maybe we weren't perched on a half-mile-square, flattened-off mountain peak, with a bottomless drop every way you looked. But we all believed that it was true. Still Alex was taking the lead and saying the sensible thing.

"Why don't we split up into two groups?" He was trying to make his voice sound like he was in command. It wasn't working, but we let him get on with it. "Jay, you and . . . Gordon, and the two lads . . . why don't you make your way around there . . . " He pointed off to the right, where the bus depot was perched on its peak and the bus had gone over the edge.

"The two ladies and the boy, Candy . . . " His wife glared at him again. "Candy and I, we'll all head along this edge in the other direction. Whoever finds a way out can come back . . . come back here, to the playing field . . . just here. Otherwise, well . . . otherwise . . . " He couldn't bring himself to say: *Otherwise we'll all meet up again when we've been right around.*

No one had the energy to object to Alex's idea, least of all me. We had to do something. So when Alex and his "team" headed off along the rough cliff edge, we did the same. No one spoke, and we walked as if we'd been on the road for weeks. As we drew nearer to the trees, I remembered something.

"What happened to the other kid?"

"What other kid?" asked Wayne.

"The kid who was crying. The one I found you with, in the school. Was he in the community centre . . . ?"

"Oh, Paulie. He's gone."

"What do you mean 'gone'?"

"He ran away. We never saw him again."

I remembered how Damon and Wayne had started throwing stones at the kid. At the time I was in no state to do anything about it, even if I'd wanted to. But now I felt sick inside. Sick and claustrophobic like I was still trapped under all that rubble. They'd chased the poor little kid away. God knows what had happened to him. I struggled with this sick feeling that I should have done something about it. Then I tried to rationalise it. Even if I hadn't keeled over and had been able to drag him along, he would have ended up at the community centre; and the chances are he'd have ended up like all the others. Burned alive. But there was another voice, one that I struggled to push down: *He might have got away, through that rear exit. Just like us. And he'd be alive now.* I shook my head, and caught Gordon giving me a funny look. Maybe being dead was the best option in the long run. Christ knew what was happening here, and what was going to happen to us now.

We reached the trees, but didn't dare go near them. We could see now that the reason they were standing at such strange angles was that most of them were right on the cliff edge, some on the verge of falling over altogether. So we skirted around to the nearest houses. We stood there at the gates and fences of the first street's back gardens, and started shouting; just to see if there was anyone in there, maybe hiding and waiting. None of us wanted to go in and see.

Everything was wrong here. The quiet. The fact that there

was no one else around. As if everyone had run away. After a while, I was so pissed off with myself for being scared that I marched up to one of the doors and knocked hard. There was no answer. It felt ridiculous. The whole of Edmonville falling apart, and here's me knocking on a door just as polite as can be. The door was open, and when I pushed inside I could see that the upstairs floor had come down, blocking the passageway with rubble. When I looked back, it seemed that the others had also managed to pull themselves together. Wayne, Damon and Gordon began checking all the other houses, knocking on doors and pushing their way in when the doors were open.

We tried the telephones, switched on radios, televisions.

None of the electrical appliances were working. When I found a battery radio, all I could get right across the bands was a continuous crackling of static. No one was broadcasting out there.

Some of the houses were wrecked, some of them relatively untouched. One of them that I went into was so untouched that it looked just like one of those stories I'd read as a kid. You know, like that ship, the *Mary Celeste*. There was a meal on the table for four people. Tea still in cups, pots and pans in the kitchen full of dried pasta. I wasn't in that kitchen long. In fact, I was out of there in double-quick time. You see, the far wall had fallen out, just as neatly as if some builder had come and taken it away brick by brick, just a small patch of plaster dust on the tiled floor, and beyond that missing wall . . . nothing. Just that empty greyness beyond, which meant that this house, maybe the whole terrace, was balanced right on the edge of the Chasm and could go over at any time, just like the church and the bus. When I got back outside, I realised just by looking at the faces of the others that they'd had similar experiences, had all seen that just being in this row of terraced houses was dangerous. And when no one spoke, I knew that they'd not found anyone in there.

We kept away from the houses as we walked after that.

But we kept calling out in the hope that someone might be in them. Christ knew what we expected. Even if we did find other survivors, did we expect that they were somehow going to wave a magic wand and make everything all right again? Maybe we'd stumble across a copper who'd give us directions, tell us where to go and what to do.

Past the trees and that row of houses was an open area. Beyond the ragged cliff edge, we could see other crags and peaks of stone with ruined houses and buildings perched on them. We didn't go near the edge; just shouted over from where we were. I guess the nearest crag was about a hundred yards, the furthest perhaps a quarter-mile. Beyond the last one, nothing but the blank greyness which you couldn't look at for too long in case it did your head in.

We walked, and shouted, but there were no replies. I tried to bring up a mental picture of what this part of the town looked like before the disaster; tried to remember what the area was like out there, where the crags and peaks were. What parts of the town had fallen into the pit? Which parts were left? I was having a hard job. Crazy, isn't it? I must have spent most of my life here, and yet I couldn't bring to mind exactly what the place looked like. I'd played football with school-friends on streets that had disappeared forever; had delivered newspapers on streets that no longer existed. But I couldn't bring the memories of those places back. We rounded a pile of rubble that had once been some kind of civic building and saw a street that suddenly disappeared over the edge. It was bizarre. Houses on either side showed no sign of damage. And then the street suddenly ended, sliced away, the cracked tarmac forming the cliff edge. A street to nowhere.

When we finally found a ruined street that I remembered, we came across the first of many dead bodies. A car had been crushed by falling masonry; the windscreen was shattered and splashed red. The driver—a woman—was hanging out of the car door, her blue-patterned dress dyed a different colour now.

And when Damon saw what had happened to her face and head, he threw up there and then. I told the others not to look, but how could we not? We followed the line of the cliff edge as far as we were able, trudging through ruined streets, past shattered buildings and stores. We saw people lying on the cracked tarmac and on the pavements, killed by falling rubble. Kids dead in prams. Bodies that had been smashed and cut up. Arms and legs lying about. Dried, black-red stains. Cars overturned or on their sides. Some still neatly parked and untouched. A garage which had caught fire and burned itself out. I'd known a kid who worked there. But I didn't go over to look inside the smoking ruins. I could see through the main entrance that there was still a car on a hydraulic lift over the maintenance pit. It had been burned out in the fire. I didn't suppose that the car owner was going to make a complaint.

In Jackson Street there was a deep crack in the middle of the road, right where the white line had been. Neat trick. We didn't cross over to look down. We just kept on going, following the cliff edge and hoping with each step of the way that maybe we'd hear an ambulance siren or something; see people waving to us, showing us the way to safety. But there were no sounds, no living people, no offers of help.

We were alone here, stranded on this rock with the dead.

The real world had gone, and had been replaced by something very like Hell.

We'd just rounded what was left of Wady Street when the kid with the guitar started to act peculiar. He hadn't said more than four or five words since we'd first met, and I guessed that it was the shock of everything. Sometimes, as we walked, I'd catch him looking at me with this really serious expression on his face, as if he wanted to tell me something important. But every time I looked, he looked away. Anyway, most of Wady Street was just a ruin, with rubble covering it and only a small path between the ruins on either side to walk through. It looked like those wartime photographs you see. There wasn't any colour now. It was like the whole place was black and white. There'd been no sign of the sun; just that big blank grey sky.

Suddenly, Gordon began to make this moaning sound. I was in the lead, picking my way through the rubble and with the cliff edge perhaps fifty feet away on our right. Gordon was right behind me, and I turned to see what was wrong. His face looked white and wild. His mouth was shut, but I could see the muscles in his cheeks moving, could see his Adam's apple going up and down; just like a ventriloquist or something. I started to ask him what was wrong . . . and he looked at me with staring eyes. Right then I felt that he *wanted* to speak, maybe even yell something out loud . . . but he just couldn't. Instead, he shoved past me and began to clamber and scramble over the rubble.

"What's the matter with *him*?" yelled Wayne.

I shouted Gordon's name, but he didn't turn back. He just kept going. A hundred yards or so over the rubble, he half-clambered, half-fell over a shattered garden wall and ran across the littered grass towards an end-of-terrace house. Half of the house had collapsed. You could see right inside the rooms from top floor to ground floor, like a cross-section of the place. By the time I'd reached the garden wall, Gordon was doing the next crazy thing.

He had scrambled halfway up the pile of shattered concrete and house bricks that lay against the side of this half-house and was tearing at the mound; throwing bricks over his shoulder, like he was trying to burrow his way inside. I stood there, watching him, as Wayne and Damon passed. They kept on moving ahead, picking their way over the rubble.

"Leave him," said Damon. "He's cracked."

I just looked at them.

"Gordon!" I shouted. "Come on. We've got to keep moving. Find a way off."

The guitar on his back was bouncing and jostling as he clawed frenziedly at the pile.

"Leave him," said Wayne.

Instead, I climbed over the broken wall and walked towards the pile of rubble. Gordon couldn't hear me. Clouds of concrete and plaster dust were swirling around him in his desperation to get into the pile. I didn't look back at the other two, but I knew that they'd stopped to watch. I kept calling Gordon's name. But he couldn't, or wouldn't, hear me. Finally, climbing up behind him, I grabbed his shoulder.

The reaction nearly sent me catapulting backwards.

Gordon whirled. He looked as if he'd gone mad. His eyes were wide and bloodshot from the dust. His hair had turned grey with it. His teeth were clenched, but he was breathing heavily. He crouched there, glaring at me.

"All right!" I snapped. "What the hell's the *matter* with you?"

Gordon screwed his eyes shut with effort. Strangled noises were coming out of his mouth.

"My . . . my . . . my . . ."

Now he was almost weeping with effort. And that's when I understood. He was trying to speak, but couldn't. It wasn't shock. This was something else. Maybe the kid had a stammer, and the shock had made everything worse.

"All right," I said. "Take it easy, Gordon. Tell me. What is it? What's wrong?"

"My . . . my . . ."

His face was turning purple with exertion.

"*AUNT!*" he yelled right into my face. "She's *here*! Buried *here*!"

Whirling away from me again, he began to claw at the rubble once more. I stumbled back down the pile. So this was where he'd lived? And someone close to him hadn't been able to get out. I dodged a salvo of bricks and shattered window frame, thrown over his shoulder.

"Gordon, there's not much point."

If anyone was under there, no way were they coming out of it alive. He either didn't hear me, or chose to ignore my voice.

Whatever, I slithered to the bottom of the rubble mound and watched him continue to pull bricks and wood and chunks of concrete away. Wayne and Damon were sitting on the shattered garden wall.

"Come and help," I called to them hopelessly.

"He's not the only one!" cried Damon, voice breaking. "I lost . . . my folks . . . *everything*. The street's just not there anymore."

"Okay," I called to Gordon. "I'll help you. For a while. But listen . . . LISTEN!"

Gordon stopped, but didn't turn to look at me. Never mind, he was listening.

"Even if someone came to help us," I went on, "which it seems they're *not* . . . it would take us days to clear this away. Now if she's . . . your aunt, yeah? . . . well, if she's down there, she won't be alive. You must know that."

Gordon began tearing angrily at the rubble again.

"Okay, okay!" I snapped. "I'll help. But listen. After a while, we've got to move on. Right?"

Gordon didn't answer, but this time when he started again, so did I. Together we slid great chunks of broken masonry and bricks and plasterboard away. I could see that there was blood on his fingers where his fingernails had cracked. I choked and coughed in the dust.

It was impossible.

I'd guessed that after a while, he would appreciate how impossible it was going to be. But he just kept going, even when I slumped back and realised that we were never going to find anyone down there. Maybe it was best for his peace of mind that we *didn't* find what was left of his aunt beneath that huge mound. I sat back, choking, and looked at his face. It was blank. No way was he going to give up until he'd burrowed his way to the bottom. And nothing I could say would make him change his mind.

"Okay," I said at last. "You do what you have to do. But

we've got to go on. Find a way off, and find out what's happened to everyone."

Gordon just kept on, pulling away the bricks and the plasterboard.

"If we find a way, someone will come back for you."

I slithered to the bottom and began making my way along the ruins of Wady Street. I didn't look back, but within a couple of minutes I could hear Wayne and Damon right behind me.

At the end of the street there used to be a job centre. It was gone now. The place where it used to stand was about fifty feet out from the cliff edge. There was a crag of rock behind it, still with part of the centre's car park on it, a jumble of bushes and a street sign showing that there was a dead end just beyond.

"No kidding," I said aloud, and continued to follow the ragged cliff edge as it swept around in front of me and off to the left, taking the line of what used to be . . . I think . . . Jefferson Avenue. The cliff edge was made up of ragged tarmac now, bordered by a bent and twisted traffic barrier. It looked like the thing had been rammed continually, part of it twisting up into the air, like a miniature rollercoaster rail. There were more of those crazy crags and peaks beyond the edge. Some of them a couple of hundred yards square, with houses and buildings in various stages of collapse on them. Others with flattened, rough areas with nothing but rubble on the top. One of them was about twenty feet square. The grass there was neatly trimmed and cut, and there was a garden outhouse—still intact and sitting nice and neat as you please right in the middle of it. Sweeping down on all sides around it, this gigantic crag of rock stretching all the way down into a darkness that I didn't want to look at for long. It was just too much for the eyes. I seemed to be drawn to the cliff edge, and I had this bloody strange feeling that if I got too close, something would make me step over the edge. Then I'd just keep falling and falling into that blackness. Forever. It made me dizzy just thinking about those depths. I shook it off and kept moving.

There were more bodies. Stuff I don't want to talk about. I heard Damon moaning at one stage, but he was quiet pretty soon after that.

An hour later, Wayne suddenly shouted.

"Look!"

The shock of his voice nearly made me jump out of my skin. When I looked at him, I saw him pointing ahead. Before I could register what he'd seen, both he and Wayne ran past me—far too close to the cliff edge for my comfort.

"They've found us!" yelled Damon. "They've come for us."

"Thank Christ," I said, and felt this great tiredness come over me.

I sank to my knees and felt all the bad stuff draining away.

| **DEVASTATION**

"**S**OMETHING'S WRONG," SAID LISA.

The boy held her hand as they walked, staring up at the blank grey sky. All around them, beyond the cliff edge on their left, was the awesome drop into the void and the surreal stone peaks and crags that had once been Edmonville.

"You don't say," said Annie with a sour expression. "The world's fallen apart, we're stranded and it looks like everyone's dead or gone. That's wrong, all right."

"No, I mean with her. That woman, Candy."

Alex and Candy were up ahead, leading the way, and out of earshot.

"You mean apart from the fact that she hates her husband's guts?"

"She knows something . . . they *both* know something. Maybe about what's happened, or how it's happened. But I can tell, and it's tearing them both apart."

Up ahead, Alex said: "I don't know, Candy. I just don't know what we're going to do."

"There must be a way off here." For the moment, Candy had forgotten that he wasn't supposed to call her that. "We can't just be . . . stranded . . . like this. It's not . . . it's just not *real*."

"Someone will come. Even if we are cut off. The whole

world can't be . . ." The word *dead* caught in his throat and would not come out.

"We've got to tell them," continued Candy after a while.

Alex didn't have to ask what she was talking about. He couldn't get rid of the images from the previous night. The man in the off-licence store, with the wooden shard in his eye. The exploding black wave that had crashed down the street after them.

"It didn't happen," he said. "It couldn't have happened."

"What the hell are you talking about? We were both there. We both saw him."

"I've been thinking about it . . ." Alex looked quickly over his shoulder, afraid lest those behind should overhear what he was saying. "Maybe it wasn't an earth tremor, or a quake, or whatever. Maybe it was something else."

"Like what?"

"Like an air attack. A bomb, or something like that. Maybe someone somewhere pushed the button at last."

"That might explain what's happened, but not the man or that . . . that . . . black . . ." Candy couldn't find the words to describe the black torrent that had pursued them.

"Maybe it was more than just a bomb. Maybe there was some kind of gas attack. Chemical weapons. That fog barrier, the clouds that were all around us last night. That could have been chemical, couldn't it? I reckon that's the answer. It didn't kill us, but it killed all the others."

"But Alex," said Candy. "That *man* . . ."

"The gas! Don't you see? Maybe it made us hallucinate. See things that weren't there."

"That black . . . black wave. Alex, *that* was what killed all those people back there in the community centre."

"I don't know about that part. About the people dying. There was . . . an explosion, wasn't there? That's what did it. A black tidal wave in the middle of the street? Think about it, Candy. How could that happen? Where did it go? It just vanished. That was because it wasn't there. We *imagined* it was there. Just like the gas made us imagine the man in the store."

"But could we both see and hear the same thing?"

"It *must* be that. Can't you see? Nothing else makes sense."

Candy began to nod her head vigorously. It was the only thing that added up. "Maybe . . . maybe *none* of this is happening." When Alex looked across, her eyes were feverish. "Maybe it's just the gas, the chemicals. Maybe we'll wake up in a minute . . ."

Alex opened his mouth to say that she was hoping for too much. But he forced himself to be silent. Maybe if he prayed hard enough, it *would* all be a dream.

Twenty yards behind, Lisa said: "Look at them. They *do* know something."

"All I know is that we haven't eaten for a long time," interrupted Annie. "And we've got to get something inside the boy."

"Are you hungry?" asked Lisa, looking down at him. The boy continued looking at the sky, unhearing. He clutched Lisa's hand as if it were a safety line.

"He needs help," said Annie.

"I think he's in the safest place possible at the moment. He's keeping the pain away."

Smoke was visible ahead, drifting up into the sky. No one believed that it could be a good sign as they skirted around the cliff edge, heading in its direction.

It didn't take them long to find the first dead bodies.

On the other side of what had once been a main road was a fast-food restaurant: Light 'n' Heavy Bite. Once it had been a single-storey building, with floor-to-ceiling windows. Now it had simply ceased to exist, the entire construction flattened by the quake. Smoke rose from the rubble, and the remains of two cars were visible beneath concrete slabs that had spilled out onto the tarmac like a gigantic pack of cards. The driver of the first car had been squashed up against the cracked windscreen when a slab had fallen over the roof, pulverising it. Somehow the windscreen hadn't been punched out and the driver's face remained screwed up against the glass in a hideous, bloody scowl. The stark white flats of his hands, fingers spread, were clearly visible against the cracked glass. Lisa walked the boy away, averting his head, refusing to let him look. The others waited at the roadside, trying not to look at the dead driver, trying not to think about whether there was anyone else inside the car, as Alex went to investigate the ruin. When he returned, white-faced, he couldn't speak.

"Anyone . . . ?" began Annie.

Alex could only shake his head, and no more needed to be said.

At the bottom of the street, furrowed and cracked by the immense forces that had rippled underground, every single window in a used-car franchise had shattered, covering the parked cars in the forecourt in shrouds of gleaming ice. The glass had spilled out into the street like fine snow. It crackled underfoot as they carefully made their way past. Someone was lying in the office, by the side of an overturned desk. The glass sheets that lay around the figure were wet with blood. Annie called as they passed, but the person—whether male or female—was clearly dead. No one else moved inside the showroom, and it was impossible to get through the fallen avalanche of jagged glass to investigate further.

The boy began humming to himself as they passed. Lisa pulled him close as they moved.

There had been an apartment block beyond, sixteen storeys high.

It no longer existed, and had been replaced by a thirty-foot-high demolition site of twisted steel cable, sundered concrete blocks and rubble, stretching down to the cliff edge, where the top six floors had vanished into the abyss. The smoke that they had seen earlier was coming from the other side of the mound. They clambered around it and saw what had happened.

A concrete flyover had come down on the main road. A

coach and five vehicles had been passing underneath when the quake had severed the concrete supports beneath ground level and the entire structure had collapsed. Petrol had spilled from the ruptured tanks, ignited, and burned through the night. The remains of the coach and two of the demolished cars were still visible, blackened skeletons still smoking in the rubble.

"Shall we?" said Annie, waving a hand hopelessly at the carnage.

"What's the point?" said Lisa. "No one could have survived that."

"Where *is* everyone?" Candy looked as if she might lose control completely. "Where are the fire brigade, the ambulances, the emergency services? Where are they, for Christ's sake?"

No one replied, and they kept moving.

Everywhere was the same.

Buildings in ruins. Cars, coaches and lorries overturned, burned or smashed. Concrete and tarmac cracked and rippled in solid waves where the immense underground fractures had sped across Edmonville, uprooting underground water pipes, fracturing gas mains, and demolishing most of the buildings. And beyond the cliff edge the same surreal sights. The plateaus of rock, containing at what had once been ground level the few remaining jigsaw pieces of Edmonville. Beneath and around the ragged plateaus, other pinnacles of rock clustered like gigantic fractured stalagmites; reaching up from the depths of the Chasm on all sides, as if striving to reach that tenuous ground level. Some spiralled upwards to sharpened points; others had flattened tops forming bridges as if trying to create some bizarre rival to Monument Valley. Had the entire city of Edmonville been dropped down onto the Grand Canyon?

Walking ahead again, Alex and Candy suddenly stopped.

Another scene of carnage? More horror?

"What is it?" asked Annie. And then Lisa gasped.

"Someone's coming!" she exclaimed. "Look! Someone's coming!"

Filled with joy and relief, Annie and Lisa ran with the boy to join the others, seeing the figures up ahead who'd emerged from the ruins and were even now running towards them.

"Thank God," said Annie, and then she saw the expression on Alex and Candy's faces. It was a look of despair.

"It's them," said Alex flatly. "It's Jay and the others."

And when Lisa and Annie looked, they saw Wayne and Damon suddenly stagger to a halt, saw their own look of joy crumple and fade as they recognised them.

"Oh, good Christ," said Candy, her voice cracking. "We've been right around the edge, and there's no way off."

There was a long, motionless silence as they all stood looking at each other.

Then Jay began yelling something at the sky, punching at the air with his fists.

Finally, he pulled himself together, shook his head—and walked slowly towards them. Although no one spoke, they all felt the same. It was as if everything in this strangely and horribly changed world was against them. They'd sensed that they were stranded here, and now they had the proof.

"Why doesn't someone *come*?" moaned Candy.

Wearily, Jay walked past Wayne and Damon, head down. When he was standing in front of the others, he looked up at them.

"I think we're stuffed," he said simply.

They heard the music before they reached Wady Street.

"It's a radio," said Damon. "Someone's switched on a radio."

But when he turned to the others, all trudging back the way that Jay's party had come, his fragile expression of hope faded. There had been elation when they thought they'd found others who might help, but the realisation that they'd been right around this bizarre, ruined plateau and discovered no way off had crushed any remaining wishful thinking in the others. There had been too much horror, too much anguish—and the remaining optimism could not be rekindled. They had been walking in hopeless silence.

"Well, it's *something*, isn't it?" Damon went on desperately.

They kept walking slowly as the sounds of the yearning harmonica drew them on. The tune it played might be Spanish. A slow, melancholic lament. It seemed somehow to resonate in the silence. Under different circumstances, it might have sounded beautiful. But not here, on this crag in no-man's-land.

"It's Gordon," said Jay at last.

When they finally turned into the ruins of Wady Street, they could see the lone figure sitting on the shattered garden wall, next to the ruins of what had once been Gordon's home. No one spoke or called out to him as they picked their way over the rubble in his direction. And if he heard them coming, Gordon showed no sign of it. He remained hunched there, guitar slung over his shoulder, playing his lament. It was a haunting, mournful sound. He finished as they finally drew level with him, but remained looking steadfastly in the opposite direction.

"I told you," Jay said to him. "There's no way you could dig her out of there . . . "

"Did," said Gordon. "Found."

"You found your aunt?"

"Dead," said Gordon.

When he turned to look at them, his face was a blank white mask from the plaster dust that had gushed around him as he'd clawed at the rubble. There were two streaks on his cheeks where he'd wiped away tears. Gordon stood up and put the harmonica back in his top pocket.

"There's no way off," Lisa told him. "We're stuck up here."

Gordon nodded. He could not react to the news. He'd tried to play the grief out, but it was still there.

"So now what?" asked Candy.

"I suppose we should eat," said Annie. "The boy needs something. I guess we all do."

"I'll never keep anything down," said Lisa. "Not after what we've seen."

"Annie's right," said Jay. "We may not have an appetite, but we need to keep up our strength."

"I need a drink," said Candy. "A *big* drink."

Alex looked as if he was going to say something, but Candy glared and he shut up.

"There's a minimart still standing over there," said Wayne. They followed his pointing finger, through the ruins of one of Wady Street's houses to a back street which ran along the eastern edge of the park.

"Someone will come," said Alex. "We just have to wait."

No one answered as they clambered through the ruins towards the minimart.

CHAPTER FIFTEEN | **TAKING STOCK**

THE FLOOR OF THE MINIMART WAS LITTERED with tins that had been shaken from their shelves. But the building had remained standing, despite a gigantic crack stretching from floor to ceiling. Even the windows had remained in their frames.

"Don't touch any of the refrigerated stuff," said Alex, as he and Lisa began clearing the tins out of the way. "The power's only been off a day, but the food might still have turned."

Wayne and Damon ignored him, charging past them into the shop, kicking tins out of the way. They reached the refrigerated units and counter at the other end of the store and began foraging.

"What happens if you get food poisoning?" snapped Alex.

Jay found what he was after and tossed it across to Alex, who fumbled the catch and nearly dropped it.

"Tin opener," said Jay. "Who's going to be Mother?"

Annie had already selected some tins from the floor and took the opener from Alex. Soon, the boy was scooping fingerfuls of minced lamb into his mouth. Wayne and Damon were eating noisily at the far end of the store as the others selected what they wanted and began to eat. Although their appetites had seemed non-existent, the sudden appearance of food made them all realise how ravenous they really were.

After a long silence, while they satisfied their hunger, Annie said: "Maybe we should light a fire or something? A beacon, to let them know there's someone alive here."

"Can't do any harm," said Jay. "And there's plenty of wood lying around."

"I don't know if that's a good idea," said Alex.

"Why not?" asked Jay.

Alex suddenly became aware that Candy was no longer with them.

"Candy?"

"What?" snapped her voice from behind the shelving unit in the centre of the littered floor. She swung around the edge, one hand gripping the shelves. There was a bottle of Scotch in her other hand. She stood for a moment, staring at him. Her eyes did not leave his face as she unscrewed the cap and took a deep drink. Alex moaned, rubbing a weary hand over his face.

"Come on, then," continued Jay, ignoring the potential conflict between them. "What do you mean? Maybe the rescue services, the others on the outside, believe there's no one alive here. We have to at least let them know there are *some* survivors."

"Tell them," said Candy, drinking again.

"Candy, take it easy with that bottle. You know . . . "

"You've *got* to tell them what we saw. What we *think* we saw."

"What the hell's she talking about?" snapped Wayne.

"Candy, please. The bottle . . . "

"You *saw* something," said Jay, remembering the nightmare back at the community centre. "Didn't you?"

Alex looked hopelessly at the floor.

"Tell them!" shouted Candy. The boy crept into Lisa's lap, burying his head.

"Last night, before the community centre blew up . . . "

Alex swallowed hard, his throat suddenly dry. "Candy and I went out . . . into the street. We saw someone . . . something . . . in one of the stores. A man with his eye . . . Christ, Candy, I *can't* . . . "

"Come on, Alex. Be a man. Try harder." Candy drank again.

"We saw a man who should have been dead. His head was . . . smashed. But he spoke to us, as if he knew us. But we'd never seen him before. Then this . . . this . . . black *stuff* . . . exploded out of him. Like black water, or oil, or something. A bloody great black wave. It just *exploded* out of the store and filled the street. It chased us back to the community centre."

"Alex thinks we hallucinated," slurred Candy. "He thinks that there might have been nerve gas, or something, in the air. Made us see the dead man, and the black stuff."

"Two people couldn't have the same hallucination," said Annie.

"Make it three," said Jay, unscrewing the top from a pop bottle and taking a deep draught.

"What do you mean?" asked Lisa.

"I think I saw that black wave, or whatever you want to call it. Just before the community centre blew to hell. I thought I'd imagined it then. Thought I saw something like a black flood exploding through the windows. Just an instant, before the place went up."

"Three people seeing the same thing?" said Annie. "You can't have imagined it."

"I've read things," said Alex. "About what they can do these days. Designer bombs that kill people and leave buildings standing. Maybe they could design a gas that makes people see the same things. Good way to start a war, isn't it? Terrify people out of their wits first, then you could move in and take over. The survivors would be glad to see an invading army then, wouldn't they? Come to save them from the nightmares."

"You think that's what happened?" asked Jay. "You think this wasn't an earthquake, but the start of a war, or something?"

"I don't know what to think," replied Alex desperately. "I just know what we saw . . . what we *think* we saw."

"I think we should light a fire," said Damon.

"But maybe we've been cut off *deliberately*," Alex went on. "Don't you see? What if there was some kind of missile strike, and some kind of nerve gas dropped here. That could be the reason why no one's come to rescue us. Maybe this whole area has been deliberately cordoned off. I've been thinking about it all. Thinking about nothing else. Maybe we're quarantined. We could be *infectious*, or something. That gas . . . "

"That doesn't make sense," said Jay. "Infectious nerve gas? I don't think so."

"Don't you see?" pleaded Alex. "If we light a fire, we might draw attention to ourselves. And maybe—just think about this for a moment—maybe, if there's some kind of invading army out there . . . Well, they might see a beacon and decide to just drop another bomb on us or something." Alex was trembling now, sweat beading on his brow.

Candy looked down on her husband with contempt, and drank again.

"I think we should light a beacon," said Annie at last. "What else can we do? The telephones are dead and it looks like the rescue services just aren't going to come. Maybe they think everyone is dead here. We've got to let them know we're here."

"You're right," said Jay. "Nobody knows what the hell is happening, whether it's an earthquake, a missile strike, or what. But whatever's happened, we can't just stay here, living on tinned food for the rest of our lives. We should all start collecting wood for our bonfire. We're going to set it up in the middle of the park, well away from the houses so the fire doesn't spread."

"Let's get started," said Lisa.

CHAPTER SIXTEEN

THE JOURNAL OF JAY O'CONNOR: THE REMEMBERED

IN THE NEXT FEW MINUTES, WE WERE ALL back out there, stomachs full. Nobody spoke much; we all had a rough idea of what was required. I found a door off its hinges, lying just behind the minimart; grabbed it and hauled it off across the stunted grassed area that led into the middle of the park. I didn't look back, but I knew that the others were doing the same: looking for anything that would burn.

I reckon it took us about two hours to build that mound, right in the middle of the park. Common sense told us that perhaps it should be closer to the edge, giving anyone over there who might be in a position to help us a good view of the beacon we were going to light. But none of us wanted to get any closer to the edge and that bottomless drop beyond. No one could tell how safe it was there. So everyone just trudged backwards and forwards to the nearest line of ruined houses, or in Candy's case back to the minimart, where she kept herself well and truly fuelled up on the booze. It was funny. Funny peculiar, not funny ha-ha. The way that Alex kept looking at her as she'd come staggering back from the minimart with some pathetic, tiny piece of broken wood or crumpled newspaper. Like we didn't know she was just bringing this stuff back as a "cover." Like she wasn't drinking at all. And it was just as funny the way Alex didn't say a damn thing to her, even when she started staggering and weaving on her way back to the steadily growing pile in the middle of the park.

Something else was happening as we worked. It was as if everyone was welcoming this chance to be simply . . . *doing* something. Up until now, we'd all been so helpless. Just survivors of this earthquake, or missile strike, or whatever. I suppose we were still all in shock, and not understanding why no one had come to save us. I reckon that Alex's words about this hallucinating gas, or whatever, had just made everyone's fears worse. But just for now, while we were all collecting this wood for the fire, the simple physical act of collecting it was like some form of therapy. And I guess we were all thinking our own private thoughts as we worked, trying to get our heads together.

Eventually, it seemed like the light was starting to fade. Things were darker now, but when I looked up and around, it was weird. There was just this huge grey blanket all around us—no sign of the sun, or the moon or stars. Night wasn't falling so much as the blank greyness all around us was *deepening*. This is difficult to describe, but there was something about it that didn't seem . . . well . . . *right*. It was going to be our second night stuck here and I knew that the others were feeling the same way I did. We didn't like this idea of the darkness closing in. We needed light.

When the debris for the beacon was about four feet high and thirty feet wide, we decided that we had enough. Annie and Lisa brought four bright red plastic containers back from the minimart, full of barbecue fuel. The boy was clutching a box of matches, but his eyes were still far away. I reckoned he was never coming back. Secretly, I think I envied him. By now, that overall greyness had become so dark that we could barely see each other.

"Have you noticed?" said Annie after the barbecue fuel had been poured all over the broken wood and she had taken the box of matches from the boy. I looked at her, realised that the question hadn't been addressed to us all but to Lisa, who just looked at her as she fumbled with the matches, trying to strike one. Everyone else was standing well back. I don't think anyone else heard her. "Have you?" They'd obviously started some conversation earlier and I'd just caught the back end.

Lisa shook her head.

"No animals," said Annie simply. "No cats, or dogs . . . or birds in the sky."

The next moment she had struck the match and tossed it onto the pile of wood.

The pile whumped into life so quickly that it took everyone by surprise, sending a cloud of billowing flame into the air. Everyone staggered back as the fireball rolled and rose into the dark grey. Our shadows leaped gigantically as the entire bonfire erupted before us. That first explosion of fire made me think about the way the community centre had blown apart and all those poor sods had been burned alive. I didn't look at the others as the first fireball rolled up into the dark greyness, and the pile of wood began to crackle and roar with flame. I didn't want to see my feelings reflected on their faces. More importantly, I didn't want to start thinking about what Alex and Candy had said about the black tidal wave that had chased them down the street and what it all meant. What we were doing with the bonfire was the sensible thing, the *only* thing to do. And I didn't want to give any kind of headroom to stuff like nerve gas attacks or the possibility that we'd been stranded and ignored; that the authorities just didn't want to know that there was anyone still alive here. Or, worse still, that if we drew attention to ourselves, someone with their finger still on the button might just decide to finish the job they'd started and blow us all to pieces.

Smoke began to rise, straight up into the darkness. That's when I noticed. There was no wind. Never had been any wind these past couple of days, just this stillness.

"Better get more wood if we want to keep the fire going," said Alex. "No point in starting a fire if we let it go out."

"Right," I said. "Wayne and Damon, you can help me." I pointed off behind them, towards the minimart. As we walked over there, looking at our long shadows ahead of us, I got to thinking about what Lisa had just said to Annie. *No cats, or dogs . . . or birds in the sky.* I don't know why it spooked me, but it did. It spooked me so much that I thought I could see the shadows of people up ahead in the darkness, shambling towards us from the direction of the minimart. But I guessed that it was only our own shadows, somehow being "doubled" by the fire against our backs. Then Damon said: "Look!"

They weren't shadows. They were people.

At first, I refused to believe it. After having my hopes built up so much last time when we thought we were going to be rescued, only to discover that it was Alex and the others coming around to meet us. I wasn't going to allow myself to believe straight away that, at last, someone had found us.

Both Damon and Wayne looked back at me as I drew level, as if they wanted me to confirm that they weren't seeing things. I strode straight ahead past them as the shadows became more solid. Yes, thank God. Someone had come to rescue us.

But the growing smile on my face was soon wiped away.

These weren't rescuers.

They were survivors, just like us.

I could tell by the way they were walking. There was a whole line of them moving towards us, and most of them were staggering and shambling. Just like they'd pulled themselves out of the ruins. I turned to look back at Wayne and Damon. They were starting to get excited, believing that rescue had come.

"Hold it!" I said, shaking my head. "Don't build up your hopes."

I turned back. Yes, I understood now. These survivors had been hiding in the ruins, probably too terrified to show themselves. Maybe they'd even heard us calling when we'd made our search, but were too traumatised or terrified to reply. Now they'd seen the fire, and had emerged thinking that we were the rescuers.

"Well, where were you all when we wanted to know?" I called to them as they shambled to meet us.

No one answered. The shadowy figures just came on, most of them with their heads down. Now I could see that most of their clothes were ragged and torn. They were all in pretty bad shape.

"*Hel-lo!* Anybody know what's happening here?"

One guy was wearing what had once been a white shirt. It was ragged and stained red down the front.

"Anybody know how we're going to get out of here?"

There was something wrong here.

"Anyone got a *tongue*?"

Other shapes were emerging from the darkness, and when I turned to look I could see that there was a whole circle of staggering people, as if they were hemming us in. I could see the face of the man with the stained red shirt, and how that shirt had become stained.

The man didn't have a face.

It was a black-red mass of bloodied muscle and gleaming white bone where the skull beneath was exposed. The woman who staggered next to him had only one arm and perhaps her legs were broken, which would explain why she had difficulty walking.

"They're dead," someone said. "They're all dead."

I realised that it was me who'd spoken.

I heard Wayne begin moaning behind me, then the sounds of running feet as Damon turned and dashed back to the others.

A young girl, maybe seven or eight years old, was crawling over the grass. Her legs had been crushed, her long red hair trailing behind from her torn scalp.

An old man, weaving like a drunk, his face as white as a

skull, holding one hand clamped to the open wound which had once been his stomach, keeping his innards from spilling out as he came on towards us.

There were dozens of them, all forming that moving cordon; and when I looked around I could see that they *were* hemming us in, the moving line of terrible figures getting tighter, shambling together shoulder to shoulder as they closed in.

For a moment, I couldn't move.

It was as if my brain just refused to accept what I was seeing.

A man in a leather jacket, with one eye hanging down from its socket onto his cheek, raised a hand towards me, beckoning. It seemed to break me out of the nightmare. I turned and ran, grabbing Wayne's arm as I passed. He too seemed frozen in shock, his mouth open, his face white. I dragged him after me and we raced back to the fire.

I shouted something to the others about getting out of there, and couldn't understand why they all had their backs to me, staring off into the darkness in the opposite direction. As I staggered to a halt, I realised what was happening. They were staring at other figures, who were staggering towards us from the opposite direction, and when I looked around I could see that the cordon was all around us now, all around the bonfire and closing in.

Candy was kneeling on the grass, both hands clamped to her mouth. Lisa, Annie and the boy remained in a tight huddle, watching as the figures staggered nearer and nearer. Gordon was holding his guitar like it was a gun or something. Alex was walking in a small circle, not knowing what to do.

"It's the gas!" yelled Alex. "We're hallucinating. This isn't real. It's not happening."

"They *are* real!" screamed Wayne, eyes popping. "They *ARE!*"

Part of me desperately wanted to believe Alex. After everything we'd all been through these past couple of days, when nothing made any sense at all, it was the nearest thing to an answer. But there was another part of me that couldn't believe it. We were here, with a fire roaring behind us and the dead closing in on all sides.

"I want to wake up," moaned Candy, still kneeling. "Alex, I want to wake up and I want them all to go away."

"God," said Alex, not hearing her. "They're going to push us back into the fire."

Candy began to weep hysterically.

I suddenly became fully aware of the heat on my back, turned quickly to see that we were only six feet or so from the flames.

And then the shambling line of corpses, shoulder to shoulder on all sides, suddenly stopped. They were still thirty feet away, right on the periphery where the light from the bonfire faded into darkness, but with every detail of their horrifying injuries still visible. Some of those bodies were . . . *things* . . . that couldn't possibly be standing. The injuries were so severe that they'd ceased to look remotely human. But there they all were, standing and waiting.

And then one of the dead things cocked its head to one side, and spoke.

"*Lisa?*"

"Oh, Christ," said Lisa.

"It's not him," said Annie, hugging both her and the boy closer. "It *can't* be your husband."

"*Still with the dyke bitch, Lisa?*" It was a man in a torn business suit. His hair was covered in plaster dust, his face white as marble and with deep, hollowed eye sockets. Blood had flowed from his mouth at one stage, drying in a dark patch over his lower jaw. "*I see you've found yourself another little boy. I wouldn't let you keep your own. So you stole someone else's. Isn't that right, bitch-dyke?*"

"It *is* him, Annie. For God's sake, look at him!"

Off to the left came another voice from the darkness, too far out of the light cast from the bonfire to distinguish, but the silhouette looked like a woman. There seemed to be the silhouette of a man next to her, with his arm around her shoulder.

"*The child is mine,*" said the woman. "*I'm his mother, and you can't have him. You took him away, when he should have stayed with us.*"

"*You had no right,*" said the man. "*You should have left him in the car. We fell down into Hell, and we're burning there. It's not right that he isn't with us. He should be burning too.*"

Suddenly the boy began to scream, the sound of his parents' voices breaking him out of his shocked and dazed existence. Lisa clung to his arm, and when the boy fell, clawing at her, Lisa fell too. Annie helped to restrain him as his cries rang out in the night. When the crying stopped and the boy collapsed sobbing into Lisa's embrace, another voice came from one of the things off to the right. A middle-aged man with a blood-stained face, wearing a bloodied apron.

"*Hello, Candy,*" said the dead man. "*Remember* me? *You looted my off-licence. You killed Ricky. And no, you're not hallucinating, Alex. The facts won't go away simply because you want them to go away. I know. We know. You both murdered your son.*"

"*Go AWAY!*" screamed Candy, rising unsteadily to her feet. "You're not real! *GO AWAY!*"

The dead man laughed and was silent, as the taunting was taken up by another figure who took a step forward on the fringes of the light. It was a woman in her sixties, grey hair tied in a bun. Of all the people who formed that hellish cordon, she seemed to be the least damaged of all. Her face was white, but there was no way of telling if there were eyes in her sockets. She held up one beckoning hand.

"*Gordon?*"

I saw Gordon flinch and freeze, gripping his guitar tight.

"*Come on home now.*"

Gordon moaned, lowering and shaking his head. Was this his aunt?

"I've got some milky coffee on the stove and it'll be boiling dry if we don't get home soon."

"'Way!" shouted Gordon. *"G'way!"*

The woman laughed then. It sounded hellish—like she was an animal or something. There was a man behind her, just a silhouette. But when she'd finished laughing, it was as if his turn had come to say something. He stepped to one side of her and although, like the others, he was keeping out of the direct light from the bonfire, there was no mistaking him.

It was Stafford, my old headmaster.

"Still making trouble, O'Connor? See what your hate's done to the school—to the whole TOWN! Don't you know that you're responsible for all this? It's all down to YOU, boy! You've turned Edmonville into Hell!"

And I knew then that Stafford couldn't possibly be standing there.

Angrily, I turned back to the fire and found a wooden spar sticking out of the flames. I grabbed it, yanking it out in a shower of sparks. Whirling the burning spar over my head . . . I flung it hard towards Stafford with an angry yell. It flew end over end like a giant Catherine wheel, hitting the ground a dozen feet or so in front of him and Gordon's aunt, sending up another shower of sparks on impact.

The effect was instantaneous.

The figures on either side of Stafford and the old woman shrank back into the shadows, away from the burning torch. But the head teacher and the aunt suddenly seemed mesmerised by the nearness of the flames and the sparks. While the woman stood rigid, arms held out at her sides and staring down at the burning wood, Stafford sank to his knees and began to moan. He raised his hands slowly to his face, and with the moaning growing louder by the instant, we all watched in horror as his body began to vibrate. It seemed as if he were having some kind of fit. Did dead people have fits? Now his head was jerking violently and it was as if I could feel a vibration in the ground beneath my feet. The woman began to judder beside him, her face a white mask. Stafford's mouth stretched wide. Too wide. It just kept opening and opening. I winced when I heard his jawbone suddenly crack. Something inside him was coming out, through the gaping black hole that had once been a mouth but which now seemed to have replaced his entire face. His body was jerking and twitching like a puppet on strings; and then we heard the noise. Like a faraway wind, gusting towards us. Like a hurricane on the way. Suddenly, with a cracking roar, a torrent of black water erupted like a geyser from Stafford's mouth. It seemed to hang there in the air above and around him, defying gravity, like a great black cloud. A squirming, undulating black mass, glinting like oil or tar. The twisting mass hit the ground at the same time as Stafford's evacuated and truly dead body slumped lifelessly forward. Suddenly there was another black liquid blur as the same stuff exploded around the woman's head, just as if someone had put a bullet into the back of her skull from short range. Another black torrent exploded from under her skirt as she fell. The black stuff from both bodies didn't move or behave like anything liquid I'd ever seen in my life. It twisted and moved like it had a life of its own. None of it splashed. Both gushing explosions of it suddenly flooded together in one great mass, and we all watched as it pooled there like tar on the grass. And then it slid away into the darkness, streaming away across the park like a glinting black river, away from the light. And as it moved, the black river was making a hellish sound. It was shrieking as if the fire had forced it out of the bodies and it was in great pain. But there was something else about the sound—it was as if there were more than one voice making the noise. It was as if a crowd of hundreds, maybe thousands, of people were all in agony. Mumbling and moaning in pain, then shrieking and screaming and hissing as the glinting black mass surged away from us. I couldn't make it out in the darkness, but I was convinced that the black liquid—oil, or tar, whatever—was heading back to the edge of the Chasm. There was no doubt that it was the same stuff that Alex said had chased Candy and himself; the same thing that I had seen exploding into the community centre.

"They don't like the fire," I heard Annie say. Suddenly she was standing right next to me, also yanking a piece of burning wood out of the flames. I helped her, and when a chunk of timber came free, she ran forward with it, hurling it underarm towards the line of figures on our right. I could see the shadows shrinking back into the night as the fire-brand fell among them. Now it was Gordon's turn. With a burning chair leg in one hand and what looked like a chunk of blazing carpet in the other, he dashed forward, precious guitar still slung on his back, throwing both his brands into the night.

By the time Alex had done the same with a smouldering bed headboard, the dead people, and whatever had been animating their mutilated bodies, had vanished back into the darkness.

We stood there, breathing heavily, looking at the burning debris we'd scattered across the playing field. I took a turn around the bonfire, to see if any of the things were behind us. But they'd all gone.

"The *fire*" said Annie again, at last. "Whatever they are, whatever *it* is—they or it can't stand the fire."

"But how long is this bonfire going to last?" asked Lisa.

"It'd better last us the entire night," I said. "Or those things will be back."

"Will it be all right in the morning, Alex?" moaned Candy. "Will we all wake up?"

I looked back at the fire and prayed that it would last through the night.

Then I looked at the others, all peering into the darkness. Silently watching and waiting. It came to me then. Were we the only ones left alive in the world?

When would this nightmare be ended?

I could hardly have guessed then what lay ahead of us.

BOOK TWO | THE VORLA

PROLOGUE	**A YEAR AND**
	A DAY LATER

THE SUN DOESN'T RISE HERE. IT JUST GETS
LIGHTER.

Ever since I got here, I've been crouching in this electrical store, dictating into this machine. Haven't checked
whether I've been using the "Pause" button properly, so God
knows whether half of what I've been talking about has been
recorded. What the hell. Does it matter? I only know that I
had to stay awake while it was dark, watching and waiting for
any sign that the Black Stuff had found me at last. Don't want
to think about those poor bastards who tried to stop my car.
Doesn't bear thinking about.

So—I've kept talking. And now I've replaced the batteries.

When the darkness became grey, I could feel sleep catching
up on me, even after everything that's happened since we
became Special Guests of the Caffneys. I never believed I
could sleep again. Absolute exhaustion, I suppose. Suddenly,
I lost three hours. Not much, but enough to keep me alert. I
could do with something to eat, but that's not the most important thing at the moment. I've got to circle around and find my
way back to the petrol plant, got to keep telling myself that the
others are still somehow alive.

I've just checked the shotgun for the hundredth time. As if

a second shell might suddenly reappear in there by magic. One shell left. No good against the Black Stuff, but it might deter any other scavengers still left alive on this city-crag. I hope I don't have to use it that way, because I'm keeping it for one of the Caffneys.

Just hope I can get back where I'm going before dark comes again.

It knows I'm still here somewhere, and it won't give up until it's found me.

If I believed in God, I'd pray.

But I don't think He lives in this neighbourhood.

The streets look clear. I'm going to head off on foot, work my way through the abandoned buildings and the ruins. There are plenty of vehicles scattered about on the streets, and it might be that some of them are still in working order. But I daren't risk using one for fear of being heard in this silent city.

Never mind the engine sound, Jay. The Black Stuff can smell your scent. It's the scent of fear.

Yeah . . . ? Well, I'll try not to think about that then, won't I?

Christ, I hurt all over. Maybe not surprising after everything that's happened. Better hurting than dead, Jay. Just keep telling yourself that. Stiff as hell, crouched down here among the televisions and the videos all night. And would you believe it? Not a thing worth watching on any of the channels. Hah-bloody-hah.

Time to move.

And this could be the last time I'll be recording anything.

In which case: Thanks for listening, whoever you are.

Good luck, Jay.

There's no one else here to slap me on the back.

So I'll do it myself.

Here goes . . .

| CHAPTER ONE | THE ORDEAL OF JULIET DELORE |

"COME OUT OF THERE, JULIET! COME OUT, YOU bitch. Or I swear to God I'll kill you!"

Juliet leaned hard against the desk which she had shoved hard up against the storeroom door. There was a lock in the door, but no chance to look around in here for the key (if there *was* a key). The door began to judder and shake again as he put his weight against it from the other side. One of the files that she had thrown onto the desk to give it extra weight fell to the floor and split, scattering papers. She gritted her teeth and kept her weight against it. She'd been on a slimming diet recently and lost seven pounds. She wished to God that she'd put weight *on* instead.

"Juliet! I'm *warning* you! Open this door or I'll . . ."

"Go to hell, you creep!"

"Juliet!"

This time when he threw himself against the door there was a muffled cry of pain.

"Good!" she yelled through the door. "I hope you've broken your shoulder, you mad bastard!"

"You . . . you . . ."

There was silence from the other side then. Juliet tried to control the involuntary noise she was making in her throat. It sounded like whimpering, and she knew that he would be able to hear it, and would take enjoyment from it. There was blood on her forehead, and she wiped away a smear when it trickled into her eye.

What was he going to do now? He was too quiet and she didn't like it.

Quickly, she looked around the storeroom again. It was about thirty feet square. There were filing cabinets of some kind along one of the cinder-block walls. On the other side, shelves containing cardboard boxes. No way of telling what was inside them, or whether there might be anything in there that could help her. At the far end of the room was a single window. The glass had shattered inwards and lay glittering on the floor. If she screamed again, would it help? Would anyone hear? That would have to wait; she could hardly find the energy to breathe at the moment. She needed something else to place against the door. The desk was heavy, but would it stop him from getting in if she took her own weight away from it?

The nearest filing cabinet was about four feet away. If she left the table and hurried, she might be able to drag it over and shove it against the door. He'd never get in then. But what the hell was he doing even as she thought about it?

"Trevor?" she asked at last, when she could find the breath.

There was no answer.

"*Trevor?*"

Still no answer.

She began to tremble then, and grew angry with herself. This was no time to be coming on with the weak female act. If she was going to get out of this alive, she had to think quickly. What if she just ran to the window and climbed out? It couldn't be that much of a drop to the ground. She tried to work out where the storeroom was in relation to the super-market entrance. She had come in through the main doors, had walked to the back before she'd found an assistant, and then when she'd asked for Trevor Blake, she'd been directed to the stairs leading up to a kind of semi-second floor, with the manager's office and the storeroom. That should only be about twenty or thirty feet from the ground if she dropped from this window. Yes, that was the way. Someone must see or hear her, and it was worth the risk of dropping that far just to get out of this place and away from this madman. She looked back at the door. Ten seconds to get to the window, another ten to climb out. It couldn't be any longer than that, could it? Maybe she'd be lucky.

Lucky? Pardon me if I say "Ha, ha."

Still trying to summon up the courage to move, Juliet thought back to how the nightmare had all begun.

Juliet DeLore was twenty-four years old with long blonde hair and a face that could have belonged to a model. But she believed her considerable good looks to be a curse, rather than of any benefit. On four separate occasions, she had fallen for the wrong man; each of them only interested in her as an "acquisition," required just to hang on their arms and look good at parties. She had been hurt badly each time; had sworn on each occasion that she'd never fall for the wrong man again. After her fourth relationship had fallen apart, she'd come to the conclusion that all the clichés were right. She had finally decided that all men were interested in her only for one thing. But somehow she'd still managed to fall for Trevor Blake. Just how she had come to be attached to him she had no real idea. He'd reacted so well when she had turned down his first advances at the nightclub. She'd been there as usual with a bunch of friends. He'd been there with two friends of his own. On that first meeting, he'd shown that he was interested but hadn't been pushy which, for Juliet, was always a good sign. Every Friday night he was there; still persevering, but not coming on too strong. Could it be that she'd finally found someone she could trust, someone who wanted to know her and not just get his leg over?

The storeroom window seemed to be shrinking; seemed to be getting further away. Juliet quietly rose to a kneeling position, still with both hands braced at the desk-edge. She winced when one knee popped, convinced that he must have heard it.

Come on, Juliet. Count to three and make a dash for it before he . . .

Suddenly the glass panel at the top of the door shattered inwards, spraying her with glass. Juliet screamed, but kept both hands braced against the desk, turning her face away as glass shards fell around her. When she looked up, she could see what he'd done. He'd found a crowbar or something, and was using it to break the window. Now he was yelling obscenities at her, and when she looked up she could see that he must be standing on something to have got up so high. Did he think that he could squeeze through the window? An arm snaked through the aperture, clawing at the woodwork. Screaming again, Juliet jumped up onto the desk and grabbed his arm, yanking it down hard on the ragged glass still in the frame. When he screamed in pain as the glass cut into his flesh, so did she, and she kept on screaming as she gripped his arm good and hard, pulling down with all her weight. He twisted then, and the crowbar lashed through the window, hitting her on the cheekbone. Instinctively, she grabbed for it. Hanging onto the crowbar and his arm, Juliet fell from the desk. Beyond, he yelled in pain again as the crowbar was torn from his grasp and Juliet fell heavily to the floor. Raging, Trevor pulled his arm from the jagged glass and fell from his perch with a thump. Juliet scrabbled back to the desk, sobbing with fear and effort, throwing herself back against it to keep the door closed, suddenly realising that she had the crowbar tightly clenched in one hand. Unintentionally, he'd given her a weapon.

"I've . . . I've . . . got it now, you bastard. The crowbar."

"You filthy, stinking *bitch*! Do you know what you've done to my arm?"

"That's nothing to what I *will* do if you stick your head back in here again."

There was a strangled sound of pure frustration from beyond the door, and then silence. Juliet struggled to keep calm, to control her breathing. The terror threatened to overwhelm her. It seemed as if some kind of animal were on the other side of the door, not the man she'd met in the nightclub; the man with whom she thought she'd finally found happiness.

"Mr. Right . . ." she said aloud, and fought to keep the tears back.

Trevor was thirty years old, medium height, with the same colour blond hair as her own, leading to jokes about the possibilities of having been made for each other. There was a scar on his right temple, which she'd laughingly called a "neat designer" scar. He said he'd got it playing rugby. He was single. When she told him that she had been working for a travel agency these past two years, he told her that he did business abroad a lot; maybe she could fix him up with some air travel?

They'd gone out for a meal, and he still hadn't come on strong. But she'd been charmed by his style and by his wit. The next time they'd met, they'd slept together. It had been after another meeting at the nightclub, and they'd left early. Afterwards, they'd gone back to Juliet's place, since Trevor shared a flat with a friend who had other friends staying over.

At last, she seemed to have found Mr. Right.

But Mr. Right didn't telephone the following week, and wasn't at the nightclub on the following Friday. And was Juliet just imagining this, or did Trevor's friends seem to be leering at her over the tops of their glasses?

———————

157

"You can't stay in there forever," said Trevor at last. His voice was cold and measured. It was so close that he might even be here in the storeroom with her. It turned her blood to ice water.

"The police will be here any second," countered Juliet. "And the fire services. When they get here, I'm going to tell them what you did. Do you hear me, Trevor? I'll tell them."

"You bitch!"

"So the safest thing you can do is run. As far away from here as you can."

"No one's coming, Juliet."

In answer, she banged the crowbar on the floor.

"I swear to Christ, you so much as poke your head round that door, and I'm going to smash it."

Trevor laughed then. It was an unhealthy, dark sound.

There was silence again, and Juliet remembered the knock on the door the previous Saturday morning. There had been a woman standing there, with a two-year-old boy. It was Trevor's wife and son. Before the woman had a chance to explain, Juliet had promised that she'd never see him again. Trevor, it transpired, was manager of Greenhaugh's Supermarket in Edmonville; this wasn't the first time it had happened.

Juliet strained to listen, but there were no further sounds from the door. When she looked up at the shattered window, there was no movement there either. She weighed the crowbar in her hand and looked across to the window. If she was going to do it, now was the time. She rose again, backing off from the desk bit by bit, keeping one hand on the edge and her eyes fastened on the broken window. When a piece of broken glass crunched underfoot, she winced and halted, raising the crowbar high and waiting. There was still no sound, no sign of movement. Carefully sidestepping the glass on the floor as much as possible, Juliet headed for the window again, not taking her eyes from the door, ready to dash back. The journey seemed to take hours. At the halfway point, she paused.

Now or never.

Even if the drop was higher than she thought, it was still worth the risk compared to staying here with him. Quickly now, she lunged to the window and began to climb out.

But what she saw out there made her reel back into the storeroom, gasping for breath.

Because the world beyond the window had simply ceased to exist.

The shattered window looked out across a vast space. Climbing out there would be like climbing out of a cable car's window. Vertigo made her head spin as she clutched at the sill, now dropping to her knees and with the after-image of the great yawning gulf still imprinted on her retinas. Unable to comprehend, Juliet rose again slowly, gingerly approaching the window and carefully looking out once more.

The world tilted again, and she moaned when she realised that she wasn't seeing things. Directly across from her, perhaps three or four hundred feet away, was a ragged cliff edge. There were broken trees there, some of them hanging over the edge by their roots. And there were ruined houses too; some of them right on the edge itself, sliced in half and with the upstairs and downstairs rooms plainly visible, like some kind of sectioned drawing. Beneath, a massive and striated cliff face of rock and clay, dropping away into utter darkness. The sight defied logic, but no matter how hard Juliet stared it would not go away, would not suddenly begin to make sense. On her immediate left, the supermarket wall curved away into grey space. On her right, the same—except that perhaps a hundred feet away she could see the beginnings of another cliff edge on her side and piles of rubble from a collapsed wall. It seemed as if the supermarket was also perched right on the edge of another cliff and that a canyon really had opened up directly beneath her.

"The tremor . . . "

———————

Juliet hadn't expected anyone else to be in the manager's office when she mounted the small flight of stairs. When she'd seen the sign, "Trevor Blake," she'd just rammed the door open hard and stepped inside. Trevor was sitting on the far side of a desk, wearing a white manager's jacket with the supermarket logo emblazoned on the top pocket. Opposite him was a small man in a business suit. Spectacles were balanced on the edge of his nose, hair parted sparsely over a balding pate. On his lap was an open briefcase full of papers. He turned to goggle as Juliet strode into the room, slamming the door behind her. But she didn't even notice him. Her eyes were fixed on Trevor. She was disappointed that he didn't look more surprised. His face was blank, and somehow more bloodless than she'd remembered. His lips were set in a tight line. Those lips had kissed her face in the darkness not two weeks ago.

"Hello, lover boy," she said simply.

The man in the business suit goggled again, as if the remark had been addressed to him.

"Juliet," said Trevor. His blank voice matched his blank face.

"Seems to me one of us has been telling fibs. Wouldn't you say?"

"Perhaps you could wait downstairs," said Trevor. "Until we've finished here."

Now Juliet's anger was starting to flare. This wasn't going the way she'd anticipated. Trevor was staring at the man now, ignoring her, when he was supposed to be jumping up from his seat in shock and trying to usher her out of the place. At which stage she could really let fly, and make the scene that she wanted the whole supermarket to witness. But no. Trevor remained blank, not responding.

"You bastard." Juliet turned to the little man. "Did you know that the manager of this supermarket was a bastard?"

"Listen," stuttered the man, hastily closing the briefcase. "Miss, I'm not sure what's happening here, but we're in the middle of a very important meeting . . . "

"I'm sure it can wait for a few minutes while Mr. Blake hears what I have to say."

"This isn't the time, Juliet," said Trevor.

"Oh, *but I think it is.*"

Trevor placed both hands on the table in front of him and began to rise, slowly. As he did, he seemed to be trembling. But to Juliet's ever-mounting anger, he was still not looking at her, or responding to her the way she expected and wanted. He was still staring at the man. And now she could see the blank face cracking; could see the ferocious anger inside him as it came to the surface. But the anger was not directed at her. Trevor was still staring at the man.

"This is the man," shouted Juliet, stabbing a finger at Trevor, "who . . ."

And then the desk began to judder and vibrate.

The large window behind Trevor, which overlooked the super-market aisles below, began to rattle. Overhead, the strip light began to sway from side to side. There was a rumbling now, like the sound of an underground train. Somewhere beyond, there was a crash of glass—and screaming. Over Trevor's shoulder, down below in the supermarket aisles, Juliet could see shoppers running. She saw a trolley spill over, saw an old lady go headlong into a pile of tins, scattering them everywhere. A man seemed to shoulder-charge one of the shelving units, toppling it over.

"Oh my God . . ." began the small man in the business suit, leaping to his feet, the briefcase clattering to the floor.

And then the window behind Trevor cracked and fell out, down into the supermarket below, great shards disintegrating as they fell. Juliet cried out, staggered back, and lost her footing on a floor that now seemed to have lost its solidity as the sounds of an express train exploded into the office.

But Trevor remained where he was, not reacting to any of the sounds of destruction, as if it had nothing to do with him. Hands flat on the vibrating desk, his eyes remained fixed on the little man as he rolled into a ball on the floor and then gave a loud yelping sound as the filing cabinet in the corner toppled over, missing him by inches, scattering its drawers on the floor.

Juliet heard tearing from above, like ripping cloth. When she *looked up, to her amazement she could see that the ceiling was being pulled apart. A widening crack had appeared from one end of the room to the other, letting in daylight and emitting a spray of plaster dust and insulation material like yellow cotton wool. Juliet cried out, heading backwards on elbows and heels until she bumped against a far wall. A slab of the roof fell inwards, the four square feet of material slamming down hard onto the desk, demolishing it and sweeping Trevor from sight in an impacting dust cloud.*

The sounds of crashing and broken glass were suddenly stilled. The rumbling beneath Juliet subsided to a low groan, and then all was quiet in the office. There was no sound from the supermarket beyond. No wailing or crying, no pleas for help. Juliet screwed her eyes shut, hoping when she opened them again that she'd see that none of this had happened. She was wrong. Her shoulder hurt and her black jeans were covered in white dust finer than flour. She pushed herself to her knees, choking, wondering whether the ground was solid again.

Trevor appeared from the far side of the desk, now edging dazedly around the chunk of roof that had fallen on it. His hair had also been whitened by the fine dust. Flinging himself away from the falling debris, he had almost brained himself on the wall behind. Without once looking at Juliet, as if she weren't even kneeling on the floor right in his sightline, he came around to the front of the desk, just as the little man—his black suit suddenly turned white—grabbed at the fallen filing cabinet and struggled to rise.

"All right . . . " said the man, strands of hair once so carefully parted over his head now white and awry. "Is everyone all right . . . ?" He looked up groggily as Trevor came to meet him. "Miss?" continued the man, rubbing the dust out of his eyes and looking for her. "Are you . . . ?"

"All right," coughed Juliet. "I'm all right. What happened?"

And then she saw Trevor stoop down to the floor and pick up a ragged chunk of concrete from the littered carpet. She wondered what he was going to do. Wondered why he was raising it to head height so methodically. And she would have screamed at what happened next, but she was still too shocked to let the sound out—as Trevor took two quick steps forward and slammed the concrete slab full into the little man's face. There was a wet crunch as the man's spectacles were impacted into his face, his nose instantly flattened and crushed. He dropped soundlessly to his knees. At first there was no blood. Just a creased and flattened and terribly skewed expression on his face. Then the redness began to spurt around his eyes, from his crushed nose, and from his mouth until his face was a crimson mask. His hands rose, juddering, towards the mutilated face.

Expression still blank, Trevor brought the concrete down hard on the man's head. It sounded like a side of meat dropped from a ten-storey building. The man went down instantly, and soundlessly. With that blow, Trevor let go of the concrete. It thumped to a rest on the man's neck, pinning his head to the floor. A dark pool began to spread on the dust-covered surface around him.

Juliet thought she could scream now, but still nothing would come. Horror overwhelmed her. Trevor was looking down at what he'd done, nodding again and again in satisfaction. Wiping the back of a trembling hand across his mouth, he seemed to notice her at last.

"You see?" he said. "You see, Juliet? Fate again. Looking after me."

"What . . . ?" Juliet had found her voice, but she choked on her own vomit; moaned and hugged herself, trying to make sense of what she had seen—if she had really seen it at all.

"Know what that bastard was going to do?" continued Trevor. "He was from Central Office. Been sent down to check out discrepancies in the accounts. Found out that I'd been creaming off some of the readies over the last year and a half. Thought it was five thousand. The stupid bastard. More like ten. That's how much he knew. Now the little fucker is dead. Killed when the roof fell in. I told him to get out of the way, didn't I? You heard me, didn't you, Juliet? But no, he was frozen there like a rabbit when the accident happened. Killed him outright." Trevor began to laugh then. It made Juliet's

163

nausea worse. "So now we're okay, honey. Just me and you. We can take what I've put away and just go. Somewhere abroad, eh? That sound good to you?"

Juliet clawed her way to her feet and fled.

But Trevor lunged across the room and caught her arm just as she yanked open the office door. On the landing outside was the staircase leading down to the supermarket, and one other door facing her. She had wanted to head down the stairs, but Trevor was hanging onto her arm, now stumbling to block her path. He yelled when she raked her nails across his face, pulling back to punch her hard. The blow flung Juliet back against the other door, which flew open as she tumbled into the storeroom. Trevor lunged for her again, missed his footing and fell on the landing. Quickly, she slammed the door shut and dragged the desk in front of it. Now, it seemed, she was trapped; and no matter how much she yelled, no one came to her assistance.

The screeching of the desk being pushed inwards jerked Juliet away from the window and her view of the Chasm below. Fear overwhelmed her bewilderment as she lurched back across the storeroom. The door had opened a crack as Trevor continued to shoulder it. Now his arm was through, fingers groping at the wall as he tried to squeeze in. Juliet hit the desk hard, trapping his arm. Trevor yelled in rage and pain.

"You mad bitch!"

"Mad?" Juliet's voice rose to a scream. "*Me, mad?*"

Lunging forward again, Juliet brought the crowbar down hard on his arm. Trevor screamed, but the sound of his voice was cut off when the second blow broke two of his fingers. Dragging his arm out, he fell back to the littered floor, hugging his hand, as Juliet rammed the door shut again.

Trevor sat with his back to the door, breathing hard. There were two parallel scratches across his cheek where Juliet had gouged her nails. His fingers felt as if they were on fire.

How long did he have before the police got here? He looked down the stairs into the supermarket. Cartons and cans littered the floor, but his view was restricted. He shook his head and tried to clear vision that had somehow become blurred. Now he could see clearly again, and think clearly. He'd had another of his "turns," just when he thought he was getting better. Normally, when the mists came, it was his wife and child who received the punishment. But when the little bastard in the black suit had arrived and it was apparent that he'd been rumbled about the money, the mists had come quickly flooding again. Trevor had found a way of shutting him up, but it couldn't possibly end there. He'd have to draw the money he'd put into his secret account, and just clear out. Maybe leave the country altogether.

How long had it been since the "accident" had happened? He looked at his watch, but the dial was shattered, only one bent hand remaining. It couldn't have been that long. He had no idea what had hit the supermarket, but surely it was some kind of sign that fate was on his side. If someone came now, to help, what would he do? What would he say? He was thinking logically now. He had to do something about Juliet, and straight away. She had seen him kill the little bastard.

But first, he had to check what had happened in the supermarket; find out where everyone had gone. Trying not to make any noise, he slipped away from the door and descended, step after careful step on the littered stairway.

The supermarket was a mess. Tins, cartons, and shelving all over the place. And the ceiling was a gigantic mass of cracks. But he could see no one. Something bad had happened—and everyone had fled. Casting glances back to the staircase and the door above, Trevor edged around an aisle to get a look right down to the main entrance. All the glass had shattered there, and sheets of jagged shards lay heaped on the tiled floor and around the revolving door. Could he see a pair of legs sticking out from under that overturned sales display? He took a tentative step forward, but his change in position made him catch sight of something that brought him up short. He stood, staring.

He knew that the bread section was on the other side of the aisle unit before him, but after that there should be a further seven aisles: fresh meat, poultry, and other cold meats.

But all of that had gone. Beyond the aisle marked "Bread," there was only daylight—of a sort. From the entrance area on his left, right across the supermarket to the rear of the building, everything seemed to have disappeared. Above, the ceiling now ended in a crumbling ridge of cracked brickwork, ragged plaster and twisted iron supports. It was as if something had come along and shorn the building in two. Trevor edged around the aisle, back to the shelving, to get a better look. Now there was what seemed to be a blank, grey emptiness around the corner of the aisle. Trevor shook his head. Were the mists coming behind his eyes again? He kept moving. And then he saw something that gave perspective to the great empty space. There was something out there, after all. Perhaps five or six hundred feet away. A cliff edge. Moving carefully forward, Trevor could see that the cliff face dropped away to an impossible depth, vanishing into darkness. Recoiling, he struggled to make sense of what he was seeing, of what had happened. Now he could see a gap between the shelving units before him, and the ragged cliff edge on which the remains of the supermarket itself were precariously balanced.

At last, he understood.

There had been an earthquake. Impossible in this country, it seemed. But there was no arguing with the facts. And the earth tremor had resulted in this gigantic pit opening up. A pit over which the supermarket had been standing. Half of the entire building had crumbled away and fallen into the abyss. The remaining half stood right on the edge of the Chasm. Realising how close he was to the edge, Trevor eased himself back around the shelving unit and then hurried to the foot of the stairs again. How long could it be before rescue came, and how much time did he have to deal with Juliet?

Then Trevor saw the barbecue section, and knew what he should do.

There was barbecue fuel there.

"Burn her out," he said aloud. "That's what I'll do."

He headed forward.

Too easy, a voice seemed to say behind him.

Trevor whirled, staring back towards the edge of the Chasm. There was no movement. No sign of anyone.

"What?"

Too easy, said the voice in his head. And now it seemed that the mists were coming back behind his eyes again. But that couldn't be. They only ever came when he was angry; maybe when that stupid bitch Theresa was getting on his nerves, or one of his many girlfriends started to get stroppy, like Juliet. Trevor rubbed his eyes. He'd never heard voices before.

That's because you haven't been listening properly, came the voice again, from beyond the cliff edge.

"Where are you? *Who* are you?"

I'm the real you, Trevor. The one you've been struggling to hear for so long. Now, something important's happened. Something that will set you free.

"I'm going mad, aren't I? I'm hearing voices, and I'm going mad."

There was a sound in his head now. Something that sounded like laughter, but was like no human laughter he had ever heard. It was the sound of a mocking wind; the sound of a crowd whispering. But somewhere in that sound he could also hear something that was very like his own voice. The sound was swept away like leaves on an autumn wind.

Mad? What's mad, Trevor? Mad is just a way of dealing with problems. Perhaps you're the only sane one left. Ever thought of that?

"Who are you?"

167

I'm you. You're me.

"Show yourself."

I . . . we . . . can't. Not yet. Not until the darkness comes. But we can speak to you, Trevor. Because you're special. What you've done today proves how special you are. And I . . . we . . . want to help you.

"Help me . . . ?"

Yes, Trevor. Everything's changed now. Nothing you've ever known, or experienced, will be the same again. You've nothing to fear.

The mists were swirling behind his eyes again, but this time they were not impeding his vision. He did not have to shake his head to clear it. Suddenly, it seemed as if he were seeing everything through different eyes with a different focus. Everything in his life had been skewed before, with bursts of occasional clarity when he went after what he desired. But now it appeared that he would see everything with that clarity, forever. The truth in the words of his invisible friend . . . or friends . . . was undeniable.

"I've got to do something about Juliet . . ."

Yes, she must be dealt with first. She's an ungrateful bitch, Trevor. Just like the others. And she deserves to be punished.

"I'll burn her out . . ."

No! You must listen to what we say. She deserves worse than that. You must make her torment last longer. She's betrayed you, Trevor. Let you down, like the others. Her pain should reflect that betrayal.

"But I've got to do it quickly, before someone comes. The police, or the fire service. I've got to finish her off before they come . . ."

Listen, Trevor. Listen to me . . . to us . . . carefully. No one will come. Listen, and know the truth of these words. There will be no one to interfere. You have as much time as you need. All the time in the world.

It seemed that the last statement by the voice had caused

it great amusement. Again there was the sound of laughter which was so unlike anything Trevor had ever heard, but which seemed to touch something inside him deep down. Somehow, the truth of the voice's words was again undeniable.

"So what shall I do? How can I make her pay?"

Burning is too fast. Too easy. She needs to be taught a lesson.

"Then how?"

Keep her locked in there. Starve her. Torment her.

"And no one will come?"

No one. I . . . we . . . promise. It's what she deserves, Trevor. Make her suffer. You've got plenty of food here for yourself.

"Yes, she should suffer. It's her own fault."

Good . . . good . . .

Juliet seemed to hear a mumbling voice somewhere beyond the door. Could it be that help was on the way at last? Hope rising, she yelled at the top of her voice:

"In here! I'm in here!"

There was a sound then—of someone hurrying up the stairs, feet crunching on the debris that littered the stairway. Juliet began to rise. Thank God. Trevor must have decided to run for it after she'd hit him with the crowbar. He wasn't crouched on the other side of the door waiting, as she'd thought.

"In here!"

Something banged against the door, making her flinch. She was just rising, to push the desk away, when Trevor's voice came through the door to chill her blood.

"I know you're in there, darling."

"Trevor, you fucking bastard!"

"You shouldn't talk to me like that, Juliet. I'm going to make you *pay* for that. Going to make you pay for everything you've done."

Juliet sank hopelessly to her knees again, keeping her eye on the shattered window at the top of the door. There was another sound now, like tins clattering.

"What are you doing?"

"Making myself comfortable," replied Trevor. "Why don't you come out and join me?"

"You can't stay there forever, Trevor. Someone will come soon. They have to. If I were you, I'd put as much distance between yourself and this place as you can."

"Well, now . . ." Trevor sighed. Back against the door, he slithered down to his haunches. He'd dumped a pile of cans beside him. Casually, he reached for one. Juliet heard the can being opened, and wondered with trepidation just what Trevor had planned. "Let's examine what you've just said. First of all, you're *not* me. Secondly, no one's coming—and I've got that on good authority. And as to staying here forever . . . well, I've got all the time in the world. More time than you, my darling."

"You're mad, Trevor. Stark, staring *mad*."

"Sticks and stones, Juliet. Sticks and stones. Why don't you come out?"

"I can stay here for a damn long time."

Trevor laughed, his mouth full of cold meat. "Think so?"

"What the *hell* are you doing back there?"

"Are you hungry yet, Juliet?"

Juliet yelled in anger, slamming the crowbar against the door.

"We'll see," laughed Trevor. "We'll see . . ."

He laughed again, and stuffed another spoonful of food into his mouth.

CHAPTER TWO

THE JOURNAL OF JAY O'CONNOR: MUSIC OF THE NIGHT

WE'D SEEN THINGS OUT THERE IN THE night that just couldn't be.

And after they'd gone, scared away by the fire, we couldn't speak. None of us. I wanted to, but I had to sort out in my mind what I'd seen. Stafford, standing there, when I knew that he was lying dead in the school rubble. I'd seen his body cut in half. But last night, there he'd been. Part of me wanted to believe what Alex had said about some kind of nerve gas, making us see things. But there was a part of me, deep down, which knew that this wasn't the answer.

Strangely, it was Gordon—the one who couldn't speak— who broke the silence.

"My aunt," he said. The sound of his voice in the silence made everyone start. We all turned to look at him. "Her," he said, pointing out into the darkness. "But not her." He wanted to explain more, but he'd dried up. He began stabbing a finger out at the two bodies which lay on the fringe of the light and the shadow, beyond the bonfire.

"What are you trying to say?" asked Candy.

Gordon moved back to the fire and, shielding his face, tried to pull another firebrand out of the flames.

"Hey!" snapped Alex. "Leave that alone. We need all the firewood we can get, to last us the night out."

Gordon was having trouble, so I stepped forward and kicked at a tangled chunk of burning rubbish, until the spar of wood that he wanted was jerked free. Gordon picked it up and looked right into my face. I could see that he was dead scared. Just as scared as me.

"You come?" he asked.

I didn't want to, but I nodded: *Yes.*

Gordon picked up the burning wood and walked out towards that figure. I followed.

"What the hell are you two going to *do*?" choked Wayne. "You're bloody mad."

"Don't go out there," said Annie.

Gordon looked back, but it was only to see if I was following. I glanced from side to side in the darkness, expecting to see shadows moving out of the night towards us. But there was only the darkness, and the stillness. When we reached the woman's body, lying face down where it had fallen, Gordon stood for a long time, looking at it. The chunk of burning wood I'd thrown at it was still lying a couple of feet away, still smouldering. When he looked back at me, I said:

"It's up to you, Gordon."

He handed me the torch. His face was white in the light. Shifting the guitar around from his shoulder to his back, he leaned down and carefully took one of the corpse's hands. I saw him wince at the touch, saw him grit his teeth as he turned the body over.

Looking at that white blood-streaked woman's face, with the dark hair straggling over her forehead and cheeks, like spider's-web cracks—well, I felt myself heave, but I managed to keep it down. Gordon just kneeled there, looking at her face. There was no expression on his own. Then he nodded, and rose to his feet. Without looking at me, he reached for the torch. I gave it to him.

172

"You going to tell me what you think, or do I have to guess?"

"Not her," said Gordon, with effort. "This. Another woman."

"It's *not* your aunt?"

Gordon shook his head. Then he stabbed two fingers at his eyes. "Saw my aunt. Heard . . . her. But not."

"You think . . . you think . . . the black stuff that was inside this body just made her *look* like your aunt?"

Gordon nodded, eyes gleaming.

"Here, give me that!" I took the torch from him and looked over to where Stafford lay, checking to make sure that we were still within easy reach of the bonfire. The others were standing silently, watching us.

"What?" shouted Wayne. His voice was breaking. "What's going on?"

"Come back to the fire," called Lisa. "It's not safe."

"Nowhere's safe," I muttered—and then I looked down at Stafford.

His body was in the same position as the woman's. Also face down, arms outstretched in the pose he'd ended up in after the black stuff had exploded like a geyser from his mouth. Now I realised that whereas this body was wearing a jacket that was almost the same colour as Stafford's that morning, this was a different jacket altogether. The hair was similar, but not the same. I didn't treat the body with the same respect I'd seen Gordon show. Holding the torch high, I stuck my foot under an armpit and heaved. The body rolled and flopped onto its back.

This had been a man the same size, shape and age as Stafford. And I knew then that he'd been chosen for that very reason. The real Stafford had been just too messed up for the benefit of tonight's floorshow. Maybe it was the same with Gordon's aunt. This man was in a hell of a mess, but at least he was in one piece. His shirt was stained black-red; his fingers were torn and ragged, as if he'd clawed his way out of the rubble somewhere. But he'd served his purpose. The black

173

stuff, whatever it was, had somehow been able to make his face *look* like Stafford.

Gordon was looking hard at me when I turned away.

"The same," I said.

Gordon nodded.

We headed back to the others.

"Well?" asked Alex impatiently.

"We all saw people we thought we knew," I said. "All heard them saying things only we knew. Am I right?"

"Gas," said Alex. "It's the gas."

"No . . . " Gordon was vigorously shaking his head.

"Gordon's right. There was no gas attack. The things we're seeing . . . well, it's *nearly* them."

"*Nearly* them?" asked Damon. "What the fuck is that supposed to mean?"

"It means that the black stuff—the stuff Alex and Candy saw, the stuff that was out there just now—got into those dead bodies and made them come here. Gordon thought he saw his aunt. We looked. It wasn't her. Same with the other body. It was made to look like Stafford, the head teacher at Burleigh High. But it was only someone the same age, the same height. I reckon the black stuff did the same for everyone else. Made them see people they knew."

"It *was* him!" snapped Candy. "The man we saw in the off-licence. It *was HIM!*"

"The man I saw," said Lisa. The boy had been moving between Lisa and Annie ever since the horror had begun, burying his face first in the folds of Lisa's skirt, then pulling Annie's arms around to cover his head and face. When Lisa spoke, he clung to her more tightly. "It was my ex-husband. He doesn't live in Edmonville. He lives with my two sons on the other side of the country. Annie saw him, knows what he looks like. But he couldn't possibly be here. What we saw only looked like him."

"Look . . . look . . . " Alex appeared to be on the verge of

174

exploding with anger. "That doesn't explain the other stuff. How could . . . he . . . it . . . *they* know things about us? How could they know things that only go on in our *heads?* That's not possible."

"Lots of things are not possible," I said. "Think about what's happened. About what's *happening* here, Alex. What the hell's happened to Edmonville, for a start? How come we're stranded on this great chunk of rock? Look at all the other peaks and crags out there. Is that *possible* in real life? Can it really happen? No use saying 'No, it can't,' 'cause it's *there*! Right in front of our eyes."

"Why . . . doesn't . . . someone . . . *COME*!" yelled Candy, like the booze was finally starting to wear off, and no way was anyone going out there in the dark to the minimart to get more for her. Her voice broke on that last word and she collapsed to her knees, sobbing.

And that's when the noises began.

At first it seemed as if that word—"*Come*"—had somehow echoed, even though there was something flat and hollow about the way sound . . . well, *sounded*, ever since the quake. It seemed to hang in the air and then drift out into the darkness and come back. Bloody weird. And everyone began looking around in the night, beyond the light from the bonfire, when we all realised at the same time that it wasn't an echo at all. It was someone moaning.

More than that.

It was the sound of lots of people, all out there somewhere, all moaning.

It's difficult to put this across, but . . . well, you know the way that kids can pretend to be ghosts and do that corny moaning kind of sound. You know, really comical ghostly sounds. Well, the voices were like that. But there was absolutely and utterly *nothing* funny about it. The voices were deliberately trying to scare us. And no matter how hard we strained to look into the darkness, we couldn't see a single person. Maybe the corpses were back again, but if they were, they stayed well away from the light and in the dark. And, one by one, the chorus was being joined by another wailing voice, then another, and another. All moaning and wailing, like some kind of crazy wind.

It chilled me. It made me feel sick with fear.

Alex rushed to the fire, yanked another chunk of burning wood from it, and threw it out into the night in a blazing arc. A cloud of sparks whumped on impact with the ground. But it didn't reveal anything. We all crowded closer to the fire. The boy was sobbing, and both Lisa and Annie were trying their hardest to comfort him. Everyone's face looked white with fear. Those wailing voices reminded me of something else now. Something I'd seen and heard on a television documentary years ago.

They sounded like timber wolves out there, all calling to each other when they knew that their prey was cornered.

"Christ," said Wayne, and he dropped to his knees. "What are we going to do?"

"Stay close to the fire," said Annie. There was nothing shaky about her voice and she looked . . . well, defiant. I remembered the way she'd acted first when those dead people had appeared, pulling a torch out of the fire. I could feel myself pulling around just by looking at her. "They can't stand the fire." She couldn't possibly know that was absolutely true, even though we'd seen how the black stuff had reacted when the firebrands had been thrown at the dead people. But, just looking at her face, I believed it was true.

Gordon walked away from the fire, just a half-dozen steps or so, and with this grim look on his face. Then he swung the guitar around from his back, got it into position to play. We could only look at him, wondering what was going on.

His hand flashed in a downward stabbing motion across the strings, making three loud chords which seemed to hang in the air. We all just stood there, looking at him. It was like . . . well, like *he* was taunting whatever was out there making those moaning noises.

And then, after a pause, Gordon began to play.

Wayne and Damon gawped at him. We all stood and listened, while Gordon played this piece of music I'd never heard before. Sort of Spanish-sounding, and angry; really angry. I'd never heard anything like it. And just as the sound of our voices had been somehow flattened in the night, it seemed that Gordon's music was somehow . . . well, I don't know the word to use, really . . . except that the music sounded boosted. Maybe by the anger and the defiance in Gordon's playing. His eyes were catching the firelight as he stood there, like there was something burning inside him, and it was coming out through his fingers, into the chords and out into the night where the things might be crouching, or prowling or lying in wait.

Suddenly we couldn't hear the moaning, keening voices anymore.

We could only hear the music.

And, somehow, the music was *us*.

We'd been traumatised, nearly killed, and had escaped death in a dozen different ways. We had lost people close to us, and had been waiting for rescue that looked like it was never going to come. The dead had come back to life to haunt us. And the Black Stuff, whatever it was, wanted to suck the life out of us. By rights, we should just be lying face down on the ground, totally fucked up by fear and terror and exhaustion, and just letting ourselves be taken by whatever it was out there in the night that wanted us.

But not now. Not right at this moment, as Gordon played his beautiful, angry music, and I could feel my own anger at what was happening to us coming right out of his guitar and stabbing out into the darkness. I could see the defiance in Annie and Lisa's eyes. Candy had risen to her feet. She stood next to Alex, the pair of them staring off into the night. They were together now, maybe for only a while, but together.

Wayne and Damon just goggled at Gordon, and they weren't terrified anymore. The boy had stopped crying as Lisa held him tight.

I don't know how long he played. Five minutes. Ten. Maybe half an hour. I just don't know, because something happened to time then.

Finally, Gordon finished—with the same flourish of chords that had started his music, the final chord hanging in the air. He looked exhausted. Beads of sweat on his forehead were glinting in the firelight.

And the howling voices had gone.

The wolves were no longer out there in the dark.

That music—Gordon's music, *our* music—had scared them back to wherever in hell they'd come from.

Now there was only the crackling sound of flames from the fire behind us.

The heat felt good on my back.

No one spoke.

And we stayed by the fire, and took turns to sleep, until the first shades of grey began to dissipate the night and bring back—grey outline by grey outline—the silence and the emptiness of our new, desolate world.

CHAPTER THREE

THE ORDEAL OF
JULIET DELORE

JULIET SNAPPED AWAKE.

In panic, she clutched at the edge of the desk to make sure that it was still hard up against the door. Wildly, she looked around the storeroom, but nothing had changed. How the hell had she fallen asleep, knowing that Trevor was sitting on the other side of that door?

There was a scuffling sound from the other side.

Juliet clambered to her feet and braced one foot against the desk, raising the crowbar in readiness. Now she could hear sounds of exertion. A final scrape and clatter. Then low laughter.

"Trevor . . ."

"Did you enjoy your little snooze, my pet?"

"What are you doing?"

"I knew you were sleeping, you know. Could have bust in there any time I wanted. But I didn't want to, did I? Got better things in mind."

"You can't keep me here forever."

"Wanna bet?"

Suddenly there was a crash against the door. Juliet cried out, bracing her foot harder against the desk-edge. Trevor began hammering at the door; repeated, methodical blows.

"I've told you, Trevor! You come in here and I'll smash your head in."

"Who . . . wants . . . to . . . come . . . in?" said Trevor, each word followed by another blow. His voice was muffled because he was speaking through gritted teeth. There were six nails in his mouth. The voice in his head had told him that Juliet was sleeping, and that he could proceed with the next stage of the plan. Quietly, he had slipped away, back into the supermarket, and found to his delight that the hardware section hadn't vanished into the pit. He'd selected a fully kitted-out toolbox with hammer and nails. Next, he had picked up half a dozen oak shelves—nice veneer, very tasteful. When he began to nail the second shelf across the doorframe, Juliet suddenly realised what he was doing.

"Trevor, you miserable little . . . "

"Sticks and stones again, Juliet. My, if I'd only known how foul-mouthed you were when I first met you, I don't think I would have let our association continue."

Juliet lunged forward and slammed the crowbar against the door.

On the other side, Trevor flinched back—and then burst out laughing.

He continued with his task, nailing the shelves one by one across the door. He laughed again when Juliet began to yell at him from the storeroom, a barrage of anger fuelled by fear.

At last he dropped the hammer into the toolbox and backed away two steps to survey his handiwork.

"There, all neat and tidy."

"Trevor, you *shit*!"

Good, said the voice in his head. *Now, come. Night is here and I have things to show you.*

Trevor suddenly realised that it had grown dark while he had been enjoying himself; he just hadn't noticed. Like when he'd been a kid, playing outside, and suddenly he'd hear his mother calling that it was time to come in and—look at that!—it had turned into evening and he'd never even seen it coming.

"Got to go for a while, Juliet. Now, you be good. Tell you what. Why don't you see if you can break out of there with the crowbar? Bet you can't."

Smiling, Trevor descended the stairs, making no attempt this time to mask the crunching of broken glass and debris underfoot. Immediately there was a banging on the storeroom door. Frenzied and repeated. He chuckled at the sounds of Juliet's cries of effort, feeling as if something in his head that had been hidden for a long time was now free and unrestrained. Idly kicking tins from his path, Trevor made his way to the bread section, and the ragged cliff edge of the Chasm beyond.

The grey had become black. This time, standing on the edge, he did not feel the giddiness previously caused by those impenetrable depths. Instead, there was just a black void; and somewhere down there, the Voice calling to him. It was as if the world ended here. It was a good feeling. Trevor felt that he'd reached an important point in his life. The destruction, the earthquake, whatever; it was all the doing of the Voice, and it was an end to his old life. In that black void below there were limitless possibilities. He could feel it with a real sense of elation.

Do you know how easily I could have taken you? The Voice seemed very near, even though Trevor knew instinctively that it was also a long way down, at the bottom of the Chasm. *How easily I have taken others, since the First Day?* The Voice went on. Trevor nodded.

"Did you see the way I took care of that little shit from Central Office?"

I did, Trevor. That's why I'm able to talk to you. That's why I haven't taken you, the way I've taken the others. Because you're very special. You have great and hidden talents inside. You've just never had a chance to develop them, to use them. Use those talents now, Trevor. Give me pleasure in the bitch's torment. Be creative.

"Please . . . can I see you?"

There was silence now, and Trevor worried that he'd spoiled everything.

"I can hear you," he went on, now unsure. "It's just that . . . I need to see your face."

I have many faces, Trevor. Which face is it you want to see?

Trevor struggled to respond, not understanding.

There was laughter in his head. A dry, brittle, crackling sound.

"There's something about your voice. Something deep down, inside my head. Something vaguely . . . "

Familiar?

"Yeah, familiar. I can't explain. Don't really understand."

You don't need to understand, Trevor. But you do want to see? You want to look on my faces?

"Yes . . . "

The Voice didn't respond, but Trevor was aware of movement. Again, even though he knew that the Voice was physically deep in the pit, it was still also very close inside his head. Even now, the Voice was catapulting up the nearside of the Chasm like a speeding elevator. Gathering speed as it came, racing up the ragged cliff face; swarming up over ragged fissures of stone and clay.

Trevor stood trembling on the cliff edge, knowing that something great was about to happen; something that he had been waiting for all his life. As the Voice came swarming up towards him from the pit like a racing black cloud, he could feel a door opening inside his head. He'd never been able to fully open the door. Sometimes it had opened a crack. Once, when he was ten years old, and for no reason at all, he'd shoved a kid into the canal. He still remembered the thrashing of water, and then the stillness with only the fishing rod floating on the surface. And then the door opening a little again when he'd overheard his father reading out the item in the newspaper about the local child who'd drowned. Again, when he was fifteen, the girl in the park. The door edging open again when he'd seen the Identikit picture depicting a face that was absolutely nothing like him at all. There had been many other occasions over the years, but the door would only open so far and no more. At last, with the Darkness below almost out of the pit, he could feel the door opening wide to the wall. At last, he would find the real Trevor Blake, the Trevor who'd struggled to be free all these years.

He felt the cliff edge tremble, but he did not stagger back, stricken with vertigo as before. He knew that the Voice was here at last, just below the ragged rim; now flowing up all around the edge, like . . . like . . .

"Treacle!" giggled Trevor, and remembered joyfully how he'd poured a tin of the stuff over his two-year-old sister's head, then blamed his four-year-old brother when his parents had come back from the pub. Sister and brother had been slapped about until they were black and blue. (*Black from the treacle and blue with the bruises,* laughed Trevor inside.) And he'd just sat watching the television (*A black-and-white movie!*), smiling while the screams had come from the bedroom.

"They had to shave her head, you know," said Trevor.

I know, said the Voice. And Trevor could feel it pooling around his feet. It spread thick and fast in the darkness. Trevor could hear cereal packets and tins and loaves of bread falling from shelves as the blackness slithered into the supermarket all around him, surveying the remains of the building and making its plans.

The Door was open in his head now.

For the first time, he could be himself.

"Your face," croaked Trevor. "Your faces. You said I could see."

First, said the Voice, *know our name.*

"Yes . . . yes . . ."

I . . . we . . . have called ourselves . . .

"Yes? Oh, please, yes."

183

The Vorla, said the Voice. But this time when it spoke, it spoke with a hungry voice. Say *it. Say my name.*

"Vorla," said Trevor. "Your name is the Vorla."

Now see my faces, it said.

And a great ebony tidal wave, darker than the night, suddenly reared up over the cliff edge in front of Trevor. It glinted black in the darkness, the spreading waves of black which had flowed around his legs and beyond also swirling and rising behind to cocoon Trevor in a rising black funnel, of which he was the centre.

The Door was well and truly open.

The Darkness had found him, had shown him what he really was; the person he'd been fighting to find, ever since he was a kid.

The real Trevor Blake flung wide his arms to embrace the glinting black mass that surrounded him. It shimmered like liquid velvet before his face. But it did not descend, did not roar down upon him like a tidal wave. Trevor trembled, waiting for the moment that would transform him, would make sense of all those dark dreams and hideous deeds.

The Vorla engulfed him.

| **WAKING NIGHTMARES**

THE FIRE WAS BURNING LOW WHEN "DAY" came; embers glowing orange in the ash-grey remains of wooden beams and the other detritus that had been piled up.

No sun rising above the surreal crags of stone and rock. No creeping, glorious light in a canyon of clouds. Only the blank grey expanse above and on all sides, lightening gradually. But as the outlines of ruined buildings and crooked trees crept back into view, only two objects drew their eyes and remained their sole focus of attention: the two bodies lying on the grass fifty feet away. The woman who had been made to look like Gordon's aunt, and the man who looked like Stafford. No one had been inclined to approach them again in the darkness.

Jay waited until everyone was awake before he spoke.

"No one's coming to rescue us," he said simply. "I think everyone should get their head around that. We're on our own, and we're going to have to look out for each other."

No one replied.

"I think that means we're going to have to do some pretty unpleasant things if we're going to survive here."

"Like what?" asked Wayne contemptuously.

"Been thinking about those bodies," continued Jay. "Those two lying out there."

Still no one replied, but they all looked at him, waiting and listening.

"We'll have to get rid of them. Can't leave them lying there like that. So the first thing I thought was—we should chuck them over the edge."

There was still no response from the others. The horror of the previous night continued to lie heavily on everyone. Jay's words only hinted at more horror, and it seemed that no one was prepared to take any more.

"Over the cliff edge, I mean," continued Jay. "Then I got to thinking about what happened last night. The Black Stuff brought those dead people back to life, didn't it?"

No one spoke.

"Seems to me it can do the same thing again any time it wants to. Throw them down where the Black Stuff comes from, it'll probably just bring them back up again."

"Not in the daytime," said Annie. "It can't do anything in the daytime."

"Now how the hell do you know *that*?" demanded Wayne.

"I don't know. I just seem to . . . sense it."

"Okay," Jay went on. "It only comes out at night. Just like the best kind of bogeymen. So that gives us a day to do the second thing I thought about."

"Which is?" asked Alex.

"We go around the rest of this"—Jay indicated the plateau on which they were marooned, unable to think of a description—"this place, and we drag out all the dead bodies we can find. Pile them up. Burn them."

There was a long silence.

Finally, Candy said: "Are you mad?"

"Yeah, bloody mad," replied Jay. "What about you?"

"I can't," said Lisa. "I mean we can't . . ."

"We can," continued Jay. "And we'll have to. Because if we

don't, I think we're in for another night like we had last night. Don't know about you, but I can do without that."

It made sense. Horrifying, but it made sense.

"Think about it," Jay went on. "The Black Stuff can only make . . . make *puppets* out of those dead people that are still . . . well, almost intact. We've got to get rid of them." Candy struggled to control her bile. Intact—such an ordinary, but such an acutely horrible word in that context.

"That won't account for any bodies under rubble," said Alex, who then felt momentarily speechless when Gordon turned to look away. He knew that he was thinking of his aunt. He went on at last, "or maybe trapped in out-of-the-way places we can't find. We can't guarantee that we'll find them all."

"So what else do you suggest? We can't just sit here and . . . "

Alex waved his hands. "I'm not disagreeing with you. What you say makes sense . . . if *anything* makes sense anymore. I'm just saying we can't guarantee we'll find them all."

"I can't do it," said Candy simply.

"Candy, we've got to try . . . "

"I just can't do it, Alex. And it's no use trying to make me do it. Christ, there might be people that we *know*."

"Wood," said Gordon, and everyone looked at him, waiting for him to continue. But he couldn't manage another word. Instead, he pointed to the smouldering remains of the bonfire. "Tonight. Come again."

"Good," said Jay. "That's a first priority. Prepare for tonight. We need to get more timber, anything else that'll burn. Pile it up here and get ready for another night like last night. Just in case we don't get all the bodies, like Alex says."

"Okay," said Annie. "I hate the idea. But that . . . that Black Stuff wants us dead, I'm sure of it. As for the dead bodies up here . . . it's not right what it's done to them. We should do what Jay says, stop it bringing them back again. So I'll help with the bodies, I mean. Obviously, the boy can't do anything. Best if he stays with you, Lisa. He seems more attached to you."

187

Lisa nodded. The boy was still in his safe place, refusing to come out and face the other horrors that surrounded them. His eyes were fixed on the smouldering remains of the bonfire. "Candy and I will collect wood," she said. "While you do . . . what you have to do."

"No way," said Damon. "I'm not collecting stiffs. You going to do it, Wayne?"

"Look . . . " Wayne struggled to control his confusion and anger. "Someone's going to come and get us out of here. They've got to! But look out there, look at it! Maybe the rescue services have got their hands full. Give them time! What are they going to do to us if they find we've been burning people's bloody relatives? It's mad. How am I going to explain why I barbecued my fucking head teacher?"

"That's not Stafford lying out there," said Jay tightly. "It's *not* him!"

"I *saw* him, O'Connor!"

"Go on out there and look at his face."

"Fuck off."

Gordon stepped forward.

"Aunt," he said. "Not her."

"So what does the dummy know?" said Wayne dismissively, turning away.

Gordon's face flushed. Emotion was flaring as he tried to respond. But no words would come.

"That's enough," said Lisa to Wayne. "You've no call to talk to him like that."

Gordon had begun striding towards Wayne.

"No, don't!" shouted Annie.

Wayne turned quickly, just before Gordon caught him by the collar. Wayne lashed out, but his blow went over Gordon's head when he ducked. Wayne yelled an obscenity and tried to kick him, but this time Gordon kicked his leg away and he fell, yelling curses. Gordon held onto his collar and began dragging him across the grass towards the corpses.

Damon hurried forward.

"Stay where you are!" snapped Jay. Damon slowed, but kept moving as if he meant to help Wayne. "I mean it, Damon."

Damon halted, his face flaring with anger.

"Stop it!" shouted Annie. "Everyone, just *stop* it!"

Wayne had twisted on the ground until his coat was a knot around his body, his collar twisted up around his neck, choking him. As he clung onto the collar with both hands he screamed abuse at Gordon.

"You dummy! You fucking dummy!"

But now Gordon had reached the man's body. Stooping down, dodging to avoid Wayne's wildly thrashing legs as he tried to kick him again, Gordon finally got a grip on one arm and forced him over.

Wayne made a strangled sound of horror.

He was face to face with the corpse.

Gordon held him there, forcing him to look. Finally he let him go, jumping back when Wayne thrashed to his feet. For a moment, it looked as if he might attack Gordon. Instead he pointed an angry forefinger at him.

"You! You're . . . you're fucking dead, you dummy. Put your hands on me. You're fucking . . . *dead*!"

"Well?" said Jay. "It's not him, is it? It's not Stafford."

Still furious, Wayne refused to look back down at the corpse.

"It's like he said. That guy . . . Alex whatsisname. It's gas. Some kind of chemical or something. Made us see that Black Stuff, and those dead people."

Jay looked at Alex. "You still think it's gas?"

Alex held his hands wide helplessly. "I don't know what to think."

"What about the bodies, then, Alex? Do we just let them come back again tonight? Or do we do something about it?"

"All right," said Alex uncomfortably. "We should do what you say. Just in case."

"You're mad!" yelled Damon. "I'm not having any part of it."

"Me neither!" shouted Wayne.

"Okay," said Jay. "Okay, everyone knows where they stand. We'll get some food from the minimart. After that, we'd best get started."

Wayne glared at Gordon as he returned to the others. Then, realising how close he was to the corpses, he angrily moved away.

"We need some kind of transport," said Alex. His mouth was suddenly dry. "We can't just do this one by one. It would take too long." He turned to look beyond the trees towards the remains of the main street. "I think . . . I think I saw a lorry, or a dump truck or something. While we were walking around the cliff edge, trying to find a way off."

"What kind of state was it in?" asked Jay.

"It looked okay. The keys might still be in the dash."

"It's worth a try."

"Fucking mad!" snapped Damon.

"You still think someone is going to come?" asked Lisa.

Damon didn't answer.

"Know what I think?" continued Lisa in a calm voice. "I think that what's happened here hasn't just happened to Edmonville. I think it's happened all over the world. That Black . . . Stuff. That's like nothing I've ever seen before. Those dead bodies walking around, threatening us. Being made to look like people we know. I don't think we can rely on anyone or anything except ourselves. Maybe . . . " She shook her head, not wanting to continue.

"Maybe what?" asked Annie.

There were tears in Lisa's eyes as she struggled with her thoughts.

"Maybe," she said, "this is the end of the world. What they call the 'Day of Reckoning'."

"Fuck me!" said Wayne. "We've got a Born Again with us. Just what we need."

"Shut up," said Annie.

"Too much talk," said Jay. "And there's a lot of work to be done."

"I'm with Wayne," said Damon. "I'm *not* putting my hands on any dead bodies. Do what you like, but count me out."

"All right," replied Jay. "You're counted out. Off you go."

"What?"

"I said off you go. Both of you. Me, Alex, Gordon and Annie are going to take a look at that lorry. See if it's in working order. But you're not a party to any of this, so . . . off you go."

"What do you mean?"

"If you don't want to be part of this group, you and Wayne can just go and start your own. Make your own way. Do your own thing."

"You can't make us go," said Wayne.

"Oh yes I can. So you make your own arrangements for tonight, when the dark comes again, and that Black Stuff comes back up from the pit. You're not staying here with us if you don't pull your weight."

Wayne looked at Damon. Between them, they tried to conjure up the courage to bluff it out. But when they both turned to look at the others, the expression on every face made them back down.

"What about her, then?" sulked Wayne, pointing at Candy. "She said she wouldn't do it. You're not making her go, are you?"

"I've changed my mind," said Candy, white-faced. "I'll do it if I have to."

Jay nodded. "Good. But we'll stick to what we've agreed. Lisa and Candy collecting wood. We'll search for bodies."

"*We'll* collect wood . . ." began Wayne, and dried when he saw the fixed expressions on everyone's face. The threat didn't have to be repeated.

"Come on, then," said Jay. "Let's get started."

He looked at Alex, his face grim. Then, quickly striding forward, he seized one of the two bodies by the arms and began hauling it away across the grass. Swallowing hard, realising that Jay was relying on him, Alex moved to the other body and repeated the manoeuvre, trying to tell himself that the body was only a shell and that they were doing the best thing. Suddenly Annie was at his side, reaching down. They exchanged a look, and now Annie was helping him, both holding an arm and dragging the body after Jay. Lisa had turned the boy away.

Wayne and Damon stood looking at each other, now cursing the blank grey sky, now making a joint run at the remains of the bonfire and kicking soot, ash and sparks high into the air. When they had exhausted themselves, the others had reached the first of the ruined buildings beyond the trees that led to the main street.

Then, heads down and without speaking, they slowly began to follow the others.

| CHAPTER FIVE | **THE ORDEAL OF JULIET DELORE** |

J ULIET HAD LOST ALL SENSE OF TIME IN THE storeroom.

There was something wrong with the sky beyond the window during the day. Grey, always grey. No clouds, no birds. No vapour trails.

No sound.

It was as if the world beyond that window had simply ceased to exist. She had tried shouting, to draw attention to her plight. The sound of Trevor laughing on the other side of the door had made her shout until her voice was hoarse, and she'd given up. The glass face of her watch had been shattered some time during her ordeal, but although she could not check the time she felt that she had been locked in this storeroom for well over two days. Why hadn't someone come? If there had been an earthquake or something, surely the rescuers would have arrived by now. The shock, the continued tension and stress, the lack of food and water—all were taking their toll. Miserably, she'd had to relieve herself in the far corner of the storeroom, creeping away when Trevor had been in one of his "silent" moods.

When the grey beyond the window had become black for the second time, and the storeroom was plunged into complete darkness, it seemed that Trevor had more energy. Throughout the night, he sat on the other side of the door, gabbling obscenities at her through the wood, deliberately slobbering over the tinned food that he'd stacked beside him, taunting her.

When Trevor slammed his hand against the door, Juliet snapped awake from the troubled half-sleep into which she'd fallen.

"Can't have you nodding off, Juliet. That wouldn't be playing the game, would it?"

Juliet replied in kind. Leaning back angrily, she slammed the crowbar against the door. Trevor merely laughed as he opened another tin and drank peach juice straight from the can, deliberately making cartoon slobbering noises for Juliet's benefit. Didn't he need sleep?

"There are all kinds of things I can do to you, if I want."

Trevor paused while he slobbered over the peaches. With eyes screwed shut, trying to ignore him, Juliet wondered how she could ever have been so wrong about someone. He'd seemed so normal, so caring. She permitted herself a rueful laugh. The others had been saints compared to the madman on the other side of the door.

"Don't you like your men to be masterful, Juliet? Don't you like them to take command? Treat you any way they want?"

"Why don't you stick your head through that broken window?" said Juliet. "And see what happens."

"Feisty," laughed Trevor. "That's the word for you, my darling. Very feisty. Now let me tell you about some of the other things we could do to pass the time . . . "

Juliet tried to shut her mind off from the obscenities that Trevor whispered through the door; racked her brains to think of another way out of this place. In the last two days she'd explored every option, even down to the possibility of just jumping out of the window and taking a chance that there might be something below to grab on to. Despair threatened to overwhelm her. She could feel the tears coming again, and tightened her grip on the crowbar.

" . . . with a broken bottle, not enough to break the tender skin down there, but just enough to . . . "

Juliet thought hard about her parents, and whether they were all right. They lived twenty miles from town, so the chances were that whatever had happened right here in the centre of Edmonville wouldn't have affected them. (*But why hasn't anyone come yet? Why am I still waiting in here?*) She thought of her workmates at the travel agency, Tricia and Jennifer. Were they all right? The agency was about five miles away. Perhaps they'd escaped.

" . . . enough to make it tight, *really* tight. And then you'll have to beg me to do it, even though it's hurting you. You'll have to beg me despite the pain and . . . "

Juliet thought about her friends in Edmonville: Kate and Janie and Becca. Were they all right? Lorraine was on holiday in Greece, so she was okay. But all of the others worked locally. My God, she really would have a story to tell them when she got out of here.

"Are you listening, Juliet? You've gone very quiet, my love."

Juliet gripped the crowbar and braced herself to slam it against the door again. But at that moment another option presented itself. One that she'd never considered before.

"Juliet?"

She remained still, now looking up at the shattered window.

"And I'll tell you what else we can do," Trevor went on. "Shall I? Shall I tell you?"

Could she do what she had in mind without making a sound?

"First we need a knife," hissed Trevor. "One of those sharp kitchen knives, with a saw edge. Know the kind I mean? Well, first we cut the . . . "

Juliet shut her mind to him. As long as he was talking, the sound of his voice might cover any noise she made. Carefully, she stood up. When a knee joint popped, she froze. But Trevor just kept on with his sick fantasy. Bracing one knee on the desk, she paused. Then, movement by careful movement, she climbed onto it. Both knees on the desk, pause. Brace the hands, pause. One foot up, pause. Then the other, so that now she was crouched there on the desk, one hand against the door for support. And Trevor was going on and on, his words sicker and sicker. There was a shelving unit to the left of the door. It looked solid enough to support her weight. Her entire plan depended on it. Juliet moved carefully towards it.

"Juliet?"

Fear spasmed in her stomach. Juliet froze again, feeling sure that he somehow knew what she was up to.

"Can you hear me, Juliet? It's not like you to stay quiet for so long."

Juliet reached the edge of the desk, put her left foot on a shelf and reached up for a higher one. It was chunky and solid, not likely to come away from the wall as she'd feared. She stayed in that position, waiting.

"Juliet? What are you doing? Are you asleep?" Trevor laughed. "That's what it is. You're asleep again! Wake up, Juliet! Wake *up*! You're not listening, and that's not fair!"

There was a six-inch shard of glass on the shelf beside her hand. Juliet plucked it up, braced herself and looked over at the storeroom window. Making three feints, to judge how hard and far it should be thrown, she pitched it. The shard sliced through the air, hitting the wall above the window with a sharp crack and tinkling to the floor in fragments.

"*Juliet!* What are you doing?"

Juliet held her breath, gripping the shelf and swinging away from the desk. She couldn't stay that way for long, but she was out of sight of the shattered window with her head about level with it at this height.

"*JULIET!*"

Already the fingers of her left hand were aching where she

gripped the shelf; the weight of the crowbar in her right hand seeming to increase by the second.

"*What are you doing, you BITCH!*"

There was a scuffling movement on the other side of the door.

Please . . . prayed Juliet. *Please . . . please . . .*

"You can't get out through the outside window. The Vorla told me that! There's only the Chasm below, Juliet. You'll just fall forever and ever. So it's no use even thinking about it. Do you hear me?"

Juliet gritted her teeth.

. . . please . . .

There was more scuffling and Juliet saw a shadow at the top of the door, through the one small section of the broken window she could see from her hidden vantage point. He was doing it. Trevor was climbing up to look through the window and see if she really was trying to make her escape on the other side of the room. But she had to wait until he was in position.

"It's no use, Juliet. You can't escape from me. We've got lots more fun and games to play . . ."

Juliet couldn't hang on any longer. She would make a noise or she would fall. Even if he hadn't made it right up to the window yet, she had to act before it was too late.

Please!

Juliet swung back from the shelving unit, bringing the crowbar up hard as she moved and jabbing it with all her remaining strength through the ragged aperture of the shattered window. Trevor was gripping the bottom of the frame, peering intently down to where she had been crouching moments before.

The two-pronged point of the crowbar stabbed into his right eye, puncturing it and lodging deep in the socket.

Trevor shrieked, hands flying to his face.

Crying in horror and shock, Juliet lost her grip and fell away from the desk, landing heavily on the littered floor, glass shards stabbing into the palms of her hands and her legs.

Trevor fell away from the window, the crowbar still embedded in his face. Juliet heard him hit the floor on the other side, still shrieking; heard the crowbar jar loose, rattling on the debris as Trevor squirmed and thrashed in agony. There was another crash and muffled thudding. In his agony, Trevor had fallen down the stairs into the supermarket, screaming all the way.

For a moment, Juliet couldn't move. The horror of what she had done robbed her of all strength.

Move, girl! This might be your last chance.

Sobbing, Juliet threw herself back at the desk, heedless of any sound she might make as Trevor's screams echoed from down below. Seizing a carton from one of the shelves to her left, she bludgeoned out the remaining glass shards in the window aperture. Was it wide enough to squeeze through?

No choice! I'm going through that bloody window even if I have to squeeze myself flat!

Juliet braced both hands on the windowsill and pushed her head and shoulders through the gap. Trevor was writhing and thrashing at the foot of the littered stairs, screaming hoarsely and with both hands still clamped to his face. Blood was oozing between his fingers. Despair again threatened to rob Juliet of her strength. How could she have done such a terrible thing?

"I had to, Trevor!" she yelled as she struggled and wiggled through the gap. "You bastard. I didn't want to, but you *made* me do it!"

She could see Trevor now, lying down below amidst a pile of tins and cartons, clutching at his face, his legs kicking and thrashing as he spun in wild circles on the floor. Sobbing, Juliet pushed harder, crying out loud again when her hips caught in the frame. It was a seven-foot drop to the floor, but that didn't matter. She twisted her body sideways and slithered through the gap. She exercised regularly, took good care of her body, but she couldn't prevent herself from falling awkwardly. There was no pain when she hit the floor; the shock and the horror of her situation anaesthetised her against it. The empty tins that Trevor had been eating from clattered all around her. The impact dazed her, but when her vision cleared she could see the blood-smeared crowbar lying on the floor. Her stomach turned, but the frenzied sounds of Trevor in agony below galvanised her into action. Instinctively, she knew she should take the crowbar for further protection, but the sight of the blood was too much; she could not touch it. Juliet started down the stairs, halting when . . .

Trevor clawed at his face, trying to gouge the pain from his eye socket. In his agony, he believed that something was in there, trying to burrow into his brain and sending him insane with pain. He had no way of knowing that his eye was gone. And as he screamed, he could hear laughter. Was it Juliet? Mocking him from behind that door? Still with one bloody hand clasped to his face, he struggled to his knees, trying to fight the pain; tried to see through his remaining eye as it constantly filled with blood.

"Juliet! You bitch! Are you laughing, are you *LAUGHING*?"

He staggered to his feet, now groping with one free hand, trying to find his way back to the stairs as . . .

Juliet stopped, three steps from the bottom. She could see the extent of the destruction in the supermarket—the fractured ceiling, the toppled shelves and units, the shattered windows at the front of the store, and the great black space over to her right where the rest of the supermarket used to be. Perhaps there was a moment when she could have made a break for it, running past Trevor as he lay in agony on the ground. But the shock of what had happened here, of what she had done to him, froze her. She was out of the storeroom now, and the bastard was insane, but . . . oh God . . . what had she done to his eye? She was about to run, about to launch herself past his scrabbling body, when he suddenly pulled himself to his feet, his face a mask of blood, one hand clamped there to staunch the flow as he screamed and staggered and groped towards her. The moment for escape was gone. He was blundering straight towards the stairs, one arm outstretched and wavering, but she could not get past him.

"Stop LAUGHING! Stop *LAUGHING!!*"

Silent, her face white and with both fists clenched to her mouth, Juliet remained on the third step from the bottom as Trevor groped his way towards her. Part of her shrieked that she must run; another, equal part told her to stay and wait. Trembling, she watched him stagger on, straight towards her.

And then Trevor stopped, realising at last that it was not Juliet he could hear laughing. Was it the voice inside his head? Was it the Vorla?

"Why are you laughing?" asked Trevor, in a voice like that of a hurt child. "Why are you laughing at me?"

Juliet almost answered. Instead, she kept her fists to her mouth and tried to keep control as Trevor stood before her, no more than six feet away.

Laughing? said the Vorla in his head. *I'm just so HAPPY for you, Trevor.*

"Happy?"

The pain is all part of the Test, Trevor. It hurts, doesn't it?

"Oh Christ, it hurts . . ."

She's out of the storeroom. She got out. Now you have to find her. You have to hunt her down and . . .

Juliet stepped carefully and quietly to the bottom of the stairs, trying not to make a noise, carefully stepping over the tins that littered the floor. Step by careful step, she moved around Trevor, who remained in front of the stairs, now silent, blood streaming between his fingers where his hand remained clamped to his face.

. . . *catch her, Trevor. She can't get far. And catching her will all be part of the Test. It's dark, Trevor. And I could take her now, oh so easily. If I wanted to. But I want to watch, and savour the hunt. I want you to hunt her down for me. I want you to make her suffer. Want to feel her terror and her pain. You can do all that for me, Trevor. That's the Test, do you see?*

Juliet headed down an aisle, away from Trevor, stepping over the detritus. Her foot caught a cereal packet, and Rice Krispies pattered over the tiled floor.

Trevor whirled in her direction.

Now no longer caring whether or not she made a sound, Juliet ran towards the shattered glass frontage of the super-market, bumping a shelving unit as she ran. Tins clattered and rolled over the floor behind her. Trevor started forward in her direction.

No! Stop! commanded the Vorla.

"Why? You want me to catch her, don't you?" Trevor groaned again as the fire burned into his skull.

Give her a few moments, Trevor. Let her believe that she's escaped. She'll soon find that she can't get far. And then you can commence the hunting. You can give me great pleasure, Trevor. And I promise you, you'll be well rewarded if you pass the Test.

At the front of the supermarket, Juliet began to pick her way over the broken glass towards a ragged hole in one of the windows. The revolving glass doors were impassable. Looking back only once, she dipped through the hole and was gone into the supermarket car park.

"*Now?*" asked Trevor.

Wait, said the Vorla. *Wait and I'll tell you the Big Secret.*

"Secret?"

About what's happened here, Trevor. What's happened to your world. And what I really am.

And as Juliet ran through the ruins of the car park shouting for help that would never come, Trevor stood with blood dripping to the floor, listening to the Big Secret, and learning at last what had happened, and the real meaning of the Chasm.

Finally, when the Vorla had finished speaking, and Trevor understood what his part was to be in this new world, the darkness began to fade.

The Vorla must return to the Chasm before that time.

But it could stay inside Trevor's head, and enjoy the chase to come.

Now, it said at last.

Suddenly, it seemed that the pain in Trevor's eye socket had been muted by the presence of the Vorla in his head.

"Now?" repeated Trevor.

Find her, said the Vorla. *Find the bitch. And do everything that you promised her.*

Grinning, his face a mask of blood, Trevor staggered down the supermarket aisle towards the frontage. Finding the same gap that Juliet had used, he stepped out into the car park.

"Juliet!" he yelled at the top of his voice. "I'm coming to *find* you!"

CHAPTER SIX | **BRING OUT YOUR DEAD**

THE TRUCK WAS WHERE ALEX SAID IT WOULD be.

It had veered off the road when the quake first hit, and crashed through a roadside fence. The twin tracks of burned rubber from the tyres were still visible on the churned-up road. Both doors were wide open, the occupants long since fled.

"Anybody ever drive one of these?" asked Jay.

"Here," said Alex. "Let me." He swung up through the door on the driver's side, slamming it shut.

"Keys?"

"Yeah, still in there." Alex twisted them and the engine coughed. Twisting again, he cranked more gas, and this time the engine caught and maintained a healthy grumbling. He looked back at Jay, as if to say something. He couldn't find the words, but Jay knew what was on his mind.

"No," he replied to the unasked question. "I don't know if this is the right thing to do. But no one's coming to help us. I don't know why, Alex. But they're not. And we have to protect ourselves."

"But . . . I mean . . . *burning* them?"

"It's the only way to stop them coming back. And before you say anything about the nerve gas theory again, ask yourself this: how long does the hallucination last? I mean, those two bodies back there by the fire . . . the ones made to look like Gordon's aunt and my old head teacher . . . they were still there this morning. They didn't disappear. Ask yourself another one: *how* did they get there? I know what I saw—they walked there."

Alex looked troubled. He turned to face the front, biting his lip.

"All right," he said at last.

"Look," continued Jay, "we'll not get far on the road. But I reckon if we drive onto the verge here, where the park perimeter is, we can move out to the cliff edge, go through the houses there, find . . . whatever . . . and drag them back to the truck. Then you can move the truck down the perimeter, keep moving it until we've covered the street between here and the cliff edge."

Gordon handed his guitar up to Annie, sitting next to Alex in the cab.

"Thought that thing was growing on you," said Jay, as he jumped down from the running board. Last night's defiant stand was still a shining memory, despite the horror of everything that had passed. Gordon smiled, and Alex drove the truck straight over the shattered fence and onto the grass verge. Yanking on the handbrake and switching off the ignition, he climbed down to join the others.

Annie, Wayne and Damon were staring at what they had just discovered on the roadside, screened by bushes.

It was another body.

A woman, face down in a dried brown pool. She was wearing a floral print dress and her hands were flung out in front of her. It looked as if she had been finger-writing in the horrifying stain. Had she been there ever since the quake? Or had she been one of the stumbling figures from last night, brought back to hideous life by the Black Stuff?

Jay, Alex and Gordon joined them.

They stood looking at the woman for a long time.

And then, bile rising, but not wanting any of the others to see it, Jay strode forward. Gritting his teeth, he stooped down and grabbed one of the hands. It was cold and hard, like a hand made of marble. Turning to fix his gaze on the rear of the dump truck where the other two bodies had been lifted, he turned her over. Annie was the first to see the pool of dried blood the body had left behind, and her sharp intake of breath made the others recoil instinctively.

"Oh my God," she said faintly, pointing down at the congealed mess.

The woman had written a message in her own blood, scrawling with reddened fingers.

"'*You're . . .* '" read Jay, sickened, turning his head to get a better look.

"*You're all in Hell*'," finished Annie.

They stood, looking down in horror. No one seemed able to move.

Then Jay angrily stooped down again and grabbed one of the corpse's legs, hauling it away. Moments later, the body was in the back of the truck, together with the other two corpses.

Jay pretended to dust his hands, his back turned as the others began moving off through the rubble towards the nearest ruined houses. He wanted to vomit, fought to control his gorge. He couldn't flee any longer. Taking a deep breath, he turned.

Alex was still there, looking at him.

Before anger could flare, Jay saw that he didn't have a "told you so" look on his face. Instead his face was grim, and he merely nodded.

"Not easy," he said.

"Never said it would be," replied Jay.

Alex nodded again, and started after the others.

Jay followed.

Gradually, they worked their way east—or what was once east, before the world beyond the outer crags of rock had faded into impenetrable grey. They moved from house to house, from room to room, catching sight of each other every time they emerged once more into the fractured streets. Their sense of unease was growing steadily and insistently as they each moved on to the next building, the next ruin—and found nothing. No one spoke, but every time they emerged from another shattered doorway or a crumbling building each strained to see if the others had found a body.

One hour into the search, and not one body had been found yet.

Could that be possible?

The search continued in the eerie silence that lay over the ruins.

And then, another hour later, a call from Alex brought the others scrambling from the ruins. He was standing in the middle of a ploughed-up road; just standing with his hands hanging at his sides, staring off into space. He looked completely exhausted. Jay was the first to reach him, could see no sign of a body, began asking him what was wrong . . . and then, without speaking, Alex pointed across the street to the wall of a half-demolished house.

It was the second message; scrawled in blood, dozens of hands working to make the letters three feet high.

Auschwitz.

"What does it mean?" asked Damon.

No one could answer. But it was clear that the vanished dead were still taunting Edmonville's sole survivors. The sight of the hideous message sapped their strength, but they continued with the search anyway. It didn't take long before Annie came across the next message, also scrawled in blood in huge letters, on a road sign that had snapped from its supports and fallen across the street.

Belsen.

"Belsen?" said Damon at last, when he'd been able to decipher the message. "What the hell is a Belsen?"

No one answered him.

The fourth message had been scrawled on the unbroken concrete of a pub car park.

Reverend Jim Jones.

"A cult leader," said Annie, before anyone asked the question. "He led his disciples to mass suicide in South America."

When their search brought them to the rear of Femmes Hardware, the message had become more personalised. There were loading bays there for the other stores. A florist's van had been crushed by falling masonry, withered flowers lying all around it like some kind of funeral tribute. Annie stood for a moment, shivering; remembering the fissure that had suddenly opened up on the other side of these buildings. Now their own property was standing on a cliff edge, everything on the other side fallen away into the Chasm that surrounded them. As they moved past it, Jay caught sight of the scrawl on the rear door of Annie and Lisa's store.

Dyke Bitches.

Annie paused. She and Lisa had put everything into making their business work. Now the quake had ruined it, brought them to the very brink of hell. But even in hell they weren't free from the hatred they'd come across in their ordinary lives. She felt sorrow and fear combining inside, threatening to overwhelm her.

Suddenly there was a hand on her shoulder.

It was Jay.

"Okay?"

Annie tried to smile, squeezed his hand—and they continued on past the ruins. She hoped that Lisa and the boy were okay as . . .

Lisa shoved open the door of the minimart, immediately

standing back when a whispering cloud of plaster dust curled down around her head from above. Coughing, she waved it away and stepped inside. The boy kept close, hanging onto her skirt.

"Candy?"

There was no reply.

Lisa stepped inside. The place was pretty much as she remembered it from yesterday. When the boy tugged at her hand and pointed to one of the shelves, she nodded and took down a can of fizzy drink for him. She handed him a packet of biscuits, popped open a tin of pears. The boy ate greedily, and she felt guilty that she hadn't thought of it earlier. Her stomach was still strained and nauseous, but she also opened a can of drink and took a deep draught.

They had been gathering wood for a couple of hours, but suddenly there was no sign of Candy. The boy needed to eat, and perhaps Candy had decided on something to "fortify" her during the search; so they'd made their way back to the minimart.

But there was no sign of her in here.

And then Candy stood up from behind the counter and made a "here I am" gesture with both hands. The sudden appearance made Lisa start. Candy laughed, and then Lisa knew that she was already well and truly plastered. One hand on the bench for balance, Candy made a wobbly descent to pick up the bottle of brandy, clunking it down dramatically, as if evidence of her condition were needed.

"Anything to say?" she asked.

Lisa drank again from her can, saying nothing.

"You sure? No lectures?"

"What you do with your life has nothing to do with me."

"Good. Now that's good. No holier-than-thou shit."

"It's just that . . ."

"I knew it! Here we go. The lecture's coming, after all."

"I was only going to say that we've got to help each other until we get out of this mess. Until someone comes."

"All for one and one for all, eh?"

"Look, Candy, none of us wants to be here. You don't, I don't. But we've got to co-operate, until we can get ourselves out of this mess. We need to pull together."

"Here we go again. Somebody else telling me what I need. You been taking lessons from Alex?"

"We don't have to like each other. We just have to . . . "

"Too fucking *right* we don't have to like each other!" Candy whirled to face her. "And I certainly don't like *you* or *your friend!*" Whirling again, she stormed away.

"We need . . . "

"I know what I *need!*"

"We need each other. But you can't help very much if you're completely pissed all the time."

"Is that it? I mean, is that the end of the lecture?"

"Yes."

"Good . . . good . . . " Candy drank again.

Lisa exhaled. It was merely a sigh of stress. But to Candy it was a gesture of contempt. Furiously, she slammed the brandy bottle down hard on the bench. A thin spiral of spirit corkscrewed from the neck and splattered on the wood.

"Don't you dare! Don't you fucking *dare* look down your nose at me!"

"Candy, I'm not . . . "

"Who the hell are you to tell me what to do? From where I'm standing, *you're* the disgusting one! You and that . . . that . . . *partner* of yours!"

"What are you talking about, Candy?"

"I mean you and her. You're lesbians, aren't you? Don't bother to deny it, you can tell just by looking at you; particularly the other one. The butch one. Does she wear the trousers, then? Is that how it works?"

"Calm down, Candy."

"It's . . . it's . . . disgusting. And that boy there. You shouldn't be anywhere near him. You or the other one." Candy staggered towards them. "You don't know what it's like . . . *can't* know what it's like . . . to look after a child. To have one of your own. Be its . . . his . . . mother."

"I have . . . " And Lisa bit her lip before she could tell Candy of her own two children. Candy's eyes were suddenly filled with tears as she fixed on the boy. He was finishing his tin of pears, was suddenly aware of Candy and regarded her with wide, puzzled eyes as she stooped down and tried to smile, wiping the tears from her face.

"Come here, darling," she said. "Come to me."

The boy moved closer to Lisa, clinging to her legs.

"Come away from there," Candy went on, her tone hardening. "You can't want her. It's not natural."

"Candy, you're frightening him."

"Someone needs to take him away from you both. It's not right."

Candy moved quickly, as if to snatch him away. The boy cried out in alarm, and Lisa pulled him around behind her.

"Stop it, Candy!"

Rising in fury, Candy screamed directly into Lisa's face: "You pervert! You disgusting animal!"

Lisa stepped forward and smacked her across the face.

Candy gasped, standing back.

And then the fury returned, even fiercer than before, raging out of control.

"Get out! Get *out!* GET *OUT!*"

"I'm sorry, I shouldn't have done that . . . "

"You . . . you . . . *lesbian!*"

"You can't stay here, Candy. It'll be dark soon. And I need help to build up the fire."

"Don't . . . call . . . me . . . Candy! Only my friends call me that."

"That Black Stuff will be back."

"Black Stuff! I don't believe it. Alex was right. It's not real. We only think we're seeing all this crap . . ."

"You know that's not true."

"Leave the boy here with me! Go back to your butch friend and do whatever people like you do to each other!"

"Candy . . ."

"Give the boy to me!"

When Lisa stood her ground, refusing to surrender him, Candy lurched to one of the shelves, seized a bottle and flung it. Her aim was bad. It smashed against the wall, spraying everyone with vinegar. There was nothing Lisa could do. Backing off carefully and keeping the boy well behind her in case Candy should suddenly snap and launch herself forward, Lisa found the door and went out onto the street. Candy lunged forward, kicking the door shut, making another plaster-dust cloud swirl.

Lisa pulled the boy close, stroking his hair.

Anger and sorrow fought inside, hurting her throat.

As Candy moved back for her bottle, Lisa realised that she was out of control. She couldn't be left alone like this. Clearing her throat, wiping her own tears away, she started back down the street with the boy clinging close as . . .

"Christ, I don't believe this," said Alex, leaning back against the side of the dump truck, pulling the tab on one of the cans they'd collected from the ruins of another store. Gordon, sitting on the running board of the truck, bit into a pre-packed sandwich. It tasted like cardboard.

Annie stood looking off into the vast expanse of grey sky, drinking from a pop bottle. She'd been very quiet since they'd found the bloody message on the back door of the hardware store. The lack of bodies and the blood messages everywhere had shaken them more than actually finding any of the dead.

"Maybe . . ." began Damon, and then dried up. He turned away to sulk when no one asked him to develop his views further.

"Maybe . . ." Wayne decided to take up the mantle. "Maybe it's like that guy was saying earlier." His hand made a dismissive gesture towards Alex. "Nerve gas."

"We've been through this," said Jay evenly.

"No, I mean this latest thing. The fact that we can't find any dead bodies when they should be lying all over the place."

"What has nerve gas got to do with missing bodies?" asked Annie.

"Well . . . maybe there *are* bodies. Lying all around here. Only thing is, we can't see them."

"Yeah." Damon had emerged from his sulk. "They're lying around, but because of this gas stuff we can't see them. Another one of them hallucinations. Like all the other things. The Black Stuff and what them two said they'd seen in the off-licence. Makes sense."

"No it doesn't," said Annie.

"What the fuck do you know?" snapped Damon.

"I'll tell you what the fuck I know," said Annie. "It would have to be a pretty specialized and selective nerve gas. First it makes all of us see things, the same things. Then it decides that it's going to *stop* us seeing things. Then it makes us see messages written in blood that aren't really there. Where the hell do we draw the line? No, the nerve gas theory fell apart a long time ago."

"Well, we think Alex is right!" asserted Wayne.

"That's more than I do," said Alex wearily. "I wanted to believe all that stuff I said. I don't anymore. Something's happened here; something's *happening* here. But we're not seeing . . . and then *unseeing* . . . things. That's not what this is about."

"Taw-taw . . ." Gordon spat out a mouthful of sandwich. "It's taun-taunting us."

"How the fuck are we supposed to understand what he's talking about?" said Wayne.

"Like. Last. Night. Black Stuff . . . tau-taunting . . . "

"I still don't know what he's talking about," said Damon.

"Like last night at the bonfire," said Jay, nodding at Gordon. "And today those messages were all put there for us to see."

"But why?" asked Annie. "Do they all mean something?"

Jay shrugged.

"How long have we been searching?" asked Annie.

"Four, five hours," replied Alex.

"We're never going to find anyone before it gets dark."

"We'd better get on with it," said Jay.

"Let's do it, then," affirmed Alex. "I'll drive the truck up ahead. Anyone know this part of town?"

"Yes," said Annie. "It's going to be harder from here. There are a lot of houses just over there, between the edge and the park."

"Why haven't *we found* anybody yet?" asked Wayne.

"That Black Stuff," said Jay. "The stuff you think you might or might not have seen . . . has hidden them away somewhere."

"Why?"

"Because it wants to use them again, doesn't it? Tonight. Tomorrow. For as long as it can before they start . . . " Jay refrained from saying *falling apart.*

Everyone understood.

Silently, Alex climbed into the cabin of the dump truck and started it up.

Silently also, the others began to pick their way down the street.

Continuing the search.

| CHAPTER SEVEN | **THE ORDEAL OF JULIET DELORE** |

J ULIET RECOILED FROM THE BRINK, ARMS thrust behind her and grabbing for anything solid. Her eyes remained fixed on the yawning chasm before her.

She'd fled across the supermarket car park, swerving around parked cars, her leather-jeaned hip smacking against the hood of one vehicle but the pain meaning nothing at all in her flight. She worked out at a local gym once a week, tried to keep in shape, but never could have believed that she was capable of such speed. She'd been freed from a nightmare; now she was in another kind of dream altogether. Like a low-flying bird she was streaking across the car park, blonde hair streaming behind her.

Nothing could stop her now.

In a moment, she'd see people—maybe dazed or disorientated by the earth tremor or the bomb blast, or whatever had happened. In a second, she'd be surrounded by crowds of protective people. Maybe there'd even be a policeman, or a fireman, in the milling crowd. She was free and she was safe and . . . she staggered to a halt when she saw what lay ahead.

The car park had suddenly ended in a ragged cliff edge.

She could see the estate agent's office across the way on Laburnum Street, could see the Chinese takeaway and the telephone kiosk outside. Nothing could have prepared her for the fact that everything from that point to what had once been the middle of this supermarket car park had vanished forever into a bottomless pit; including one hundred and twenty square yards of tarmac, the twenty-two vehicles that had been parked there, a main road, a taxi rank and the one hundred and fifty-three men, women and children who had fled the supermarket when the first tremor had hit Edmonville.

Juliet teetered on the edge, saw the vast space yawning before her—and then fell back, breathless, to the cracked tarmac.

Disorientated, panicking, she scrabbled back further on elbows and heels.

This couldn't be right.

Now she was on her feet again; crouched and running around the cliff edge, looking for the point at which she could cross to safety. Okay, something terrible had happened. There'd been an earthquake. Impossible and unheard of in this country. But it had happened. She could handle it. But first, she had to get away from that bloody supermarket and find where the people had gone and . . .

There was no one here.

No one behind her when she whirled to look (and, thank Christ, no sign of Trevor loping across the car park in her direction), and no one over on the other side of the huge fissure. That couldn't be right. There *had* to be people. She just had to keep following this cliff edge, and she'd see somebody. Fire fighters, maybe. Or men in bright yellow oversuits, directing people to the nearest emergency station, or . . .

Juliet was still running, now in an arc around the supermarket, following the cliff edge, and looking out over the two-hundred-foot fissure that separated her from the other side, and it was just going on . . . and on . . . and on.

And where, for Christ's sake, were all the people?

Now the ragged edge seemed to be taking her back towards

the main supermarket building, which was the last place in the world she wanted to see again.

She was panicking now. She knew it.

She stopped. Bent double, hands on thighs, she drew deep, sobbing breaths.

This didn't make sense. She had to get control. Had to sort herself out.

Looking back again, she saw at last what had happened to the supermarket.

It really had been shorn in half.

The missing half had fallen away over the cliff edge into the Chasm. She tried to think what had been there. A furniture franchise. An electricals section. A music department. All gone over the edge into that terrible rift. She could see now where the roof had slumped and torn, ragged brickwork and shattered timbers marking the split. Rubble and detritus marking the interior of the supermarket and the irregular cliff edge on which it now stood.

And now, picking his way over the broken glass that had once been the front windows of the supermarket, she could see a familiar figure with a mask of blood for a face.

She froze as he spotted her and put one hand up over his empty eye socket as if this could somehow focus the vision in his one remaining eye.

Could she see him grinning, even from this distance?

"*Juli–ettttttttt!*" he called. "*I'm . . . coming!*"

Ducking behind a ruined wall, Juliet ran frantically along the cliff edge, looking for a way across. Deep inside, some hopeless and lost part of her was weeping; telling her that the supermarket and the surrounding buildings were stranded on this one pinnacle of rock less than four hundred yards square and with a bottomless pit on all sides.

No, that was impossible.

She must find somebody who could help.

. . . somebody . . .

"Juli-ettt!"

Trevor's voice seemed somehow to be echoing from all around.

"You can't run, my darling! I'm coming to find YOOOOOOOUUU!"

| **THE JOURNAL OF JAY O'CONNOR: GRAFFITI**

WE'D COVERED MAYBE HALF OF THE OUT-side edge of the plateau that we were stranded on; at least the buildings that were still standing, or were only partly in ruins. But even I could tell that there were places in the rubble where the Black Stuff could have hidden bodies and we'd never be able to get to them. I kept telling myself that if we couldn't reach them, then surely that meant they couldn't get out to get to us—if that makes sense. But time was creeping by, and it looked as if the job I'd bullied everyone into was hopeless. All the time we searched, I kept asking myself whether I was really up to what I'd told everyone we should do.

And all through our search, we were constantly being taunted by the Black Stuff, using the dead people as its messengers. There were other messages for us; splashed on alley walls, daubed on clear patches of street, free from rubble.

On the remains of a store wall: *Charles Manson.*

Daubed on a cobwebbed store window: *Fritz Haarmann.*

On a clear patch of pavement: *Gilles de Rais.*

On the side of a car: *Peter Kurten.*

On the roof of an overturned bus: *Ed Gein.*

Most of the names meant nothing to anyone. But we were

pretty sure that they wouldn't be the first names on any garden party invitations. We knew that it wanted to scare us badly; wanted to taunt us. And maybe there were supposed to be clues in the names to what was going on. But we remained none the wiser as we continued the search and came across more and more of the names splashed about the ruins. The dear, dead departed of Edmonville had certainly been busy after they left us last night.

From time to time, when I'd finished searching a ruin, I'd step back out onto the street and see one of the others. And each time, they were doing what I did too—searching the sky, looking for some sign up there in that great blank greyness that someone was searching for us. But there were no planes, no sounds of distant engines. Just the great empty quiet that lay over everything on this isolated chunk of rock.

Then, when I saw Alex and Annie sitting on the roadside, I knew that we were reaching the end of our tether. Slowly, I picked my way over fallen masonry until I'd reached them. Alex had parked the dump truck on the remains of someone's front garden.

"We're never going to be able to cover all the buildings before it gets dark," said Annie.

"I know."

"We haven't done half of the houses and the stores on the outside edge," said Alex. "Any idea how many other buildings there are in the centre?"

"All right . . . all right. We'd better get back to the others at the fire. Make sure we've got plenty of wood to keep it burning all night again."

"Maybe nothing will happen," said Alex. "Maybe the Black Stuff . . . and the others . . . won't come back again."

"I hope so too," I said. "But I'm not going to bank on it."

"What the hell *is* it?" Alex wasn't talking to us. He was talking to the empty street. "What the hell does it *want* from us?"

"I think it just wants us dead," said Annie, flatly. "Like the others."

"You think it's like this all over the world?" asked Alex.

No one had an answer for him.

Gordon suddenly emerged from around the shattered frontage of a pub. The inn sign hung crookedly overhead: The Fallen Oak. No one seemed able to appreciate the joke. Head down, he walked over to us. When he realised that we were all waiting for some kind of response, he held his hands wide in a "Nothing at all" gesture.

"How long does everyone reckon we've got?" I asked. "Before it gets dark again. We don't want to be stuck out here when it does."

The three of them just looked at me uncomfortably.

I waited for someone to say something.

No one did.

And then I got it. Now I knew how the situation had turned around. They didn't want to hear me asking questions like that. They wanted me to be giving them answers.

"Now wait a minute," I said. "Don't look to me for all the answers. Don't wait for me to tell everyone what they should be doing."

Still no one spoke. They all just looked at me.

"What is this? I'm not your leader."

"You've been doing a good job so far," said Annie.

"No, no, no. Look . . . that's not the way it is."

"Someone has to lead . . ." began Alex.

"What the hell are you talking about? No one voted for anyone. You're the oldest, Alex. You should be taking charge."

"No, you're the one," said Alex.

I stared at them.

Then Gordon said simply "You," and pointed his finger at me.

As if the conversation were over, Alex said: "I'll drive the truck around to . . ."

And then Annie exclaimed: "Lisa!"

The others turned quickly to see Annie's partner and the boy approaching down the ruined street they'd just covered on the latest "leg" of their search. Annie hurried to meet her, but it was Alex who got there first, vaulting over a wonky garden fence in his hurry. I hadn't realised he was so fit, but I knew why he was worried.

"Where's Candy? What's happened?"

"Someone had better come," said Lisa breathlessly. I watched the boy skip across to Annie, take her hand and begin to pull. "I can't do anything with her."

"What's wrong?" Alex's face had turned the same colour as the sky. Drab grey.

"She's in the minimart, drinking."

"She's supposed to be helping gather wood," said Alex through gritted teeth.

"Look . . ." I began.

And that's when Wayne and Damon came scrambling around the corner, waving their arms and yelling like hell. Damon tripped on a brick and fell full length. Wayne didn't stop to help; he just came straight on, eyes wide. When he reached us, he couldn't speak. Chest heaving, he tried to draw breath and speak at the same time.

"Slow down," said Annie. "Slow down . . ."

And then Damon came up behind, with a look on his face that was partly bewilderment, mostly fear.

"Found them," he said—and then he was sick.

"The dead people," said Wayne, finding his breath. "Jesus. God. The dead people. I think it's . . . it's *all* of them."

"Where?" I asked.

Whatever they'd found, it was so bad that the pair of them hadn't got the words to explain. I could see it in Wayne's eyes, like he was still seeing it himself; now in Damon's, when he staggered around to the front again, wiping his mouth.

Was it just me? Or was the grey blankness of the sky much darker than it had been before? How much time did we have?

"Right," I said. "Come on."

"What about the dump truck?" said Alex. "Can I get it through?"

Wayne and Damon just looked at him as if he'd arrived from the moon and was speaking a foreign language.

"Can he drive it to where you've found them?" I snapped.

Damon nodded. "Yeah, down that side street there. And around to the right."

"No rubble on the road?" asked Alex. "I can drive it through?"

"Yeah." Damon nodded again, eyes far away. "Drive it through. Yeah."

"Okay, take us there," I said. The pair of them looked at me hard, like they were having trouble understanding. Then Damon said "Yeah" again and they started off down the side street beside The Fallen Oak. Behind us, I heard the snorting of the dump truck and turned to see the vehicle rounding the corner after us. Alex seemed to be handling it well.

At the next main street, Wayne and Damon paused and looked at each other, as if they didn't really want to go on. Then, heads down, they turned left and we followed. I'd already covered some of the terraced properties along this street. A few of them were right on the edge of the cliff, some of them had crumbled apart and fallen over. Beyond was the usual blank grey, but I could see two towers of rock through a gap in the houses, both of them about two hundred feet away. There were houses on one, most of them ruined and collapsed. On the other was a grassed space and some tarmac. I still couldn't get my head around how bizarre it all looked.

Wayne and Damon were heading for the houses at the end of the terrace. I hadn't been in any of those.

At the end of the terraced street was a semi-demolished building with white walls. I was sure I had been in this neck of the woods some time in the past, but I was damned if I could remember what that building had been. There was a sign hanging up there, but something had smashed across it, maybe a section of the roof from next door, and obliterated everything except " . . . AT MA . . . " Even before we got there, I knew this was where Wayne and Damon were taking us.

They kept turning to look at us as we hurried on, as if somehow there might be a change of plan and we could all walk away and make everything okay again. I knew they were terrified about what they'd found or seen. My own guts were churning with fear. But I knew that we had to go on.

To whatever horror lay ahead in the white-walled building.

| CHAPTER NINE | THE ORDEAL OF |
| | JULIET DELORE |

JULIET SEIZED A CHUNK OF RIPPED PIPING from the ground as she moved; and turned to look back. It felt solid in her hand, a good eighteen inches long. But then she remembered what she'd done with the crowbar, and the memory of it turned her stomach and threatened to rob her of her will.

There was no sign of Trevor.

She clamped her jaw shut to stop her teeth from chattering together and moved from side to side, trying to see if she could flag where Trevor's voice had been coming from.

"*Frightened, Juliet?*" His voice seemed to come from everywhere and nowhere. "*You should be . . . you should be . . .*"

"Trevor, you bastard! Keep away from me or . . ."

"*I've only got one eye . . . but it's . . . ALL THE BETTER TO SEE YOU WITH!*"

The Citroën, over there beside the shopping trolley rank. He must be hiding behind it. Juliet took a short three-step run and hurled the piping at the car. The back window imploded in a shower of glittering shards, glass hissing to the tarmac. But now Trevor was laughing; he seemed to be way over to her left, somewhere in the bushes. Juliet ran on along the cliff edge, swerving as she followed its ragged line, back towards the supermarket. On her right, she could see other chunks of rock like bizarre mountains jutting upwards from empty space, some as near as a hundred feet or so, others half a mile away, isolated against a blank grey backdrop.

"Over here!" she yelled as she ran. "Someone! Over here!"

But there was no movement on any of the bizarre crags, and it seemed that her own voice was flat and hollow compared to the unnerving echo of Trevor's taunts.

"*Yes!*" laughed Trevor. "*Come on over here, someone. We're waiting for you, aren't we, Juliet? The thing is, my love, there's no one over there to COME! Now, isn't that a funny thing? Just you and me stuck on our own little love island. Having a great party time.*"

The cliff edge furrowed away from the supermarket building and Juliet felt a wave of renewed hope. Her instincts were wrong. She wasn't stranded. Behind the supermarket was solid land, and beyond that there would be help. She knew that there was a shopping precinct beyond. Surely there'd be rescue services.

But why no sirens? Why is everything so quiet?

She silenced the small, terrified voice inside. Now she could see the building that stood behind the supermarket. She saw the sign, Radio Edmonville, and then the communications mast, covered in aerials and discs, standing three hundred feet tall. There must be someone in there. Someone who knew what had happened; someone who, even now, would be broadcasting details of the disaster and what people should do. The cliff edge curved directly up to the side of the local radio building and for a moment it seemed to Juliet that this building, like the supermarket, was also balanced on the edge of the crevasse—and that perhaps there was nothing beyond these two buildings after all.

"No, I don't believe that!"

She jumped over a low wall, staggered on fallen rubble, and then headed directly towards the radio station's main entrance. There was a small drive, with a low wall all around. Up ahead, a reception door; another swing-door like the supermarket's. She set her sights on the door and ran hard.

Somewhere behind her, something clattered.

But she wasn't going to turn and look.

She was going to reach that door, and find someone.

Suddenly Juliet knew that Trevor had broken cover; had emerged from his hiding place back in the car park, and was racing after her. She could not hear his footsteps, couldn't hear any frenzied ruffling of clothing, any displacement of air, but she *knew* that he was hurtling down upon her as she raced for the entrance. Fear was upon her again, threatening to slow her down, sap her strength.

At any moment, his hand would be on her shoulder.

His fingers would tangle in her hair.

She'd be yanked backwards to the ground.

And then her worst torment would begin as . . .

"No, this can't be happening."

Up ahead, Juliet could see that the radio station was perched on the edge of a cliff. The same cliff edge that ran from here to the supermarket building.

"It's not . . . it's just not possible."

Which meant that there was nothing beyond the broadcasting building and that she was stranded on this small chunk of a devastated Edmonville. A supermarket, a car park, a local radio broadcasting company and its three-hundred-foot mast, a ruined warehouse and tumbled outbuildings. Beyond the radio station and the supermarket was a bottomless chasm, separating this plateau from the rest of the city beyond. Behind her and beyond the car park, nothing but ragged peaks of stone and rock, like some alien landscape. And no survivors.

Other than herself.

And Trevor.

"Juliettttt!" came his mocking voice, echoing in the stillness. *"I'm coming to find youuuuuu . . ."*

| CHAPTER TEN | THE JOURNAL OF JAY O'CONNOR: ABATTOIR |

DAMON AND WAYNE STOOD IN FRONT OF THE white-walled building, and clearly didn't want to go any further. No one seemed inclined to do anything but stare at the building, me included. Now I could see what the place was. That damaged sign on the front—" . . . AT MA . . . "— made sense at last, because there was a complete version on the side of the building, in big stencilled letters: "WHOLESALE MEAT MART." Something told me that the Black Stuff was laughing at us again.

The dump truck snorted around the corner and made everyone jump.

Alex brought it to a halt and slid out of the cab, dusting his hands. He looked different somehow. Like everyone else, he was struggling to come to terms with everything that had happened since this nightmare began. But now he looked worse. I knew that he was as worried as hell about his wife, but he wasn't making any attempt to leave. He was going to stay around a while and see what happened. Right about then, I realised just how much I had been underestimating him.

"Right," I said, and marched straight on into the ruins of the entrance yard ahead. The others followed me. When I saw that Lisa and the boy were also following, I turned back. "Maybe . . . you know . . . maybe not the kid."

Lisa nodded and held back as I crossed the yard.

Let's get this part straight. I wasn't being the leader, wasn't playing the hard man, or the hero. Frankly, I was scared shitless.

Ever since that first tremor, when I'd been trapped underground with Wayne and Damon, something had happened to me. Something I thought I'd put behind me a long time ago. Ever since I was a kid, I'd been bothered by the fact that, at heart, I was a coward. My dad used to yell it at me when I'd hold back on the playing field, or when I wouldn't stick up for myself in a schoolyard fight. And knowing this fact sometimes made me do the things I'd done. Sometimes I'd be so ashamed of my fear, of knowing how shit-scared I was, I'd deliberately put myself into situations that my friends would admire me for. Someone once called me a brave bastard because I'd abseiled down from a railway bridge on a frayed piece of rope. I was ten years old, and it was four hundred and seventy feet. But what they didn't know was that I was terrified. More terrified than any one of them would have been. But—and this was the important thing—I was more terrified of how I'd feel about myself if I didn't take up the dare of dropping down that fraying rope in the first place. Always been the same.

It was the same then, walking into that entrance yard; knowing that there was something really bad inside that building. So bad that Wayne and Damon couldn't even bring themselves to talk about what they'd seen. The prospect of what we might come across, after the terrors that we'd all been through these past few days, made my legs feel weak. They felt like rubber now as I walked on ahead. But the anger was there too; that old enemy of mine. Flaring up when it wasn't needed, spoiling everything for me; keeping the things I wanted most at arm's length. Sometimes working for me, like now. I was angry that I was afraid. Angry at myself for being such a bloody coward. And that anger and that shame were making me do the brave thing, at least maybe in the eyes of other people.

But it wasn't brave at all.

It was never like that.

There was a lorry ahead, tilted on its side at a crazy angle. Now I could see what had happened. The concrete forecourt had cracked—more than that; there was a bloody great fissure zigzagging right through it. The lorry had slid partly into it, its cab and front wheels pointing up at the blank grey sky. Both doors were open, as if the driver and his mate had made a leap for safety when the tremor had hit. But there was no sign of anyone around. No bodies, anyway.

Well, there wouldn't be, would there? I thought. *The Black Stuff has been making use of every dead body it can find.*

There was a ramp here, leading up to corrugated metal doors, which had been pulled back from a loading bay. Inside, it was dark. No way of seeing from here what we were going to find. I decided that I wasn't going to push Wayne and Damon any harder on what they'd discovered. We'd find out for ourselves soon enough. But at least I had to know where the hell we were headed. I turned back on the ramp and looked at them. Was this the way? Damon looked as if he was having trouble swallowing. I pointed into the darkness and looked at him.

He nodded.

"I can't," he said, shaking his head. "I just can't go in there."

Annie came striding up the ramp, slapping Gordon on the shoulder as she passed. Gordon winced, feeling as jumpy as everyone else. But, hoisting his guitar around to the middle of his back, he walked on up. Alex followed.

The fear again, gnawing inside me.

And then the anger.

Never let the fear eat you alive. Hate the fear. Use that anger to face it head on.

I turned and strode quickly into the dark.

When my eyes got used to it, I could see that we were

in some kind of loading area. Large, lumpish shapes were hanging from the ceiling, swaying and creaking. When my eyes adjusted, I could see ribbed patterns in each of those shapes—realising at last that they *were* ribs, and that I was looking at dozens of gutted cow carcasses hanging by hooks from overhead rails. Right then, we became aware of the smell. The refrigeration units in here had broken down and, although it had only been a few days, the meat had begun to rot. Not enough to make anyone gag yet but getting there. Maybe the meat was loaded from lorries outside, via those hooks and chains on the overhead rails. The carcasses swayed and rattled as if there was a wind blowing through the building. But there wasn't. There was just us, the cold and the quiet creaking and rattling.

"It's up ahead," said a strange voice from behind.

When I turned to look, I could see that Wayne had followed us in after all. Damon was still framed in the entrance, unable to step inside. But Wayne's voice didn't sound like his voice at all. It was as if his fear had made it drop to a lower tone.

"There," he went on. "There's a door up ahead."

I turned to look where he was pointing. There was some kind of sliding door in the wall. It was pulled halfway open.

Whatever lay ahead of us was in there.

Fear of fear.

Anger at fear.

Cowardice.

I headed for the sliding doors. Was I bringing my feet down hard and making the echoes louder because the quietness in here was scaring me? Was I stamping out my anger on that fear? I wanted to stop then; maybe take a breath and build myself up in front of the doors. My anger wouldn't let me. Not even a peep around the half-opened door first. Instead, I grabbed the handle and heaved it aside, shoving hard until it clattered like some giant concertina into the wall brackets on my right.

There was a collective gasp from behind me.

I took my time raising my head. One concession to the fear.

The room beyond was about a hundred feet square and must have been some sort of loading area for the cold storage room. The iron rails and hooks overhead went straight in there, through ratchets at the top of the sliding doors and across the room to the actual cold storage unit itself. The door to the refrigerated section was directly opposite me, set into the far wall, and it looked like the vault door at Fort Knox. Want to know how I took in so much detail of the architecture? Because I had to keep looking away from what was in the storage room, and at what had been clawing and scratching at the cold storage door, trying to get in.

The room was filled with corpses.

Of all the bad things we'd seen—even the scary things that couldn't possibly happen—this was the worst. The dead people, those who had been left lying in the ruins and the rubble after the earthquake and had somehow been brought back to life to taunt and terrify us, were all here. Somehow, after we'd scared them away from the fire, they'd been brought to this place by the Black Stuff. They'd shambled in here, maybe piling up on top of each other as they staggered into the storeroom; and then they had groped and clawed and beaten at the cold storage door when they couldn't get it open. It was covered in bloody smears and handprints. The same hands that had left those scrawled messages for us to find. Finally, when the Black Stuff had given up, it had left them lying there. Waiting for night to return. There must have been a hundred, a hundred and fifty bodies; some of them damaged so badly that you just couldn't look.

"Why . . . ?" began Alex.

No one else spoke for a long time. Then I said: "Where else would you put dead bodies? Somewhere to keep them fresh. Why not meat freezers, cold storage? Makes sense."

"They couldn't get inside," said Annie. I glanced back at her.

She couldn't look anymore. She was staring away at another wall.

"But the power's off," said Alex. "The refrigeration in there will be shut down."

"Still going to be colder inside there than out, isn't it?" Did my face look as white as the others' when I turned back? Why were they all staring at me? I got it then. They were waiting for me again, waiting for me to tell them what to do.

"I'm . . ." I bit down on what I was going to say: *I'm not your leader!* Instead, I said: "I don't know how long we've got before it gets dark again. So we've got to move fast. You all head back to the park. Make sure the fire's started and we've got lots of fuel and firewood. Alex, you sort Candy out. Get her out of that minimart and back to the fire. Take a crate of booze with you, if you've got to."

"What are you going to do?" asked Annie.

"What we set out to do. There's petrol in the dump truck. And these bodies are all in one place. So, I'm going to bring the bodies from the truck, dump them in here with the others. And burn them."

"Is there time? Before it gets dark?"

"I don't know."

"I'll stay and help you . . ." began Alex.

"No, you go and get Candy organised. Annie, you take Lisa and the boy back. We've got to make sure there's enough wood and stuff to keep that fire burning through the night. Whatever happens, we know the Black Stuff doesn't like the fire."

Gordon stepped forward. He was still staring into the storeroom. This time, as if he couldn't look away.

"Me," he said. "I'll help you."

"Okay. Wayne and Damon, you help Gordon get the cans from the dump truck. Bring them in here, quick! I'll see if there's other stuff we can throw in there to start a good fire. You others—go now! Get back there as quick as you can!"

I braced my hands against the door and stared into the

hellish room, listening to the echoing footsteps of the others as they hurried off. And fuck me, hadn't I just gone and done it again?

Taken charge.

Become the leader.

Was this all bloody crazy, or what?

There was a long, thin window in the storage room, with security wire and mesh on the outside; a thin, grey light washing over the bodies that lay sprawled over each other in there. White and bloodied masks leered from that sickening pile; white, claw-like hands stuck out from that mass, as if they'd been trying to claw themselves free before they'd seized up again.

Even as I looked, it seemed that the grey light was fading.

Growing darker.

Terror froze me to the spot. The anger had burned out.

I was alone with the dead.

Who wouldn't be staying dead for much longer.

CHAPTER ELEVEN | DELIRIUM TREMENS?

I T WAS AUTUMN IN CANDY'S HEAD.
It was always autumn in her head. No matter whether
the sun was blazing down outside; whether they were in the
middle of a heat wave, with clear blue skies and no breath of a
breeze. Or whether the streets were covered in snow, and the
trees and shrubs in the garden were hidden beneath mounds
of white. Inside her head, frozen in time, was the garden in
autumn. Rust-brown leaves falling around her from the trees,
sweeping around her feet as she gazed back at the house.

Alex, walking towards her from the house. Slowly at first,
not understanding.

Quickly now, as he began to understand that something
was wrong.

She wanted to tell him, wanted to scream. But there was
nothing she could do.

The wind was swirling around her feet, the leaves were
dancing there. And she felt so light inside. Surely the wind
must snatch her up and blow her away? To another place
where what she had seen could not possibly happen. A dream
place, perhaps. Somewhere light and quiet and peaceful. So
that when she opened her eyes, she would be in bed again. The
day would not have started yet, and she'd have that wonderful

feeling of relief on waking from a nightmare, with the realisation that none of the bad stuff had happened and that there was a new fresh day waiting. But the wind could not sweep her from where she stood. On the inside, she might be as light as a feather. But her body was as heavy as stone, and she remained rooted to the garden like a statue as Alex came running right up to her. Even her face was carved from stone, and no matter how much he shook her by the shoulders, she couldn't respond.

Alex, running past her, mouthing something that she could not hear. Hearing the garden swing swaying gently in the wind, the chains squeaking against the metal poles. And now, knowing that he'd be seeing what she had just seen.

Ricky, still there.

Still looking as if he were trying to climb up one of the chains of the swing; one hand clutched in it as he twirled slowly, his feet hanging high above the seat. In her mind's eye now, Alex doing exactly what she'd done: turning Ricky slowly so that he could see his face at last. A face that was purple and blotched. Eyes wide, puzzled. Tongue protruding. And then, there were only the sounds of Alex's screaming.

But she couldn't scream; couldn't make a noise.

Because she was made of stone, like a statue.

And statues didn't cry.

Did they?

Candy came back from the bad place again. That autumn scene was always there in her head. Sometimes it was vivid and real, and no matter how much she tried to blot it out, it wouldn't go away. More often, it was behind a locked door in her mind. And although the picture was not there, its existence couldn't be denied. She could feel its presence with every waking second. Sometimes the drink made it easier for her to open that door and look at the scene. The grief was still there, of course; but numbed by the alcohol. And for the time that she was drinking herself into oblivion, it dulled the hurt. The pain never went away. And the hangover afterwards always seemed to make it worse. But for the time she was drinking, like now, it made life bearable.

Candy lifted the bottle to her mouth and realised that her cheeks were wet. Suddenly she was back from that terrible moment in time.

"Statues can't cry."

Candy wept as she looked around and remembered where she had come. She was sitting down on a littered floor, her back up against the glass door of a soft-drinks cooler. It was the minimart, and there had been an earthquake, or something. There were cracks in the ceiling. Pieces of plaster on the floor and dust all over the place. Tins and packets lying where they had fallen from the shelves.

"I'm not anything to do with what's happened . . . I mean, what's happening . . . outside. This is my world, in here. Where I've got everything I need." Candy brought the bottle to her chest, patting it with love.

Something scraped on the floor, nearby.

"Nothing," said Candy, "to do with me. Outside is outside. Those who want it can stay outside. Inside's where I am. Away from it."

Something light and fragile, but made of glass, tinkled on a shelf just out of sight.

This time, Candy looked up. There was nothing alarming about that sound. It was too gentle, non-threatening.

"Ten green bottles . . ." Candy began to hum.

And then something clattered against the broken front window.

Candy sat up straight, clutching the bottle.

Three different sounds now, from three different places in the store.

Something whispered, a breath of air—as if something very fast had suddenly flown through the air overhead. A sparrow, maybe. Trapped in the store, or taking refuge.

But there was no sign of anything, and now an empty bottle

237

was rolling across the floor. It bumped against the edge of the counter where Candy sat and spun lazily to a halt. Candy shrank back from it. Now the alcohol was no longer keeping the fear away. Another image cut through the blur, bringing sobriety of a plain and terrified kind: the storeowner, standing behind this self-same counter, with a shard of wood embedded in his eye and with that Black Stuff gushing from every orifice as he screamed with laughter.

Something beyond the counter, out of her vision, seemed to rush from one side of the store to the other. A small cloud of plaster dust rose above counter level. A single sheet of newspaper flapped in the air, making Candy wince and pull her knees up to her chest.

"Who's there . . . ?"

Silence now.

As if the several invisible presences on the other side of the counter who had been exploring the store had suddenly frozen in their tracks. Even now, were they turning their heads slowly and with horrifying interest towards what might be hiding with its brandy bottle on the other side of the counter?

"There's no one there." Candy unscrewed the top from the brandy bottle and took a deep swallow.

Something giggled in the store, out of sight.

Candy froze, the bottle still raised to her lips. Breathless, she waited to hear if the sound would come again. It had sounded just like . . . just like a small child. Doing something secretive and naughty.

Now something was whispering on the other side of the store. Like another child, answering the first.

Something scraped on the floor.

And then Candy saw the shadow slowly approaching around the end of the counter where she sat. It was vaguely human in shape. There seemed to be a head and shoulders; moreover the head and shoulders of a child, or a midget perhaps. The shadow paused, and Candy saw an arm raised; now it was placed carefully against the side of the counter as the shadow slowly came on. Secretive, furtive, knowing that she was hiding on the other side. The alcohol had ceased to be a protective barrier. Candy was shuddering in fear. Could the shadow hear her breathing? Now its small head was cocked to one side, listening.

Another child's voice giggled from somewhere in the store.

The shadow made an unmistakable gesture.

Half-turning its head back so that Candy could see the profile of a child's face, with tight, curling hair, the shadow placed a forefinger to its lips in a plea for silence from the others.

The giggling stopped.

The shadow turned to look back towards the corner of the counter.

Candy was no more than five or six feet from the edge, but she could not move.

Silently, the shadow crept towards her.

CHAPTER TWELVE   NIGHT FALLS

"I DON'T LIKE THIS," SAID ALEX, AS THEY drew level with the dump truck in the rear yard.

Lisa and the boy were waiting there for them. The boy was climbing on the running board of the truck, just like any other kid his age. But he still acted as if there was no one there when they approached. As if the only real people in his make-believe world were Lisa and, sometimes, Annie.

Gordon pulled open the passenger door and began to lug cans of petrol out from where Alex had stored them. Annie looked to see that Alex was staring at the grey, unchanging sky. Wayne and Damon had pulled down the flap at the rear of the truck and were lifting cans to the cracked concrete yard, trying to ignore the bodies there. They stopped when Alex spoke.

"Why?" asked Damon. "What's wrong?"

"Everything's wrong," answered Annie. "Come on, we'd better get back to the others."

"No!" snapped Damon, betraying the tension they all felt. "What does he mean?"

Alex wished he hadn't spoken. It was an unguarded comment. He'd suddenly been struck by the notion that whatever passed for day and night, light and dark, in this strange new world, didn't seem to abide by the normal rules. And he had been overcome by the possibility that maybe there would be no gradual change from grey to dark grey to utter darkness "tonight." What if it was like someone flicking a switch? One moment, the blank greyness. The next, utter darkness. And how long would it take the Black Stuff to come swarming up from the Chasm? How long before it exploded in a hideous torrent around the corner of this meat mart, engulfing them? How long before Jay's cries from within the building told them that Edmonville's remaining dead were dead no longer?

He said: "Nothing. I'm just spooked."

"Come on," said Annie again, tugging at his sleeve.

Alex hesitated, looking back at the meat mart.

"Your wife needs you," said Lisa. "There's nothing I could do to get her out of that store." She took the boy's hand, and the next moment Annie had joined them as they headed back in the direction of the park. Alex nodded then, and with a last look back at the meat mart set off hurriedly after them.

Gordon grabbed two cans of petrol and hurried back up the ramp into the building. The weight of the cans, the sound of his footsteps echoing in the darkness, the rancid smell—all physical evidence that these things really *were* happening. But he still felt as if he were acting a part. Since he'd played that lament over the mound of rubble that was his aunt's grave, he'd felt himself turning inside out. Was it the grief that had done that to him? His relationship with her had been far from easy. But nevertheless, she was the only person he'd been able to relate to. And even though his bedroom seemed to have become a prison for him, cut him off from his peers, part of him wanted to be back there again. In the real world. Had he wished too hard to be free? Was that the reason why his wish had been granted with such spectacular success? Not only was he free from his bedroom/prison, but that prison . . . that house . . . hell, the entire town—had been blown apart.

Suddenly, Gordon wanted to drop the cans and run.

He'd suddenly realised what they were about to do.

Pour petrol over dozens of dead people.

Set them alight.

His stomach tightened. Fear clutched in his chest and throat.

Shaking his head, Gordon ran on ahead, the petrol sloshing inside the cans.

Jay was standing in the sliding-door aperture, staring into the charnel house. One hand was braced against the edge of the door, and there was something about his stance that made Gordon's stomach lurch again as he banged the cans down behind his silhouette. Was Jay ill? Gordon didn't look into the storeroom. He kept staring at Jay, waiting for him to say something.

Jay, he wanted to say. *Jay, what's wrong?*

Nothing would come.

Do something, Jay. For Christ's sake, do something. Or else I'm only going to be able to stand here and do nothing.

Jay opened his mouth. But the fear inside made it impossible for him to speak.

And then Jay turned to look at him. His face seemed terribly white in the darkness, like one of the dead people lying in there.

"Hit me," said Jay in a blank voice.

What? Gordon's mouth formed an "O," but he couldn't ask the question.

"Do it," said Jay.

"What . . . ?"

"For Christ's sake, Gordon! Just do it! *Hit me!*"

Jay's voice stabbed in the darkness, shocking Gordon.

"*HIT ME!*"

And this time Gordon stepped forward and smacked Jay hard across the face, galvanised by the fury in Jay's voice.

"Again!"

Jay, what . . . ?

"Again, damn it!"

Gordon hit him again, with the back of his hand, snapping Jay's head back. It hurt Gordon's hand where he had caught his knuckles on Jay's teeth. When Jay turned to look at him again, his eyes were glittering. There was blood on his lip. Gordon stood back, convinced that Jay was going to attack him. Jay wiped the blood from his mouth and nodded.

"Good."

The anger was back. Jay was roused from his immobility. Stooping, he grabbed a can and unscrewed the top. Stunned, confused, Gordon watched the top clatter and roll on the cold concrete of the floor, hypnotized by its glittering motion. When it stopped, he looked up to see that Jay had moved down into the storeroom. Step by careful step, he was moving over bodies and scattering plumes of glistening blue petrol over the bloodied corpses. The pungent smell masked the other rancid smell, and suddenly Gordon wondered whether the smell of decay had been coming from the racks of meat swinging back in the storeroom or from the dead people in here. He reeled to the wall at the thought, bile rising in his throat. When Jay had emptied the can, he stood for a long time, not looking at anything in particular. Did he need *hitting* again?

Suddenly he gestured up at Gordon, without looking round at him.

Gordon realised that he needed the other can. Still shaken, he grabbed it. Holding his breath, he stepped carefully down into the storeroom—and stood on an outstretched leg. It felt hard and solid; more like a piece of wood than human flesh. Clutching the can, he cried out, staggering. Then Jay had moved quickly forward to take the can out of his hands.

"Go and get the rest," he said, without looking at Gordon. His face tight, he unscrewed the top. "And the matches. Don't forget the matches."

Was it getting darker in here? Was the grey deepening to black?

"Hurry up, Gordon. And where the hell are Damon and

Wayne? Tell them to drag those three bodies from the dump truck in here."

Gordon clambered back out of the storeroom. Head down, he ran back across the warehouse, dodging the hanging carcasses, to the ramp. Both doors of the dump truck were open. The remaining cans from the rear had been stacked at the bottom of the ramp. But there was no sign of Damon and Wayne. Gordon looked anxiously around, but they were nowhere to be seen in the yard.

It was getting darker, no doubt about that.

And it was getting darker fast.

Gordon clambered into the driving cab and grabbed handfuls of matchboxes. They were the big domestic kind. Stuffing them into his pockets, he ran to the back of the dump truck, saw that the three bodies were still there, seized up another two cans and ran back into the warehouse.

Something clattered and bounced, making him flinch as he ran. Were Damon and Wayne in the warehouse somewhere? But there were no signs of movement in the deepening shadows as Gordon reached the storeroom once again. Jay was waiting for him, both hands braced against one of the walls, marshalling his will and his strength. Gordon saw the second can lying against the wall where Jay had thrown it in anger or disgust, or both. That had been the sound he'd heard. Jay reached for the next petrol can.

"Where are the others?"

"No . . . no . . ." *Nowhere.* "Gone."

"Gone?"

"Can't. Find. Them."

"Shit!" Jay took his arm and they ran back to the dump truck.

"Ready?" Jay turned from the back flap and looked Gordon hard in the eye.

Gordon nodded.

"Right!"

Between them, they dragged the bodies up the ramp, through the storehouse and rolled them over the door track to join the others. Jay unscrewed the cap from another can and staggered around the horrifying pile of bodies, scattering more of the petrol, trying not to get it on himself. "Wayne and Damon. I might have bloody known. This is down to you and me now, Gordon."

Again, the flaring of fear in Gordon's guts. Gritting his teeth, he twisted the cap off the remaining can and jumped down into the storeroom. He couldn't bring himself to look as he began pouring the petrol on the dark, huddled mass. He kept telling himself that these weren't real people anymore; they were abstract shapes. He tried not to look at the white and ghastly faces; terrible indeed if they were recognisably human, worse still if by accident he should see a face that he thought he knew. The smell of petrol made him choke. He could hardly believe that he was in this nightmare, or what he was doing now. What if they were wrong? What if the rescue services were landing right now? What would they say about what they'd done, about what they were doing? Only Jay's strength was pulling him through. He had to believe in this nightmare, had to do something about stopping it. Sitting still and covering his head with his hands wasn't going to make it all go away. He staggered when something caught the hem of his jeans. Gordon pulled, not wanting to see what he'd stood on this time. The material remained snagged. He would have to lean down and pull it free. He stooped and turned.

He looked, and saw . . .

Oh God . . .

A ghastly white hand from the entwined mass of bodies had caught in the hem.

Gordon looked over at Jay, who was still scattering petrol. Should he call for help?

No, he'd try to be strong. Not let him down.

Gordon grabbed at the hand, yanking hard.

The hand would not come free. It felt cold and hard, like stone.

Christ . . .

He couldn't understand how the fingers had caught like that. They were gripping the cloth tight. Some kind of muscle spasm caused by rigor mortis? He would have to pry the fingers off one by one.

But this time, when he reluctantly picked at the claw-like fingers, the hand suddenly let go of the hem.

And fastened on his wrist.

Gordon couldn't breathe.

Instinctively, he scrabbled at it with his own free hand, lunging backwards. But the grip was tight, and as he lunged he saw with horror that he was pulling the hand's owner out of the contorted jumble of bodies on the storeroom floor. It was a man. Or what had once been a man. He was wearing a dark business suit, smeared with dried blood and concrete dust. His hair was matted and straggling, with a wound in his centre parting, wide enough to show a grey-red mass of exposed brain. Gordon yanked again, this time succeeding in pulling the corpse out completely. The hand would not let go. But the sound of the movement had drawn Jay's attention. Gordon's eyes locked on his; Jay looked as if he were suddenly about to say: *What the hell are you doing?*

The corpse braced its other shredded hand on the bloodied storeroom floor and, still holding Gordon tight with the other, raised its head to look him full in the face.

Gordon stared at the white, blood-streaked mask and saw that where there had once been eyes were now two small orbs of glistening blackness. It was the very same blackness that had come up from the Chasm to inhabit these dead shells and reanimate them. He could not move, could only stare, as the corpse smiled up at him; a horrifying, leering death-mask . . . and then the other bodies heaped in the storeroom began to stir.

Someone or something within the hideous pile moaned. Arms and legs began to writhe, hands clutching at the air. The dry slithering of fabric, the rustling of skirts, the scuffling rasp of shoes on concrete.

Day had suddenly become night once again in Edmonville. And the dead were returning.

Gordon watched the dead man clamber awkwardly to his knees, retaining his grip on him.

The blackness in his eyes seemed to swirl and bubble like black geyser mud. His teeth were clenched, as if he had lockjaw, the face smeared with a dried bloody mudpack.

Gordon knew that the corpse was going to take him to Hell.

Jay vaulted over writhing bodies and brought the petrol can down hard on the thing's arm, breaking its grip. Gordon staggered back. Jay caught and steadied him, at the same time planting his foot on the corpse's chest and shoving hard. Without a sound, the dead man fell back amidst the churning mass of newly awakened bodies and thrashed, trying to rise as Jay dragged Gordon to the doorway. Gordon was free of his enervation as they clambered out of the storeroom.

"Matches!" yelled Jay. "Where's the matches?"

Gordon didn't know, couldn't think. Christ, had he let them fall back there in the storeroom?

"Gordon, *think*!"

Inside the storeroom, figures were beginning to rise; pulling themselves out of the hideous pile and staggering to stay upright as others awoke and began clambering from their entanglement.

"*Gordon!*"

There was a box of household matches on the floor beside the sliding door. Gordon couldn't recall leaving them there, but snatched them up, hands shaking. The box opened in his trembling hands, scattering its contents onto the concrete floor. Moaning, he dropped to his knees and tried to pick them up. His fingers were too large and clumsy. He felt as if he were wearing thick gloves.

The corpse of a young woman braced its hands on the concrete edge before him. Her long dark hair was matted and straggling, her eye sockets bubbling with black liquid. She opened her mouth and hissed at him, like a snake about to strike. Once again, he couldn't move. The woman began to climb towards him, raising her face as if she wanted him to kiss her.

And then something flared beside him, a burst of bright light.

The dead woman reared back from him, white claw-hands covering her face.

Jay lunged forward with the handful of matches he'd scooped up and scraped on the concrete floor. The corpse's petrol-soaked sleeves and hair ignited with a rippling Bunsen-blue flame. Shrieking, the woman blundered back into the rising mass behind her, arms flailing as she became a stumbling pillar of fire. The fire surged and roared on the floor, leaping and enveloping the dark, shuffling mass. It gobbled hungrily up the walls on all sides, racing to the ceiling. With a coughing roar, the storeroom suddenly became a raging furnace. Within, arms and legs flailed; figures staggered and spun in a fiery danse macabre.

Heat blasted Gordon's face, singeing his hair and eyebrows.

Then something had him by the collar and pulled him away. Yanked to his feet, Gordon swung around to see Jay's white face.

"Help me!" shouted Jay, lunging away to the sliding door and beginning to pull it across the aperture.

Gordon felt weak. His eyes were drawn to the furnace.

"*Help* ME!"

This time Gordon managed to drag himself from the awesome sight and throw himself at the sliding door. Together they yanked it closed. The roaring of the fire from the other side was muted now. Smoke began to curl under the door.

They staggered back.

"Jay. Those pee-people. What if . . . I mean . . . maybe . . . *alive?*"

"No! Don't think about it. You saw what they were like. Saw what happened last night, didn't you? They're dead."

"But . . ."

"They're dead, not alive! It's the Black Stuff. Didn't you see it in their eyes?"

Gordon nodded, wiping a trembling hand across his mouth.

"Come on, let's get out of here and back to the others. We're not safe yet."

Together they ran back towards the ramp, knocking the swinging carcasses out of their path. Both remembered the sight of the black flood swarming over the park like some serpentine living animal. Perhaps, with the advent of darkness once more, it was already gushing through the ruins towards them.

Something screeched behind them; a grating crash. Heat blasted against their backs and suddenly the meat mart was awash with flaring yellow light; their shadows leaping gigantically ahead of them. They looked back as they ran.

Jesus, Jay . . .

"Keep running, Gordon! For Christ's sake, keep *running!*"

The burning dead had dragged the sliding door back open.

Flames crackled and leaped into the factory from the storeroom; smoke gushed and billowed as the first of the blazing shapes staggered out of the inferno. The air was filled with a multitude of shrieking voices, the same insane cacophony that they had heard on the night they'd thrown the blazing torches at the approaching shapes in the darkness.

Gordon slithered on the factory floor, regained his footing and looked back again.

The first of the terrible burning figures had fallen to its knees. Was it the woman? Flame-wreathed arms clawed at the burning mass that had been her head. And then something deep inside the blazing shape burst, and black, steaming liquid erupted from a dozen places; from the head and mouth, from the torso, the pelvis, the arms. The liquid spattered on the concrete like incandescent mercury. Globules swarmed and gathered into one glistening pool. Hissing, it streamed quickly away from the blazing mass, desperately hunting for the safety of darkness. The burning husk of the woman tottered and fell face forwards onto the concrete.

But the other burning shapes behind the woman were even now staggering past the lifeless corpse, blazing arms outstretched towards Gordon and Jay as they came. As they blundered against the hanging carcasses, flaming handprints transformed the wildly swinging meat into dripping balls of fire.

"Gordon, *don't stop!*" yelled Jay.

And Gordon turned to follow him as they ran for the ramp.

The meat mart was filled with the blazing flames of Hell.

Like the very denizens of Hell itself, the lurching pillars of flame that had once been the citizens of Edmonville came after them.

| **THE ORDEAL OF JULIET DELORE**

JULIET FLUNG A SHOPPING TROLLEY OUT OF HER way as she ran once again across the supermarket car park. For an instant, she considered running back into the supermarket, finding somewhere to hide. But it would be like running back to the prison from which she had escaped. And perhaps there were bodies in there . . .

Glancing back over her shoulder, she could see that Trevor was not in pursuit. She couldn't see him at the glass frontage of the radio station, but that didn't mean that he couldn't see her. Ducking behind a car, Juliet paused to get her breath. She had to find somewhere to hide. It couldn't be long before help got here. If only she could find somewhere to keep out of Trevor's sight. She sneaked a look around the corner, keeping on her haunches. Still no sign of Trevor. But she was far from safe here. She dipped down again, moving hand over hand behind the car, looking around the car park and beyond to see if there was anywhere she might have missed.

And almost fell over the body that had been lying beside the car.

Juliet retched, turning quickly away. There was no time to tell whether the bloodied mass had been a man or a woman. But he or she had been hit by a flying fragment of concrete.

"Don't!" Juliet hissed, a hand over her mouth as she looked away. "Come on, Juliet! Keep cool. Don't make a noise."

She looked back at the radio station again, and then over to her right. There was a glass-recycling container there. Keeping low, and averting her sight from the body, she ran between cars until she'd reached the container. Once behind it, she braced her back against the cool metal and tried to control her breathing. She scanned the sky. No vapour trails, no clouds. No circling helicopters, looking for survivors. Just that same blank greyness that she had seen from the storeroom window. If not for the fact that she was hurting so much, she might be tempted to believe that this was a nightmare and none of it was happening.

But where the hell was she going to go? She'd already been around most of the cliff edge, and she knew that the supermarket and radio station were balanced on the brink of the Chasm.

There's nowhere else, Juliet. Nowhere else to run.

She fought off despair.

And then heard the car engine turning over.

Someone else *was* alive, after all. Just when she had been giving up hope. She glanced back at the radio station again. Still no sign of Trevor, and it seemed as if the noise was coming from the row of parked cars just ahead. Once they had been parked neatly side to side. Now the tremor had shifted and jolted them against each other so that they were standing haphazardly, their paintwork scratched, side windows splintered. Supermarket trolleys lay scattered all over the cracked asphalt.

Again, the engine turned over, this time coughing into life.

Juliet pushed away from the container and ran towards the sound.

A Land Rover edged out of the haphazard rank.

"Wait!" Juliet waved her arms as she ran, trying to flag it down.

The Land Rover jerked to a halt, engine stalling.

"Please, wait!"

The engine roared again, and the vehicle swung towards her, juddering to a standstill, engine idling.

"Thank God . . ."

Trevor leaned forward over the steering wheel, smiling that ghastly rictus of a smile. Fresh blood was leaking from his ragged socket down his cheek and dripping from his chin. He scratched at the itch it caused, as if the terrible pain in the socket itself meant nothing. Suddenly, it was as if the Trevor Blake she'd known no longer existed. What sat behind that wheel was some kind of ravaged shell; something that now barely looked human. Something that existed only to torment her to death.

Juliet staggered to a halt, hair flying. It wasn't possible!

Trevor barked out a laugh, then jammed his foot down hard on the accelerator. The Land Rover shot forward.

Juliet couldn't move. The terrified part of her wondered whether she shouldn't just let the vehicle ram into her. Would the pain be so bad, and wouldn't it put an end to this nightmare one way or the other? But another primal and instinctive urge made her flip aside just before impact, twirling almost gracefully like some kind of matador. Trevor anticipated her move, twisting the wheel hard. The vehicle swung after her. This time, not so gracefully, Juliet scrambled up over the hood of another parked car. She fell badly, grazing the palms of her hands. As the Land Rover slammed into the skewed car, shattering its already crazed windscreen in a shower of glass, Juliet launched herself through two tubular rails of the trolley-parking bay into the cluster of trolleys beyond. An instant later, the Land Rover jammed the vehicle right up against the rails, where she had just been crouching.

It reversed noisily, gears screeching, then rammed the car again. The tubular rails buckled. Did Trevor think that she was still down there, crushed up against the rails? Shoving a path through the trolleys, Juliet repeated the manoeuvre on the other side of the bay. Now she was out in the open car park again, and could hear the Land Rover reversing and turning to follow her. Directly ahead of her were two parked cars. She ran for them, lungs bursting, breath sobbing in her throat. She saw the reflection of the Land Rover in the rear window of one of the parked cars as it roared around towards her, swaying on its suspension in the tight turn. There was no time to veer to either side, nowhere to run if she did. Between the cars was a two-foot space, leading to a low wall and a hedgerow, with no way of knowing what was on the other side.

There was no choice.

With the roaring of the Land Rover engine filling the air, Juliet ran between the cars and hurtled on ahead. Using the small wall as a step, she lunged forward through the hedgerow as the Land Rover smashed into the rear of both cars, shunting them forward with her. The brambles tore at her clothes as she fell, the car on her right bursting completely through the hedge and nose-diving the three feet down the other side with a noise like another earth tremor. Juliet hit the ground, staggered, but did not fall. Now she could see where she was; she'd curved around towards the radio station again. There was the forecourt and glass frontage from which she'd just run, further down on her left. The Land Rover engine was making a grinding sound, as if something under the chassis had been damaged. Juliet saw smoke rising from over the roofs of other parked cars as Trevor headed for the car park exit, hunting for her again. She wouldn't have time to reach the main entrance of the radio station before he found her, and it would mean running in the same direction as he was headed.

Head down, Juliet ran for the nearside of the broadcasting building, constantly glancing to her left. When the Land Rover roared out of the car park, she cried out aloud and tried to run harder. The vehicle screeched to a halt and paused, smoke rising from its hood. Juliet prayed that there would be an unlocked side entrance at the edge of the building, prayed that there was someone still alive there who could see and hear what was happening and could help.

The Land Rover hadn't moved. It was still pointed in her direction. Was Trevor playing with her again?

When she reached the building, she heard the engine roaring and knew that Trevor had recommenced the chase. She hurtled around the corner and found herself facing the broadcasting mast right next to the building. It was set into a six-foot-high concrete base, and there was an iron door set squarely in the centre before her. Juliet staggered to it.

Please!

It was locked.

Tugging at the handle, Juliet yelled for help. She kicked at the metal door.

Out of sight, the Land Rover closed.

There was a metal ladder at the side of the door, leading up to the roof of the concrete platform. From there, a steel maintenance ladder ascended on the outside of the mast.

The Land Rover engine growled like a living beast.

There was no time for anything else.

Quickly, Juliet climbed to the top of the concrete base.

You've no head for heights, Juliet. What are you doing?

"What else *can* I do?" she shouted aloud, and scrambled to the base of the maintenance ladder. She looked up, and the height of the mast made her dizzy before she had even begun to climb. "Oh, God . . ."

And then the Land Rover came around the corner of the building, screeching to a halt before it could slam into the concrete base.

No time.

And nothing else for it.

Juliet climbed, not looking up or down, concentrating hard on each metal rung as she gripped it. Her footsteps seemed to clang preternaturally loud, as if she were climbing inside some great metal cylinder. She heard the Land Rover door slam down below as Trevor climbed out. She refused to look down, and kept on.

"Now *where* do you think you're going?" came Trevor's voice.

Juliet gritted her teeth. Already the voice seemed to come from a long way down.

Don't look down. Step after step. Just do it.

"This isn't the beanstalk, Juliet. What do you expect to find up there? A way out? A magic castle, maybe. A golden goose? A magic harp?" He began to laugh then; as if he'd just made the best joke in the world.

Come on now. You can do it. Step, step, step.

"You couldn't have picked a better place!" Trevor's voice was even more distant now. "Only one way to go now. And that's *down!*"

Juliet reached for the next rung.

It wasn't there.

"Oh no . . . "

Gripping the ladder tight, she forced herself to look up.

There was a metal rail above her head, slightly higher than where the next rung should be. She would have to reach for it. But suddenly she felt as if she were frozen to the ladder. She hadn't looked down, but she knew that she was high. And just the thought of it terrified her.

"What's wrong, Juliet? Stuck?"

Juliet hugged the ladder tight, eyes screwed shut.

"Shall I come up there and help you?"

"*No!*"

She reached with her left hand. For a moment, it seemed that the rail was higher than she'd thought. A sickening fear gnawed at her stomach. She was going to fall. Her fingers closed around cold steel. The chill of it seemed to suck the energy right out of her body. Did she have the strength to go on, or was she going to fall backwards off the ladder? Hauling herself up, she grabbed with the other hand. There was a steel mesh inspection platform ahead, perhaps five feet square.

Frantically, she clambered up onto it and collapsed there, hugging herself tight. From below, she could hear the distant sound of Trevor laughing.

"You couldn't have picked a better place!" he said.

Juliet forced herself to the rail and looked down. Her senses reeled. She couldn't believe that she'd managed to climb so far; perhaps a hundred and fifty feet, half the height of the mast. It seemed very still up here; unreal, without a breath of wind. Down below, Trevor was standing with his arms folded, looking up. Steam still rose from the hood of the Land Rover to his rear.

"Behind you!" shouted Trevor. "On the other side of the mast!"

Carefully, fearfully, Juliet shuffled on all fours to the other side of the platform. Above her, the maintenance ladder continued up the side of the mast. And at the edge of the platform it was as if she were back in the supermarket storeroom again, balanced precariously on the window ledge and looking down into a great void. Giddiness threatened to overcome her as she clutched at the metal rails. In her panic to get away, she hadn't seen the most obvious thing. Her refusal to look down had perhaps been a big mistake.

Because now she realised with overwhelming horror that not only the broadcasting building but also its communications mast, and the concrete base in which it was set, was balanced on the edge of the Chasm. Below was nothing but the hideous, mountainous drop into darkness. Hundreds of feet away, on the other side, was the ragged cliff edge of the nearest "plateau," rimmed by torn trees and ruined buildings.

"Seen this, Juliet?" asked Trevor. He pointed to the base of the mast. "No? Maybe you didn't notice it when you started to climb." He walked casually forward, still pointing. "It's cracked. See? Right there . . . and there . . . and there. Big cracks, too. I reckon that mast could go over any time."

"Oh, sweet Jesus . . ."

"Like I said: Well done! Couldn't have picked a better place. Question is . . . what happens next?"

Juliet looked around angrily for something to hurl down at him. There was nothing.

Trevor walked back to the steaming Land Rover and leaned his back against the front grille, as if he had all the time in the world.

"Oh dear," he said at last. "I think it's getting darker."

"Trevor! Leave me alone! Get the hell away from me!"

"And bad . . . *bad* things can happen in the dark."

"You *bastard*!"

"Can't they?"

| ## THE CHERUBIM

"IT SHOULDN'T BE GETTING DARK SO QUICKLY!" They had reached the outskirts of the park and Alex gave voice to what was worrying everyone. "We haven't even had six hours of 'daylight' yet."

The journey back through the ruins had been like a stage-managed effect solely designed to enhance the nightmare. Shadows had descended amidst the ruins, the grey becoming black, the shadows growing deeper and longer. Just as if someone somewhere really *was* turning off switches as Alex had fantasised. No one spoke as they hurried through ruined and empty streets back to the one place where they might find a fragile safety. Every shadow was a threat; every darkened corner a possible hiding place for further horrors. Were there still bodies in the rubble? Would they turn another corner only to find another shambling line of the dead blocking their way? Even the boy, in his safe place, could sense it; and he clung tight to Lisa as they hurried on.

"If we . . ." began Annie angrily, then stopped herself from saying make it *through another night.* Instead she said: "When it gets light again, Lisa and I are *definitely* going to get something sorted. On the lights front."

There was no time to ask what she meant.

They could see the dark mound of the bonfire up ahead, still smouldering but not yet alight. Stacks of splintered wood and other flammable debris had been stacked beside it, at a safe distance. Cans of paraffin and petrol had been positioned carefully out of the way behind one of the piles.

"That's good," said Alex as they hurried across the grass.

"Mostly my work, I'm afraid," replied Lisa, without pleasure. "Look, I'm sorry. Maybe I should have stayed and got the fire started. But Candy . . ."

The sound of running feet made them whirl in alarm. It was Wayne and Damon.

"Have you done it?" asked Annie.

Breathing heavily, both looked back the way they'd come.

"Is it finished?" asked Alex.

"Finished," said Damon. "Yeah."

"Where's Jay and Gordon?" Annie strained to look back.

"They're . . ." Wayne waved vaguely back in the direction from which they'd come. "They're coming." Before anyone could ask further questions, they both ran on ahead to the bonfire, seizing cans of petrol.

Alex stopped to look back, searching for any sign of Jay or Gordon.

"Where . . . ?"

But now flames were leaping high as the first pitched stream of petrol ignited on the still-smouldering embers from the previous night. Annie and Lisa began to pick up timber from one of the piles, throwing it into the centre of the bonfire. Clouds of sparks soared high. The boy threw a small stick, and missed the fire completely. The unfurling tongues of flame bathed them in bright orange light, but now seemed to accentuate the darkness that had fallen all around the ruins and on the shattered crags and pillars that had once been Edmonville.

"I'm going for Candy!" said Alex, when he was sure that the fire was well under way, and he headed off in the direction of the minimart. Lisa looked back and waved to wish him luck, then grabbed more wood from the pile and threw it into the flames. Alex didn't look back, concentrating on the growing darkness beyond.

Something wasn't right. Something about Wayne and Damon's demeanour. But there was no time now to stay and ask further questions. He had to get Candy back to the fire straight away. Was the Black Stuff even now seeping over the rim of the Chasm and heading their way?

The minimart was less than five minutes away, on the periphery of the park. But as Alex ran, it seemed to him that the first outlines of the ruined side street were getting no closer as he ran. Suddenly, he was overwhelmed by the feeling of how isolated they were on this bizarre plateau. He could feel the immensity of the Chasm on all sides; could feel how pathetically small they were in their new and hopeless situation. Was he really running frantically on the spot, not moving at all? And hadn't that been what their lives had been like—Candy's and his—running on the spot, wearing themselves out, tearing each other apart? Candy trying to wash away the pain with liquor, just as she was doing now. And no matter how hard he tried, no matter how much he persevered, no matter how much he argued, it seemed that everything he did was no good at all. Every one of his responses only seemed to enrage her further.

"Candy!"

He began to shout even before he cleared the park and reached the first rubble on the grass. What if she'd left? What if she'd wandered off somewhere and fallen asleep in the ruins? *Oh Christ, let her still be there!* He paused for breath at the corner, leaning against the cracked brickwork of a rear wall before heading off down the side street. At the next bend, he could see the frontage of the minimart just ahead.

"Candy!"

There was no sign of movement in the darkened windows.

Alex struggled on, looking around on all sides. The words of the dead man in the liquor store seemed to echo in his head.

The real truth is simple. You see, you both killed your son.

"Candy, for God's sake, are you in there?"

There's a darkness in you both that will destroy you.

Alex stumbled and fell in the rubble. He clawed forward on hands and knees. Was there something moving in the darkness on either side of him as he ran?

Alex, your wife thinks that you killed your son. And Candy, you think that Alex is responsible. That's why you hate your husband so much. And don't you know that no matter how much forbearance you show—you hate her just as much as she hates you. That's the darkness.

"I don't hate you, Candy. It's not true what he said!"

And then, in his mind's eye, he could see the dead man with the smashed face, standing in the darkness just beyond the light of the bonfire: *The facts won't go away simply because you want them to go away. I know. We know. You both murdered your son.*

"You didn't kill Ricky. Neither did I . . . Christ, Candy, we only let him out into the garden on his own for a minute. A *minute!*"

Alex was clear of the rubble and up on the fractured pavement.

Something moved beyond the darkened windows of the minimart. Something bright that flashed too quickly to register.

"Candy!"

Alex shoved the door open and stood in the doorway, getting his breath back and trying to adjust his vision to the gloom inside. He was overwhelmed by the feeling that there had somehow been a great deal of movement in here only moments before he'd shoved open the door. There was a silent expectancy, the feeling that someone or something other than Candy had fled into hiding at his sudden appearance.

"Candy, are you in here?"

Something whimpered in the gloom.

Had the sound come from behind the serving counter?

With growing apprehension, Alex moved into the shop, carefully stepping over the detritus that littered the floor. Had something happened to her?

"It's all right, love. I'm here."

A bottle rattled on a shelf to his right, for no apparent reason. Once again, he felt that there was not one but several presences in the dark. Watching him, and waiting. The air was too still. Or was it that the approaching night and the horrors they had all endured were fraying his nerves even further?

Behind him, the door juddered. Alex whirled in alarm, heart racing.

There was a silhouetted figure standing in the doorway.

Flinching back, he looked around desperately for some kind of weapon.

And then the figure asked: "Well, is she in here, or not?"

It was Wayne.

"What the hell are you doing here?"

"Lisa's got some food and bottled water back at the bonfire. Collected it while we were searching. But that's *all* she's got. And your wife isn't the only one who needs a proper drink."

Wayne strode brusquely into the store and began searching the shelves. Alex relaxed, but remembered the whimpering and moved quickly to the counter. Behind it there was a shape huddled on the floor, knees drawn up to her chest, head down. A brandy bottle rolled at her feet.

"Candy, it's me."

"Oh *Christ* . . ." Candy looked up at him from the floor, and he saw the tears gleaming in her eyes. More than that, he saw the naked fear there.

"It's all right," he said, carefully leaning down and holding out a hand, as if any sudden movement might make her fly into a panic. "Come on, I've come to take you back to the fire."

263

"Christ, Alex. *Don't move!*"

Now he could see that she wasn't staring in fear at him, but at something that seemed to be directly behind his right shoulder. Alex could feel its presence. Fear prickled in his neck and down his spine.

"Here," said Wayne from the gloom. "Look what I've found. A torch and batteries." There was a fumbling and rattling as he unscrewed the torch and began to fit the batteries. "Might come in handy."

Slowly, Alex began to turn.

At first he could see nothing but the shelving set into the far wall, perhaps four feet from where he stood. The shelves were deep and high, stocked with breakfast cereal packets and other comestibles. Strangely, there was a doll's head resting on top of a packet of cornflakes. One of the larger type of dolls, the head about the size of a two-year-old's. Short but extravagantly curled blond hair. It had a cherubic expression, with rosy cheeks. The gender was indeterminate, in the way of some politically correct children's playthings. The blue eyes seemed to have an eerie luminosity in the gloom.

And then those eyes blinked, and the cherubic face smiled. The head shoved itself forward and the packet fell from the shelf to the floor, spilling its contents.

Alex could not move.

Impossibly, a completely naked two-year-old child was pushing forward on all fours to the edge of the shelf and smiling that impossibly angelic smile at him. He could not react, could not take in this sudden and bizarre sight. The child braced its smooth pink arms on the shelf, perfectly formed fingers gripping the edge. It looked down to where the cornflake packet had fallen, and then back up to Alex again.

With shocking swiftness, the child slithered its legs around and pushed itself over the shelf edge. Instinctively, Alex lurched forward to save it from the fall. But in that instant, something

264

seized his trouser leg, making him wince at the pain where his flesh had been pinched. It was Candy.

"Alex, don't *move*!"

He saw the fear again, and turned back to look.

The child wasn't hurt. It had fallen miraculously and lightly on all fours in the littered cornflakes. Now Alex could see that it was a boy, its small penis curled in the groin, testicles not yet descended. It was still smiling up at Alex, who watched in ever-mounting incredulity as the child, without taking its big round eyes from him, took a handful of the cereal and brought it up to its mouth. The boy sniffed . . . and then opened his mouth to cram a handful of cornflakes inside.

In that brief instant, Alex saw the child's teeth.

They were not the teeth of a two-year-old boy.

There was a full set top and bottom. Dentally perfect, white and aligned. All the same size.

And each one pointed, like the teeth of some wild animal.

The boy continued to smile, not taking his gaze from Alex, cramming more cornflakes into his mouth as he crouched there.

"That's better," said Wayne. A beam of torchlight swung around the store.

The boy reacted instantly. In a flurry of cornflakes, he was suddenly gone. Moving almost too fast to register, he was halfway up the shelving unit again; one small foot braced on a lower shelf, one hand gripping an upper shelf, with the other arm and leg dangling in space at his side. He hung there, peeping around the outside edge of the unit to where the torch beam explored the store, and with all the agile grace of some beautiful feral creature. His eyes glinted impossibly blue in the reflected gleam of the torchlight as Wayne scanned bottles on the other side of the store. Now Alex could see two fleshy protuberances on each of the boy's shoulders, two raised ridges of bone which couldn't be seen from the front. Whatever Alex was looking at, it surely couldn't be a human child.

Candy was trying to rise. Carefully, Alex stepped back and, without taking his gaze from the boy, began to help her up. The child gave him no more than a glance before returning his attention to Wayne and his torch. The smile was gone, and there was an uncannily adult expression of wariness on his face now.

Wayne moved to the liquor shelf and hoisted down two bottles, shoving them into his jerkin pockets. "That'll do for now. Better move fast."

"Wayne . . ." began Alex.

And suddenly there was movement all over the store.

"Don't move, Alex!" gasped Candy, her voice breaking. "Just keep still."

Bottles crashed from the top shelf where Wayne had gathered his supply. He jumped back as they shattered on the floor. Something seemed to fly through the air from the top shelf to the units on the other side of the store, too fast to see. The strip light on the cracked ceiling began to pitch and sway from its chain fastenings, as if it had been hit by the invisible passing. Now other packets and containers began to fall from other shelves, all over the store; a packet of flour exploded on the floor, sending up a powder-white cloud.

Wayne staggered back, spinning now in alarm at the commotion, the torch beam swinging wildly around the store. It came to rest on something that had emerged from hiding on the top of a freezer unit.

"What the *fuck* . . . ?"

It was another child. Naked, like the other, with the same tightly curled blonde hair and cherubic face. The same small ridges of bone on either shoulder. But this was a girl, perhaps three years old. She raised one arm to shield her face from the torch beam and then, with the same astonishing speed and agility, leapt from the freezer unit to the shelving beside the window. Jars clattered from the shelf on which she had landed as she quickly pushed herself out of sight on all fours.

When Wayne swung the torch beam away to a clattering of tin on the floor, the girl poked her head out again. Wayne had caught another figure on the floor; another naked boy, the same age as the first boy, hair slightly darker but with the same cherubic face and bony ridges. Wayne flinched when the boy hopped, skipped and jumped across the floor, raising a cloud of flour dust as he moved. Pausing to crouch on all fours, he suddenly disappeared from sight, moving so swiftly as he leapt that his passage was invisible. Bottles rattled as he vanished somewhere on the booze shelves.

Small heads and figures were appearing all over the store. From around crates stacked in corners, on the tops of units, hanging from shelves. Two were peeping through the bead curtains behind the counter, which led into the living area of the store. And each time that Wayne swung his torch beam to shine on one of these bizarre children, he or she would vanish from sight in a blur of motion. Not one of them could be more than four years old.

"It's the light!" Alex had found his voice. "Wayne, they don't like the light."

Wayne ignored him, swinging the torch again when a small figure sped through the air from one of the shelves in a blur, heading for the front window or the door. Using his torch as a club, Wayne struck out. The blow connected. There was a sound not unlike a small child crying out, and the next moment one of the small figures was lying on the floor at Wayne's feet; by the look of it, it was perhaps three years old. It struggled to rise as Wayne shone the torch directly down on its writhing body.

Wayne raised his foot.

"No!" shouted Candy. "Don't . . ."

But it was too late.

Wayne stamped down hard on the child. Whether it was a boy or a girl was difficult to tell. When the child screeched, Candy cried out, and Alex moved forward to the counter in horror. It twisted to get away. But Wayne followed it, his lip

curled in disgust, and stamped on it again. The creature began
to croak, waving its arms feebly. Wayne stamped again.

It was dead.

Something hissed in the darkness, flashing through the air.

Wayne was flung back against the shelves, hitting them so
hard that bottles began to fall around him. Dazed, he tried to
push himself away, as the boy who had hit him in the chest
with both feet suddenly appeared on the floor next to the
dead creature and began pulling it away across the store floor.
Something else streaked towards Wayne from the other side
of the counter, and when a naked little girl suddenly appeared
crouching on the front windowsill, Wayne yelled in pain and
grabbed at his side. He brought his hand up to his face, shining
the torch on it. His fingers were wet with blood, and when he
looked down at his side he could see that a chunk had been
bitten out of his shirt, and out of his flesh. Moaning, he shone
the torch at the little girl.

Her face was the face of the angel.

But her lips were bared in a snarl, revealing the sharp teeth,
and the blood on her chin.

"You little *shit*!" shouted Wayne.

He grabbed a bottle from the shelf and hurled it at the girl.
But in a puff of flour dust she was gone. The bottle smashed
through the front window.

"Wayne!" shouted Alex, moving around the counter. "For
God's sake, don't move!"

But both Alex and Candy reared back when a small figure previously hidden from sight suddenly bounded up in the
air from the other side of the counter. In one lithe motion, a
naked two-year-old boy was suddenly crouching on the counter
before them. They could not see the details of his face, but knew
that he would have the same angelic countenance as the others.
Blue eyes glinted in the darkness, his lips parting to reveal the
same pointed teeth as he gave a low snarl at them both. The
body language was unmistakable. Don't make another move.

Beyond, Wayne screamed, clutching at the back of his neck. He staggered away from the shelves as more bottles began to fall around him.

"Oh Christ," said Alex.

Suddenly the air was full of flashing movement as Wayne began to whirl violently on the spot, his arms lashing out around him. Shadows leaped and pranced, the torch beam swinging crazily all over the store. Tins, packets and bottles were falling all around Wayne as he shrieked and beat at the air.

"Don't," said Candy weakly. "Please don't."

The boy before them did not respond, merely inclining his head marginally over his ridged shoulder to look briefly at them as Wayne made a break for the door.

Another flash of movement, and suddenly the door was slammed shut, sending the flour gusting into the air again. Another flash, and Wayne shrieked once more, clutching at his face but refusing to let go of the torch. Something hit him hard from behind. He straightened in pain, his back arching as he was flung forward. He flailed with the torch. The sounds of ripping fabric and rapid, invisible movement all around him filled the air.

"Please," said Alex. "Make it stop."

The boy on the counter did not move.

And suddenly, Wayne was hugging his body with both arms and tottering to a standstill in the centre of the store. The flashing movement stopped. Wayne was still moaning, but no longer thrashing. In shock, he tried to take a step forward. The torch was shining up from below into his face, making it look like a Halloween mask. But in that short moment, Alex and Candy could see what damage had been done to him.

Wayne's face had been bitten in several places. A flap of skin hung from one cheek. Three diagonal gashes on his forehead were bleeding copiously, the blood running down into his eyes and dripping from his nose. It pooled at his chin, splashing down his shirtfront—a shirtfront that was also ragged, bloodied and torn where the creatures had bitten further chunks out of him. His hands were lacerated. Small bite-sized chunks had been taken out of his jeans and the flesh of his legs.

Somewhere out of sight, one of the children mewled in distress over the body that Wayne had stamped on.

Wayne took another step towards them.

"Help me," he said simply, and fell to his knees.

The torch fell from his nerveless fingers and rolled across the floor in an arc of light until it bumped against the serving counter. From below, the light shone up onto the boy who was keeping Alex and Candy back. He flinched only slightly, raising an arm to cover his cherub's face.

And suddenly, the air was alive with flashing movement again. All around Wayne.

He pitched forward, out of sight.

This time they could see the children. Bouncing down from shelves to where Wayne lay. A ripping of cloth and another guttural moan of pain before a small figure flashed away into the darkness. Another angelic but bloodied face, snarling before it vanished once more. Like a wild and feral pack, the children continued their remorseless assault. Striking, flashing out of sight. Striking again, and vanishing into the darkness.

Finally Wayne stopped making any kind of sound at all.

Now there was only the ripping of cloth and a flurrying of flour dust.

Then, silence.

No movement. And no sign of the children, apart from the boy who crouched on the counter, standing guard.

His pulse pounding in his temples, Alex looked at Candy.

Her face was drawn and white. But there was more than an expression of horror on her face now. Throughout the encounter, she had clutched Alex's hand, like him too afraid to move lest they should also be attacked. But now her gaze remained levelled on the one remaining boy. And it was a gaze that spoke of other things. Something way beyond the horror they had witnessed. Some kind of awful, impossible revelation, even more bizarre and terrifying than anything they'd yet seen in the hellishly transformed city that had once been Edmonville.

The boy was looking around the store, still shading his face from the torch beam. Was he checking to make sure that all of his companions had gone now? Was it his task to be the last to leave?

"Alex," said Candy. It seemed that she was using all of her remaining energy to utter just that one word.

The boy turned to look at her. This time there was no threat. This time it was just the curious face of a young child, or an angel.

"Oh good Christ, Alex," said Candy. She seemed to be on the verge of hyperventilating. "Look."

Alex looked at the boy.

And refused to believe what he saw.

"No," he said simply. "No, I won't believe it."

They recoiled in alarm at a flurry of motion.

And then the boy was gone, raising plaster dust from the counter. The strip light swayed crazily; the front door of the store jarred open.

They were alone.

"No," said Alex simply again, moving carefully around the edge of the counter in case any of the "children" were still in the store.

Wayne lay face down and still amidst the debris on the floor. It was impossible to tell whether the dark pool in which he lay was from the myriad broken bottles or whether it was his own blood. But Alex didn't have to examine him closely to know that he was dead. Stooping carefully, looking all around, he switched off the torch and picked it up.

"Come on, Candy."

He held out his hand.

"Alex, did you *see* . . . ?"

"Come *on*, Candy!"

Fingers trembling, Candy reached out and took his hand. Step by careful step, they made their way over the broken bottles and littered floor. Candy refused to look at Wayne, keeping her eyes tight shut and letting herself be guided.

Outside, night lay heavily on Edmonville, the ragged and fractured outlines of ruined buildings all around them as they clambered away from this latest nightmare.

"We've got to hurry," said Alex. "The Black Stuff may come back."

Candy was silent as they made their way back down the rubble-strewn street. Suddenly, it was as if she'd never had a drink that day.

In silence, they reached the end of the street and turned in towards the park. They could see the flames leaping from the bonfire. It evoked a deep and primal response within them both. To get back to the light and take refuge by the roaring flames. To keep the darkness and the terror that hid in the dark at bay.

"It was," said Candy simply as they moved.

"It wasn't!" snapped Alex, hanging onto her hand and dragging her after him. And then, later: "Christ, Candy! It *couldn't* be!"

They plunged on through the darkness, towards the light.

But both knew what they had seen, even if they could not comprehend it.

The cherub on the counter, the one that had kept them back while the others killed Wayne. The face of an angel. A face they knew only too well.

The face of their own son, Ricky.

Killed at the age of two in a garden accident over two years ago.

CHAPTER FIFTEEN | **FLIGHT**

JAY AND GORDON BURST OUT OF THE MEAT mart, staggering on the concrete ramp.

There was a howling behind them. It was the same insane gibbering sound they had heard the Black Stuff make when it had burst out of the dead the previous night by the bonfire. It was exploding out of the burning dead now, but some of them were still staggering after them like blazing marionettes, hungry to take them in their hellish embrace.

Back inside, the factory was lit up like Hell. Mad shadows writhed and flailed against the flames. Ahead of them, beyond the yard, utter darkness had fallen on the remains of Edmonville.

Gordon made to dash on ahead. Jay held him back.

"I don't think we'll get far out there. We don't know whether that Black Stuff has come back from down below."

"Jay!" Gordon looked back at the flailing torches in the factory. Another figure, utterly consumed in crackling yellow flame, pitched forward onto the concrete floor. Sparks showered on impact. Feebly, it groped and crawled on towards them. Something deep inside the corpse cracked, and the next moment the "life" went out of it. Black tar spattered from the flames, pooled all around the burning mass, and then swarmed hissing into the darkness like glistening black snakes. Gibbering and howling, other figures stepped over the fallen body, groping forward with arms of flame. They would soon be upon them.

"The truck!" snapped Jay. "We can get a straight run to the park from here. I know we can."

"Jay?"

"Get in the fucking truck, Gordon."

There was no time to argue. Gordon jumped on the running board on the passenger side and yanked the door open. When there was a flurry of motion at the rear of the truck, he jerked back to see that Jay had seized one of the remaining petrol cans that had been stacked there by the missing Wayne and Damon.

"Get in!" yelled Jay again. Twisting off the cap, he ran at the ramp and flung the can two-handed at the entrance. The can clanged against a wall, spraying petrol and rattling to the ground. It was a hell of a shot. The petrol instantly erupted in a cloud of fire, filling the entrance. Tongues of liquid blue fire began to lick down the ramp towards the truck. Whirling, Jay ran to the vehicle and flung himself into the driving seat.

The engine turned over straight away.

"Thank God for that," he muttered grimly, and stepped on the gas.

Just as the first of the figures erupted through the flames at the top of the ramp and began tottering down after them. The burning petrol had spread down the ramp to the remaining cans. Gordon flinched, waiting for the explosion as the cans were engulfed in the fire. Jay headed straight for the opened gates, realised that he was driving too wide, swung the wheel around hard—and stalled the engine.

Just as one of the blazing marionettes staggered through the flames and tottered straight towards the dump truck, arms held wide.

Jay saw it coming for the driver's side. No more than ten

feet now; a man-shaped, roaring mass of flame and smoke, intent on yanking the door open and dragging him into its embrace. The air was filled with a mad gobbling, hissing sound as Jay twisted the key. The engine coughed and juddered as if it were going to stall again.

Fire filled the side window beside him, blackening the glass.

A shrivelled hand closed on the door handle.

A hideously burning face, flesh crisping away from the skull, leered inches from his own.

And then the dump truck roared forward.

The burning shape was left behind, its smouldering hand yanked from the thing's arm and still clutching the door handle. In his rear-view mirror, Jay saw the body stagger and fall to the ground in a flaming mass. Other shapes were staggering and weaving out of the flames, trying to locate them. Somewhere within the flaming chaos, another corpse burst apart. Black ichor splattered high in the air; jet-black droplets pattering to the concrete, swarming together again and snaking away from the fire into the night.

Something bumped on the back of the truck as they roared out of the meat mart. The vehicle hit fallen rubble and Jay fought to regain control of the wheel as it spun in his hands. The headlights picked out great chunks of disintegrated wall directly ahead. Jay swerved, tyres screeching. Behind them, the remaining superheated petrol cans exploded. A cloud of oily flame erupted into the night, reflected in their rear-view mirror, sending gigantic shadows leaping amidst the ruins.

Again, something bumped and shuffled from the rear of the vehicle.

"On the back!" shouted Gordon, turning in his seat to look through the rear window. He couldn't see anything, since the dumper was lowered, but he knew that some of the burning monstrosities must somehow have clambered into the back as they left the yard. "Jay! Some . . . some . . ."

"I know!" yelled Jay, and swerved around the corner of the

street, heading for where he thought the "flat" route might be between the ruined houses, leading them back to the bonfire. The truck hit a fractured pavement hard, jolting them in their seats and throwing Gordon hard against the windscreen. The guitar on his back gave a teeth-jarring, ragged chord. As Gordon scrambled around to face the front, rubbing his head, Jay looked in the rear-view mirror again, to see that they'd left the meat mart behind and none of the dead had been able to follow. Had they been consumed in that last explosion? They surely couldn't get any further before the animating Black Stuff was driven out of them.

Something bumped on the cab roof above them.

Twisting furiously at the wheel, Jay strained to look up through the side window.

"Jay!" Wide-eyed, Gordon pointed ahead.

The side of a house loomed large in the headlights.

"Shit!" Jay twisted again, and this time they just missed crashing. No matter what other passengers they'd picked up, he'd have to concentrate on driving, and getting them to the others as quickly as he could. There was no time to stop.

A burning arm smacked down across the windscreen.

One of their passengers had managed to climb from the dumper to the cab roof.

Jay slammed on the brakes.

A burning shape catapulted down over the hood and flapped out of sight in front of the truck. Smoke wafted over the hood and obscured the screen. Jay put his foot down again, and the truck jolted forward. Straight over the body. Now he could see which way they were headed and remembered clearly the route he had in mind. It couldn't be far now.

There were more scrabbling noises from the dumper behind.

Gordon's hands began exploring the floor, frantically searching.

"What the hell are you doing?" snapped Jay.

Gordon couldn't speak, quickly smacked Jay's shoulder as a

way of telling him to shut the hell up, and continued searching. Jay slapped out at him.

"Gordon, stop pissing about!"

And then he'd found it. A lever and handle by the side of Jay's seat.

Gordon yanked it back.

"Gordon!"

The dumper began to lift behind them, the mechanism cranking as they raced on through the night. Jay looked anxiously around, not knowing in their panicked flight just what the hell was going on. When he saw in the rear-view mirror that two burning bundles were bouncing around on the road in the darkness behind them, he realised at last what had happened. Now the figures were lying still and smouldering as the truck raced on ahead.

"You clever bastard," he breathed. "Now why didn't I think of that?"

The dump truck screeched around the gable of another ruined building, the headlights picking up the park ahead.

The bonfire was three hundred yards away, blazing in the darkness.

Moments before, the fire had been their enemy.

Now it was their beacon to a fragile safety.

Jay put his foot down again, and the truck lurched on ahead over the grass.

CHAPTER SIXTEEN | **THE ORDEAL OF JULIET DELORE**

J ULIET COULD NOT BELIEVE THAT SHE HAD SLEPT again.

She snapped awake, still clutching the cold iron rails on the inspection platform. Crying out, she jerked around to look down the ladder, certain that Trevor must have taken the opportunity to climb up after her. It had grown dark again, but there was no sign of him. The dark shape of the Land Rover was still below, but no sign of her tormentor. Was he inside, sitting behind the wheel? Quickly, she looked all around, but there was no other way that Trevor could get up here. The darkness was now hiding the terrifying drop into the Chasm on which the broadcasting mast stood, but she could still feel it; could feel its power, like invisible waves of energy drawing her to the edge. She remembered feeling like that when she was a child, when her parents had taken her up to the top of Greys Monument. Her father had held her close to the railed barrier; she had seen the immensity of the city below, and felt the horrendous drop pulling at her. Just as the Chasm was pulling at her now.

How could she have fallen asleep? It had to be the stress and the shock, ambushing her. She looked out into the growing night, searching the sky. There were no searchlights, no sounds of aircraft or helicopter engines, no evidence that anyone was searching for survivors. Despair choked her. There was a bitter taste in her mouth.

Something splashed, somewhere below.

Juliet looked down anxiously, through the steel lattice of the platform on which she crouched. Only darkness. Was Trevor up to something? She shuffled forward again and looked back down at the Land Rover. There was no movement. She heard it again. A soft lapping, like a wave on a beach. Was something leaking down the mast? She looked up, but again there was no sign of anything. But there was definitely a continuous liquid sound now, difficult to pinpoint: a sighing, gentle sound. Now much closer, no longer as gentle, dribbling and splashing. As she listened, it became the sound of hot water in a pan, hissing and bubbling on the stove. Juliet reluctantly pulled herself to her feet, listening to the sounds coming nearer. She looked all around in the darkness, down the ladder in case Trevor was coming up. But there was no sign of him.

"Trevor!" she hissed. "Don't come near me, you bastard. I'm warning you. It's a long way down for *both* of us . . ."

Something moved beneath the steel lattice of the observation platform.

Juliet's heart leaped. In an instant, she grabbed the railings of the platform and pulled her feet up into the air, bracing them on a lower rail. There was something directly below, but she could make no sense of it. Trevor? No, this movement wasn't being made by any human form. It was where the liquid sound had been coming from. Now she couldn't see down through the lattice. It was as if there was a pool of black oil or tar rising up through the grille even as she looked. Swirling and bubbling beneath her, it suddenly stopped. Juliet looked out into the night. This didn't make sense. How could a black pool rise up the centre of the broadcasting mast like that? Again there was the lapping, splashing sound—and Juliet recoiled when she saw that the black liquid was somehow flowing up the platform railings.

For a moment, she couldn't move. Now her vertigo was being made even worse by the impossibility of what was happening below her. Black water, or oil, or tar—whatever this stuff was—didn't move like that. Liquid flowed down, not up. And for a moment, it was literally as if her world had been turned upside down. Was *she* the wrong way round? Was the liquid flowing *down* over those rails towards her? Juliet screwed her eyes shut, and willed her world the right way round. But when she opened them again, the black stuff was still running up the rails the wrong way. Worse, some of the liquid was dripping up from a lower rail to a higher rail.

Juliet grabbed at an overhead rail and stepped up higher as the black liquid funnelled and dripped along the rail on which she had just been standing.

This isn't happening. You're just not seeing this right. You're on a maintenance platform. So this has to be oil. Maybe stuff the engineers use for equipment up here or something . . .

Where there had once been a steel platform was now a glinting black pool of bubbling tar. It began to rise.

This CAN'T be happening! The rails around the platform are open on all four sides! It should be running out through them, down to the ground!

But the black pool continued to rise towards her in a steady column.

She knew then.

It wanted to engulf her.

It wanted to fasten onto her legs, swarm up around her body, suck her down into its horrifying blackness. Swallow her body and soul. Drag her back down to the Chasm. Devour and digest her alive, revel and delight in her screaming.

Something flared in the darkness.

Even though her attention was fixed in terror on the ascending black horror, the sudden light made her snap her head away to look for it. It was way off, on the other side of the Chasm. Somewhere on the other plateau. Now there was only darkness, and Juliet looked down again in terror, expecting the black liquid to be lapping at her boots.

It had stopped.

Inches below her feet, it bubbled and swarmed and churned, as if on a slow boil.

But there was no doubt that it had ceased for the moment to climb towards her.

The flare of light came again, and this time it stayed.

Juliet had no idea how far away it could be. But she could see the outlines of a factory wall and ruined buildings. As if someone were building a fire in there. And now there was another light; this one much bigger than the first and growing larger all the time, revealing outlines of trees against the steadily growing flame. It stood out brilliantly against the utter darkness of the night. And despite the terror that Juliet had endured, the light meant that there *was* someone out there after all. She and Trevor weren't the only people left in this new and horrifying world. And that meant there was hope of rescue after all. There could be many other reasons for the fires. A short circuit in one of the many ruins. A petrol leak, suddenly igniting. But Juliet would not allow headroom to these thoughts.

She was not alone.

For the first time there was hope.

Beneath her, the black liquid hissed and spat as if hot coals had been dropped into the pool.

Juliet braced herself to climb.

And then the liquid began to drop away.

Clinging tight, Juliet watched in growing relief as it descended to the steel-lattice base of the maintenance platform; saw the criss-cross metalwork appear as the black pool sank away beneath it. Now that liquid on the railings beneath her was behaving as liquid should behave, running and dripping away after the descending pool as if gravity had suddenly remembered the way it should be working. Ribbons of oil spattered and twisted away down into the darkness; spattering globules of tar burst and fell like black rain into the void.

It left nothing of itself behind.

No smear on the railings.

Not a drop on the maintenance deck.

No spatterings on the mast or the metalwork.

Nothing dripping from the rails.

Slowly, hesitantly, Juliet descended to the platform. First, one careful foot. Then another. But nothing swarmed out of the darkness to engulf her. The metalwork all around her was bone dry, as if it had never been wet at all.

"Didn't like it, did you?" Juliet spat down through the platform, to wherever the black stuff had gone. Instantly, she wondered why she had spoken to it as if it were alive. And almost immediately, another thought came to her. Something that didn't make sense, but the truth of which seemed undeniable.

Because that liquid stuff was alive.

And it didn't like what was happening over there.

Juliet hunched up against the rails, staring out across the void to the rapidly growing light of the bonfire. There were still flarings of light off to the right, somewhere in the ruins. But these were sporadic, and not as frequent as before. No, the bonfire beyond the trees (perhaps half a mile away?) was where hope lay. In this world of utter darkness, it brought the possibility of salvation.

Juliet looked down.

She could see the Land Rover. No sign of Trevor. And absolutely no sign of the moving black liquid. Perhaps she'd never seen it at all? Perhaps it was the product of her ordeal and all the terrors she'd been forced to endure? For now, she didn't want to think about that.

She just wanted to concentrate on the light.

When morning came, and there was more light, she would be able to see the people who had made the fire.

They would save her from this living hell.

| **NIGHT RIDERS**

"DEAD?" SAID DAMON, HIS FACE WHITE IN the light of the bonfire.

He stood there, his hands hanging at his sides, a piece of wood in one of them. He had been in the act of throwing it into the flames when Alex and Candy had told them what had happened in the minimart. He'd said nothing throughout.

"Wayne's dead," he said again in a flat voice. He was standing as if someone had taken him by the inside label of his shirt collar and hung him on the peg of an invisible door. The label snapped and he sagged to his knees. "Wayne's dead." He was running the two words over and over as if repetition would make sense of them.

The dump truck was parked close to the flames. Gordon had wanted to tell everyone what had happened back at the meat mart but couldn't, as usual, find his voice; not even for one-word descriptions. He couldn't understand why Jay wasn't regaling them with all the details of their nightmare encounter. He seemed content merely to tell them that what needed to be done had been done.

Between them, Alex and Candy had recounted their tale of the feral children and of Wayne's gruesome death. When they'd finished, Jay said: "Tell it again."

Alex drew breath and squatted down beside the fire, looking off into the night. Carefully, he told the story again.

"It was him," said Candy, after a long pause when the only sound was the crackling flames; the only movement the dancing and twisting of long shadows. "It was Ricky."

The boy cuddled up close to Lisa, taking an obvious pleasure in the nearby warmth of the fire. "I don't hear anyone talking about drugs," she said. "Or nerve gas, or hallucinations. I take it we're all agreed that whatever's happening here is really happening to us?"

"Hallucinations," said Alex, "don't bite chunks out of you. They don't savage you to death."

Jay stooped, picked up a piece of panelling, and threw it into the flames. A cloud of sparks flew up into the night. "And they don't bring dead people back to life."

"Wayne's dead," said Damon again. The chunk of wood slipped from his fingers to the ground.

"Those words," said Annie. "The graffiti that was all over the place. They're clues. Bad people. Bad places."

"It *was* him!" Candy ignored her. "It *was*!"

Alex had seen his son with his own eyes. There was no denying it. But as Candy stared hard at him, wide eyes reflecting the light, he found that he had nothing to say. His silence seemed to enrage her. She turned and stared into the flames.

Annie was about to speak, but bit her lip. She had remembered the dead bodies that had appeared the previous night. The bodies that had somehow been made to look like people they knew. Whatever these bizarre children had been, could it be that the same trick had been repeated on Alex and Candy? Had they been made to see their dead son? Was this all part of the same insane game, trying to drive them all mad? Speaking her mind now was not going to help matters.

Everyone was silent then, not knowing what to say.

They stared into the night and looked into the fire.

"Wayne's dead," said Damon quietly.

And then there was a hushing sound in the darkness. Like a wave rushing up onto a beach and breaking against the sand. It came again, and again. The darkness was filled with the sound, now like a wind, although there was no motion of the air.

"It's back," said Jay.

When he spoke, they all saw it at once, out beyond the gleam of the bonfire.

The Black Stuff was flowing up over the ragged rim of the Chasm, pouring up from the impossible depths in pulsing black waves. It glinted like tar or oil as it came, now flowing across the parkland towards them like some vast ebony sea. There was movement and agitation on its surface, as if the firelight reflecting there was causing turmoil and pain in its inky vastness. And as it came, rippling waves began to spread across its immensity, flowing hungrily towards them. Defying gravity, it continued to surge and lap up over the cliff edge.

"Oh Christ," said Candy. "It's going to get us this time."

"No it's not," said Annie. "Not if we keep close to the fire."

"Annie's right," said Jay. "It doesn't like the light. Gordon and me saw it all again back at the meat mart. Just like last night."

Carefully, slowly, they backed off from the oncoming black sea, closer to the fire.

Just beyond the edge of the bonfire's flicker, where the light met the darkness, the sea suddenly halted, rippling and bubbling softly like hot tar. It began to flow around the periphery of the light, spreading on either side to encircle them like some vast living, liquid creature.

"It's trying to find a way in," said Alex.

The Black Stuff reached the dumper truck. They saw the oil flowing and lapping behind it.

"My God, look!" Lisa pointed unnecessarily as black streamers of oil suddenly appeared on the cab roof, trickling down the windscreen. The Black Stuff had flowed over the rear of the vehicle, where it was in shadow from the bonfire. But now, with the firelight shining full on the front of the truck, they watched as the streamers hissed angrily, like black water on a red-hot stove. Suddenly they slid back from the windscreen and into the safety of the darkness behind. The waves kept moving past the truck, still on the periphery between light and dark, still searching for a way in.

Silently, they watched as it flowed around them on either side of the bonfire. Jay and Gordon walked with it as the black sea moved, edging around the left-hand side of the bonfire; watching the Black Stuff flowing and lapping over the cracked earth, flattening the grass in its oily morass. Alex and Annie followed their lead, moving to the right, around the fire.

On the other side, they watched the black tide as it joined itself again, flowing together and forming a glinting ebony surface way back into the night.

They were surrounded.

Just as they had been stranded on this bizarre half-mile crag in what had once been the centre of Edmonville, they were stranded again. Cut off on a burning island, in the middle of a black and poisonous sea. They stood watching as the black waves roiled and swirled, the hideous tide lapping at the edge of the light, testing for a way to break through and engulf them. Jay looked back at the fire. It was burning well, and they had enough fuel stacked close by to see them through the night.

There was a noise from the other side of the fire. One of the others, crying out in alarm. Keeping their eyes on the Black Stuff, their backs to the fire, they ran around to the other side. Wave ridges chased them as they moved. The liquid was watching their every move, waiting for someone to make a mistake and step out of the circle of light.

"What's wrong?" Jay scanned the others. But no one seemed hurt, everyone was still close to the relative safety of the fire, looking out across the black sea that had engulfed the entire park.

"Someone's coming," said Lisa in a flat voice, and she pointed into the darkness.

Was it more of the dead? Perhaps bodies they hadn't been able to retrieve, buried in the ruins and hidden from sight? Now finally dragged free and brought back to taunt them again?

"We got rid of most of them," continued Jay, moving forward. The Black Stuff seemed to surge and ripple at him as he did so, bubbling and swirling on the edge of the light. "But we might not have got them all. If we didn't, it'll be like last night. But they won't like the light, just like this Black Stuff. And they can't get us. Not as long as we stay close to the fire. Just remember that." *There you go again, Jay. Taking charge. Why not just shut the hell up . . . ?*

A single figure was walking through the night towards them.

Unhurriedly, and without the staggering gait of the living dead that they had seen before. At first, it was a vague man-sized shape, but now, as he drew nearer to the light (and they could see now that it was a man, not a woman), his silhouette was becoming more clearly defined. Head down, arms swinging casually at his side, he came on.

"He's . . ." began Lisa, and her voice dried up. She coughed to clear it, a ridiculously ordinary sound in this hellish night. "He's . . . *walking* on the Black Stuff."

And yes, they could all see now that the silhouette was walking on the tide of rippling ebony. He was not splashing through the stuff, not kicking up plumed gouts of black water. It was as if he were walking through the night on a rain-washed pavement. Beneath his feet there was no liquid; only the glinting solidity of hardened tar.

The figure came on.

Damon groaned.

When Jay looked over at him, he was rising from his knees. His face was still blank, but his attention was riveted on the approaching figure. Jay looked back out into the night. The figure had stopped, right on the shoreline of the Black Stuff. Waves lapped around his feet now. His head was still down, but everyone knew who it was, even before he looked up.

"Wayne," said Damon, relief in his voice.

It was as Candy and Alex had told them. They could see the chunks bitten out of his arms and legs. The ragged tears where savagely sharp teeth had ripped the fabric of his shirt and trousers. The dark gleaming of exposed wounds beneath. The flap of skin hanging down from his cheek. The blood on his face. His hair awry, as if he'd just woken from sleep.

Even from here, they could see the dark boiling movement of the Black Stuff in his eye sockets.

"Wayne," said Damon again, and began to move forward.

Alex took him by the arm, holding him back.

"Stay there, Damon!" snapped Jay. "It's not him."

"What do you mean, 'It's not him'?" Damon yanked his arm away from Alex, whirling on him. "You were lying! You and that drunken bitch!"

On the edge of the firelight, the thing that had once been Wayne grinned.

"He's not dead," Damon went on. "You just left him there, in the mart."

"Look at him!" shouted Alex. "You can see it for yourself. He's not alive."

"Liars!" screamed Damon, and he began to run towards the silent figure.

Gordon brought him down in a rugby tackle before he'd gone two yards. Damon screamed and cursed, thrashing and kicking. Jay and Alex ran to help. Pinning his arms, Alex tried to reason with him. But the sight of Wayne had snapped something inside. Twisting his head furiously from side to side, yelling at the top of his voice, Damon refused to listen.

"*They left me, Damon,*" said the figure on the rippling shore. "*They just left me there.*"

"Let me up! Get off me, you fucking dummy!"

"*They hate us. They all hate us. Right from the beginning. Just 'cause we're young or something.*"

"Help me, Wayne! I'll . . . I'll . . . fucking *kill* you, O'Connor!"

"*There's a way out, Wayne. A way off this place. Just come to me, and I'll show you the way . . .*"

"Wayne! Help me!"

Wayne held his arms wide as the black waves flowed and surged over his feet, around his shins, always flinching back from the direct light. He grinned then, a ghastly rictus. The blackness in his eyes writhed and squirmed like boiling pitch.

"*Give him to me,*" said the Wayne-thing.

"Here," said Annie, striding forward. "Have this!"

In one swift and angry motion, she flung the burning tree branch she'd taken from the fire directly at him.

The result was instantaneous as the branch whirled through the air and landed at Wayne's feet. He screeched in a voice that was not human. It was the scream of some terrible, primordial creature, up from the depths of the Chasm. His bloodied white hands flew to his face as he recoiled from the light, the Black Stuff at his feet hissing back into the darkness. Bent at the waist, hands and arms covering his bowed head, Wayne was suddenly travelling backwards at speed. It was a bizarre, surreal sight. His legs weren't moving, yet he was speeding away from her. When Annie looked, she could see that the black liquid on which he was standing was carrying him away with it, suddenly solid again beneath him as he was borne off on the surface of the retreating black flood.

"Wayne!" yelled Damon from beneath his captors. "Don't leave me."

Annie shook a fist defiantly in the air, watching the tidal edge of the Black Stuff shrinking back on all sides.

Jay made sure that the other two still had a tight grip on Damon, and stood back. They had made the Black Stuff retreat the previous night by throwing torches into the darkness. Why the hell hadn't they just started doing that straight away? Realising that the relentless approach of the Black Stuff from the edge of the Chasm, and the sudden appearance of Wayne, had frozen them with fear, he strode to the fire. Was it always going to be like this? The first sign of something to fear, and fear itself would make everyone forget what they had to do? He remembered how the fear had overwhelmed him at the meat mart, making him unable to function and bringing him close to the edge—and he hated himself for it. Anger flaring, he jammed his hand into the flames, felt pain as the fire blistered his wrist. Yanking out a ragged, flaring chunk of firewood, he ran to where Annie was standing and flung the firebrand underarm into the night. It sputtered in the darkness, arcing through the air and throwing out sparks like some failed firework. When it hit the ground, the hissing and screeching came louder in the darkness. The Black Stuff fled from the burning wood on all sides, retreating into the darkness and leaving the grass around it with no evidence that it had ever been there. Unsmeared, unstained, no sign that it had been engulfed by the sickening black mass.

Wayne's figure suddenly came to a halt, so far out that he was barely a silhouette on the black water. His body straightened from its contorted and doubled-up posture. Even though they could no longer see him clearly, they could tell that whatever he had become, whatever was inside him, was engulfed by a ferocious rage.

"You'll all die! Every one of you! Not quickly. But in agony! Slowly, and in AGONY!"

Suddenly, Damon was quiet, no longer fighting Gordon and Alex. The voice that emanated from Wayne's silhouette was no longer his voice. It was a hundred voices, all filled with abominable hatred for them. It was all the hatred and evil that existed at the bottom of the Chasm.

"You want to know? You want to know what's happened to you and your world? You want to see? You want to UNDERSTAND? Then . . . then . . . SEE!"

The silhouette flung its arms wide in a gesture of rage.

All around it, the black sea had been infused with the same rage. It swirled and eddied around his body. Glinting black waves funnelled and sped through the darkness. Whirlpools swirled and sucked, even though the Black Stuff that covered the parkland could be no more than two or three inches deep. The blackness boiled and blistered, churned and raced around the bonfire. The effect was at once terrifying and dizzying. Annie clung to Jay's arm. He held her, feeling that he too might fall. Behind them, Candy threw herself flat on the ground, arms outstretched as if she feared that she might suddenly be spun up into the air by some dark and powerful centrifugal force.

"Jesus . . ." said Alex in a hollow voice.

"SEE!" screamed the silhouette, as if in some body-racking contortion that was summoning up all this hate. *"SEE!"* The black tar swarmed quickly over Wayne's legs, slopping around his torso and greedily engulfing his entire body as he remained standing there, arms flung wide.

All around him, the Black Stuff suddenly reared up into huge obsidian waves of frenzied activity. The twisting, roiling tar seemed to be struggling to take shape, squirming masses of black muck churning to form grotesque images. Four columns emerged from the undulating mass, two on either side of Wayne, perhaps twenty feet apart and twenty feet high. There was a groaning sound now, from beneath their feet. As if the Black Stuff were putting all its energy into this new activity, and the vibrations were drumming into the very soil of the parkland. The air was filled with the hissing, gabbling voices again. A horde of the damned was howling their hatred at those who crouched by the bonfire.

And then, at almost exactly the same time, the four undulating columns of grotesque black mud found their shape. Exultant with hatred, the four shapes became living statues of hardened black tar and oil. They writhed and twisted and exuded Hate.

They were four black horsemen.

Astride four gigantic black horses.

The horses reared and pawed at the air with their forefeet, now dropping back to the tar, now rearing again and spinning as the black-garbed riders, with expressionless faces like carved ebony, clung tight to their steeds. The riders pulled hard at the reins, dragging the huge horse heads around time and again to face the bonfire. Their flanks glinted, their nostrils flared. The jet-black harnesses and spurs stretched and jangled in the night. Cloaks fashioned from tar flapped and dripped around the riders' shoulders, swarming and reforming around their torsos, as much a part of the riders as their newly fashioned black limbs. The night was filled now with the screaming of human voices, the shrieking of maddened wild horses. But the black faces of the riders were impassive and implacable, somehow more deeply terrifying than if they had been screaming the same hatred that emanated from the black sea and the thing that had once been Wayne.

"*The sun has become like coarse black cloth!*" screamed Wayne. "*And the moon is red with blood! The stars have fallen and are no more, the sky disappeared like a scroll rolled up and every mountain and island moved from its place!*"

"Fuck this," said Jay, pulling away from Annie.

When he turned, he could see that Gordon and Alex were no longer holding Damon down. They had risen to their feet, standing over him, and all three were gaping out at the four lunging figures in the frenzied ebony sea. Jay held Gordon's eye as he strode to the fire. His fixed expression seemed to break Gordon and Alex out of their trances. As he began to yank another firebrand out of the flames, they hurried to him and began to do the same.

"*Now you know!*" screamed Wayne in his hundred voices as the horses reared and lunged on either side of him, the black waves undulating in their mad frenzy. "*Despair, before you die! Despair, despair, despair!*"

"Go to Hell!" yelled Jay, and in the next moment three firebrands were blazing through the darkness towards Wayne and the horsemen.

The screeching grew louder.

The firebrands fell short of the figures, but suddenly the horsemen were gone and four dissolving pillars of darkness flopped and fell apart in writhing torrents on either side of Wayne. Screeching, the Black Stuff dissolved all around the impact of the torches. Funnelling waves fled from the sparks that showered on impact.

This time both Annie and Candy—galvanised by terror—were at the bonfire, pulling out makeshift torches in clouds of sparks. The boy clung tight to Lisa. If not for his need to hide from the nightmare shapes, she too would have grabbed something from the flames.

More fire arced into the night, falling into the black ocean.

Patches of dark green began to appear in the blackness as the sea retreated.

Suddenly, Wayne had fallen forward, both arms above his head. He vanished into the Black Stuff, and when it recoiled from where he had been standing, they could see that he had been taken with it as the blackness fled away to the edge of the park. The screaming and hissing began to die away, growing fainter as the Black Stuff began to pour back over the edge of the Chasm, disappearing into the bottomless depths below.

Relentlessly they kept up their bombardment with blazing firebrands, Jay and Gordon moving around to the other side of the bonfire to repeat the exercise. There was hardly any need. Already, most of the rippling black liquid had slid away, anticipating their move.

In minutes, the black ocean had gone. There was no evidence that it had ever been there.

Damon remained where he was, sitting and staring into the darkness.

For a long time they stood looking at the smouldering torches scattered around the park, listening to the silence.

"So now we know," said Annie.

"Know what?" asked Jay.

"Lisa was right in the first place."

"Right?" Alex turned to look at Lisa.

"Those horsemen," said Annie. "The riders that the Black Stuff showed us. They're . . ."

"The Four Horsemen of the Apocalypse," said Lisa flatly.

"Oh, good Christ," said Candy, her face white in the glare of the bonfire. "No one's coming for us, because there *is* no one to come for us."

Lisa looked at Jay, and knew that he needed more explanation.

"The things Wayne said? They're from the Bible—the Book of Revelations." Lisa stroked the boy's head, felt tears trickling down her cheeks. "War, famine, disease. Just like the Bible says. It really is the End of the World. That's what's happened here."

For yet another night in this hideous new world, they waited silently by the bonfire.

Lost in their own weary thoughts.

Trying to make sense of the nightmares they had experienced and endured.

And waiting for the growing greyness that would herald the arrival of yet another day in Hell.

CHAPTER EIGHTEEN | THE ORDEAL OF JULIET DELORE

J ULIET REALISED THAT THE SKY WAS
lightening.

Gripping the rail of the inspection platform, she had kept her attention equally divided between the fire beacon somewhere off on the other side of the pit and on the Land Rover still sitting silently facing the concrete platform of the mast. Her throat was sore from the calls for help across the darkness. There had been no replies, no offers of help. But she refused to believe that it was hopeless. There was no real way of telling how far off the fire was. When day came, she would see. And perhaps then they might hear her calls.

(What makes you think they'll hear you any better in the light, Juliet? Surely they would have heard you, even in the darkness? If, that is, anyone was there?)

She refused to listen to that inner voice.

Once, she had resisted the urge to call for Trevor; just to make sure that he was down there somewhere. If she did, it would be too much like giving in, and after the most recent night terrors she needed all the courage she could muster. Had she really seen that oil, dripping and flowing the wrong way? No, she could not allow herself to think about that. There was nothing to suggest that it had happened at all. No oily marks on the railings, no smudges on the platform, no stains on the ground around the concrete base. She had to keep her attention fixed on the beacon.

But as the skies lightened, the only darkness now being the darkness of the pit at the foot of the broadcasting mast (which she steadfastly refused to look down into, lest vertigo should swamp her again), Juliet realised that she wasn't going to get a clear view after all. She could see smoke rising from where the fire had started, but her view of it was obscured by a ragged screen of tilted, fractured trees and the ruins of buildings. The ravine was perhaps three or four hundred feet wide, with the smoke rising perhaps half a mile inland on the other plateau. Surely if there was someone over there they must have heard her yelling in the night?

"Over here!" Juliet began yelling again. She looked anxiously down again for any sign of Trevor, but there was no movement. "Please, someone! Help me!" She looked out across the Chasm again to the rising smoke.

There's no one there, Juliet.

"There *must* be someone!"

Everyone's dead.

"Help me, please! Over here!"

And from down below, from the Land Rover, came an answering scream . . .

"I'll help you, Juliet! I'll fucking HELP you, my darling!"

The Land Rover engine coughed into life. Trevor rammed it into first and revved hard. During the darkness, the fearful pain in his ragged eye socket had muted, but now, with the coming of "day," the terrible agony had returned. He took one hand from the wheel and slammed the heel of it against the socket, shaking his head like a wild animal, as if he could cast the pain aside. But it was only making things worse as the pain ate like a living thing into his head, into his face.

297

It was time now.

Time to prove to the Vorla that he was worthy. It was incapable of action in the light, but he would show it that he could do its bidding when it was at its lowest ebb. Deep inside his soul, that small part of the Vorla that remained hidden squirmed in anticipation.

"*I'm sending you to meet someone, Juliet!*"

Trevor began to laugh manically.

"*A very, very good friend of mine.*"

He lifted his foot on the clutch. The Land Rover shot forward, roaring across the grass.

Up above, Juliet clung to the rails of the maintenance deck, looking down. Now she realised that Trevor had been in the Land Rover all night, silently watching and waiting. She could hear him screaming inside, but couldn't make out the words. Frozen in fear, she could only watch as the vehicle came straight at the mast. She gripped the rail tight, not understanding.

"Trevor, *no!*"

The Land Rover smashed into the concrete base.

Juliet felt the ringing impact in the rail she was clutching. The mast shuddered with echoes. When she looked down again, steam was rising from the buckled hood.

Inside the Land Rover, Trevor gagged against the wheel. He hadn't fastened his seatbelt and the impact had thrown him forward. His neck had whiplashed and there was a crushing pain in his chest where he had hit the steering wheel. The pain was good. The Vorla would know that he was trying to prove himself. Trevor shook his head and looked up. The windscreen was covered in cobweb cracks. Was that steam rising from the hood or was his vision out of focus? No matter.

Laughing again, Trevor jammed the Land Rover into

reverse and roared away from the concrete base. When he saw that the cracks at which he had been aiming were wider and that there were fragments of concrete scattered on the grass at the base, he began to shout *"Yes, yes, yes!"* When the vehicle lurched to a halt, he was much further back. Had Juliet realised what he was planning to do? Trevor wound down the window.

"*Games are over, Juliet!*"

He revved the engine again as . . .

Juliet braced herself against the rail once more. At that moment, as the Land Rover roared forward again, she finally realised what Trevor was trying to do. She saw the widened cracks at the base of the platform, the chunks of concrete. But surely—*surely*—it wasn't possible? He would wreck the car first. The engine block would fracture. He couldn't believe that it would be possible . . . and then Juliet felt the pull of the Chasm on the other side of the mast; knew that it was balanced right on the edge, that the platform was cracked, that the soil all around the mast was crumbling. And then the shivering echoes rang in her ears, the entire platform beneath her feet shuddered, the rail to which she was clinging stinging her hands with its vibrations when . . .

The Land Rover slammed into the concrete base again. This time the windscreen exploded out across the buckled hood. The cracks in the platform widened, ran up to the foot of the inspection ladder and onto the centre of the base. Steam gushed from the hood now. And surely it must all be over; the vehicle was wrecked and Trevor's mad plan to topple the mast into the Chasm was at an end. Juliet's legs felt weak. She leaned forward to look down, the steam from the vehicle rising to meet her. Should she risk climbing down now? Perhaps she could make another break for it; find somewhere else in the ruins to hide? Below, the Land Rover was still. Yes, she had to give it a try. Maybe Trevor had knocked himself senseless. Juliet gritted her teeth and stepped forward to the top of the ladder as . . .

The Land Rover growled into life, reversing away from the platform. Sparkling fragments of glass slithered in sheets from the hood. Something had broken beneath the chassis, the gears grinding, the engine racing as it lurched away in a shroud of steam. Inside, Trevor spat out a tooth and felt more pain in his gut. For a second time, he had been slammed forward against the wheel. This time he had cracked a rib. But he still wouldn't fasten his seatbelt. He knew that the Vorla inside him was watching and waiting. He would not fail the Test. The Land Rover swerved and wobbled back over its own ragged tyre tracks. Trevor could see that the cracks had spread. Chunks of concrete littered the grass.

"GOING *DOWN, JULIET!*" he screamed, revving the wavering engine madly. He began to laugh again; wild, ringing peals of laughter. Now growing even more manic when the laughing made the pain in his gut match the hideous agony in his eye socket, his neck and his broken rib. He jammed down the accelerator once more and the Land Rover roared forward again as . . .

"*Then DIE, Trevor!*" yelled Juliet. "Smash yourself to pieces you mad, sick, stupid *animal!*"

She braced herself against the rails. The ringing echoes from the last impact were still quivering, whispering and shivering in the ironwork, growing fainter. But there was another sound now that filled her with sick fear. It was a low grinding sound. Wildly, Juliet looked around to see where it was coming from.

But it was all around her, and she couldn't pin it down to one source. Stretching, grinding, slowly groaning.

"Oh God . . ." said Juliet, and then . . .

The Land Rover smashed into the concrete base again.

Trevor was hurled from his seat, out across the hood.

He bounced in a tangled flurry of limbs, hit the concrete platform hard. Arms flopping, he slid lifelessly from the hood as steam gushed around him, hiding his body from sight on the grass at the side of the Land Rover.

Despite the damage that had been done to the vehicle, the third impact was the greatest by far. Cracks radiated around the platform on all sides. A massive chunk of it had fallen away by the side of the vehicle. Something inside the platform gave a massive, rending groan as . . .

Juliet was flung from the rail to the maintenance platform deck. The impact snapped her jaws closed, blurred her vision. Sprawled face down, looking through the metal latticework. It took her several seconds to make sense of who she was, where she was, and what was happening. Down below, she saw the Land Rover wreathed in steam.

Trevor was out of the vehicle, crawling on all fours out of the steam cloud. She tried to shout down at him again, but the impact had knocked the breath from her lungs as . . .

Trevor staggered to his feet, weaved from side to side like a drunken man and fell back against the side of the Land Rover. His bottom front teeth had been loosened. He spat out bright red blood, wiping his chin. He knew that something else inside had been badly damaged, but didn't know what it could be. He knew only that inside, where the hurt was, the Vorla was smiling. He returned the smile, spat blood again, and fumbled at the door handle. When he looked up at the mast, at first he thought it was swaying, ready to topple over the brink. But when he steadied himself on the Land Rover roof, he realised that he was the one who was swaying.

"Nexsht . . ." Trevor spat out another tooth. "*Next* time."

He pulled the door open, pausing like a drunk to get his bearings.

And then Trevor fell inside, as . . .

Juliet pulled herself to the rails again.

Even from that height, she could see that Trevor was badly hurt; could see that nevertheless he still wasn't going to give up. All around her, the groaning, grinding sound had become louder. She could feel vibrations in the metal platform beneath her feet. It seemed impossible, but Trevor was going to succeed. If she was going to act, going to do anything, then she had to act *now*! She saw Trevor fall into the Land Rover and knew that she had to get down, no matter what. Suddenly the immensity of the drop into the Chasm behind her was no longer paralysing her, no longer holding her back. Even the drop from the maintenance ladder to the ground wasn't as daunting as she lunged at the top rails. Turning, she stepped hurriedly down and then paused. Taking two quick breaths, steeling herself, Juliet started down the ladder as . . .

Trevor started the engine again, couldn't seem to locate the clutch, and stalled the vehicle. He tut-tutted, another tooth falling from his mouth in the process. He started again, dragged the damaged gear lever into reverse. When the vehicle began to lurch away from the concrete base something cracked, and Trevor looked up in delight to see that a fissure was opening right across its top. The door was buckled outwards. With the joyful sound of grinding and cracking filling the air, Trevor guided the Land Rover back over the rutted ground as . . .

Juliet felt the ladder tilt beneath her. She pulled herself hard against the cold metal, hanging on grimly. Her face was pushed up against a rung. She could hear the groaning, deep inside the mast; like some great animal, trying with a dying effort to raise itself.

I can't move! I can't open my eyes and I can't look down because if I look down I'll be paralysed or I'll fall or . . .

"No!" Juliet banged her head against the rung.

She began to descend again as . . .

Trevor saw Juliet climbing carefully down the ladder and began to laugh again.

No! said the Vorla deep inside. *Don't let her. It's time.*

The laughter died. Trevor's face was a blank and bloodied mask.

"Time," he said, and then stopped the Land Rover. With the precise and mechanical actions of a robot, Trevor engaged first gear, revved—and then brought up the clutch. The Land Rover roared over the churned grass.

His face set, Trevor aimed straight for the largest fissure that had appeared in the base.

One second before the Land Rover slammed into the concrete base, he yelled Juliet's name as . . .

Juliet screamed, feeling the terrifying impact as it shivered and rang in the ladder rungs. The groaning sound became a roar, like some gigantic avalanche. Beneath her, the Land Rover was wrecked beyond repair. It had mounted the fractured platform, both front wheels off the ground, steam gushing from the hood now, the chassis fractured and ravaged. The side and back windows had shattered. Glass lay around the wreck like snow. Juliet looked down and saw that, impossibly, the vehicle was beginning to rise. Its nose was tilting slowly up, like some animal trying to stand on its hind legs. The groaning had become a screeching of steel on steel. The ladder moved. Juliet clung tight again, her heart hammering. The Land Rover stood upright—and then slowly fell over onto its back with a juddering crash.

Something was rising from the ground beneath it.

Something that had flipped the vehicle over onto its back.

A gigantic metal strut, one of the broadcasting mast's support structures, now tearing open a great chunk of earth, sending furrows of ploughed earth in all directions.

Oh God, no, this can't be happening . . .

But it was happening.

Juliet clung to the ladder, still a hundred and fifty feet from the ground, as the broadcasting mast pitched over towards the Chasm.

Her screams were lost in the screeching, rending cacophony as the mast toppled over the edge, the concrete base crumbling as the other steel supports burst from the fractured earth in explosions of soil clods and spewing clay. The cliff edge around the base disintegrated, the out-facing wall of the broadcasting studio falling apart in an avalanche of bricks and dust, showering down into the abyss. The mast was no longer on a smooth trajectory. It juddered and swung out like a crane, hit the edge of the studio with a shivering crash. The base became tangled in the remaining rubble.

And then the mast fell out across the gaping fissure, dropping with a rending screech into the Chasm.

| THE JOURNAL OF
JAY O'CONNOR:
THE MAST

SUDDENLY, I WAS AWAKE.
  I hadn't been able to stop the bad dreams, but something had woken me up. When I looked around, I wished that I was back in that other nightmare place. Because this was the land of *real* nightmares. A place that I really couldn't escape from. I screwed my eyes shut, and willed myself awake. It wouldn't work, because I was already awake—and the reality of where I was, and what was happening, couldn't be wished away.

The bonfire was still burning steadily. The pile of wood had lasted well through the night. Overhead, the sky was its blank and alien grey. Grey smoke from the fire seemed to be drawn up into the blankness, like it was feeding into the sky or something. We were still surrounded by the same ruined buildings and crooked trees. The dump truck stood where we'd left it, with no evidence of the previous night's horrors. No smears or smudges where the Black Stuff had tried to cover it and had been driven away by the light. Aching all over, I pulled myself up and remembered that we'd worked out a "night shift" to watch for any sign of the returning Black Stuff or remnants of the walking dead. I must have crashed out as soon as it was my turn to lay down my head. Apart from all the up-front horror that had burned me out, I was suffering from the same thing that everyone else seemed to be suffering from. Too much happening, too many things that didn't make sense. The Black Stuff. Burning dead people. Little kids with teeth like wolves who could move faster than you could see. The Horsemen. Annie telling us that the quotes the Wayne-thing had been shouting at us were evidence that we'd died and gone to Hell. We couldn't talk about these things yet, couldn't give them headroom without it all threatening to send us round the twist. Maybe everyone thought that with the return of "day" in this place, someone might be able to put it all together and make sense of everything.

But it still felt like Hell this morning.

Now everyone was awake, and looking around for the same something that had woken me up.

"Listen!" said Lisa.

And then I heard it.

A faint cry for help.

"Where's it coming from?" asked Alex.

It was impossible to tell. Everyone got up and began walking around, looking. But the way sound carried in our new world, it could have been coming from anywhere.

There was another sound now—the racing of a car engine, as if someone were pumping the accelerator.

"Look," said Annie, indicating the boy.

He had left Lisa's side and was standing over by the wood-pile, not far from the dump truck. He was pointing, looking back with an anxious expression on his face. He still couldn't use his voice, but was using that expression to tell us we should look where he was pointing.

"What is it?" asked Lisa, hurrying to him.

The boy stabbed a finger out hard again, grabbing her hand when she came close and shaking it. We all looked. There was a ragged screen of trees off to the right, but nothing else to see. When it was obvious no one was able to see what he could see, the boy became agitated, yanking at Lisa's sleeve. The sound came again. A woman's voice? Obviously in terror. And now the racing of the car engine was cut off with a faint crump. There was silence for a moment. Again, the cries came. Again, the sound of the engine.

Then Alex saw what the boy was pointing at.

"Look! Look there . . . just above the trees. It's a radio mast or something."

It was hard to see through the screen of trees, but at last I could make something out.

More cries for help. More racing of an engine. And then another crump.

Gordon caught my eye, then pointed to the dump truck.

"Good idea," I said, hurrying to the cab. Gordon followed. "We'll take the dump truck. You others stay here . . ." Mentally, I caught myself again. *Shit! There you go again. Giving orders.*

"I'll come, too," said Alex.

"This a men-only affair?" sneered Candy. "Racing to the rescue while the 'women' hold the fort and look after the kids?" Annie looked away, and Lisa just shook her head. For the first time, I realised that Candy was finally suffering from a long-delayed hangover. It still didn't give her any excuses. She slumped to her knees on the grass, looking down between her legs, maybe returning to thoughts of what she and Alex had seen in the minimart last night. Damon hadn't said a thing. He looked sort of pathetic now, as if Wayne's death had done his head in. I couldn't work out whether I felt sorry for him now or not. There was no time.

We climbed into the cab, me in the driver's seat, and the engine turned over straight away. The next moment we were bumping over the churned parkland towards the ragged trees and the radio mast beyond. Last night this grassland had been a churning black sea.

"Do you believe it?" I asked Alex as we headed on.

Out of the corner of my eye, I saw him turn to look at me. He knew what I was talking about. Somehow I couldn't look him in the face. I concentrated on the steering as the dump truck pitched and lurched over ruts and cracked earth.

"Are you expecting me to go on again about all the old stuff?" he asked. "About nerve gas, and hallucinations?"

"No. You ditched those ideas yesterday. Remember?"

I felt, rather than saw, Alex nod.

"So, did you see your dead son?"

"Did you see your old teacher?" he asked.

We were silent as the dump truck jolted on. We would soon be at the trees.

"Those things were real," said Alex at last. "Real enough to kill Wayne. But I still don't know whether one of those things was *made* to look like Ricky—the way it made those dead people look like someone else. Like the fella we saw in the shop. Your teacher. It might have put Ricky's face on one of those things. Just to make Candy and I despair even more."

"Difference," said Gordon.

"What difference?" I asked.

"Black Stuff wuh-was . . . wasn't . . . *there.*"

We waited, giving Gordon a chance to explain further, get more words out.

"Wayne kuh-killed . . . one . . . those things."

"Yes," said Alex. "He stamped one of them to death."

"Eh-any . . . Black Stuff? Come . . . come *out?*"

"Black Stuff? You mean . . . you mean like when it came out of those dead people? When the fire came near?"

Gordon nodded his head energetically.

"No," replied Alex.

"Then it . . . wuh-wasn't . . . *there.*"

"Yeah, I see it, Gordon," I said. "The Black Stuff was in the dead people, making them move around. Just like it did with Wayne last night. When the torches came near them— the light, I mean—it burst out of them. Just the way it was

308

bursting out of them at the factory last night. It didn't happen in the mini-mart when that . . . thing was killed."

"Suh-so . . . it . . . wasn't . . . *in* . . ."

"So it wasn't in those children," finished Alex. "Wasn't animating them, or creating them, or giving them new faces. If it was, we would have seen the Black Stuff coming out of the dead one."

There was logic there, but it still didn't give us any real answers.

And now we were in the trees, driving around the twisted boles. There were ruined buildings ahead. A side street seemed to be the only way through, and there was fallen rubble there.

"Hang onto your seats," I said.

Then the dump truck was lurching and swaying over the fallen masonry and shattered wood. It was a rough ride. Above the roaring of the engine and the crash and clatter of the truck as we bounced in our seats there was no way to tell whether those cries for help were still coming. But the boy had pointed out the aerial or the mast or whatever it was, and that was where we were headed. A thought flashed through my mind then. Pointless, maybe. But it seemed to make sense. We didn't know whether this was a trick, or really someone in trouble, or even if we were just imagining it. But at least, right now, we were *doing* something. We weren't just sitting around, letting things happen, waiting for the end. Maybe it was unfair on the others who were left back there, but right at that moment I felt as if the simple action of driving, of finding out, of maybe being ready to offer help, was enough to start making me feel good about . . . about . . . well, about being *human*. There was something else. It had to do with the fact that, until then, we all thought we were the only ones left alive. But here was the possibility that there was someone else, after all. Another survivor. Maybe more than one. And just the prospect of finding that someone else was important. Probably the most important thing since this nightmare business had all begun. I don't know if Gordon and Alex felt that way. Something inside seemed to tell me they did. I hoped they did.

I twisted the wheel and we rounded the corner between houses.

Now we had a clear view of the cliff edge on our side, and the cliff edge over there, on that other island of rock. The Chasm between us was about three, four hundred feet wide. And the island across the way was a hell of a lot smaller than the one we were on. But there was the broadcasting mast, standing right on the cliff edge opposite, next to a building whose facing wall had fallen out and down into the Chasm. I supposed that was a radio station next to it. Maybe I'd passed that place a hundred times in my life, but I didn't recognise it. I'd had a continual problem with that, working out where places were after the quake. Just beyond the radio station, I could see another half-demolished building that was most definitely a supermarket. I recognised the sign: "Greenhaughs." Cars were still in the car park. But no sign of any people.

I brought the dump truck to a halt and we climbed out.

My feet had just hit the ground when I heard that car engine roaring again, and Alex said: "Jesus Christ *Almighty!*"

I looked at him, saw where he was looking, then heard another crump.

This time it was a hell of a lot louder. A cloud of dust sprayed up around the concrete base of the mast, and I heard the crump come again, this time fainter. It was coming from the Chasm, an echo of the impact. Then . . . *crump*, even fainter. Like the Chasm was swallowing the noise or something. Alex and Gordon moved towards the edge. I followed, as the dust cloud on the other side began to settle. There was some kind of movement over there, but it was difficult to make out.

"Mast," said Gordon, pointing.

I looked—but couldn't see anything.

"Woman. On the mast."

I looked again, and now I could see someone up there.

Looking through the gantries and the multiple aerials to the other side, I could see a figure, clinging to a ladder about two-thirds of the way up. And yes, it was a woman, in dark clothes and with long blonde hair. We could hear a screeching sound now. Thin and distant, like metal on metal.

"What the hell is . . . ?" began Alex.

And then the ground around the mast began to move. It was a strange kind of movement, not seeming to make sense at all. The grass and the soil began to furrow and burst all around the concrete base. Something lifted on the other side of the concrete base, and when I saw shattered headlights I realised that it was a car, moving up like it was on a hydraulic lift. We all flinched when a steel girder suddenly burst out of the ground beside the concrete base, showering soil. The base cracked and split.

"Christ," said Alex. "The mast is falling."

And then the concrete base split apart, cables and metal struts burst out of the ground around it, and with that screeching echo filling the air, the entire mast shuddered and tilted. For a moment, it seemed as if it was going to drop straight down into the Chasm. But suddenly the entire structure tilted and hit the side of the building next to it. Rubble exploded out into the Chasm and the impact made the mast change direction. It was falling straight out across the gap, the remains of the concrete base, the anchoring steel girders and cables becoming tangled up in the cracked soil and clay on its own side of the cliff.

"Oh God," said Alex. "The woman on the mast. She's had it."

The mast was directly opposite us now, falling straight down and across.

"How tall is . . . ?" I began.

The mast seemed to be falling all wrong, like the whole thing was in slow motion or something.

"How wide is . . . ?"

I never finished. Because at the same moment, the three of us *knew*.

We turned from the edge, and ran like hell.

The mast was taller than the Chasm was wide. It was going to slam down on our side, tearing a great chunk out of the cliff edge, and taking us down into the pit with it. We didn't look back as we ran, but I could feel the mast coming down, right overhead. I could see Gordon next to me. He glanced back and winced—and I thought: *This is it! We're going DOWN!* I knew that the Black Stuff was somewhere down there, in the darkness, waiting. I hoped we'd be dead as soon as the mast hit. I didn't want to be alive when we fell into that stuff.

There was a terrific crash behind us.

The ground shivered and I whirled to a staggering halt. There was another crash, and a squeal of tearing metal that sounded like an elephant trumpeting or something. The mast had hit our side, just as I'd thought. But not nearly so far in as I'd guessed. It had torn a ten-foot chunk from the edge before disappearing into the Chasm. If we'd stood our ground, we'd have been all right after all. But I don't think anyone could blame us for not taking the chance and just standing there to watch it come down.

"Bloody hell," said Alex. "Bloody *hell!*"

We stood, wiping sweat from our faces, looking back across to the broadcasting station.

Something wasn't right.

We could still see the shattered concrete platform on the other side, and the tangled girders and cables that had erupted from the ground. They were still snared at the edge of the cliff over there; a huge twisted knot of steel, embedded in the cliff edge.

Carefully, I began to walk forward.

As I did so, I could still see the broadcasting mast, projecting down and out into the Chasm. Was it hanging from the edge by that snarled mass of girders and cable? The others followed, equally puzzled. And the closer we got to the cliff edge, the more of the mast was revealed.

It hadn't fallen into the pit.

It was still anchored to the other side in that tangle of metal, lying out across the Chasm like some crazy bridge. Right at the edge, or at least as close to the edge as we were prepared to go in case the ground there had been softened by the impact, I saw what had happened over here.

The top of the mast had hit our side, gouged out a great chunk and then, instead of collapsing into the darkness, had carved out a great gash down the ragged cliff wall. Twenty feet or so below the edge, it had become stuck, its end jammed into the impacted clay. It really had become like some tilted bridge to the other side. The woman we'd seen clinging to the ladder must have been flung down into the Chasm on impact. Step by careful step, we edged forward to look.

And the woman was still there, still clinging to the mast.

She was struggling now, pulling herself around on the ladder and trying to climb up to what was now the topside of the mast. I could see straight away how she'd managed to save herself from being torn off. She'd pushed her arms and legs through the rungs of the ladder, wrapping herself around tight. She couldn't have known that the mast was going to wedge itself as it had, but I admired her coolness for hanging on like that when all she could count on was the entire structure just falling down into the darkness. Luckily for her, the ladder up the side of the mast hadn't been yanked free on impact.

"Hang on!" I yelled, and realised how stupid my words were. As if she was going to do anything else. She looked up at us then, and even though she was a long way off I seemed to feel waves of relief coming from her. She shouted something, but we couldn't hear her words.

"Someone else!" said Gordon, and when we looked across the Chasm to the other side, we could see that another figure had appeared beside the shattered concrete base of the mast. It was a man, and he didn't look to be in good shape. He staggered on the cliff edge, falling to his knees beside the tangled cables and girders. Even from that distance, I could see that there was blood on his face. Had he been on the mast too? Come to think of it, what the hell had the woman been doing up the mast in the first place if it was balanced so close to the cliff edge?

"What are we going to do?" said Alex, looking down into the pit and out across to where the woman still hung onto the mast. "I don't see how we can get to her."

He was right. Like I said, it was about twenty feet down to the mast on our side, but with no way of telling how safe the gouged cliff edge would be.

"She's going to have to do the work," I said to Alex. "No way of knowing how long the mast is going to stay like that. Even if one of us was able to get down on it, the extra weight might just be enough to drag it loose." I shouted to her: "Climb along to us! We'll pull you up!"

But what the hell with?

Then I remembered.

"There's rope or cable or something in the dump truck. Next to a toolbox in the cab . . ."

Before I could head back, Gordon was already running to the truck.

"Bloody hell," said Alex. "I don't believe it."

"What . . . ?"

When I looked back across the Chasm, I could see what had surprised him.

The injured man was yanking and pulling at the nearest of the tangled cables.

"What's he doing?"

"I think he's . . . no, he *can't* be!"

But he was. The man was trying to yank the massive tangle free. Now he was behaving like a maniac, cursing and shrieking at the twisted cable. Kicking it, beating at it with both hands. He *wanted* the mast to fall into the pit.

"Leave it alone!" I yelled. "Are you fucking *mad* or something?"

"*Yes!*" Now we could hear the woman's voice as she finally managed to climb around to the "top" of the mast. Her long blonde hair was flowing around her head as if there were a wind coming up from below. "*He is! For God's sake, help me!*"

Something clanged on the mast, raising a small cloud of dust about fifty feet behind the woman. It was the man. In a complete rage at his inability to do anything about the tangle, he had begun scooping up loose stones from the cliff edge and was throwing them at her. Now he was screaming at the top of his voice, like an animal.

"*Please!*" yelled the woman again, and she began edging along one of the struts on the mast, on all fours.

Another stone whanged against steel.

What the hell was going on here?

Gordon reappeared with the rope, quickly unspooling it to see how much we had. More than enough to reach down to the mast if the woman could reach our side.

There was a cry. When we looked back, she was clinging tight to the mast. She'd either slipped, or the mad bastard on the other side had hit her with a stone. Slowly, she rose to all fours again and came slowly on. Giving another yell of rage, her attacker began prowling backwards and forwards on the cliff edge, looking for more ammunition. This time he was able to find a chunk of heavy-duty pipe. If he hit her with that it would knock her straight off and down into the Chasm. Now she was about fifty feet out from our side.

"Tie this around me," I said to Gordon, shoving an end of the rope into his hands. "Loop the other end around yourself and Alex."

"What are you going to do?" asked Alex as Gordon whipped the rope around my midriff.

"I'm going down onto the mast. See if I can get hold of her."

"But the extra weight . . . ?"

315

"If he hits her, she'll go over . . . *shit!*"

Whirling end over end, the heavy-duty pipe flew through the air, missing the woman and the aerial by less than six feet before vanishing into the Chasm. She saw it flash past. Her hair flew in a blonde cloud when she jerked her head back, either in anger or fear, and then yelled: "*Go to hell, Trevor!*"

He's already here, said a little voice inside me.

Then I saw the Crying Kid in my mind's eye, being chased away with stones.

"Move well back from the edge!" I said to Alex and Gordon. "Give me about ten feet . . . that's it. Now let me have more when I shout for it."

I saw Trevor whatsisname hunting for something else to throw.

Then I turned my back and lowered myself over the edge.

I concentrated hard on the mast, tried to convince myself that the iron gantry was ground, and there wasn't a sickening, stupendous drop into God knew what just beneath it. The cliff edge was cracked and crumbling. Clods of earth showered from the edge as they lowered me down. The soft soil that formed the upper part of the cliff edge didn't seem to have any solidity at all. But I couldn't allow myself to think about that.

Quicker than seemed possible, my feet made contact with steel.

I scrabbled around, found handholds on a bent aerial dish that looked pretty solidly screwed into the gantry, and yelled: "Okay! Keep it there!" Now I could see that the edge of the mast had carved out a deep V shape in the cliff wall. I prayed that it was as solidly anchored there as it looked.

The woman was about forty feet away from me, and still coming ahead on all fours. Behind her, something clanged again. We both ducked instinctively and I felt the vibration shivering in the mast beneath me. Her friend had found something else to throw.

"You can make it!" I shouted across to her, looking for some

316

way to move closer. There was a snarl of wiring, difficult to get through. One way or the other, it would have to be cleared if she was going to make it over to this side. I began yanking it to one side, trying not to think about what the extra weight and my actions might do to the way the mast was balanced.

I could see the man on the other side now. He'd gone completely apeshit. He was shrieking and jumping about over there. The woman turned to look back. I had to keep her attention focused on our side.

"Friend of yours?" I called.

When she looked back, I saw her face properly for the first time.

She was hanging in space on what was left of a four-hundred-foot broadcasting mast. By rights, she should already have been flung down into the Chasm. There was a madman over there, trying to do everything in his power to make sure that she fell. I was hanging over the edge on a rope that hadn't been tested, with a cliff edge that seemed to be made of soft loam, crumbling all around me. Below us somewhere was the Black Stuff. We were in a bizarre new world—Hell, if the Wayne-thing was to be believed—with horrors on every side.

So the next thing that happened might seem ludicrous. But it happened anyway.

She smiled at me, and I smiled back.

And she was the most beautiful woman I'd ever seen in my life.

"Just got to choose my friends more carefully in the future," she said.

"Some new friends over here if you think you can make it." Head down now, concentrating hard, she came on.

"Jay!" yelled Alex from up above somewhere.

"Yeah!"

"He's coming down—*on to the mast!*"

I shoved more wiring from my sightline. Sure enough, the

madman was clambering hand over hand through the tangled wire and girders on the other side, trying to find footholds so that he could lower himself down onto the mast. As I pulled and shoved at the wiring, I saw him manoeuvring himself down. He moved as if he didn't care whether he fell into the Chasm or not. I knew what he was going to do even before he started to do it.

"What's your name?" I tried to keep my voice calm, but it didn't come out that way.

Without looking up, she answered: "Juliet." She was about thirty feet away now.

"Juliet, you'll have to move faster. Don't panic. Don't worry." I finally managed to yank the wiring away, and began to crawl out across the mast towards her.

And then our friend Trevor reached the mast on his side. Bracing his back against the crumbling cliff edge, he began to stamp down hard on the gantry with both feet. Again I could feel the juddering impacts in my hands through the metalwork. Juliet cried out and tried to look back.

"*Don't* . . . don't look back," I said. "Just keep on coming."

I moved forward again. Was I going to help the situation by moving out to her? Or should I just stay where I was? The mast tapered near its top end, with only enough room on the thin girders for one person to move. If I went out to meet her, I'd just end up having to back off again, maybe impede her progress.

Mad Trevor was shrieking again when the mast showed no signs of collapsing into the pit. His feet were drumming on the metalwork. I realised then that I was stalling. I had to get out there across the mast.

"Alex? Gordon?"

"Yeah!"

"Give me another twenty feet. I've got to go out there. If the mast falls, get ready."

I waited until I saw the rope looping down from above. The sight of it made me feel weak, aware of the drop beneath. Where the hell was the anger when I needed it? Gritting my teeth, I gathered up the rope and pushed myself out across the mast. If Trevor did succeed in knocking it loose, I had to make sure that the rope didn't snag anywhere. If it did, and Trevor did succeed, then we were *all* going down into the Chasm, Alex and Gordon dragged over the side with us.

Twenty feet out, Juliet and I met face to face.

As if the whole thing had been stage managed, just to make everything worse, the mast gave this moaning sound. It was as if every part of it was groaning under the pressure, ready to fall away. Juliet's hand flashed out and I grabbed it. Right at that moment, it was like electricity passing between us, welding our hands together.

The mast shuddered, and was silent. Unmoving.

From the other side of the Chasm, Mad Trevor began to scream in frustration again.

We had both been holding our breath, and exhaled at the same time. Juliet's skin was cold, and I could see from her face that she was suffering. It was marble white, probably from shock, and there were scratches on her forehead. I heaved a coil of rope over her head, pulled it down around her waist, under one arm. We put an arm around each other like we were in some sort of crazy clinch, and I began shuffling back along the girder. Juliet kept pace with me.

I didn't have to say anything about hurrying.

From the other side, Trevor had stopped screaming. He'd also stopped stamping on the gantry. I didn't feel like thanking anyone for small mercies.

We clung together close, breathing into each other's faces as we moved. And something else strange was happening. We were in fear of our lives, *real* fear. But our physical closeness, stuck out in space on this girder and with horror waiting for us far below was . . . well, it was the most *intimate* thing I'd ever experienced in my life. For a moment, the feeling was so intense that I couldn't move. Then I heard her teeth chattering, and forced myself on.

I knew what was going to happen next. We'd just get to the cliff edge, and the whole fucking thing would screech and groan and fall away, just when we thought we'd made it. Which is why I couldn't believe it when I felt the snared wiring behind me that I'd shoved aside to get to her. We were nearly there. The rope was coiled and looped behind me. I twisted around and yelled:

"Take up the slack!"

Both shuddering, we watched the rope being pulled up. When it was nearly taut, I yelled again: "*Whoah!*" The rope halted. Part of me wanted to get up there as fast as possible before everything turned bad again, the way things had of turning bad in our new world. Another part told me to take it easy, don't rush, don't make a mistake at the last minute.

Forehead to forehead, I said to Juliet: "I'm going to have to stand."

"I can't let go of you."

"I've got to stand, Juliet. So I can get a proper grip on the rope."

"I want to let go, but I don't think I can."

"Then, when I'm up . . . you're going to have to stand too."

"What's happened to everyone? No one came. Trevor had me trapped over there. And no one came."

"Someone's here now. There are others. Up there. Waiting for you."

Juliet screwed her eyes shut and nodded her head.

"Okay," I went on. "Now, I'm still going to hold you, but you've got to let go of me. Just for a moment."

"I know the rules for this sort of stuff."

"What?"

"Don't look down."

"Right, yeah. Here I go. Are you ready?"

"Yeah . . ."

"Okay."

"Okay . . ."

"Juliet?"

"Yeah?"

"You've got to let go."

"Okay . . ."

Slowly, I raised myself on my haunches. Still slowly, and praying that the mad bastard wasn't going to start throwing stones again, I began to rise. I was concentrating so hard on the cliff face that I couldn't even look back over there to see if he was up to anything. I braced my hand against the crumbling soil and clay. It didn't seem like there was anything solid there to reassure them.

"Alex, Gordon! Tighter!"

The rope tautened.

Both feet braced on the girder, I leaned down to take Juliet's hand.

A noise from out across the mast made me look up.

Mad Trevor was shuffling along the gantry towards us on all fours. Moving a hell of a lot faster than we had, because he didn't really care whether he fell off or not.

"What is it . . . ?" Juliet had seen my expression change; was beginning to look back.

"No, don't look back! Or down. Just give me your hand. Stand up here next to me."

Juliet reached up slowly and took my hand. Slowly again, she began to rise. I could feel the drop beneath us, could see how fast Trevor was moving. He was halfway across the mast, in no time at all. If he reached us before we could be pulled to safety . . .

And now Juliet was standing, each of us with one arm around the other's waist while I held onto the rope, and she looked back to see what had scared me.

"Oh, *Christ*!" I felt her seize up with terror. We wobbled on the girder. Leaning heavily on the rope, I righted us again.

"*Julietttt!*" screamed the madman. "*You're not playing the game, you bitch! You've got to suffer!*"

His face didn't look human when he glared up at us. Something terrible had happened to him. It was a white mask streaked with blood. He lowered his head again and crawled on.

I kicked my foot into a twisted coil, hoping it would act like a toehold. But I couldn't loop any more of the loose rope between Juliet and me around us to try to bind us together.

"Hands around my neck!" I hissed at Juliet. I grabbed her waist tight. Again that crazy, out-of-place intimacy. Then I yelled: "Pull us up! *Now!*"

Maybe I'd expected it to be a slow climb, with the weight of two people on the rope. What I certainly didn't expect was that we'd be hauled straight off the mast and slammed into the cliff wall. The impact winded us. We clung tighter, spinning and dangling there as showers of dirt and soil fell around us, crackling down on the mast and spraying off into the Chasm. I tried to brace my feet. But now we were being yanked again.

And there was the cliff edge.

The next part is confused. Just a breathless, frenzied clambering to get up there. I remember that Juliet had raised a leg, so I grabbed the lower part and shoved her hard. Alex was shouting words of encouragement. Then there was less strain and for a horrible moment I thought I'd lost her. But there she was, now topside, on her knees. Leaning back for me as I kicked my leg up and tried to get my knee on the edge.

And then something seized my foot and dragged me back down.

More soil showered around me. Up above, there was more yelling. This time Juliet was shouting too. But I was dizzy and whatever had grabbed my foot now had hold of my calf. I spun, dirt in my eyes, clawing at the cliff edge with my free hand and trying to find something that I could hang on to. Below, something screeched and I felt sure that the mast was falling away. The rope was tangled. We'd managed to save Juliet, but I was going to be dragged down into the darkness, kicking and screaming, while that Black Stuff boiled below like a black sea, waiting to swallow me.

Now I was going up again while the screaming and yelling went on all around me.

My head was slammed against the cliff wall. Everything became even more confused. I was flying upwards like I had wings. Now the great grey sky was tilting and I could feel solid ground beneath me. Had they managed to pull me up after all? I tried to turn, still dizzy. There was a lot of activity. People were shouting, someone was screaming like an animal. There was some kind of fight going on around me, none of it making any sense. I saw Juliet's hair flying. Then someone kicked me in the ribs and I felt sharp pain there. I rolled over.

I was back on the cliff edge.

And Mad Trevor was standing over me, his face a leering mask of blood.

He began to laugh. How the hell had *he* got up here?

Then there was a strange sound. Like a heavy, clunking blow, and a loud jangling, like bedsprings breaking.

Mad Trevor looked puzzled. Then he fell sideways, out of sight.

Behind him, I saw Gordon, holding his guitar by the neck. He'd used it like a club, slamming Trevor over the head.

"Shit!" he said, ignoring me and hastily turning the guitar around to look at the strings. Two of them had broken, curling away from the fret board. "*Shit!*"

"Nice . . ." I started to say . . . *music.*

But the grey backdrop behind and above Gordon faded to black, and suddenly I wasn't there anymore.

| **THE JOURNAL OF JAY O'CONNOR: THE END OF THE WORLD AND OTHER INCONVENIENCES**

WHEN I CAME AROUND, ALL I COULD SEE WAS THE grey sky.

But there was something different about it now. It wasn't just the same monotonous grey. There were . . . cracks . . . in the sky. Thin cracks. I shut my eyes, opened them and tried again. The cracks were still there. Now I realised that it wasn't grey at all. It was a different shade. And there was light shining from below. Light from the bonfire? No, this wasn't the stark light from the fire. It was more of a comforting orange light. I looked around.

Was I really awake?

I closed my eyes, and tried a second time.

I wasn't lying out in the open under the grey sky, next to the bonfire.

I was in a small bedroom, on a bed, with a neat quilt tucked in around me. The grey above me was the ceiling of the bedroom, with small spider's-web cracks in the plaster. Something had happened. But not the quake, not all the horrors that had followed. That had all been part of a bad dream. Thank Christ for that. No, all I had to do now was lie here and think; try to work out where I was, and what had happened to me to give me such bad nightmares, or hallucinations, or whatever. My mouth was dry, my head hurt, and when I tried to turn to have a better look at where I was, my side ached like hell.

"You're awake," said a female voice.

She was sitting not far from the bed, in the corner, slumped back in an easy chair. The same long blonde hair, the same dark clothes. This time her face wasn't white. It was bathed in the warm orange glow from the lamp on the bedside table. And she was smiling the same beautiful smile. The girl from the dream.

"Juliet . . ."

"Juliet DeLore. I would have introduced myself properly, but what with one thing and another we just didn't seem to have the time. Your name's Jay O'Connor."

"It's the only thing I think I'm sure about."

"Just a moment." Juliet slid out of the armchair. When her hair moved around her face, I could see that there was a sticking plaster on her forehead. There were others on her fingers, and a white bandage around her wrist. She moved to the bedroom door, opened it a crack, and said: "He's awake."

The next moment two familiar faces appeared in the doorway, now pushing through and smiling. Gordon and Alex.

"How are you feeling?" asked Alex.

I groaned.

"Tell me it's all a dream . . ."

"Sorry," said Alex. "Can't do that."

Gordon smiled again, thumping a fist on his chest as if to prove that he was solid. He held up his forefinger and thumb in an "okay" sign. Juliet moved back to the armchair and curled there, catlike, with her legs drawn up.

I gestured around the bedroom, waiting for some answers. Now I was more aware of the pain in my head, and in my side. Alex went on.

"We're still in . . . or I should say *on* . . . what's left of Edmonville. No change, apart from the deluxe surroundings.

With any luck, we should have spent our last night out in the park, next to a bonfire."

Gordon moved to the bedroom window and gently pulled aside a curtain. It was daylight outside. Juliet switched off the bedside lamp.

"How did you do that?" I asked, stupidly.

"Easy," she replied, smiling. "Finger and a thumb on the switch. See?" She switched the light on again.

"But you shouldn't be able . . . I mean *we* shouldn't . . . oh Christ, I don't know *what* I mean."

"We've just used the talent at our disposal," Alex went on.

"Talent?"

Annie and Lisa had appeared in the doorway.

"Us," said Lisa. "Or I should say Annie, with a little assistance from me."

"Wait a moment, wait a moment! This is too much, too quick. Start again. How long have I been out?"

"Three days," said Gordon, holding up three fingers just in case I hadn't heard him right.

"What?"

"He's right," said Alex. "Three days. Ever since Juliet . . . how shall I put it? Ever since she dropped in on us."

"Three *days*?"

"You had a bang on the head from our other visitor. Must have been concussed."

"You've had us worried," said Annie. "On the second day, you were raving and ranting. Had a high fever. We weren't sure if you were going to come out of it. Then today the fever dropped and your pulse evened out. How do you feel now?"

"Like I'm still waiting to wake up."

"Join the club," said Lisa.

I tried to sit up and felt the pain stab again. Juliet leaned across and pushed me down with the flat of her hand, the smile changing into a look of real concern. I hadn't seen anyone look that concerned about me for a long, long time.

"Rest up," she said. "Give it some time."

"How are you doing?" I asked, remembering the mast. "You okay?"

"I'm okay . . . "

"She's not telling the whole truth," said Lisa. "For two days she was shaken up so badly she could hardly talk. When she did start talking, it was like she couldn't stop. Juliet's had an . . . " Lisa looked to her for a description.

"An *interesting* few days," replied Juliet. "Not something I'd want to put in a travel agent's brochure. Where I used to work, by the way."

Lisa saw the cloud appear on her face and quickly continued. "Anyway, she talked it all out. And she's okay now. We're *all* okay."

"Speak for yourself," slurred a voice from the next room. It was Candy. I pretended not to see the tense expression on Alex's face.

"Candy's anaesthetic," he said, trying to keep things light. From a starting point where I hadn't cared too much for his attitude, things had changed a lot. Alex was okay in my book.

It was all coming back to me now. The fallen mast. My first sighting of Juliet. The haul on the rope. And the madman who'd thrown stones and who now, I realised, had caught up with us at the last and tried to drag me back down into the Chasm.

"That bloody madman . . . Trevor?" I looked over at Juliet. She looked away, kneading her fingers in her lap, now stroking a strand of hair from her face. She was trying not to react.

"He was hanging onto you," said Alex. "Gordon and I dragged you both back up. Then he attacked Juliet. I brought him down. For a while, I thought he was going to get the better of us. There's something . . . well, something . . . " Alex was suddenly looking uncomfortable. Juliet was still working hard at giving no reaction—" . . . not *right* with him."

There was a silence, and I could sense there was something

327

they either weren't ready to tell me yet, or were unable to deal with.

"I saw Gordon belt him with his guitar," I said. "It was the last thing I *did* see. Cheers, Gordon."

"Two strings," said Gordon, sadly shaking his head as if he'd lost two dear friends.

"Now tell me about the light," I said, pointing to the bedside lamp. "And please tell me I'm not dreaming about that." It looked *great*.

"We've had two nights by the bonfire," Annie went on. "The Black Stuff didn't come back. And there weren't any more . . . well, you know, any more of *them*. But we decided, Lisa and I, that we weren't going to have any more of it."

"So," Lisa said, "we did something about it."

"We got some stuff from our hardware store, and after two hard days searching through the rubble we were able to rig up a petrol-driven generator in the basement. Sorted out the electrics in here. Well, most of it anyway. Hey presto! They said 'Let there be light.' And there was light." Annie was pleased with herself, and didn't care who knew it.

"Where exactly are we?" I asked.

"Promise you won't laugh," said Alex.

I just looked at him.

He cleared his throat, guiltily wiping the smile away.

"We're in a three-star boarding house. Rooms for everyone, with *en suite* facilities—not that there's any running water, of course. But I guess you can't have everything.

"Except a fleet of rescue helicopters."

"Well, there's that, I suppose."

"But the Black Stuff . . ." I began.

"It has a name," said Alex.

Everyone was trying to stay light, but the tension kept creeping in.

"A name?"

"It's called the Vorla."

"And how exactly do we know that?"

"Our new arrival, Trevor. He told us."

"How the hell does he know?"

"Because . . . well, because . . . " Alex looked at Juliet.

She was still looking down into her lap. With a measured voice, trying to keep calm, she said: "Because it's inside him."

Everyone waited for her to go on. She was having difficulty, but now I had to know.

"Trevor kept me . . . locked up, after the earthquake. I don't know how and when it happened. But some time during that time, what he calls the Vorla got inside his head, inside his body. It's still there, controlling him."

"You've seen it?" I asked Juliet. "The . . . what is it called, the Vorla?"

"It came up the mast after me. Black liquid, flowing up against gravity. Horrible. Something happened to stop it, but I still don't understand that part."

"I mean, you've seen it in Trevor?"

"Not when I was over there, but since I came here . . . "

"We've all seen it, Jay. In his eyes."

"Where is he?"

"There's an extension out back with two or three extra rooms. We put him in one of those because . . . well, because we didn't want him in the house. No one would feel at ease. We've got him locked in a room there. Tied up. Curtains drawn for the light. He had agonies during the day because of it, but the stuff—I mean, the Vorla—didn't burst out of him the way it burst out of the dead people in the light. We've seen it in his eyes. For the most part, he keeps them shut, and that keeps the light out. We don't understand what's happening to him but . . . "

"But it's horrible," said Candy, appearing in the doorway. She had a bottle in her hand, and was well on the way to oblivion. No one said anything for a long time. And then the boy also appeared in the doorway, yawning. He had been in the room beyond, asleep. He pushed past Candy and moved to his usual comforter, Lisa, snuggling in the folds of her arms.

"You've got him tied up good and tight?" I asked. "No way he can get free?"

"Trussed like a mummy," said Lisa. "When I tie a knot, it stays tied. Believe me."

"Should . . . should . . . " Gordon smacked a fist into the palm of his hand. "Shoulda th-thrown. Him. Over the edge."

"We thought about it, Jay," Alex went on. "But . . . well, you know. That would be murder. That stuff is in him. But he's not dead. And he's still *human*, whatever he's done."

Juliet remained silent.

"Is there enough light here to keep the Vorla away?" I asked.

"You've woken up just in time," said Annie. "Lisa and I have worked out a little surprise. You feel like getting up?"

"Try and stop me."

Groggily, I rose from the bed. With a little help from my friends.

Heavisides' boarding house was a small bed-and-breakfast establishment that had suffered relatively little damage in the quake. Some cracks in the plasterwork, a fallen chimney, and a few slates. That was it. It was a detached house, and had maybe been a private residence in the past, converted to its present use. It had just the right number of rooms. Like it was custom-built for us, really. The others had already christened it the Rendezvous. I never did get around to asking why.

Annie and Lisa were bursting with pride, wanting to show off their petrol generator in the basement, and tell me how they'd gone about hooking everything up. But they could tell that I wasn't up to a long tour, since I had to hang onto Gordon's shoulder for most of the time. So they decided to go straight to the most important part.

"This *is* going to be a good surprise, isn't it?" I asked, when they opened the front door and everyone moved out into the garden. Slates were still embedded in the grass like bizarre ornaments. "Most of the surprises so far haven't been what I would have asked for on my Christmas list."

"Keep your fingers crossed," said Annie, and she walked out of the garden into the middle of the street. She stepped over thin cables on the way, kicking them as if wanting to keep them apart. Now I could see that the same cables were lying all over the street, stretching away on both sides past ruined houses, a shattered bicycle repair shop, and another garage. Some of the cables went into the garage. Others headed back to the house and around the garden wall, vanishing around the side of the Rendezvous. We had searched this part of the town, hunting for dead bodies. And the cables hadn't been there then.

Annie headed for the garage, kicking the wires as she went, the way that some people buying a new car might kick the tyres. I looked at the others, and saw how tense they'd become again.

Lisa was standing in the doorway of the boarding house, like she was waiting for a signal. When an engine started up in the garage, and Annie appeared in the entrance with a wave, I knew that was just what she had been waiting for. Lisa waved back, and vanished inside. Now both women were gone.

"What happens next?" I asked.

"Just wait," said Alex.

Someone took my hand. I recognised the coolness of the skin.

It was Juliet. She didn't look at me. We just stood there, holding hands and waiting.

Something fizzed and sparked halfway down the street. A shower of sparks fell from nowhere into the street.

"Shit!" said Gordon.

Had those sparks fallen from one of the streetlights? From the garage, I heard the growing whine of an engine or another generator.

And the next moment most of the streetlamps still standing

on the street suddenly began to glow. There were other lamps there, strung out along the fractured pavements and all connected, like the streetlamps, to the tangle of cables that ran down the middle of the road. There were two great round contraptions that looked like searchlights. They'd been aimed, not at the sky, but directly across the street at different angles. I could see that streetlamps behind the boarding house had also been connected and were also beginning to glow.

Suddenly the entire street was lit up, and even though night had yet to fall on what remained of Edmonville, it seemed that the blank grey of the sky overhead was disappearing. For the first time since the quake, we had proper light thanks to Annie and Lisa.

Annie appeared in the garage doorway, hands on hips. She dusted her hands extravagantly and came back towards us, grinning. Lisa stepped out into the garden, holding the boy's hands and swinging him around in joy. The boy laughed out loud. They embraced. Candy turned away to swig at her bottle and Damon sat on the garden wall, swinging his legs and looking at nothing in particular. But everyone else was . . . well, we were ecstatic.

"I don't think the Vorla is going to like that one little bit," said Alex.

If I'd felt good about seeing that small bedside table lamp and its beautiful orange glow, I felt like my heart was going to burst or something. I can't tell you the way it felt. All of us standing in the ruins of this God-forsaken place, not knowing what was going to happen next. By rights, none of us should have made it. But here we were—thanks to Annie and Lisa—standing in the light that they, that *we* had made. A single street in the ruins. A street that had seen death and horror and the walking dead. But now we'd brought life back to it again.

No one spoke.

Juliet squeezed my hand harder, and we looked at each other. She'd been through her own hell before getting here, but knew that she could feel that . . . that . . . *blaze* inside. This wasn't Hell anymore. Hell was where the Vorla lived, down in the Chasm, in the darkness. Not up here in our light.

I looked at Alex. There were tears in his eyes, reflecting the light.

Gordon slapped him on the shoulder.

"Drink?" he said.

"A bloody good idea," Alex replied. "Let's celebrate."

Back in the boarding house, in the living-room area, we opened some bottles of champagne that Gordon had found in a nearby shop. We tried to ignore the bits and pieces of everyday material that were still lying around the place, evidence of the people who had boarded here. Photographs on windowsills, clothes hanging in wardrobes. We also tried not to think about what had happened to those people. We just felt good about the lights outside, and the knowledge that the Vorla would be kept away from us as long as they were burning.

We all shared our stories again, for the benefit of Juliet. When it came to the Black Stuff, I mean the Vorla, it was clear that she could relate to that. But I couldn't tell what she was thinking when we told her about the living dead people, and the burning, and the high-speed kids with the teeth. Eventually Juliet told me her own story. About Trevor Blake and her ordeal over on the other side. It was a story that needed no exaggeration, and I knew that only someone special could have got through what she'd endured without just giving in completely, surrendering to that mad bastard, or just cracking up altogether. Her voice never wavered.

"How long can we keep the lights going?" I asked at last.

"Well, not forever," said Annie. "We'll have to be careful. Keep them maintained. But the main thing is the fuel supply. We've found quite a bit in the garage, and there's a depot full of the stuff. We'll need to siphon what petrol we can find from the tanks of all the other vehicles still lying around here."

"And what happens when it runs out?" slurred Damon. He'd taken to sitting next to Candy, who was well out of it by now. But he seemed to be wanting to catch her up, bottle in hand.

"We'll just have to think about that nearer the time," said Lisa. "If everything else fails, we just go back to lighting bonfires again."

"There are other things to think about, as well," I said. "We have to find out how much food we've got here. How long it'll last."

"And what we're going to do about basic things," continued Annie. "The conveniences—or should I say inconveniences. Like if you'll pardon my French, *le pissoir*."

"What?" slurred Damon.

"Toilet," said Gordon.

"Up until now," Annie went on, "we've all been, well . . . making do. But now we're under one roof, we're going to have to come up with something a little better than potties under the bed. Needless to say, I hope no one's been using the toilet facilities in here, since there's nowhere for anything to go. Tomorrow, I'm going to have another look at that factory unit, see if I can find a portable toilet. The kind they use on building sites. There's bound to be something there."

"The electrics are fixed . . . " I said, suddenly getting an idea. "In the house, I mean." I looked around, saw the television set in the corner. "Maybe . . . "

"First thing I did," said Alex. "As soon as we had power, I switched it on. Nothing on any of the channels. Just static. Like the time we tried the telephones and the radios."

"Not good," I said, and everyone was quiet for a long time.

I knew what had to come next. "There's something else to discuss," I said. "Unless you've discussed it while I was out." They all knew what I was talking about, and I could tell by the silence and the way everyone had found something else to look at that maybe they'd been avoiding the issue. Even the blank televisions and radios hadn't prompted anybody to start talking about the obvious. "Something that we haven't got round to," I went on. "Maybe because we don't want to think about it."

Lisa cleared her throat. "You mean when we saw the Four Horsemen. And what Wayne . . . or at least whatever Wayne had become . . . quoted from the Bible at us."

"We need to decide for ourselves," I went on. "Well, whether . . . whether . . . "

"Whether the world has really ended," said Alex. "Whether this is the Apocalypse. Or whether it's something else."

So we talked on, aware that the night was closing in beyond our circle of light. And during that talk, we went over the same old ground, without getting any nearer to the truth of it. Either this was the End of the World, what Lisa had called the Day of Reckoning, or else . . . well, or else it wasn't. One thing was for sure. This was no fantasy. We didn't have to pinch each other to believe that we were made of flesh and blood, that we could bleed, that we could die. That we were terrified. Alex and Candy had seen Wayne killed, and no one doubted that. Fantasies didn't kill people.

We talked in circles.

"Trevor," I said. It seemed I had a way of bringing the conversation to a stop. "If the Black Stuff . . . the Vorla . . . is inside him somehow, then it must have the answers. Has anyone spoken to him? Asked him questions?"

Silence again.

"Then that's who we have to speak to," I went on. "Show me where he is and . . . " I tried to stand up, but my head began aching like hell. I slumped back again. "Must be the champagne." I gave a hollow laugh.

"Sit back and take it easy," said Alex. "And no, we haven't had a question-and-answer with our mad friend. Just being in the same room as him is enough to freak anyone out."

"Okay," I said. "Show me where he is and . . . "

Gordon laughed, pointing a finger at me.

"Wh-who said. You. Leader."

I must have looked at him like a gormless idiot, because it set him off even louder. "No one! Voted! You!"

Then I realised. I was doing it again. Taking charge. I laughed and the pain hurt my head *and* my side. I put my head in my hands, trying not to laugh. And suddenly, Annie and Lisa, Alex and Gordon were all laughing. The boy burst out laughing too, even though he couldn't understand what was so funny, was hugging his sides and curling up next to Gordon on the sofa. Even Juliet, who hadn't been here from the beginning, was laughing. Damon gave vent to a loud snort and suddenly everyone was laughing fit to bust. It wasn't such a great joke. But we were laughing and laughing, and feeling good. Maybe it was the lights outside, bathing the street and keeping the darkness away. Maybe there were shadows of grief in there, and huge relief that we were all still alive after everything we'd been through. Maybe it was the champagne. But it was good, and it was healing, and very, very special. There was something else there too. It was like that first night at the bonfire, when the dead had come to taunt us and Gordon had played his music. That music had been special—it had somehow bound us all together, and it had kept the nightmares away. The laughter was doing the same thing now.

When it settled down, there was a glow in the room. No other way to describe it.

"Okay," I said. "I'll speak to him in the morning. See if I can get something out of him."

"See?" said Alex. "Doing it again. Bossing every fucker about."

And the laughter had begun again. My head was banging like a bloody drum, my side burning. But I couldn't stop it. No one could stop our laughter. Candy emerged, bleary-eyed from her sleep. Wiping tears from his eyes, Alex moved to her.

"The hell with it," I said. "I'm going back to bed."

"Breakfast in bed in the morning, sir?" asked Annie.

"Of course," I said, trying to adopt a snotty accent, and failing completely. "And don't forget my early-morning call."

"When Hell freezes over," said Lisa, and we were all laughing again. Candy was awake now, looking at us as if we'd all gone mad. Perhaps we had.

I headed for my room. Annie was confident about the power setup, but she and Lisa decided to go and check in the garage. Perhaps it was the laughter and the lights outside, but the boy seemed confident enough now to let them go without running after them. He sat next to Gordon, fascinated by his guitar, and Gordon let him pluck at the remaining strings. He still wouldn't talk. Still wouldn't come out of that place inside his head where he had been living since the day of the quake. But the smile on his face looked good. Damon remained out of it, sleeping on the sofa, and as I headed upstairs Alex carried Candy to their room. Gordon indicated that he'd stay up with the boy until the others came back.

We were all of us too exhausted to even think about some kind of "watch." Part of me almost suggested it, but the laughter about the "leader" thing had taken the sting out of everything. If no one else thought about it, I was going to say nothing. Maybe it was foolish, what with Trevor out there somewhere in the extension. But I had to take them at their word, that he was trussed up and safely stowed away. And—I don't know—just raising the issue now was like putting a damper on the good feeling we'd experienced. I went back to "my" room.

I suppose I slept as soon as my head touched the pillow, bathed in that wonderful, strangely comforting orange light.

Some time later, God knows how much later, I was suddenly awake and alert.

Fear stabbed through me.

The light was still on, but I glanced around the room,

listening for that sound the Vorla always made when it was near. Like a black sea on the move; like a hundred thousand mad, whispering voices.

"I'm sorry," said the silhouette in the doorway.

It was Juliet.

"Oh, God. Yeah. Juliet . . . "

She remained there, saying nothing else.

I sat up, groaning, waiting for her to go on.

She brushed a long strand of that backlit golden hair from her face. I couldn't see her expression, only her silhouette.

"What's wrong?" I asked. "Are you all right?"

"Jay."

"Yes?"

"I don't want to be alone tonight."

Neither of us spoke for a while.

Then I said: "Neither do I."

She pushed the door closed when she came in.

And I found something then, and for the rest of that night, that I'd never even known I'd lost. Something about the real me. Something that I was able to share, and give, and I knew that from then on I would never be the same person again.

NIGHT VISITORS

ANNIE AND LISA HAD FIXED UP A ROOM ON the ground floor for themselves, giving them good access to the basement and the generator, should they need it. A bed had also been set up in there, in the corner, for the boy. Candy had glared at them throughout, clearly feeling that it wasn't right that he should be sharing the same room. But nothing had been said.

The others had already gone to bed when Annie and Lisa decided to check on the garage across the street, leaving Gordon and the boy on the sofa. The boy seemed happier, more aware, than usual. Gordon allowed him to pick at the guitar, becoming lost in his thoughts, now examining the room and hardly believing that it had been only a matter of days since everyone's world had been turned upside down. He couldn't bring himself to think of his aunt, or of what had happened to her when the dead had returned to life in Edmonville. Had she remained trapped down there in the rubble of their former home, or had she been forced to climb out and join the others? Gordon shut down on those thoughts again. The pain was too vivid.

But you're out of prison, Gordon, another part of him seemed to say. *Despite the fear and the horror and all the nightmare happenings, you're out of that bedroom now. This may not be the world you remember, but you aren't sitting every night with the curtains closed, picking at those guitar strings. And for the first time, the things you've done here have made a difference.*

He'd remembered the nights they'd thrown stones at the windows when he'd practised his "uncool" music. And then he remembered the night by the bonfire, when he'd put everything of himself into playing his guitar at the horror hidden in the dark. All his fear, all the loneliness, all the frustrated emotion that had led him to taking up the guitar in the first place. Something had happened then; something that he wasn't sure about. Perhaps for the first time the monkey at the typewriter really had performed a work of genius.

Gordon heard Annie and Lisa coming back, and looked down to see that the boy had fallen asleep, slumped against him with the guitar in his lap.

The generators were fine. Outside, the streets surrounding the boarding house were bright as day. Lisa smiled when she saw the boy, carefully lifting him from the sofa as Gordon retrieved his guitar.

"Look out," said Gordon, and pointed at the window.

"Okay," said Annie. "I'll spell you in . . . what? Three hours?"

Gordon nodded, and the two women quietly moved to their room at the end of the ground-floor corridor, carefully edging the boy around the door and into his bed. Gordon watched them go, waving once as the door closed. He thought about Candy's reaction to Annie and Lisa's relationship, which was hostile to say the least. Was it the loss of her own child that had made her so bitter about them? Couldn't she see that the boy had clung to Lisa and Annie as his only hope? He was lost somewhere in his own mind as a result of what had happened to his parents. The two women had shown nothing but protection and affection. Gordon moved to the window, refusing to think about it further lest he be judging Candy in the same way that she had judged them. He picked up her empty brandy bottle and dropped it into the bin beside the window, looking out. The glare from the streetlights and the floodlights hid everything of the night beyond the street outside. Was the Vorla out there somewhere, lapping at the edges of the light like a great black sea?

Gordon returned to the sofa, put his guitar in his lap, and looked at the dent in the base where he had laid it across Trevor Blake's head. Were Annie and Lisa really sure about their work on those generators? How could they be so confident that the lights wouldn't suddenly go out and the Vorla wouldn't come sweeping down that street, engulfing them like some great black tidal wave? They needed a contingency plan, just in case.

Thinking these things, aware of the danger, of the need for vigilance, Gordon, like Jay in the room above him, was instantly asleep. It was a gap in their plans for protection, but exhaustion had taken its toll not only on their physical state, but on everyone's mental resources. They must sleep, even if the Chasm should rise up and devour them all.

Gordon dreamed, but his dreams were formless and he could make no sense of them. Taunting faces when he was a child. Keeping the pain and the tears inside. Voices, yelling: "Dummy!"

He was cold.

Was it the cold that suddenly woke him up? He could feel the hair on the nape of his neck. Felt a cold chill in his shoulders, under his armpits, down his spine. And in that emergence from sleep, he suddenly became aware that something was moving in the room.

Something that had stopped moving as soon as he shuffled on the sofa.

Still barely awake, Gordon realised that the feeling he was experiencing was not from the cold. It was warm in here. The temperature seemed to have remained at a constant level ever since the day of the earthquake, now he came to think of it. No, this feeling was something else. Part of his unconscious, sleeping mind—the instinctive part—was telling him not to wake up; that he should return to sleep, not connect with whatever was going on around him. But it was too late now.

Because Gordon knew that the cold feeling was fear.

There was something with him in the room, and even though his conscious mind did not know what it was, a primal part of him was reacting instinctively.

Gordon slowly opened his eyes.

A naked child, about two years old, was crouching on the windowsill opposite him. It was a boy, with ash-blond curly hair, and bright blue glittering eyes. Something about the child's eyes, something about his expression, seemed almost adult. He was frozen in that crouching posture, on his way in or out of the opened window, and it had been Gordon's shuffling from sleep that had alerted him and made him pause. Gordon could not move. This was the same sort of child that Candy and Alex had seen in the minimart, the same kind of child that had killed Wayne.

The boy raised an eyebrow, as if waiting for Gordon to do something.

Gordon kept still, hardly daring to breathe.

The boy cocked his head to one side, and then looked quickly over to the other side of the room. Moving only his eyes, Gordon now saw what the boy was looking at.

There was another child, crouching on the television set.

It was a girl, perhaps slightly younger than the boy. But for that she could have been his twin sister. The same curling ash-blonde hair, the same glittering eyes. Her attention was also riveted on Gordon, and from her position, delicately balanced there like a cat, he could see the bony ridges on both her shoulders, as if something was growing there beneath the skin.

Something scampered over Gordon's feet. Involuntarily, he flinched.

And suddenly the room was filled with snarling, naked children baring sharp, pointed teeth.

A three-year-old boy was on the back of the sofa, not two feet from where Gordon sat, glaring at him. Even with that look of ferocity, the sight of those savage teeth, there was something indescribably beautiful about him—about all the children who had crept into the living room through the window and had been silently examining the room and its contents before Gordon had awoken. Directly in front of him, on the living-room carpet, was another two-year-old boy—green eyes, curled yellow hair. He stood swaying, arms at his sides; ready to leap at Gordon's throat if he should show any sign of attacking them. Frozen on the sofa, Gordon's eyes moved warily around the room. There were perhaps a dozen children in here, perched on the table, clinging to the backs of chairs. Physically no younger than eighteen months, no older than three, perhaps four at most. But all of them possessing the same strange feral agility and instincts.

Something flashed in the air, too rapid to register.

The next instant, a two-year-old girl was swinging from the light fixture overhead, glaring down at him.

Behind him, Gordon was aware of further movement, but dared not turn around to look. Something was climbing up the back of the sofa, was now balancing on the edge and shuffling forward to sniff in his ear. Heart hammering, he felt wetness there as it sniffed cautiously, then retreated . . . sniffed, and retreated. When it edged back to the boy crouched on the end of the sofa, Gordon looked to see that it was another boy, perhaps eighteen months old. The older boy put his arms around him, and the younger boy snuggled up close to his chest, looking back at Gordon. The movement and expression were at once like the behaviour of some hybrid human-ape, and also intensely human. Their attention remained fixed on him. Now he could see that the look of ferocity had softened. Could it be that they meant him no harm? Could they be as frightened of him as he was of them?

Gordon moved his hands in his lap.

Instantly, the twelve children hissed.

He was motionless again, waiting.

The eighteen-month-old pulled away from the older child and began to shuffle warily along the sofa towards him once more. Gordon waited for it to come near, for the sniffing to begin again. But suddenly the child hopped down onto the sofa beside him. Gordon's guitar had fallen there while he slept. The child hit the fret board with both feet, making a jangled chord ring in the air as it bounced to the carpet. Instantly alert, full defensive ferocity on every face, each child's attention swung from Gordon to the guitar.

The children began to move around the room, the guitar remaining their centre of attention. To Gordon, it seemed that they were circling like a pack, ready to attack. He was forgotten now as the pack paused and waited for further sounds, perhaps waiting for this strange thing to move. The child who had swayed on the carpet before Gordon, as if daring him to move, suddenly darted forward and slapped at the guitar on the sofa. It shifted, but there was no sound. The children circled, and waited.

Afterwards, Gordon would be unable to understand why he did what he did next. Every instinct told him to keep still and not antagonise the creatures, given what had happened to Wayne. But the next moment he found his hand creeping slowly over the sofa to the guitar. This time the children did not react to his movements. The guitar remained their sole focus of attention. When he reached the remaining strings, Gordon plucked one.

The children flinched, looked at each other, and then back at the guitar.

Gordon plucked another string.

This time they did not move.

Gordon began to pick out a tune: "Baa-Baa Black Sheep."

Eyes wide, entranced, the feral children watched and listened.

Slowly, Gordon leaned down and edged the guitar onto his lap with his other hand, plucking out the tune as he did so. Sweat was running down his face, trickling down his back. He was convinced that if he made one awkward or unexpected movement, the pack would fall on him with their sharp teeth bared. With two strings missing, Gordon slowly and carefully reached for the chord combinations available to him—and began to play.

It was one of his "mentor's" pieces: "Ninna Nanna Sul Nero," which some music reviewers had said was too close in style to Ravel's "Pavane (For a Dead Polish Princess)" for comfort. Since Gordon had never heard the "Pavane" he didn't much care. So he played anyway: a gentle, melodic, very sad lullaby.

The children watched and listened with wide eyes and open mouths.

The little girl on the light fixture spun slowly upside down, hanging by her legs and listening.

And suddenly, these were no longer feral children who could tear a human to pieces in moments. They were children, entranced by the sounds they were hearing. Behaving like children who had never in their lives heard music before.

Gordon lost track of time. It seemed as if he were playing for hours.

His fingers were aching. But he feared what would happen when he stopped.

Later, when noises came from Annie and Lisa's room, as Annie prepared to relieve Gordon's watch duty, the children suddenly became alert again. Attention fixed on the door at the end of the corridor, they flashed through the air, over the furniture and towards the window with an incredibly fluidity of motion and eerie grace. Pausing only briefly to look back at Gordon and his guitar, they slipped silently out of the window, dropping down out of sight into the floodlit night. The light fixture gave a quiet rattle and spun violently as the little girl vanished, reappearing on top of the television set. She glanced at him curiously, then cocked her head to look at the guitar, as if seeing it from a different angle might answer some of her questions. Then she vanished in a flurry of air. A slight bump on the window glass, a brief fogging as if something had breathed there . . . and now the children were all gone.

Gordon stopped playing.

The bedroom door opened and Annie slipped out, careful not to disturb Lisa or the boy. Gordon kept looking at the window.

"That was nice," said Annie as she approached, and she meant it.

Gordon nodded, unable to speak.

"Time to get some sleep."

He nodded again. Picking up his guitar, he walked up the stairs to his room like a sleepwalker. The lights were on when he entered, as they remained on in every room. For a moment, he paused on the threshold, expecting that the children would all be in here somewhere, waiting. But the room was empty. When he lay down and put his head on the pillow, Gordon didn't know how he'd ever sleep again with all the questions that buzzed through his mind.

Instantly, he slept.

CHAPTER TWENTY-TWO

REVELATIONS

THEY PAUSED AT THE DOORWAY TO THE extension, and although Jay was the only one not knowing what to expect, he could feel and share their anxiety. "Morning" had come, and it was the time for answers.

Alex stepped forward, and unlocked the door. He didn't want the others to know just how badly frightened he'd been by his encounter with Trevor Blake. He remembered the way that he—that *it*—had hissed in his face as they had fought on the cliff top. He remembered his first real look at that horrifying, mutilated mask, so close to his own that the very nearness of it threatened to rob him of his strength. After Gordon had delivered his top-ten hit, they had trussed him up straight away, with the rope they'd used to haul Jay and Juliet up from the mast. But Alex still couldn't forget the touch of Trevor's skin, even the feel of him through his ripped and bloodied clothes. Although it still looked like human skin, it felt as if he were touching something utterly inhuman. Something dry and cool. Like the time he'd once touched a snake's skin. They'd left him bound beside the smouldering bonfire. But he'd writhed and twisted, trying to get free. Annie had volunteered at one stage to give him water. Like an animal, he'd tried to bite her hand. While they'd ministered to Jay and

347

looked after the newcomer, Juliet, Trevor had behaved as if he were in agony throughout. From then on, his one remaining eye remained screwed shut, as he writhed in pain. For the next two days it had been the same, until they'd found the Rendez-vous and locked him in this extension.

They entered the small corridor that led to the three rooms which comprised the extension. Lisa stayed at the main door with the boy, as the others clustered around Alex. Alex paused only briefly, making sure that everyone was ready. No one spoke. He unlocked the door.

As they entered, Trevor looked up slowly from the large armchair in the centre of the room, and grinned.

Jay was unprepared for the extent of the injury to Trevor's face, even though Juliet had told him all about it. The five lamps that Annie and Lisa had rigged up were still shining, giving Trevor multiple shadows. His arms were tied tightly to his waist with some of the rope from the dump truck (it had been one hell of a job, and had taken all of them to subdue him). There was dried blood on the ropes now. His legs were bound together and tied to the chair legs. The chair itself had been anchored. They could see that the carpet around his feet had been worn threadbare where he'd constantly scuffed with his heels, trying to rise.

"Hello, my angel," he said. His remaining eye was screwed shut, but it seemed that somehow he could still see, and was looking past Alex and Jay at the person behind them.

It was Juliet.

She stepped into the room, her face tight. She opened her mouth as if to speak, but nothing came out.

Trevor hissed in agony. The sound of a striking snake, or of coals on a fire. He began to twist his head from side to side.

"*You're damned!*" The voice that broke from his mouth was not his; it was a hundred voices, radiating hate. Now he was speaking in the voices of the Vorla.

"*You're all damned! You're in Hell and we're going to feast on your souls!"* Now Trevor's face was a mask of pain again, the voices hissing away. When the spasm passed, his cracked face smiled. It was as if he had been playing a game with them. "Please," he asked in his normal voice. "Put the lights out."

"Why?" asked Jay.

Trevor turned to "look" at him, still with his one eye shut. It was uncanny.

"Because I'm asking you nicely?"

"Trevor," said Juliet. Again, the mask turned to "look" at her.

"Sweetheart. Won't *you* at least draw the curtains for me?"

Juliet said nothing. She stood looking at him; then put a hand over her mouth in distress. "It's not him anymore," she sobbed. "It's not Trevor."

Trevor laughed. A hideous, dry, crackling sound.

"Want me to put my cock in you, Juliet? You used to like that so much. If you let me fuck you again, I'm sure you'd change your mind. Come on, you don't have to untie me. Just zip me down and . . ."

"Shut *UP!*" Juliet turned away from him. Jay moved to her, put an arm around her shoulders.

"Ah-HAH!" said the Trevor-thing in its myriad voices. *"A new boyfriend? Didn't take you long, slut! Even in Hell you can find someone to fuck. Tell him what we used to do, tell him what you liked best, tell him . . ."*

"SHUT UP!"

Laughter burst from Trevor's throat; the sound of a hundred damned souls.

Jay plucked up one of the lamps, trailing its flex. Grim-faced, he marched across the carpet and held the lamp up to the Trevor-thing's face. The effect was instantaneous. The laughter stopped as Trevor flung his head back, breath hissing from between clenched teeth as if some bizarre pressure valve inside him had broken. Frantically, he twisted to keep his face from the light. Angrily, Jay kept the lamp shining full on him.

"Take it away! Take it AWAY!"

Jay stood back.

"Tell me the truth," he said. "Whatever you are, inside there. You know what's happened. Tell us!"

"You're damned and you're in Hell . . . "

Jay swiped the shade from the lamp and thrust it forward again. The naked bulb touched Trevor's cheek. Smoke curled from his flesh. Trevor shrieked in a hundred voices as his head snapped back.

"Tell us!" shouted Jay.

Trevor's one good eye opened wide.

And Jay lurched back in alarm as a spout of black ink erupted from Trevor's eye socket. It ribboned in the air, black-beaded globules splattering back onto his upturned face. Alex flattened himself against the wall as Jay pulled Juliet back to the door. Trevor's entire body was juddering now as the black liquid swarmed and bubbled like hot tar on his mask-face. Unlike any earthly liquid, it left his face and poured down around his neck. Gathering itself, it suddenly surged and flowed down over the bloodied ropes, settled on the armchair between his legs and began to splash into a pool around his feet like molasses. It writhed and bubbled there, gathering sticky streamers of itself from above, leaving no trace behind on Trevor's body.

Jay shoved Juliet outside with the others, and slammed the door. Only he and Alex were in the room now.

The Vorla which had erupted from Trevor looked like no more than a couple of pints of spilled pitch. It pulsated . . . then began to send creeping liquid tendrils of itself out over the carpet, like a spreading ink stain on blotting paper.

"Now what?" said Alex, still flattened against the wall.

Jay moved back again, still holding the lamp.

The black pool looked like a live, painted spider on the carpet. Its questing liquid tendrils drew back from the light all around it, recoiling all the more as Jay advanced with the naked bulb. It probed and tested, hissing like a tarantula when it found only more light. There was a sofa on the other side of the room. Withdrawing its tendrils, the liquid surged in a thin, glistening-black flow towards it.

"It's trying to get away from the light!" Jay ran forward as the blackness vanished under the sofa, hunting for shadow. He bent and seized the edge of the sofa, trying to lift it. Pain stabbed in his ribs and he fell to his knees. A thin black tendril shot out from under the sofa, inches from him.

"Christ, don't let it touch you!" Alex pushed away from the wall, grabbed the sofa and spun it away across the room on its castors as Jay staggered to his feet again. Alex kicked hard and the sofa fell over onto its back.

Revealed to the light once more, the Vorla shot across the carpet towards the door.

"Grab a lamp!" shouted Jay. "Don't let it get away!"

The black pool spread at the foot of the door, stretching itself thinly like some bizarre, glistening draught-excluder. Alex grabbed a lamp and advanced on it.

And then the Vorla shrank at the base of the door—and was gone.

From the corridor, Juliet cried out, followed by Candy and Damon.

"It's gone under the door!" Alex flung it open in time to see the others flattened against the corridor wall, looking down to their right at what had slithered into view. Alex stepped out into the corridor and the lamp in his hands went out as the flex was yanked from its socket.

"Shit!"

Lisa snatched the boy away as a black rivulet flowed out through the open door and into the garden. And now Alex and Jay were out of the room and hurrying with the others to follow the Vorla as it pooled and bubbled on a cracked flag-stone path, looking for somewhere to go. A hissing, glistening patch of tar no more than two feet across and a millimetre thick, it writhed and undulated in the "daylight." It flowed to a bush in the garden for shade, found none that could end its agony, and began to flop and bubble as if it were on a hot plate.

They stood watching it.

"There's nowhere for it to go," said Annie.

Smoke began to rise from the black patch. Tentacles formed and quivered, dissolving and hissing. The pool began to shimmer, black ripples spreading across its surface. The smoke became thicker. Now the thing began to make a sound like a rattlesnake. It gathered itself, tried to rise in a column, as if reaching for the sky. Glistening black tentacles continued to open all around it, shivering; like some bizarre black sea anemone, flowering in an underwater current. The tentacles dripped and disintegrated. Smoke engulfed it as it flopped back to the ground. Now there was no black pool. Just a hissing, writhing cloud of noxious gases. The smoke swirled and parted.

And the Vorla was gone, leaving nothing behind but a burned and smouldering patch on the grass.

"I think that's one up to *us*," said Jay.

"*Too late*," moaned Trevor from inside the extension. He sounded grief-stricken. "*Too LATE!*"

As one, they all turned and headed back through the main door. Alex paused only once, looking back at the blackened patch on the grass as if to make sure that the Black Stuff had really gone.

Inside, Trevor was where they had left him. Tied to the armchair, head hanging down on his chest. He looked up when they entered the room, his eye screwed shut again. His face twisted in a snarl. Foam flecked at cracked lips as he tried to push forward, towards them. He still looked inhuman.

"There's more of you inside there," said Jay, retrieving his lamp and switching it back on. "Isn't there?"

He stepped forward. The Trevor-thing hissed.

"The stuff that got out," continued Jay. "I mean, the part of you that got out. It didn't escape. You know that, don't you?"

Trevor leered again, hissing. Jay waved the lamp at him. Trevor recoiled, slapping his head back against the armchair. The hissing stopped. His cracked teeth were bared.

"It's daylight outside," Jay went on. "Nowhere to hide. That's why you're in so much pain, isn't it? That's what you mean by 'too late.' You've been trapped inside Trevor too long, and now you can't get out. Not during the day, when it's light. Not during the last few nights, too close to the bonfire. Last night, all these lamps were keeping you inside. Now . . . it's daylight outside. And there's nowhere for you to go. So all we have to do is repeat the process, to *force* you out where we can deal with you. Bring the light *really* close . . ."

Jay stepped forward, holding out the bulb, checking that he wasn't stretching the flex. Trevor twisted his head from side to side and moaned.

" . . . and wait for more of you to come out. We'll just keep on doing that, until there's no more of you left in poor old Trevor."

"Juliet," groaned Trevor. "It's me. Don't let him hurt me. I'm sorry for what I did. Really. It was the Vorla made me do those things to you. Just make him go away and stop hurting me . . ."

"Jay," said Juliet. "Maybe I was wrong. Maybe . . ."

"You know you were right," said Jay, not taking his eyes from the figure tied to the armchair. "It knows it's stuck, and it's using Trevor's voice because it thinks it might help. Well . . . it won't."

Trevor was still then. The pleading expression was gone. His face was fixed where Jay stood. Waiting.

"But there *is* a way out for you," continued Jay. "Only one way. And I can set you free. If I want to."

Trevor remained motionless, his face set.

Jay waited again.

At last, the Vorla inside Trevor said: "*How?*"

353

Jay nodded, a grim smile on his face. "I'll take you back. Back to the pit. Back to the Chasm. Where the dark is. You can go back down there."

"*Back to the others?*"

"Yes. Back to the rest of the Vorla. But there's a condition."

"*Which is?*"

"You've got to tell us the truth."

"*The truth?*" The Trevor-thing began to chuckle. The sound was liquid, as if the black tar inside were churning in his lungs.

"You've got to tell us what's happened to Edmonville. What's happened to us. Where everyone else has gone. And what you . . . what the Vorla really *is*."

The Trevor-thing stopped chuckling. It was silent again for a long time. Grim-faced, Jay waited. Behind him, the others stood tensely, mesmerised, waiting.

"*You've been shown the truth,*" hissed the thing. "*Don't you see? You've been SHOWN! This way* for *the sorrowful city! This way for eternal suffering! This way to join the lost people! You're in Hell, you're—*"

"You're a fucking liar," said Jay, and he stepped forward, holding the naked bulb out towards the Trevor-thing's face. Instantly, he was silent, twisting his head back again in a frenzy. "So I think we'll just squeeze every last drop of you out, and watch you evaporate like that thing out there."

"*You'll let us go back to the Chasm? You'll set us free?*"

"I'll take you to the edge, chuck you right over myself. How about that?"

"*You promise?*"

"Cross my heart . . . and hope to die." Jay stood back again.

"*There may be punishment. If we reveal what all the Vorla has hidden.*"

"Your choice. The truth and nothing but. Or else . . . " Jay held the lamp up to his own face.

Trevor made a noise in his throat then. Like a ventriloquist trying to suppress several voices that wanted to erupt from his mouth at the same time. A strangled, squirming sound. He swallowed, and the noises were still. And then a sly smile came over his horrifying face, a hideous travesty of the face that Juliet had once known. A face that had kissed her. A face that she once thought she might have loved.

"*You're wrong, Juliet,*" leered that face, and Juliet had to look away. "*About Trevor being gone. He's deep down here somewhere. The . . . important . . . part of him, that is. What he's done, what he is . . . it's all a part of us. When we return to the Chasm, all the fear and the pain and the misery that Trevor gave . . . will all be a new part of the Vorla.*"

"Make your mind up!" snapped Jay. "Now!"

"*We've made our minds up,*" said the Trevor-thing. "*We'll tell you . . . and we'll tell darling Juliet . . . the others must go.*"

"They're staying," said Jay. "They've as much right to hear what you've got to say."

"*No.*"

Jay stepped forward angrily. Trevor hissed.

"Let me out of here!" snapped Candy from the corridor. "I need a drink."

"You'll tell us all!" shouted Jay.

"*NO!*"

"Why?"

"Jay," said Alex. "It's okay. The important thing is to get the truth. Annie, maybe it's best if we . . . "

Annie nodded. Whatever the reason why the Trevor-thing wanted them all out, at least Jay might get the truth out of him and he could tell them all later.

"*But you must draw the curtains,*" said the Trevor-thing. "*And turn off some of the lights.*"

"No," said Jay simply.

"Tuh-trick," said Gordon.

Jay looked back. "He's tied tight. And you saw what happened to the Black Stuff in the light. Annie, maybe you and Lisa could make sure that the generator's okay." Annie nodded.

The last thing they needed now was for the lights in the extension to fail.

"Outside," said Gordon, backing towards the door as the others left the room. "Me. Right outside. Any tuh-trick and . . ." Gordon slammed a fist into the palm of his other hand.

"Thanks." Jay nodded, and turned back to the Trevor-thing. Juliet, gritting her teeth, moved to sit on another chair.

The door closed.

Now all the others were outside. Waiting.

"*Sitting comfortably?*" leered the Trevor-thing, his eye screwed shut but "looking" directly at Juliet.

"Get on with it," said Jay.

"*If there wasn't a Hell before,*" said the thing, and laughed, "*then there is now . . .* "

| **THE TRUTH**

GORDON, ALEX AND ANNIE SHUFFLED AND paced in the garden, watching the day grow lighter and trying to think of something to say to each other that might make some kind of difference, or give some kind of general comfort. No words of comfort would come, and the fact that the answers to what had happened to them all might even now be coming out of the thing that had once been Trevor Blake was adding to their agitation. Annie had checked the generators. There would be no problem, and she was going to leave the back floodlights burning all the time, given the nature of their prisoner in the extension. Lisa was still holding the boy, casting anxious glances out at them from the back garden door of the boarding house. Damon was leaning against the back wall, still nursing his hangover and pretending that nothing he'd seen or heard that morning had anything to do with him. Alex moved back to the burned patch, where the small part of the Vorla had evaporated, and began pushing at the shrivelled grass with the toe of one shoe. He thought again of what had happened in the minimart, and of seeing what seemed to be the son they'd lost. Candy had retreated to the bottle and hadn't been able to discuss it with him anymore. But he knew that despite the alcohol she was pouring into herself, she couldn't help but think about it. Neither could he. But what was the point of playing and replaying the events of that night in their heads, over and over? There was no answer.

But now there might be answers. Answers to everything.

From the mouth of the thing that had once been Trevor Blake.

"Al . . . Alex."

He looked back at Gordon, and at his troubled expression.

"It'll be okay," he said, walking slowly back to him. "If they need us, they'll yell."

"No," said Gordon. "Not that."

"We're all under strain, Gordon. Everything that's happened . . . "

"No!" Gordon struggled to find words. "Want . . . Alex . . . "

"Okay. Do it slowly."

"Tell . . . tell you . . . something."

"All right, I'm listening."

Alex watched Gordon struggling to find the words. He looked as if he might begin to weep.

Alex raised a hand, almost put it on his shoulder.

Then Gordon shook his head and whirled away; confused, angered to the point of tears at his inability, and disgusted with himself. Alex tried to say something reassuring, but couldn't come up with anything that wouldn't be mistaken for a patronising attitude.

Gordon walked to the extension, and stared hard at the door, listening for any sounds within. It seemed that he just needed one excuse, the slightest noise, or evidence that the Trevor-thing was trying some kind of trick, and he would burst in there and strangle the Vorla's host with his bare hands. He'd wanted so much to be able to tell Alex. No point in even approaching Candy. But Alex needed to know. Needed to know what had happened the previous night after everyone had gone to bed, when the night-children had visited. And yet wasn't there another part of him that didn't really want to share it with anyone? Gordon shook his head, and squatted down in front of the extension door, confused.

Alex looked away from him and moved back to kick dirt over the burned patch. Annie had gone into the house once more, presumably to check on Lisa and the boy. All around, the floodlights still glowed, making it seem as if the entire house and its surroundings were on some kind of movie set.

Gordon chewed his lip.

Should he write down what had happened the previous night, and then show it to Alex? Would it help? Or was it simply going to make things even more complicated for Candy and him? Shouldn't the others know that these potentially dangerous kids were able to come and go as they pleased, searching the house when everyone was asleep? Were they looking for something in particular, or were they merely curious? Where in hell had they *come* from? What did they want? Gordon was still pondering what to do when sounds of shrill screaming made him start so abruptly that he fell backwards onto the garden path.

It was impossible to tell whether it was Trevor or one of the others.

Scrambling to his feet again, Gordon looked back to see that Alex was already running towards him. Head down, Gordon threw himself at the door and burst it open. The sounds of screaming were shrill, but this time there was no agony. There was something horribly triumphant about that sound. It filled Gordon with horror as he flung himself at the interior door.

"Knew it! Tuh-*trick*!"

The door slammed against the wall as Alex clattered into the hallway behind him.

Something horrifying and bizarre was taking place in the room.

Trevor Blake was still in the chair, still bound. But he was no longer moving. His head had sagged forward on to his chest, and it looked as if he was dead.

Juliet was bracing both hands behind her against the windowsill, kicking at the sink unit set into the far wall. Jay was crouched on the floor beside her, yanking hard at something under the sink. Cursing, he fell back in a shower of plaster as Gordon hurtled into the room. Alex shouldered past, scanning the room for any sign of the crawling black mass. Gordon jumped over a chair and saw what Jay was doing. He had seized the pipework under the sink and had pulled a huge part of it out from the wall. Giving hoarse cries of effort, Juliet was sitting on the sill now and kicking at the washbasin with both feet. The pipework came away in Jay's hands and he threw it down on the floor as if it were somehow alive, stepping warily back from it. Juliet skipped away from the sink unit, also standing at a safe distance.

"What is it?" said Alex, looking back and forth between Trevor's still body and the bent piping on the floor.

Jay nudged the pipe with his foot, then stooped to look into the ragged hole in the wall beneath the unit. Juliet was leaning forward now, warily examining the sink unit.

"Too late," said Jay at last. To Gordon, it seemed like an echo of Trevor's agonised words that morning. He looked at Juliet, as if for confirmation. She leaned back from the sink unit, shaking her head.

"Gone," she said.

Annie suddenly appeared in the doorway, gasping for breath.

Wearily, Jay and Juliet moved away from the sink.

"Come on, everyone," said Jay. "Let's go outside. I think we need some air."

"Trevor?" asked Alex.

"He's dead," said Juliet. "At last, he's really dead."

"And the Vorla?"

Jay gestured back to the sink unit.

"It all came out of him. This time, it—or should I say *they*—learned from their mistake outside in the light. Headed straight for the one place it would be dark, the one place that would take them back to the Chasm. I should have thought about it before. Straight down the fucking plughole, down through the waste pipes and into whatever's left of the sewer system. All it needs to do is follow the sewer to where a broken underground pipe sticks straight out of the side, over the Chasm—and it's home."

"Did he . . . I mean it . . . ?" Annie relaxed in the doorway, running a hand through her hair. "Oh shit, I mean . . . did the Vorla tell you anything?"

"Get the others," said Jay. "Outside."

Alex, Gordon and Annie stood looking from Jay to Juliet, as if there were some kind of answer to everything on their faces. They both looked tired beyond words.

Jay saw their expressions. He nodded again.

"Outside," he said again. "There's a lot to tell . . . even if I don't understand half of it myself."

"I think I know why Trevor wouldn't start speaking until everyone else was out of the room," said Juliet at last.

Both Jay and herself had been trying to find a way to start when everyone was assembled in the back garden. Neither felt comfortable going back inside the Rendezvous, as if their ability to come to terms with what they had heard would be somehow inhibited by the enclosed space. Even outside, under the alien sky, they were feeling claustrophobic and stressed. Jay leaned against the garden wall and waited for her to continue. The tension emanating from the others was palpable.

"The Vorla wants to cause us as much misery as it can," Juliet went on. "I think even at the last it wants to split us up. What it told us is so crazy . . . well, so crazy that you might not believe us. I think it wants that. If we'd all been in there with him, you would have felt the truth of it . . . " Juliet dried up and looked at Jay for assistance.

"Go on," he said.

"Christ, I don't know where to start."

"All right, let's start at the beginning. We wanted to know where everyone's gone. Why no one's come to help us. The answer's the other way around. They haven't gone anywhere; the world outside Edmonville hasn't gone away."

"What the hell is that supposed to mean?" asked Damon.

"They haven't gone away. *We* have."

The others looked at each other and shuffled. Jay could feel the sky pressing down from above.

"What hit Edmonville was more than an earthquake. Even the Vorla couldn't explain what kind of earthquake. Not only did it smash the town up the way we can see it all around us now, but it . . . it . . . well, it smashed Edmonville right off the face of the earth."

"Off the earth," said Alex, in a hollow voice. "What do you mean, 'off the earth'?"

"I mean what I said. The whole of Edmonville has been uprooted . . . literally. The entire town has been shattered, and transported somewhere else."

No one spoke.

"For God's sake," said Jay after a while. "Somebody say *something.*"

"You mean . . ." Lisa let the boy go. He began to play in the bushes—unhearing, unaware and unconcerned. "You don't mean . . . like . . . well, you know. Outer space, or something?"

"No," said Juliet. "Not outer space. Nothing like that."

"Then where?" asked Annie.

"To what the Vorla calls a No-Place," said Juliet.

"Look around you," continued Jay. "We've seen how Edmonville has been split apart. These bloody peculiar peaks and crags. We know the way the town has been cracked up can't be natural. And the Chasm on all sides. Now we *know* that's impossible. But think about what's beyond all that. Sometimes where we can see gaps between the crags. What can we see past them? Nothing—except the same grey nothingness that's up there." He pointed up. "That's because there *is* nothing out there. Edmonville, all that's left of it—that's all there is. The real world just doesn't exist anymore."

"Duh-dimension?" asked Gordon.

"Something like that," said Jay. "Whatever this earthquake was, when it hit Edmonville, it *shifted* the entire town out of reality—I mean, out of the world we know. And it slammed it right down here in this other place. This No-Place. This different . . . dimension, I suppose we'll have to call it. Like Gordon said."

More silence.

"It's working, isn't it?" asked Juliet hopelessly. "You don't believe any of it. That's just what the Vorla is hoping for."

"And what the hell *is* the Vorla anyway?" asked Alex.

"It lives here," said Jay. "It's been living here for thousands and thousands of years."

"Yes, but what is it?"

"It's us," said Jay.

"Christ," said Damon. "You two been swigging bottles in there or something? None of this makes sense."

Jay looked at Juliet. "You think you can handle this part? I'm still trying to get my head round it."

Juliet cleared her throat nervously, as if she were having to deliver a difficult lecture on a subject about which she knew nothing in front of thousands of people. And her life depended on it. A flush had risen around her throat. Her hand played there while she spoke.

"Basically . . . well, basically it's Evil. With a capital 'E'. Every evil thing that's ever been done on our . . . on our side. I mean, our world. Well, there's more to it than that. But I think it means that every act of violence, every killing, every massacre has much more of an effect than we think. I mean, apart from the people who actually suffer from it. It's as if there's an *energy* released when that act takes place. An evil energy, like

363

electricity or something. And that energy doesn't just dissolve or disappear, it's drawn or pulled . . ."

"Or maybe just dumped," continued Jay. "In this place. In this No-Place that we're in now. The Dumping Ground."

"Not just the big things," Juliet went on. "Like killing and rape and murders. But even the smallest things. Spitefulness. Meanness. Everyday cruelty. Harsh words. Aggression. I don't know . . . maybe even kicking your dog." She tried to laugh. It didn't work.

"It all creates this 'energy'," continued Jay. "And for thousands of years, maybe from the first day humankind walked upright on the earth, it's been released and 'dumped' over here."

"Those names," said Annie. "The graffiti that we saw splashed all over the place in blood . . ."

"Madmen, murderers," said Jay. "That was the Vorla, taunting us with a few clues."

"Then the Vorla is . . . it's their souls?" said Annie.

"No," said Juliet. "I don't think so. Not if we can believe what Trevor . . . I mean, that thing . . . was telling us. It's the evil that they created, the energy that was released by their cruelty and their horrors. That's what's down there in the Chasm. The acts, the consequences, maybe even some of their personality. But not *them*. That's what makes it so difficult to understand when the Vorla talks about itself in the plural all the time."

"There's a great big bloody sea of that Black Stuff down there in the Chasm," Jay carried on. "And somehow, all that evil energy—whatever you want to call it—knows what it is. It's *become* alive. Over the thousands of years, it's grown and grown and it's evolved. Like those amoebas and things they used to talk about when I was at school. You know, how life began and all that stuff? Well, somehow that blackness has become a living thing. Alive enough to even give itself a name: the Vorla."

"Why the Vorla?" asked Lisa. "What does it mean?"

"We don't know," said Jay. "We just know that by some

incredible accident, a hole's been ripped in the life we knew and we've been transported to a place where humans have never come before."

"And the Vorla's glad," said Juliet. "Glad that we're here. Don't you see? It really *is* a part of us. The evil side. The bad side. And here we are, the very things that create it—dropped right on top of it in its dumping ground. Right from the beginning, it's been on its own. Growing and growing as more and more of that energy is dumped here. But all it's had has been itself. All the evil and the cruelty and the hate. Seething and feeding on itself, with nowhere to go. Nothing to take out its horrors on."

"But now," said Jay, "it has us."

"So this . . . " Lisa held her arms wide. " . . . is a kind of . . . limbo?"

"The Vorla said something, just after you left. It said: 'If there wasn't a Hell before, then there is one now.' It's got the opportunity to create one for us."

"Then how do we get back?" asked Damon. His Adam's apple was wobbling; he looked as if he might burst into tears at any moment. "I mean, how do we get out of this fucking place?"

"We don't," said Jay.

"We're here forever," said Juliet. The flush around her neck had risen to her cheeks.

"The petrol won't last forever," said Annie. "The generators won't work indefinitely. And we could end up burning every last scrap of wood on this plateau. After that, what happens?"

"Not to mention food," said Alex.

"This is crap," said Damon, and he turned away to walk down the garden. At the bottom, he vaulted the wall and vanished from sight.

The boy began poking in the dirt with a twig.

For a while, nothing more could be said about these revelations—not until everyone had had a chance to think.

"What about Trevor?" asked Juliet at last. "What are we going to do with . . . ?"

"I'll take care of it," said Jay. "We can't have him lying around, when night comes again. Just in case . . . well, you know."

"Petrol?" asked Alex.

Juliet turned away.

"No. We need every last drop of it from now on. Annie, we'd best have the floodlights and streetlamps turned off now. We'll have to check out the meat mart and see if there's any petrol left, though I doubt it. We'll also have to make sure that we don't have any of our night-time friends left there. But I guess the petrol for the generators is the most important thing."

"Then how . . . ? Trevor, I mean."

Jay looked at Juliet, who was still turned away.

He gestured towards the Chasm, and made a diving motion with one hand.

And then, confused, bewildered, stunned, lost in their own thoughts, trying to come to terms with what they had heard, they went back inside the Rendezvous. Now that it was all out, there was no claustrophobia. Only a tenuous security, an imitation of normality when the door was shut and they were turned from the window.

The greyness of the sky pressed down, hard and relentless.

BOOK THREE | THE CAFFNEYS

ONE YEAR, TWO DAYS LATER

A NOTHER DAY AND NIGHT HAS COME AND gone as I crept through the ruins, searching for the others. During the day, I've had to be careful; making sure that I didn't blunder into any of the Caffney tribe. During last night, it was the same as before. Crouching in the dark, whispering into this tape machine; watching and waiting for any sign of the Vorla, and telling the story of what happened to us all in New Edmonville. Maybe trying to take my mind off the fear of what may be happening—what may already have happened to Juliet and the others.

I suppose my sense of direction must be okay, because I just kept heading in the direction that I felt was going to take me back to the petrol plant. I didn't find that main street littered with the tortured dead, but signs of the Caffneys and their favourite pastime were all over the place. Late this afternoon, I rounded a corner and nearly walked straight into the tribe; crouched in the rubble and behind fallen blocks of concrete.

I froze, right in the middle of the street.

They were facing away from me, their attention fixed on the cliff edge of this crag, right next to the ramshackle "bridge" they'd managed to get to the petrol plant on the other side. Still spooked after what happened, I think. But still mad enough and dangerous enough. If any one of them had been facing in my direction, I suppose that might have been the end of it for me. If Henry or his brothers had managed to wind them up again, they wouldn't be held off by this shotgun, even if they thought I had a whole bag full of ammunition, rather than its single remaining shell.

I hopped back around the street corner, throwing myself against the wall, heart hammering. I expected to hear yelling and running as they came after me. But there was no sound. I stayed there, overcome by the urge to glance around again; at least to get a look over to the plant and see if there was any sign of the others. Surely there must be someone still alive? Why else was the tribe's attention fixed on that far crag? But I knew that I'd be pushing my luck if I tried it. Far better to somehow get up high; somewhere that overlooked it. They'd already stayed one night by the bridge safe from the Vorla. After all, despite what Alex did to Old Man Caffney, they're still supposed to have this deal with the Black Stuff. Or would they treat it warily when night fell and find some place away from the edge to sleep? Maybe one of the ruined buildings nearby? If I was going to find a building overlooking the edge and the bridge, I'd need to be pretty damn careful about not stepping on any sleeping tribe members.

It took me a while, creeping through the ruins and trying not to make a noise. But eventually, I found a department store that overlooks the bridge and the Chasm. A lorry carrying oil drums had crashed into the frontage, and provided a perfect cover for me. Those drums had fallen from the back and were all over the road, so I was able to slide from one drum to the next without being seen; screened by the wreck of the lorry itself as I sneaked into the building.

And that's where I am now. On the fourth floor, and I don't like it one bit. The walls have bloody great cracks in them and most of the ceiling in here has come down. God knows how steady this building is. The staircase was a nightmare, and it ends at the fourth. Just high enough up here for me to see down and give me a pretty clear view of the cliff-edge up ahead, all the places where the tribe members are hiding. I can see the bridge and the plant on the other side, with its giant canisters and twisted metal wreckage.

There's a low fire burning on the other side of that bridge, and that's where the tribe's attention is fixed. I saw Henry and Patrick a little while ago, pointing over there and giving directions to the other tribe members. They've got some kind of plan up their sleeves. The fact that they haven't rushed the bridge yet means that some of us are still alive over there, and somehow holding them at bay. It's growing dark again, and no matter how hard I strain to look—and I've got to be bloody careful I'm not seen—I can't make out which of us is still alive over there.

Now that I'm here, I have to do something.

But I just don't know what I can do. I have to think . . . think!

What if the Vorla comes?

Christ, I don't want to think about that.

So here goes, with the next tape. Talking and remembering will help me stay awake, maybe give me a fresh idea about what I have to do. Risk running at that bridge in the daytime, when I know the Vorla can't come, but I've got to contend with our Caffney friends down there? Or try it during the night, sneaking past them, but risking what might come up from the Chasm below? And if I make it, what then? I need time. Time to think, time to remember, time to try and put a few more pieces of this nightmare together. For a time back then, after the Vorla that was in Trevor Blake told us just what kind of Hell we'd found ourselves in, it seemed that we were never going to pull ourselves out of this daze, trying to come to terms with the craziness of it all, and the horror of everything that happened; knowing that we were never going home again. In the days that followed our confrontation with the Vorla that was in Trevor Blake, we talked everything inside out . . .

| CHAPTER ONE | THE JOURNAL OF JAY O'CONNOR: ACE OF HEARTS |

SOMETIMES I THINK IT WAS AS IF TALKING would help us to find other answers; other ways of explaining what it was that the Darkness in Trevor Blake had told us. (And yes, I got rid of Trevor's body, just like I said I would. When Juliet wasn't around.) Stuff like this wasn't supposed to happen. But there were no other answers. No other reasonable and acceptable explanations for everything that had happened to us. Still no one came to rescue us. Nothing moved overhead in that grey sky. No aeroplanes, no searching helicopters. No clouds. No sign that there was anything out there. The world as we knew it no longer existed.

There were lots of things to be done if we were going to make the Rendezvous a safe place to live. And we set about those practical problems and those physical jobs, throwing ourselves into them as we'd thrown ourselves into those other tasks as a way of trying to stop thinking and talking about it all. Even Damon, who remained isolated and hostile, began to muck in and do his share. Something had happened to him after Wayne's death. It was as if his last hold on reality had gone. And it was obvious, just by looking at his face, that he hated me more than he'd hated anyone in his entire life. Maybe he somehow blamed me for Wayne's death, even though I wasn't there when it happened. I underestimated him and what he had in mind for me. Little did I know what a bad mistake I was making.

The one thing we drew a blank on, since the Vorla had said nothing about them, was the savage little kids who had killed Wayne. Whatever they were, Gordon's idea that they couldn't be controlled or be a part of the Vorla seemed to make some sort of sense. Lisa had a name for them, based on how Alex had described what they looked like. She called them Cherubim. Out of the Bible. Little angels, with sweet faces. Except that these little angels had a much more dangerous attitude than the sweet plaster statues you see in churches and religious places like that. Of all the things we discussed, the Cherubim were the one aspect that we didn't dwell on, maybe because they didn't fit in anywhere and no one had seen them since. Candy and Alex remained convinced that one of those angels had the face of their dead son, Ricky. And the more we talked about them, the more pain it seemed to give Candy. I remember thinking also how strange Gordon looked when we did talk about them. He looked distant, thoughtful, maybe even a little bit anxious. But I didn't dwell on it, which, as it turned out, was another mistake.

Because there was a lot more going on there than any of us realised.

Fuel, both for the generators and for our stomachs, was the most important consideration. So we organised new searches of the plateau. Annie was right about the depot she'd spotted. Fortunately for us there wasn't much damage there. We began draining the petrol out of the remaining cars. And Gordon came up with something that none of us had thought about. The sewer system. He got the idea from hearing how the Vorla had escaped from Trevor Blake, down the sink. Why the hell no one else had thought about it, particularly me, I don't know—especially since it could have held more danger for us than anything else. He reckoned that if the Vorla could escape down there to the Chasm, then there was nothing to stop it coming back *up* through those underground pipes that hadn't been shattered. Up through the sewer gratings and the manhole cover in the middle of the night. That was another big job. Sealing everything down as tight as we could, particularly at the Rendezvous and the surrounding streets.

It was hard, but not as bad as our search of the meat mart to find out if we were finally rid of Edmonville's walking dead. The place had burned to the ground. And everything inside and just outside the building had burned with it. I'm not going to paint a picture of what we found in the ruins. You can probably fill it in yourselves. But at least we weren't going to get any more of those visitors in the night. During the search, we realised just how lucky we had been. The fire hadn't spread from the factory. If it had, maybe if sparks had carried over to the other buildings, we could have been completely burned off the crag we found ourselves on.

There were twelve remaining stores on our plateau, three of them mini-supermarkets. All with a good supply of tinned and preserved foods. Some of them you could hardly get near, because of the smell. But we had to force ourselves, nonetheless. Clearing all the rotting stuff out of the place, and getting to the tins and the preserves. We would have to ration them, while we thought of ways of growing our own. We had soil here. A wrecked library with a good horticultural section, and plenty of crop potential from the ruins of a garden centre, provided that we got down to studying hard and planting early. At that stage, we had no way of knowing whether crops would grow in our new climate or even whether the crop seasons were the same in this "No-Place." If there was no sun, then there'd be no ultraviolet light. How could *anything* grow? Still, the trees in the park and other surroundings seemed to be managing okay, so why not? But these were things that we didn't dwell on too much either. We just had to get ahead and do it. For the time being, no one talked about the supermarket on the other side of the gorge. Because if we did, then someone would have to suggest that one of us go out over the broadcasting mast, which remained wedged between both sides, and start organising the transfer of surviving preserved food with no way of knowing when the mast would break loose and plunge down into the Chasm. We knew we'd have to get around to discussing it eventually, but in the beginning no one seemed inclined to raise the matter.

And so it went on, for those first few weeks; then the first few months.

We worked hard during the day.

The floodlights burned at night. The Vorla showed no sign of returning.

For a while, it looked as if we might be making a go of it. Starting afresh in our New World. Trying hard not to think about where we were, the nothingness that lay beyond, and the horrors of the Black Sea that lay in the bottom of the Chasm. That was the way to cope. Not thinking about it. That, and hard work.

I only knew that, despite the unknown, I had found something with Juliet that I had never experienced before. It was the first really good thing that had happened in my life, and I could feel it changing me. Turning me into someone else, maybe even someone half good, as each day went by.

No one could have known the ultimate nightmare that lay ahead of us, no one could have expected the way things were going to turn out. All the time we hoped and prayed that the Vorla would just leave us alone was time wasted. We'd underestimated just how much it hated us, just how much it wanted us to suffer, and to what lengths it would go to ensure our destruction. If we'd known then what we were to subsequently find out, maybe we would have just switched off all the lights and let it take us.

But in that first year together in what Lisa started to call the Realm of the Chasm, there's one memory that stays in my mind. Something that Juliet gave me. I've had it in the chest pocket of my jacket for nearly a month now—ever since that day we went "shopping."

It started with another one of those "leader" talks.

I thought we'd managed to avoid it, since the matter hadn't been raised in some time. We'd cleared some land within easy reach of the Rendezvous which was also covered by floodlights. This was the place we'd decided to start raising our own food, although no one knew whether we were wasting our time or not. The floodlights here were vital, since we didn't want the Vorla flowing in over what we'd done during the night. We'd had a good sign the previous day. It had rained. A thin drizzle, but rain nonetheless. Not some bizarre bloody chemical, or acid. Just good old rainwater. It didn't make sense. Where the hell was it coming from out of that empty greyness up above? We didn't question it, or whether there was anything in it that might have long-term effects on us. We took another chance in drinking it. Our bottled supply from the ruined stores wouldn't last indefinitely and we hadn't found anything in the library about making our own. If it was going to poison us, so be it. Anyway, in good spirits, we'd brought back a whole pile of stuff from the garden centre in the back of the dump truck, and everyone was helping to unload sacks from the back. Alex and Lisa had begun "ploughing," most of us had been reading up on the do-it-yourself farming bit, and we were ready to go.

When I yanked a sack of seeds down to the ground, Alex said something simple, like: "Okay, boss."

"What?"

"Nothing. Just thanks."

"No, what's with the boss thing?"

Alex dropped the sack, dusted his hands and looked at me. Wiping sweat from his forehead, he turned and called to the others: "Okay, everyone. It's time."

"Time for what?" I asked.

"Time for the talk that you've been avoiding."

I looked up to see that the others were all stopping what they were doing and coming back to the dump truck. The way they were walking, the way they were holding themselves, I could tell that something was up. Only Juliet seemed as puzzled as I was. She'd been driving the dump truck. Seeing my puzzlement, she jumped out of the cab and came to join me as the others crowded round.

"What's wrong?" I asked, at last.

"Nothing wrong at all, really," said Alex. "Well, I mean apart from the fact that we're stranded in another dimension or something, with no chance of ever getting home. Possible starvation at best, all kinds of other worse things that can happen. But apart from that, nothing wrong."

"So what . . . ?"

"It's the way you react whenever any one of us talks about having a leader, or someone being in charge of what we have here," said Annie.

I opened my mouth to say something. I never got a chance to speak.

"You get angry every time it comes up," said Lisa. "So most of the time it never comes up. But we've been talking among ourselves, when you—and Juliet—haven't been here. And we've come to a decision."

I waited.

"First," said Gordon, holding up a finger. "Not angry."

I shuffled uneasily and looked at Juliet. She shrugged.

"Okay," I said. "I promise not to get angry."

"We've had a vote, since we've decided we're a democracy," said Annie. "And it was a unanimous decision."

"We need a leader," said Candy, looking at the sky. "And you're it."

"Look, I've told you all before that I . . ."

"Promise!" said Gordon, waving his finger again.

"The fact of the matter is," said Alex, "you're the one who comes up with the way forward that everyone feels confident about. You're the one we look to. You're the one who comes up with the ideas . . ."

"That's bollocks. I was never cut out to be a leader. Look, we all have a say in what happens. No one tells anyone else what to do."

"But you've been doing that since the beginning, and getting it right most of the time. And yes, we discuss things and decide a way forward. But it's you we look to, Jay. And you're who we want."

"I don't want to talk about this anymore."

"Did I say this was a democracy?" asked Annie. "Maybe I was wrong. We're not asking you, Jay. We're *telling* you. If it wasn't for you, we wouldn't have made it this far."

"Can't you see?" asked Lisa. "We need you to accept it. It's not going to make any difference to the way things are working now. And they *are* working. You just have to accept it. We know you'd never abuse it. We need your strength, Jay. It holds us together."

"Alex," I said tightly. "You're twice my age. *You* be the leader!"

"You saved us at that community centre, Jay," Alex replied. "You got us out of there before the place blew up. Everything that happened back there at the meat mart. That was all down to you."

"Gordon." I turned to him, still trying not to fly off the handle. "You were there. Didn't you tell them how terrified I was? How I couldn't move?"

Gordon shook his head. "You," he said simply, echoing what he'd said the last time this bloody stupid discussion had come up.

That was it. I couldn't keep it in any longer. I was just about to tell them all to take a running jump off the cliff edge when Juliet grabbed me by the shirt collar. For someone so slender, she was also very strong. She slammed me back against the dump truck. The sheer abruptness of her action not only took me completely by surprise, it also seemed to knock most of the anger right out of my system.

"And you pulled me off that radio mast, Jay. If you hadn't come down for me, I would have fallen."

"Juliet, it was Gordon and Alex who pulled us up. They were the ones who . . ."

"Shut it, Jay! You're the one who came down across the mast. No one said you had to. You did it, because you couldn't do anything else. So if they—if we—want you to be the leader of our own little rat pack, just . . . say . . . *yes.*" And with each of those last three words she banged me against the dump truck by my shirt collar.

When she'd finished, we just stood looking at each other, her fingers fastened in my shirt collar. And then she pulled me forward and kissed me hard on the mouth. There was loud laughter and applause. When she pulled away again, I tried to say something more, but Juliet crushed her mouth on mine again and this time there were whoops and wolf whistles with the applause.

"Try getting out of that," she said again, when we pulled apart.

She was the most beautiful woman I've ever known. And I was deeply in love with her. What the hell was I supposed to say, except: "All right then."

If nothing else, it seemed to put everyone else in a good mood, no matter how mad I thought they were. Okay, then, I'd said yes; but nothing was going to change, so far as I was concerned.

The best thing that happened was later in the afternoon.

We'd made a pretty good first job of getting some vegetables planted. We'd just have to keep our fingers crossed. There was good compost—we'd followed all the instructions. Gordon had stuck up a handwritten sign, *Sons and Daughters of the Soil,* which gave everybody a good laugh. With any luck we'd have more vegetable stew out of that lot than we needed.

There was still lots of "daylight" left when Juliet and I decided to go "shopping."

I needed a new jacket—the last one had been torn on the dump truck. She wanted new shoes. And there was a store on the other side of our plateau (well, half a store). Things like forgetting to take our credit cards just didn't seem to be a problem.

We were wary of most of the buildings still standing. There was no way of knowing how sound the structures were, but the department store looked to be okay. There was a car showroom next door. Everything in there had collapsed, except part of the frontage. Miraculously, the massive glass windows were completely undamaged and, standing centre-stage, unscratched, was a gleaming red Aston Martin.

"How about that?" asked Juliet.

"Very nice, but expensive."

"You mean you won't buy it for me?"

"When I win the lottery, it'll be the first thing on the list."

Juliet began to laugh.

"What is it?" I asked.

"We could drive that car out of here and back to the Rendezvous. We can . . . *afford* it. But what we can't afford is to use the petrol."

Both laughing, we entered the building.

The ceiling had come down halfway into the store on the ground floor, burying whatever had been there. But just through the main entrance, just off Wady Street, there had been a men and women's clothing section, and a bedding department. We stepped carefully over the cracked and littered floor. Rainwater was dripping from the shattered ceiling way across the store, like miniature waterfalls. Ridiculous, I know, but it looked beautiful. I found a rack of jackets and began trying them on for size, leaving Juliet to hunt for shoes. It didn't take me long to find what I was after, and when I went to look for Juliet, I found her beside one of the counters beyond the clothing section. There had been several Plexiglas stands on the counter, containing department-store jewellery. Most had fallen to the floor, but there was still one standing. When I reached her, she was looking at the necklaces thoughtfully.

"Can I help you, miss?" I said, like a store assistant.

"Hmmm." She put a finger to her lips. "Not sure about these. Haven't you got anything more expensive?"

"Have you tried our ground-floor selection?" I asked, pointing down to the jewellery lying around her feet. She smiled and linked her arm with mine, dragging me away across the store with surprising strength towards the shoe section. While she set about selecting some boots, I wandered to a toy and games department. The ceiling had come down on most of it, but there was still a rack of tricycles and some kids' games. For a moment, I had a mental flash of the Crying Kid. It threatened to ruin my good feeling, so I pushed it away. Maybe it was longer than just a "flash," because Juliet seemed to come up behind me only moments later, even though she subsequently told me that she'd had to push her way into a storeroom at the side of the shoe section to find a pair of leather boots her size.

"A penny for them," she said.

"Not worth it. You find what you're after?"

Juliet indicated the boots with a sweep of her hand. I murmured approval. A box had slid from one of the games shelves, spilling packs of playing cards all around. I stooped and picked up a packet. "Maybe something for everyone to do during those long nights at the Rendezvous."

She didn't say anything. She just took my hand and we walked back through the racks of clothes to the bedding section. There was a double bed there, called "The Honey-Mooner"; a four-poster done up with velvet drapes. The frilled sheets and pillows were whiter than white.

"Think we need playing cards for those long nights?" she asked, and she wasn't smiling.

"No, Juliet," I said; and I picked her up, carrying her to the bed.

As we undressed each other, she suddenly held both my hands by the wrists. Our faces were very close.

"Did you feel it, Jay?" she asked. "When you came out over the mast? And we were holding each other?"

I didn't have to ask any questions. I was just utterly amazed. First, that I could have felt that way about someone I'd never met, even though we were dangling over a hellish drop and all I should be concerned about was getting the hell out of there. Secondly, that *she'd* felt something. For a moment I couldn't speak, even though I wanted to ask her a hundred questions; about exactly *how* she'd felt. Part of me was frightened; scared that she'd felt something completely different. So different that it might crush the way I felt about her. I was full inside. My heart was beating fast, my mouth was dry. I was incredibly happy, but I was afraid. And even though there were so many things I needed to ask and needed to say, I could only nod.

"Trevor was right. I haven't . . . haven't been lucky with relationships."

"Juliet, you don't have to . . ."

"This is *serious, Jay!*" she said, now gripping both sides of my face. We were so close that our lips were touching when we talked. "In the past, I've only ever been wanted for the way I look. For one thing. You know? So don't lie to me, Jay. Don't hurt me. And don't just want me for the one thing."

I struggled to find my voice again. "Juliet," I said. "It's *you* I want."

We made love then in that department store, in that "HoneyMooner" bed.

It was different and special. We had the closeness that we'd felt on that first, dangerous meeting. We were truly *together*. I can't discuss it anymore, can't give you any more explanations without everything seeming clichéd. I don't know, maybe cli-chés *are* clichés because they very often touch on the really true things in life, and people get sick of hearing and reading about them. Something wonderful had happened. Something wonderful and special.

And all I know is that was the Best Thing.

Afterwards, when we'd lain together for a long time, she leaned across me and picked up the pack of cards that I'd left on the side table. She unwrapped the cellophane carefully. I watched as she took the cards out and began to flip through them, discarding them on the sheets before us.

"This is you," she said. "The King of Hearts."

"Oh, yeah . . . ?" I began.

Juliet put a finger to my lips, her face serious.

She began flicking through them again; found one that she wouldn't show me and put it to one side. Then she found another and said: "This is mine." It was the Queen of Hearts.

"And this," she said, picking up the hidden card as she dis-carded the remaining pack, "is ours."

I didn't have to look to know that it was the Ace of Hearts.

Juliet took the Queen, and pressed it into my hand. "Promise me you'll keep it forever, Jay."

"I promise."

I took the King, and pressed it into Juliet's hand. Her eyes were shining, and she was utterly beautiful. She picked up the Ace, kissed it, and gave it to me. "One of us will have this one for a month, then give it back to the other. As long as we're in love."

I kissed the Ace, leaned over and kissed her.

We lay together for a long time, and then she said: "It's all I can give you, Jay."

"I don't want anything else, Juliet."

We made love again.

And this time it didn't matter which world we were living in.

| CHAPTER TWO | DAMON DREAMS |

ALMOST SIX MONTHS TO THE DAY AFTER Wayne died, Damon had his first "new" dream of the Vorla.

Up until that time, all his dreams had been bad; most of them based on the memories of things that had happened since the quake. How could nightmares "improve" on those things? And when he dreamed of the rolling Black Sea that came up from the Chasm, flowed over buildings and ruined cars and cracked earth to engulf everything that lived and left no trace of itself behind afterwards, it was with a stabbing anxiety that brought him awake, shuddering and bathed in sweat.

But he was still dreaming, because now he could see Wayne rising from a glistening black pool at the foot of his bed. Damon screwed his eyes shut before he could see his friend's face properly. He kept them shut, his fingers clutching his shirt front, intensely relieved that he had left the dream behind. He opened his eyes.

And Wayne was still standing there, arms folded across his chest like some corpse that had been dredged from a vat of black oil and laid out vertically in front of him. Wayne's eyelids opened, but Damon could not see his eyes. Only the black, hollowed darkness of an ebony statue's face. Damon desperately willed himself to wake, and could not.

The statue grinned, and it was an expression that Damon remembered well. He'd seen it so many times before, when Wayne had a cool idea. The last time he remembered seeing it was when he'd written on the school toilet wall "Stafford Sucks Shite," and then they'd pushed the "informer's" note into the head teacher's pigeonhole, telling him that they'd seen Jay O'Connor deliberately avoid cleaning it off the wall tiles.

"*Neat, wasn't it?*" said the sculpture, and suddenly it wasn't a statue anymore. It was Wayne, through and through, only a different colour. Rivulets of blackness flowed continually over his face and down across his body, as if he himself were the rippling surface of some strange black pool. Or as if he were standing behind a shimmering barrier.

Damon tried to answer, but couldn't find his voice.

"*That's all right,*" said Wayne. "*I thought that it was scary as well. At the beginning. But it isn't like the others say it is. Evil, and all that other crap. It . . . well, it feels . . . good.*" And he hugged himself then, with that familiar smile on his face. For a while he swayed from side to side, and despite his fear Damon could see that he was truly enjoying himself.

"*I am enjoying myself. There's stuff down here, at the bottom of the Chasm, that you wouldn't believe.*"

Now Damon could feel Wayne's reassurance taking the edge off his nightmare.

"*That's because there's nothing to fear. They've got everything wrong. And the things they've told you? All fucking lies. We're in a new life now, Damon. No doubt about that. But everyone's keeping you at arm's length, keeping you away from the Truth. While you're sleeping, they all get together and whisper about what they're going to do. They don't tell you anything. The truth is, they're frightened of you. Just like they were frightened of me.*"

"But, Wayne, aren't you . . . I mean . . . aren't you . . . ?"

"Dead? Yeah, of course. But 'dead' doesn't mean the same over here as it does where we came from. There's no big deal about dying. Nothing to be afraid of. See, once you're dead and with the Vorla, that's when you see the real Truth, that's when you really start living. I'm telling you, the living I've done since I died . . . well, you have to experience it yourself. No, the thing that's wrong is the way I died. Those fuckers, Alex and Candy. They just left me to die. Just like the others'll leave you to die, eventually. They don't want you around, Damon."

Damon could feel the anger swelling in his breast, as if it had somehow been implanted there by an outside force.

"Of course you're angry. That's because you're better than them. Well, we're not going to let them get away with it."

"What do you want me to do?"

"I knew it. Knew you'd understand. Listen . . . " And Wayne leaned forward confidentially, placing one dripping hand on the bottom of the bed. The movement defied gravity as he swayed forward at the hips, legs bound together in one black column; like some black cobra swaying forward out of its basket. For a moment, Damon was hypnotised by the streamers and globules that ran from Wayne's fingertips onto the mattress, as if exploring the material, before flowing back to the fingers once more. *"Listen,"* said Wayne, to get his attention. *"They think they've got the Vorla where they want it. They think the light's keeping it away. They think they've won the fight. Well, they fucking haven't."*

"I can smash up the generators. Fix those floodlights."

"No, the Vorla's got bigger plans than that. But it knows who its friends are, Damon. I've put a word in for you. No, you've just got to bide your time a little longer. You just have to wait for the right moment."

"When will it be? When will the moment come?"

"Someone's coming. They're on their way now."

"Who?"

"People who know the Real Truth. People who know what the

Vorla really is, and what it wants. People like us, who understand. And when they get here, you'll know what to do and when to do it."

"Wayne, I don't know what you . . ."

"It'll be a test." The smile was gone from the black statue's face. Damon felt the fear again. *"You'll have to pass it if you want to stay here with us, Damon. There's going to be a new world, but not the one that Jay and all the others want. They're going to pay, Damon. The Vorla wants to make them pay for all they've done. And you can be with them, or you can be with me. It's up to you."*

"I don't want to be with them."

"Good. That's what I want to hear. Just remember, you've got to watch them and wait for *who's coming. You've got to be ready for the Test when it comes."*

"All right, Wayne."

"You know this is a dream, don't you?"

"I think so."

"Well, it is. But it's real. Don't question it. I'll be coming to you in dreams from now on. We'll talk, and you'll tell me what's been happening here. And we'll work out what we're going to do . . . for the Vorla."

"Anything you say, Wayne. I want to be with you. On your side."

"And that's the winning side." Again, the familiar smile. *"Just remember . . . "*

"Yes?"

"Someone's coming."

388

CHAPTER THREE | CLOSER TO HEAVEN

GORDON SAT IN THE RUINS OF WHAT HAD once been a church hall.

His throat was dry, and his heart was beating fast. Only part of him knew what he was doing here; the rest was driven by a strange impulse that both elated and frightened him. No one had questioned him that afternoon, when he set off on his own with his guitar slung over his back. Everyone knew the rules, about making sure that they were back at the Rendezvous and the safety of the lights well before that greyness began to grow dark. Night had a way in this new world, not so much of falling as suddenly being there and taking everyone by surprise. But it was "early afternoon," and experience had shown that there would be at least another four or five hours of safety left.

That morning, during one of her forages through the ruins, Annie had come across spare guitar strings. There were no music stores on this crag; the only one in Edmonville that Gordon frequented had been over a half a mile away to the west and had vanished into the Chasm when the quake hit, along with an entire shopping centre, the town hall offices and three thousand people. She'd been keeping an eye open for strings (among many other "needs") during her foraging trips (at which she'd become quite expert) and had discovered that a general store they'd previously searched had a small music section behind a fallen wall. Nothing extravagant. No guitars there, and it seemed that the chance of there being any guitar string replacements was remote to say the least. But there they were; amidst fallen shelves and the crushed remains of a baby grand piano. On her return to the Rendezvous, Gordon was so overjoyed when she'd dropped them in his lap that he'd jumped from his seat and gone to kiss her. Suddenly embarrassed, he'd paused in midair.

"What's the matter?" Annie had laughed. "Speechless?"

She'd kissed him then.

A good day and a good feeling.

But afterwards, when the strings had been fitted and he'd had some practice, the strange impulse had come over him. Lisa had looked up when he'd started off down the garden past the extension.

"More puh-practice," he'd said, waving back. "And . . . walk."

Lisa smiled, and nodded.

And he was gone, down past Yardley Terrace (or what was left of it), on past The Fallen Oak pub and the grisly reminder of the burned-out meat mart somewhere behind, down rubble-strewn Wady Street, past the overturned bus and its scrawled graffiti on the roof: *Ed Gein.*

And finally, to the Church Hall, standing on what had once been a main street; but now was the only building left standing with four walls. There was a mound of rubble inside—the remains of the ceiling, which had collapsed. To Gordon, this building had special memories. Not pleasant memories, exactly. He'd often walked past this building in his previous existence. Posters were still there, advertising a Line Dancing Special Event that had never materialised. How could they have known what was going to happen to Edmonville when the posters went up? Gordon wondered if any of the people in the community centre on the night that it burned had been intending to go along. And then he'd pushed the thought from his mind.

His special memory came from the time he was seven years old. He'd been walking past this place with his aunt and he'd heard the sounds of a youth band rehearsing inside. They'd been playing rock music, and Gordon wanted so much to be a part of it. They'd walked on. And he'd never heard music like that coming from the church hall ever again. Who'd been playing? What was that rock music? He'd never heard it before or since on the radio. Did the memory of it have something to do with him and the loneliness that had led him to the guitar after all these years? It was a melancholy puzzle.

But, for what he had in mind, it seemed to be the only place to go.

He'd never been inside the place before.

And he would never know what it had really looked like before the quake. The windows had burst out. The walls were fractured. He could see the blank greyness of the "sky" through the remaining, shattered roof timbers.

This was the place. The only place.

But would it work?

Sitting on the pile of rubble, Gordon unslung the guitar. He didn't want to start with any practice-stuff. He wanted to start with something straight away. "Ninna Nanna Sul Nero"? No, he had done that the last time. What about the piece he'd played by the bonfire on the night of the dead? No, that was too special; he didn't want to ruin the memories of the special bond that seemed to have been formed that night; in many ways, the most important night in his life, when the music that had been his only, lonely companion had reached out and he'd been able to share it with others. No, this must be something different.

Gordon strummed the first chord: "Closer to Heaven." A good choice, given who he was trying to attract.

He looked around. What did he expect? That they would

suddenly appear, as if by magic, just as they'd appeared that night back at the Rendezvous.

Give them time, Gordon, he thought. *And keep playing.*

The music filled the shell of the church hall, swirling out through the ragged timbers and into the greyness. The acoustic effect was strange; like playing in a funnel. But the resonances were wonderful.

And while he played, Gordon thought about the strange creatures that Lisa had christened Cherubim. Were they really angels? If they were, what did it mean? If they weren't—then what the hell were they? No one doubted what Alex and Candy had seen, or that they'd killed Wayne—least of all Gordon, who seemed to remain the only other person to have seen them so far. And why couldn't he bring himself to raise it with anyone? After all, they were potentially lethal: Wayne was testimony to that. Why couldn't he raise it with Alex and Candy, knowing the grief that kept their relationship so badly shattered and unresolved? What if one of those creatures really was their dead son, Ricky? The Cherubim fascinated and worried Gordon, and he had sat alone at night on more than one occasion since their first visit, ostensibly on guard; actually waiting to see if they would return. So far, he hadn't the guts to play the guitar in the house again. Another puzzle.

So he was going to try this out. Away from everyone else.

Would they come?

There was no movement in the rubble. No secret, scuffling noises; no sixth sense telling him that there were other presences.

He played on.

He could see things so much more clearly when he was playing. Not only had most of Edmonville been wiped off the map, but also according to what Jay and Juliet had been able to get out of Trevor, the map didn't exist anymore. Even so, since the terrible time of the quake and the loss of his aunt, it seemed that Gordon had had more dealings with people on a one-to-one basis than he'd ever had in his previous life, in that other world. They might be living in a new kind of Hell, but at least he wasn't alone anymore.

A sound from above. A piece of stone or plaster, falling from the ragged hole in the roof. Nothing more. Plaster dust swirled in the air and Gordon watched the stone roll down the rubble mound on which he was sitting, causing a miniature landslide.

The music came to an end. Gordon paused. Then began to play the same piece again.

Two hours later, he stopped.

What had he expected? That they'd come swarming again? What then? Did he expect them to speak, when he knew in his heart that they had no voice? Was he expecting them to give him answers?

Still unsure, Gordon hauled himself down the pile of rubble, and hoisted the guitar over his shoulder. He paused only once to look back, as if expecting to see small faces with bright, intense eyes; staring through the ragged hole in the ceiling. But there was nothing. Only the echo-memories of that day long ago, when he had walked past here with his aunt and had heard the music.

Back on the ruins of the street, head down, Gordon made his way slowly back to the Rendezvous.

Inside the church hall, plaster dust pattered down on the mound of rubble, swirling in a cloud. The cloud twisted and dispersed, as if something that moved faster than the eye could see had suddenly flashed through its centre.

A hinge creaked on a shattered door.

It sounded like the fading laughter of a small child.

CHAPTER FOUR | NEW SOUNDS

L ISA CAUGHT CANDY WATCHING THE BOY through the downstairs window of the Rendezvous. Perhaps she had been drinking again; it was hard to tell these days. Her life seemed to have blurred almost to the point of non-involvement, although she assisted with the practical requirements wherever necessary.

Lisa had just left Annie back in the garage, checking over the generator, and was making her way back towards the house and its front garden. The boy was sitting on the ground, digging a hole with a plastic spade he'd found, just like any other kid his age. Candy was sitting inside the house at the window, just watching him. Was she thinking back to her own boy? Or maybe to the strange encounter with the Cherubim in the minimart? Since the boy showed no sign of ever talking again or giving any details of his name or family, Lisa had decided to "christen" him Michael. They couldn't continue to depersonalise him by calling him "the boy," so it was time that he had at least a temporary name. No one except Annie knew that it was the name of Lisa's father. Unfortunately, the boy— Michael—never responded to his new name.

Lisa waited for Candy to spot her as she approached the Rendezvous, remembering the confrontation they'd had the night when she refused to leave the minimart and the "Cherubim" had appeared. She knew what Candy thought about Annie and herself. They were "unnatural." Lisa was well used to the arguments back home about lesbian and homosexual partners adopting children. Perhaps, then, there should be reasons to dislike Candy. The drinking, making her less than a valuable contributor to their survival situation. The way she despised her husband. The dark jealousy about the boy, as if by rights he should become her own surrogate son to compensate for the loss of Ricky. Couldn't she see that Michael had "adopted" Annie and herself, and that it wasn't the other way around? And what the hell did it matter, in any event? As long as the boy was loved and protected. But as Lisa reached the gate, she could not find it in herself to hate Candy. Instead, an unbidden wave of pity seemed to overwhelm her. Lisa tried to push it aside. Everyone had their troubles in their former lives, but those troubles had been dwarfed by the cataclysm that had overwhelmed them since the quake. There was no time for the old ways, no time for the old grievances. Only time to pull together, to learn, and to set about creating a new life for themselves in this place; never losing sight of the horrifying and ever-present threat of whatever lurked deep down in the darkness of the Chasm.

Candy's face was blank as she continued to watch from the window, but Lisa seemed to feel the anguish inside; seemed to sense the hidden grief. No one could help her with it, not even her husband. She had locked it down tight, afraid that it might destroy her and, as a result, it was destroying her.

Candy saw Gordon before she saw Lisa, as he hopped over the garden wall. He'd been on another of his "practice walks"; finding a quiet place to play his guitar and to think. Lisa waved as she opened the gate. Gordon walked over, and when Lisa looked back at the window, Candy was gone. The boy ran over to Lisa, took her hand and pulled her across to the hole he'd been digging. He'd been making a small village of mud houses. After she'd praised him for it, she asked if anyone was hungry.

Gordon and the boy nodded vigorously.

"Then I guess . . ." Lisa looked up at the window again. Candy had definitely vanished back inside. " . . . I guess I'll be Mother. What colour tin today?"

Gordon laughed. Since most everything they ate came from tins or bottles (until such time as their home-grown food was ready), they'd developed comedy routines between themselves on the colour-coding of tins based on everyone's mood that day. Gordon waved his hands—any colour.

"Alex tried his hand at baking bread this morning," said Lisa. "Packet stuff from one of the shops. Smelled great this morning, so it might turn out okay. What do you think?" Gordon and Michael nodded again, and Lisa went inside.

There was no sign of Candy but Alex was standing at the bottom of the stairs looking up. Lisa had seen that despairing expression before. She'd seen anxiety on everyone's face since the quake, had seen terror when the night horrors had threatened them. But it seemed that none of it matched the despair that Alex felt in trying to get close to his wife and in helping her. He looked like that now in the main hallway, as if still listening to the words that had been exchanged before Candy vanished to her room. Lisa hadn't heard anything, but deliberately made a noise as she entered. Startled, Alex turned around. He looked old this afternoon.

"Bread smells good," said Lisa. "Anyone tasted it yet?"

Alex dusted hands that had already been washed of flour, and tried unsuccessfully to smile. "Be my guest."

Lisa touched him on the shoulder as she moved to the kitchen. Three loaves had been laid out on plates, on the kitchen bench, one already sliced. She tried one of the slices. It tasted like heaven. Alex came in behind her as she picked slices for Gordon and Michael, opening a tin of corned beef from one of the cupboards. "I don't know what you used to do for a living," she said, without turning. "Back in the real world, I mean. But I reckon you were born to be a baker. We should celebrate tonight. Our first real bread. A few expensive bottles from our 'cellar.' What do you say?" When there was no reply, she turned.

Alex was leaning against one of the kitchen units, head down.

"Are you all right?" Concerned, Lisa moved towards him.

Alex held out a hand, shaking his head without looking.

Lisa stopped. Alex took a deep breath.

"What is it, Alex? What's wrong?"

"Nothing that hasn't been wrong for a long time."

"Candy?"

"Yeah, Candy. Every day that goes by . . . well, it just gets worse."

Lisa struggled to find something to say, but could find nothing.

Alex laughed. "Do you know where she is now?"

"I saw her from the garden. Watching Michael."

"But do you know where she is *now*?"

"Upstairs?"

"Yes, upstairs. With Damon."

"With *Damon*?"

Alex looked up, and now Lisa saw the real extent of the grief in his eyes. He nodded emphatically, so that she wouldn't misunderstand. When he screwed his eyes shut, tears squeezed out and fell down his cheeks. He could still see the image of Candy storming past him in the hallway, cursing him. He could still see Damon standing at the top of the stairs, holding his hand down to her as Candy snapped her head back to glare at him; then reaching for Damon's hand as they both vanished from sight around the top of the landing.

"How long . . . ?" Lisa struggled to find the right words. "I mean, how long . . . ?"

"Weeks now. Five, six. I don't know."

"I don't understand."

397

"Join the club. What am I supposed to do? Go up there now, fling open the bedroom door? Drag the little bastard out of bed and break his nose? Give him a good kicking? I could do that. No problem. Grab Candy, throw her around. Shake her and shake her until I can get all the pain and the hate out of her. No, I don't see that solving anything."

"If it's hurting you, then make it stop."

"Yes, it's hurting me. It's tearing me up inside. And it's just like it was before, in our other world. The agonies, and the hurting. The drinking. Candy's young pick-ups. We've had more than our fair share of broken windows, shattered crockery, cuts and bruises. But where does that lead to, except splitting up? You see, Lisa—I *love* Candy. And when things got so bad between us that we were laying hands on each other all the time, I knew that I had to stand back, had to let her get on with it. Maybe burn out all the pain with the alcohol. Let her have her one-night stands, hoping that she'd realise it was all emptiness compared to the way I felt—the way I *feel*—about her."

"It can't be right, Alex. Not if it's giving you both so much pain."

"And then, God help me, after the quake hit Edmonville, after all the death and the horror that we've seen, I thought that it might even bring us . . . well, bring us together again. But now . . . " He waved a hand at the ceiling. "Now, it's just like before."

"I don't know what to say. Don't know how to help you."

"You know that the boy makes it worse, don't you?"

"Yes."

"It's worse because he's chosen to love you and Annie."

"I know."

"That night, in the minimart. Those children—what you called the Cherubim."

Lisa nodded.

"They were real, you know. We did see them. Even though

no one else has. They *did* kill Wayne. And we *did* see Ricky. He had become one of them, whatever they are."

"No one doubts it, Alex."

"You'd think that seeing him again, even like that, would make a difference. Once, he was dead. Now . . . well, now . . . he's *here*. It doesn't make sense. But even though he's changed, he's alive. *Alive!*" He gave a weak laugh. "It hasn't helped. It's just made things worse. Candy wants him, you see. And she still can't have him."

"Alex . . . I'm so sorry."

"That bread's getting cold. Come on, let's take it out to Gordon and Michael."

Alex held the door open for her. She paused with the two plates as she passed, and kissed him on the cheek, moving quickly on in case he didn't want her to see his expression.

Outside in the garden, Gordon was sitting cross-legged beside the boy, helping him with the mud houses. The ever-present guitar lay alongside him on the ground. Lisa walked towards them, a plate in either hand. She could get used to this mother-figure business, if only she could do something about Alex and Candy's grief. She tried not to think of Candy and Damon upstairs. Someone called from the main street. It was Jay and Juliet, returning from their wanderings in the ruins. It didn't take a genius to realise that something important was happening between them. They made their way, hand in hand, towards the Rendezvous.

Lisa bent down, ready to hand the plates to Gordon and Michael.

And then the boy looked at Gordon and said: "You can't speak very well, can you?"

Lisa froze. For a moment, she couldn't believe that the words had come from him. Almost a year since they'd first been stranded on this rock and not a single word from the little boy they'd saved from the Chasm. Her eyes flickered to Gordon, as if he were somehow a ventriloquist, throwing his voice.

"No," said Gordon, and in that instant Lisa knew that she was not imagining things. Her heart was hammering in her breast. What if Gordon didn't say the right thing in response? Would that break the magic? Would it send the boy back into his world of silence? She struggled to say something. Struggled to think of something quiet and natural so that she wouldn't frighten it all away. She opened her mouth, but nothing would come out. Now her inability to speak seemed as if it had bound her to the other two.

"Why?" asked the boy.

Please, Gordon! thought Lisa. *Say something. Say anything that'll make everything all right. Don't hesitate, don't stammer. Please bring him back to us . . .*

"Like you," said Gordon. "I . . . had a bad fright." And Lisa could see the effort on Gordon's face. She could see the contortion in the muscles of his cheeks, could see his Adam's apple wavering; could see the beads of sweat appearing on his brow. "Just like you. My . . . muh-mother and fuh-father. They were both killed."

"How?"

"Car crash. Juh-just like you."

"Did it make you sad?"

"Yuh-yes. So sad, I couldn't speak. Suh-still can't speak very well."

"I was scared," the boy went on. "So scared. I was . . . was . . . "

Lisa tensed, plates still held out and gripped tight.

Please, not now. Keep speaking. Don't stop!

"I was in a different place," the boy went on. He had only been pausing to think, trying to find a way of expressing himself. With a gesture so natural that it almost broke Lisa's heart, he brushed a strand of hair from his eyes and reached out to take a piece of bread from one of the plates. He bit into it, and began to chew. "Like . . . I was here. But not here. Funny thing. I think it's because I was so sad. Are you still sad?"

"Yes." Gordon also reached out and took bread from the other plate. "You?" He began to eat.

"Yes."

They ate in silence then. Lisa felt as if every nerve in her body was screaming. The plates began to tremble in her hands.

"Wuh-what's . . . your name?" asked Gordon.

The boy chewed fast, and swallowed.

The pause was agonising for Lisa.

"Lisa and Annie call me Michael. But my real name is Robin MacKenna. I live at a hundred and thirty-three Kings Park. You have to know where you live in case you get lost and have to ask a policeman to take you home. My mummy says."

There was another silence while they ate. Lisa felt sweat trickling down the small of her back.

"Teach me," said Gordon, at last.

The boy looked up, chewing.

"Tuh-teach me," continued Gordon. "To talk the way you can."

"How?"

"We'll just tuh-talk together." Sweat was streaming down Gordon's face now, dripping from his chin as he ate. "About . . . anything, eh-everything. And I'll . . . I'll copy the wuh-way you talk. Okay?"

"Okay." The boy nodded, and continued eating.

Tears blurred Lisa's vision, flowing down her cheeks. Trembling, she placed the plates on the ground and leaned forward to stroke the boy's—Robin's—face.

"Nice bread," he said, cramming the last of it into his mouth and turning his attention back to the mud houses.

Lisa put her hand on Gordon's damp face, felt the tension in the muscles beneath his cheek.

"God bless you, Gordon," she said.

Gordon looked down. For a moment, he had difficulty swallowing.

When Lisa looked up, she saw that Jay and Juliet had

been watching from the garden gate. Behind, Alex had been standing over her. The look of distress had gone from his face, replaced by something resolute and strong. He took her hand and helped her to rise, nodding his approval as she wiped the tears from her face.

Down below, the boy said: "Think we could make a river through these houses, or would that be wasting our water?"

"Maybe wasting," said Gordon, and began to help with his excavations. "Draw one instead." He took a twig and began scrawling wave shapes in the dried mud.

"Yeah," said the boy enthusiastically.

And then everyone heard the sounds of an engine, distant and buzzing. Lisa looked across to the garage, expecting to find that Annie had found yet another way of coping with the inconveniences that the End of the World had brought. Everyone seemed to have the same idea, but now it was clear that the sound wasn't coming from there. And it was getting louder.

"Oh my God," said Juliet. "I don't believe it."

She was looking up at the sky.

Everyone looked up.

There was a shape up there in the greyness, heading their way. And the sound of the engine was getting louder as it came closer. An aeroplane, a helicopter?

Lisa's heart was hammering again as everyone's attention fixed on the indeterminate shape flying their way. Annie emerged from the garage, paused to look, and began to run towards them.

"Someone's coming," Lisa shouted to her. "Annie . . . someone's *coming!*"

CHAPTER FIVE | THE JOURNAL OF JAY O'CONNOR: THE OTHERS

I T'S IMPOSSIBLE TO DESCRIBE HOW I FELT.
There was the special something that Juliet and I had found, in spite of our situation. Then there was what we'd just seen between Gordon and the boy—I mean Robin. If that wasn't enough, the sound of the engine from overhead. Annie began whooping and waving her arms as the shape floated closer. Then we were all doing it, like we'd gone mad.

Candy and Damon came running out of the Rendezvous just after that. Maybe I should have put two and two together then, but the only thing that anyone could see or hear was the prospect of rescue, coming closer.

"Is it a helicopter?" asked Robin in his new voice. I saw Candy staring at him. She was looking at the kid and then at the shape in the sky, as if what she could see up there was somehow responsible for giving him back his voice. Damon stood, hands on hips and shirttail hanging out. It was, as usual, almost impossible to read anything on his face.

Gordon shook his head emphatically. "Muh . . ." He looked down at Robin guiltily, as if another stutter might change everything. All the kid was interested in now was the thing in the sky. "Microlight," finished Gordon.

As soon as he said it, I knew he was right. Not exactly the

fleet of rescue helicopters we'd been expecting, but the first signs we'd had that there was something else out there.

"A what?" asked Candy.

"Motorised hang-glider," said Juliet. "Looks like a two-seater, but there's only one person in it."

The microlight circled us as we continued to wave, like some great big kite. Perhaps a thousand or so feet high in that dense greyness. It was impossible to tell whether the pilot was a man or a woman. It dipped and continued to circle, dropping lower each time.

I knew what everyone was thinking then. We'd all had to accept what that small part of the Vorla had told us about what had happened to Edmonville. Under threat of being wiped out forever in the daylight, we had to believe what the Black Stuff in Trevor had told us if we were going to come to terms with living in this new place. We thought that it had originally wanted us to despair, to believe that we were experiencing a biblical End of the World, complete with its self-created Four Horsemen of the Apocalypse—this time with Evil winning out. But Juliet and I also believed that we'd given that small part of the Vorla its own reasons to be terrified. It knew what had happened to the part of it that had escaped into the garden, and into "daylight." And it knew that we were prepared to do it again. That's why we believed its new explanation that we had been catapulted out of one existence and into another by some sort of "psychic" earthquake.

But now I knew the others were thinking that maybe the arrival of this newcomer meant that its second story had also been lies, after all. There *was* something out there. We hadn't been transported to another fucking dimension, and help *was* coming.

"It's all lies," said Candy, giving voice to the thought. "What the Vorla said about us not being in our own world anymore . . ."

"Don't count on it," I said, feeling like a shit. But someone

404

had to say what came next. "It's just a microlight. It could be another survivor on another crag somewhere. Maybe he or she's found some petrol, been able to get up into the air. Maybe they're looking down thinking *we're* going to be their rescuers."

What I'd said didn't seem to wear down anyone's optimism. Annie continued to whoop and wave; everyone was all smiles. Alex was ruffling Robin's hair, and everyone still felt pretty good.

And then the microlight banked, and began to fly off.

"What the hell . . . ?" said Annie.

"Where's it going?" asked Lisa.

"Christ," said Alex. "Maybe we frightened it off."

The drone of the engine began to fade as the microlight dipped again and vanished over the semi-collapsed roofs of buildings on the other side of the street. No one had expected that to happen, and the mood began to change.

"But there still might be others," said Juliet. "Other survivors, Jay."

I nodded.

So we followed the microlight as it vanished from sight over the ruined rooftops, catching up with it again when it had reached the edge of the park. It droned and circled once more, as if it were encouraging us to follow, waiting for us to catch up. And as we hurried, the others were all yelling encouraging noises, trying to get the pilot to come down.

We passed the site of the bonfire, and it was a bloody strange feeling looking at the charred remains. We'd been here for nearly a year, but it seemed as if that first night we'd stood by this fire, surrounded by the dead and by a living black sea, was a hundred years ago. Maybe we would still be spending our nights here if it hadn't been for Annie and Lisa.

"He's going again," said Alex, and we followed once more, heading off across the furrowed grass of the park towards the west. Past the bordering fringe of trees was the remains of the apartment block that had fallen into the Chasm and the collapsed flyover. We'd been over every square inch of our plateau, hunting for food and fuel. Alex had called it "maximising our resources," and when everyone had looked at him he'd apologised and pointed out that he'd been a senior policy officer in local government before the earthquake. He'd burst out laughing then, and everyone had followed suit. Another good moment.

But the others weren't enjoying themselves so much now as the microlight swung around in the sky, circled over the trees and disappeared once more.

"What the *hell* is he doing?" demanded Candy.

I looked at Damon. Still with his blank face. It was strange. After everything we'd been through, I expected him to be just as filled with hope as the others—no matter how thin that hope might be. I thought back to the early days, and realised how much he'd changed. Withdrawn, certainly since Wayne's death. Not hostile anymore, but with this air of waiting.

If only I'd known what he'd been waiting *for*.

We reached the trees and there, circling over the ruins of the apartment block, was the microlight again. Still there, still waiting for us to catch up. People were getting angry now, as we climbed over the shattered concrete blocks and rusted iron girders that had once formed the base of the block. From the top of the mound, we'd be able to see the fallen flyover and the rusted wrecks of vehicles that it had come down on.

But that was not what drew our attention when we climbed to the top of the mound.

"Good *Christ*!" breathed Lisa, grabbing Robin with a look of joy on her face.

"I don't believe it," said Alex breathlessly.

"They came." Candy was on the verge of weeping. "After all this time, someone *came*."

How do I describe the way I felt? Well, I can't. I just know that this wave came over me as Juliet and I hugged on top of the mound. Hope, yes. Relief, certainly. I know that in that one moment, it was as if everything that had happened after the quake destroyed Edmonville . . . well, it was like *none* of it had happened. It all belonged to some nightmare time. There wasn't time to think everything through, only time to feel the joy of knowing that our ordeal was over.

About four hundred yards or so away, just beyond the collapsed flyover, lay the cliff edge. Two hundred feet or so from that cliff edge, across the Chasm, was the nearest plateau to ours. It wasn't possible to see its extent because of the destruction. From our standpoint on this side, we'd guessed that it was maybe a quarter-mile long, but the exact breadth of it was hidden by the other pinnacles and crags surrounding it. The blank greyness framing the ruins gave everything a false perspective. It could be a hundred yards or so wide, a quarter-mile, anything. There was no way of telling. As with every other peak or crag in New Edmonville, we'd spent time yelling across, trying to find out whether there were any other survivors. But there had never been any response. So we went on believing that we were the only ones; everyone else was either dead in the earthquake, or devoured afterwards by the Vorla.

But we had been wrong.

There *were* other survivors.

Dozens and dozens of them.

And they were all here now, standing on the cliff edge at the other side. Waving and cheering and yelling and hooting as we clambered down the mound, eager to get free of the rubble so that we could run the remainder of the way across the shattered highway and onto the open grass leading up to the cliff edge. The microlight was still circling overhead, and now we knew why it had been flying on, circling and returning. It had been leading us to these other survivors. I saw Gordon swinging the guitar around his head as he ran jumping over a concrete block and falling full length on the grass. But then he was up and running again, still swinging the guitar as he ran. Alex swung the boy—I mean Robin—up onto his back, piggyback style. Robin was laughing wildly, the first time we'd ever heard him make that noise. Even Candy was smiling as she picked her way over the ruins, and no one had ever seen *that* expression before. Annie and Lisa had their arms around each other, and I couldn't resist grabbing Juliet and swinging her round.

They were cheering even louder on the other side as we drew nearer.

Something made me look back, I don't know what.

Damon was still standing up on the mound, hands on hips and looking down. It was hard to tell from that distance, but I think he was smiling.

"Come on, then!" I yelled back at him. "Aren't you coming?" He didn't move. He just stood up there, watching.

I looked at Juliet as we ran.

"There are others," she breathed. Her face was . . . I don't know . . . *bright*. I'd thought she was beautiful before. But now she was like no other woman I'd ever seen in my life. My chest was suddenly tight and I felt so good I could hardly breathe.

And then, fifty feet or so from the cliff edge, we all stopped. Everyone's smile faded at the same time.

We stood and we watched as the crowd of people on the other side continued to whoop and cheer and yell.

And everything was wrong.

No one spoke. We just stood, and watched, and listened.

Not understanding at first, then disbelieving. All our hopes, all our joy. All the good feelings about finding someone else alive on these surreal peaks and crags of stone. All of it fading and dying as we realised that New Edmonville had found new nightmares for us. We saw, and we listened.

And then, once again . . .

We despaired.

CHAPTER SIX | WELCOMING COMMITTEE

THERE WERE ABOUT FORTY, PERHAPS FIFTY of them.

It seemed that none of them could be older than fifteen, the youngest perhaps eleven or twelve. And it soon became apparent as they ran and leapt on that far cliff edge that the whooping and cheering had not been to welcome the residents of the Rendezvous.

They were jeering and yelling abuse at them.

Most of their faces were painted; horizontal finger-streaks on the cheeks, vertical streaks on the forehead; reds, greens and blues. The clothes they wore were ragged and stained, looted from the department stores and fashion shops that they had managed to find in the ruins. Some wore extravagant jewellery around their necks and on their arms; others had tied designer belts around their heads, like improvised sweatbands, with the buckles fastened tight at the back and the ends of the belts hanging down. The overall effect was as if they were wearing some kind of tribal costume.

Alex tried to shout something across the abyss, but the jeering and yelling grew louder, drowning his voice. One of the youngsters, a girl aged about fourteen, picked up a rock from the cliff edge and threw it across. It came nowhere near the other side, dropping into the Chasm below. But suddenly another figure had appeared behind the "tribe." He was larger than the rest, and before anyone on either side could react, he seized the girl around the waist and stepped forward to the edge.

Annie was the first to guess what was going to happen, and yelled: "No!"

But there was nothing anyone could do.

The larger figure suddenly pitched the girl forward.

She screamed, twisting in the air as if she might be able to grab the cliff edge and save herself. But she had been thrown a good six feet out, and dropped screaming from sight. Instantly, the other youngsters were silent, looking down and listening as the girl's screams faded and faded . . . and were gone.

"You . . . you . . . *bastard*!" yelled Jay.

The figure looked up from the edge of the Chasm and smiled.

It was a man.

He was about thirty years old, and dressed in the same sort of garb as the others. A black waistcoat from what had once been a trendy designer suit. No shirt. Blue jeans, torn at the knee. Motorbike boots. A red leather lady's belt tied around his head. The other kids were looking up at him and waiting. This clearly was their leader. No one seemed to be concerned about the girl who had just been flung into the abyss.

The man smiled.

And then he yelled across at the others. It was a wordless, wild shout. And at his call, his followers began yelling and screaming too, carrying on just as before. Taunting and hurling abuse across the gap.

Overhead, the microlight was still circling. Now it seemed to be sharing the manic glee of the newcomers. It had not been leading them to safety or the comfort of other survivors. It had been searching for them, had brought them here to the edge so that they could be taunted.

Jay tried calling across again. But the constant shouting and jeering were meant to drown out his voice. Whoever they were, they were not interested in any kind of civilised contact. Throughout, the man—their leader—stood and smiled across the Chasm as his "tribe" continued their abuse.

When Lisa tried to make contact, hoping that a woman's voice might make some kind of difference, the man slowly raised an arm and pointed in their direction. As the cheering and the dancing on the cliff edge continued, he pointed at each of them in turn. Slowly, deliberately, and with the smile never wavering from his face. His motive was clear. He wanted them, each and every one.

Jay moved towards Alex.

"There's no reason why we should stay here any longer. Is there?"

Wearily, Alex looked back at the whooping crowd on the other side, and shook his head.

When everyone turned and began trudging back the way they'd come, the yelling and cheering grew louder, prompted by their retreat.

The man on the other side folded his arms and watched them go.

Up on the mound that had once been the apartment block, Damon smiled as he watched them climbing back up to him.

"Someone's come," he said aloud.

He seemed to sense that, somewhere, Wayne was laughing.

| THE JOURNAL OF
JAY O'CONNOR:
THE TOWER

BACK AT THE RENDEZVOUS, IN THE COMMUNAL
room, we had what I suppose you could call a "council of
war." Feelings were running high, and no one could be blamed
for that. After all, there'd been new hope when the microlight
made its appearance, even if, to my mind, there'd been little
real chance of rescue. I think everyone really knew that. It was
just the prospect of seeing new faces, of having new people
to share experiences with; just the knowledge that others had
been able to make it on their own and gotten this far in New
Edmonville without having fallen prey to the living dead and
the Vorla. To have it all dashed by the appearance of what
seemed to be a tribe of wild kids who only wanted to get over
here and do God knows what.

No one could forget the sight of that one adult; the guy who
had thrown the young girl into the Chasm. Maybe he'd given
instructions about throwing stones, or making direct contact,
or maybe he just did it for the hell of it. Whatever, it was this
act that convinced everyone of the tribe's hostile intentions.
No one thought they wanted to come over and share polite
conversation. Fortunately for us, the fissure between their side
and ours was wide enough to ensure that they couldn't come
over and visit.

"Know what I think they want?" asked Alex.

Everyone looked at him.

"I think they want everything we've got. Food, fuel, everything."

"Those kids didn't look scrawny," said Annie. "For the most part they looked pretty well fed. Maybe they've got more over there than we've got here."

Lisa laughed derisively. "Maybe they've come to share what they've got with us."

"The man," I said. "The big fella. I think his body language told us everything we wanted to know. I think dropping the girl over the side was supposed to tell us something about what they have in mind."

"Why haven't we heard or seen any of them before?" asked Annie. "I mean, it's been nearly a year now. And there're plenty of them. Why suddenly show their faces after all this time? There's been enough going on over here to let them know that there were survivors on this side."

We talked everything through, looked at it from every angle imaginable. But, as in the past when considering the bloody strange things that happened in New Edmonville, we ended up talking in circles and getting no nearer any of the answers. We did agree on one thing. In the morning, we'd head back to that cliff edge and try to make contact again, if that was possible. If they were still there. At the very least, we could show them that they weren't the only ones capable of making threatening noises. Perhaps it wasn't such a positive plan, but we couldn't think of anything better. The generators had been checked, the floodlights and streetlamps were illuminating the Rendezvous in preparation for the night. We were all set to take our worries to bed when the noises began.

Gordon was the first to hear something, pausing just ahead of Juliet and me on the stairs, on our way to our rooms. At first I thought he was turning back to tell us something he'd just remembered. But by the way he held his hand up and cocked his head I knew that he was listening.

It was a thin and distant clattering, somewhere way outside.

"What the hell was *that*?" exclaimed Annie.

It came again—the sound of metal on metal, a long way away.

By this time, everyone had heard it, and we hurried back down to the communal room to look out of the window into the darkening sky. Annie was in the kitchen area, peering out, but couldn't see anything. Now the sounds were coming more frequently. Irregular, erratic. Crashings and clatterings, as if someone were at work in a distant junkyard.

Moments later, everyone was in the front garden, looking every which way for some sign of what was making the noise. The floodlights and streetlamps made it impossible for us to see anything beyond the immediate area because of the glare.

"Where's it coming from?" asked Candy.

No one answered. The acoustics in New Edmonville caused constant confusion. Sounds here were sometimes flat and hollow; sometimes they seemed to echo off into the vast greyness forever. It was as if there was a whole new set of rules about sound. It was impossible to tell where the junkyard sounds were coming from. They were almost constant now. But, thank God, they didn't seem to be getting any nearer. Even so, given what I've said about the acoustics, this didn't offer anyone a great deal of comfort.

"The Vorla?" said Juliet.

Again, no one answered. It had been a long time since the Black Stuff had put in an appearance, but that didn't mean that it wasn't out there somewhere beyond the lights, swirling all around us and looking for a way in. But this wasn't the sound that the Vorla usually made. This wasn't a sea of voices, mumbling and hissing and screeching at us.

"The crops," said Lisa. "Maybe it's ruining the crops."

But that wasn't right either, because we could see the floodlit

414

area where we'd toiled to raise our own food. There was no sign of the slithering black sea flowing over the furrowed ground.

"What about our new arrivals?" said Alex. Everyone looked at the ruined line of houses on the other side of the street, as if it were somehow going to be possible to see all the way past the park and the ruined apartment block to the cliff edge where the newcomers had made their intentions so plain.

"Working outside in the night?" I said. "If they've managed to survive this far, then they must know all about the Vorla coming out in the dark."

"Maybe," said Gordon. "Bonfire."

"Yeah, I suppose they could have built one," I said. "The way we did. But I can't imagine it's going to make them very comfortable, watching that Black Stuff all around them, waiting for a way to get to them through the light."

"I'm going to check the generators again," said Annie.

"Do you need to?" I asked.

"No, but I don't like that sound. And doing something will just make me feel a little better."

Alex joined her as we all made our way back into the Rendezvous. When they returned, the noise was a constant banging and jangling. Still distant, but near enough to get everyone's nerves jangling nonetheless.

It was a bad night for everyone. We all stayed up longer than we'd intended, just for the company. But we'd already talked everything through, and no amount of speculation was going to give us any more answers. Maybe they were just having some kind of wild party out there?

Only Robin managed to get any proper sleep, lying across Lisa's lap on the sofa. I sat opposite with Juliet, both of us putting away a couple of brandies as we listened to the noises in the night. I watched him sleep; examined his young, innocent face. It brought back images of the Crying Kid. I don't know why I was still so disturbed about that. The poor little bastard, being driven away. But it still got to me. I looked around for

Damon, but he was nowhere to be seen. I was aware of Juliet then, watching me. She gave me a faint, worried smile, and I knew she wanted to ask me what was wrong. But she didn't, and I was glad, because this was a part of me that I couldn't understand, couldn't give any answers for.

Later, when we went to bed, we lay awake in each other's arms for a long, long time. I'm not even sure if we slept. But the noises just went on and on, as we waited for the darkness to become grey again, and for another day to dawn in New Edmonville. When it did, maybe then we'd have our answers.

The buzzing of the microlight woke everyone early.

When Juliet and I made our way down to the communal room, we could see that everyone was already out in the front garden, looking up at the sky. Sure enough, there was that big motorised kite again, circling the Rendezvous; first swooping low as if whoever was flying it was trying to get a better look at us all, and then flipping back up into the sky like he or she was showing off. I couldn't tell whether the banging metallic noises were still going on or whether the droning of the microlight was covering up the sounds.

"I think it's time to find out whether our friends were making that noise in the night," I said.

Everyone was ready. After a night of jangled nerves, we all wanted to discover just what the hell had been going on out there as quickly as possible. This time the microlight was following *us* as we made our way over the street and past the ruined houses that bordered the park. No one felt inclined to wave or cheer up at it as we made for the cliff edge. As we picked our way through the ruins, there was no sign that the Vorla had been up to anything in the night. The ploughed-up area where we'd planted seemed okay. Behind us, there was the familiar whining of the generators as Annie switched off the lights. We waited for her to catch up, then we all started off across the park towards the ragged trees on the other side.

The microlight circled and followed.

That was the first time I noticed that something was going on between Damon and Candy. Alex was walking ahead of us; Candy and Damon were at the rear. Then I realised that Alex was deliberately not looking back, as if he didn't want to see. When I glanced back, Candy and Damon pulled apart. They'd been holding hands. It was a strange sort of reaction, them pulling apart like that. If something was going on between them, then it was going on—and it had nothing to do with me or anyone else. But I did feel bad for Alex. I knew how hard he'd been trying to make everything work between them, and if he knew what was happening now then it was bound to be tearing him apart. But the way Candy and Damon acted when I looked back—it made me feel like I was a disapproving parent or something. If this was what being a leader involved, then they could keep it.

Beyond the trees, the demolished apartment block.

Beyond what was left of the apartment block, the ruined flyover.

Gordon hurried ahead when we reached the pile of rubble that was hiding the cliff edge. For the first time, as he climbed hand over hand, I realised how much he'd changed since we'd been stranded here. His sleeves were rolled up and I saw with surprise that his skin was tanned, and healthy looking. Now how was that possible in a world where there was no sun, just the surrounding greyness? Even his hair seemed lighter, the way fair hair is sometimes bleached in constant sunshine. He'd lost a little weight, and was well muscled beneath his shirt. It was the same with Alex when he began to climb. He looked fitter and healthier than I remembered from the time when the quake first hit. Hell, it was the same with everyone. Annie had been a little overweight at the beginning; maybe Lisa had even been a little underweight. But now they both looked to be in the same shape, at the same weight and looking really good. I suppose all the physical work we'd had to do, making a life for ourselves here, had been better than any health-training programme. That, and the fact that the luxuries of junk food had been denied us. We were all looking good, and I could see the funny side of it.

Nothing like a good earthquake to get you fit again, I thought, as we all climbed to the top of the mound.

I was the last to see what the others saw as soon as we reached the top of the mound. Everyone stood silently, watching. Now we knew that the junkyard sounds had been coming from over here, after all.

Our new arrivals *had* been busy throughout the night.

And quite how they'd managed to do what they'd done, without any interruption from the Vorla, was anybody's guess.

They had been building a tower.

They were still building it now, and we just stood there and gawped at the little figures who clambered all over its ragged, angular frame.

"What the *hell* are they doing?" said Alex.

It wouldn't win any architectural awards, but clearly they'd been working right through the night. Even from where we were standing, we could see that they'd scavenged through the ruins to find every piece of scrap metal or solid wood or iron tubing they could find. They'd begun with some kind of platform made out of heavy-duty pipes, a sort of solid criss-cross frame, maybe thirty or forty feet wide. From there, they'd begun to build scaffolding, lashing ironwork and wood together with ropes and wire. There were cables on all four sides of the tower, anchoring it to the ground. Since we'd seen them on the previous day, and since the construction noises had begun, they'd managed to build their tower up to about eighty or ninety feet. They must have been working hammer and tongs to get it to that height.

"They're taking a hell of a chance," said Annie.

I looked at her.

"Well, look at it," she went on. "They haven't dug any foundations for it, and they're no more than twenty feet or so from the cliff edge."

"They've done it before," said Alex. "Look at them. They know just what they're doing."

"Oh Christ," said Juliet, and when I looked at her face I knew straight away what she was thinking, and that we knew what they were planning. It brought me out in a cold sweat, and I cursed myself. I should have put two and two together a lot faster than I had.

"The broadcasting mast," Juliet went on. "Remember?"

There was a shocked silence when everyone else finally got it.

"That's why we haven't heard from them before now," said Juliet. "Because they've just arrived, from another crag or a plateau out there. They've worked out how to travel, how to get from one cliff edge to the other. Build a tower like that . . ."

"Push it over," continued Lisa. "Across the Chasm to the other side."

There was no doubt about it. But there was one other little detail that worried the hell out of me. There was no sign of a bonfire, no evidence that our newcomers had made any kind of defence against the Vorla. They had worked right through the night, right next to the edge of the Chasm . . . and it looked as if they'd had no interference from the Black Stuff. I looked all around the cliff edge, but couldn't see anything. I didn't like this; not one little bit.

"Come on," I said at last, heading down the mound towards the cliff edge. "Let's see if we can at least get through to them."

The day before it had been as if they'd been waiting for us; all the cheering and yelling and abuse they'd hurled in our direction. Today it seemed that they were too engrossed in what they were doing to notice that we were paying a return visit. It was the microlight buzzing overhead that alerted someone on the ramshackle tower that we were on our way. Were there more kids on the other side than there had been the day before? There seemed to be, hanging or clambering on the tower; lashing ropes and squirming between the scaffolding poles. On the ground, several dozen were working on the base, hanging on the four cables that presumably kept the entire thing from tipping over before it was ready.

The kids on the ground began to make an excited commotion as we approached the cliff edge, but no one ran to their own edge to make the same threatening noises at us. They were calling back into the ruined houses and buildings behind them. And I knew they were calling the big man whom we'd assumed to be their leader, if only for the reason that he was the sole adult among them.

I was right. It didn't take long for him to put in an appearance.

He emerged from one of the ruins, surrounded by teenagers. They were clamouring for his attention, pointing across to us. But he ignored them, and with the air of someone who was completely in charge, he just walked slowly through them and around the base of the tower. The kids became quiet, gathering behind him as he moved right up to the cliff edge. Same black waistcoat, same red belt for a headband. The kids still up on the tower stopped what they were doing and looked down eagerly.

Now this was what you might call a leader.

Snap my fingers, do this. Snap my fingers, do that.

I don't think I've ever seen anyone look as confident as he did.

He just stood there on the edge, waiting for us. The kids were making no noise at all now, just waiting for something to happen.

Suddenly I realised that I was in the lead. So this was it, then? I'd agreed to be the leader of our own bunch, so now it was down to me to say or do something. Right then I didn't feel very much like I was in charge of anything. Even though it was a couple of hundred feet across to the other side, I could see every detail of the big man. I'd seen that blank expression before, on the streets. This was the kind of dangerous bastard who was so sure of himself he didn't feel the need to give anything away. There was nothing soft about him. If I had to guess, I'd say that he was into working out; probably long before the quake had hit Edmonville.

"Nice job," I said, pointing up at the tower. Not the best opening line I've ever come up with, but right then I was stuck for something to say.

The big man just stood there and looked at me.

"You look like a caring kind of guy," I said. "Taking it on yourself to look after all those kids. Gives them something to do during the night. Keeps them out of mischief, eh?"

No reaction. He just stood and looked.

"You a scout leader?"

Nothing. But it was clear that the big chief of all these little Indians was trying to stare me out, psych me out. Well, with two hundred feet between us at the moment, it was a game I was prepared to play. Mouthing sweet nothings, or appealing to the possibility of a better nature, seemed like a complete loser from the very beginning.

"Yes, it's a nice piece of work," I said, returning my attention to the tower. "Bit lacking on the health-and-safety angle, though. And most of these kids look a little young to be members of the union. Hope you're not breaking any child labour laws."

Silence; just that slow, evil smile appearing on his face.

"So . . . you build it up to . . . what? Two hundred feet or so. Reinforce it a little more, maybe. Then you cut the four cables that are holding it there. Give it a hard shove, and over she goes. Instant bridge, and party time. Am I right?"

Slowly, the big man raised his hand and pointed at me.

In exactly the same manner as the previous day, he pointed

to all of the others on our side. One by one. The threat was unmistakable. They were coming over here to get us.

"You think that's what's going to happen?" I asked.

The big man looked back at me, still smiling.

"Wrong," I said. "Want to know why?"

Nothing.

"Because it's going to take you another day to get that tower as high and as strong as you need it to be before it can take the impact. I've no doubt you've tried it all before, and it works. But you see . . . we're just not going to let you do that."

Suddenly, the man flung his arms up to the sky and howled.

It was a wild animal's cry; savage and full of hate, and mockery. At the sound of it, all the kids behind him began to howl too. The kids up on the tower began yelling and screaming, whooping and banging on the metal poles and the support structures, like they didn't really care whether the ramshackle thing was going to pitch over into the Chasm or not.

I don't know whether the big man gave a signal or not, but he must have done, because in the next instant all the kids over there were grabbing up rocks and stones and pelting them over at us. I backed off, trying not to make it look as if I were being chased away—a hard job when you've got chunks of concrete and pieces of lead piping dropping all around you.

While the mad tribe howled and shrieked and jeered at us, we made our way quickly out of their throwing range and climbed the rubble mound of the apartment block once more.

"Want to pick another leader?" I asked them all when we reached the top and looked back down. It looked like big party time over there now as they pranced and jumped and leaped all around the big man. He remained still and silent, watching us; even from there trying to psych me out. "As you can see, I've got that mad bastard scared shitless."

"What are we going to do?" asked Candy.

"We're going to stop them," I said.

"How?" asked Juliet.

"What goes up," I said, "can also come down."

We looked at the microlight circling above us.

When we headed back to the Rendezvous, it followed us all the way.

| **TRUE COLOURS**

THE SIGHT OF THE TOWER ON THE OTHER side of the Chasm had a profound effect on Juliet. All the way back to the Rendezvous she was silent; trying to shake off the sick feeling of fear that overwhelmed her. Jay was silent too, as the others engaged in agitated discussion about the wild tribe of newcomers on the other side. Juliet knew that Jay was thinking about whatever plan he had in mind and was glad that he couldn't see how badly shaken she was.

It had taken her a lot longer to get over her ordeal at the hands of Trevor Blake than she had let on. And there had been a time, on the broadcasting mast when it had fallen out across the gulf, when Juliet thought she'd lost her mind. First when it fell. She had been unable to believe that she'd survived, was still clinging on. Then the perilous journey across to the other side when Jay had come out to save her. What had happened between her and Jay was real, and completely unexpected. But for a long while, everything else about their situation in New Edmonville had seemed to her to be just a long bad dream from which she would eventually wake up. When she thought back to their confrontation with the Vorla that had possessed Trevor, and to the revelations about their predicament, it barely seemed real. Only one thing kept her from wishing too hard that the nightmare would end. If she did, would Jay vanish too? Their love had effected a great deal of healing. Step by step, she'd come to terms with their new life; even accepted the knowledge that they were here in the Realm of the Chasm forever, with no escape back to the real world.

But the arrival of the wild tribe and, in particular, the erection of the ramshackle tower had brought her terrors into sharp focus once more. It reminded her vividly of the broadcasting mast, and brought all the horrors of that ordeal back with shocking clarity. Something of the teenage kids' sheer ferocity, more like a tribe of wild animals than kids, reminded her of the insane sadism and anger that had possessed Trevor as he'd pursued and tormented her. But, in particular, there was something about their leader, the big man, that worried her more than anything else.

Juliet gritted her teeth as the Rendezvous came into sight once more.

She'd got this far. She wasn't going to give up now.

The microlight buzzed overhead, circling the boarding house as they drew near.

"Wish I had a bloody rifle," said Alex, looking up as they entered the house.

The communal room had become the place where the important talking always seemed to be done. By unspoken mutual consent, they wearily found their usual places, slumping on sofas and chairs. No one had eaten that morning. Perhaps no one had the appetite for it, but Lisa and Alex made their way into the kitchen anyway and began preparing cold food.

"So?" asked Annie.

Jay ran a hand through his hair. "I need a drink. Anyone else?"

"Bottled water, pop or beer?" asked Damon. He rose from the sofa, rubbing his hands nervously on his thighs.

Christ, thought Jay, unbelieving. He *wants to do something for someone.* It was the first "community" gesture that he'd made in all their time together, ridiculously small though it was. It seemed as if the sight of the wild tribe and the utter hostility of their intent had suddenly made him realise where his loyalties must lie.

"Beer for me," said Jay, still bewildered. Damon took everyone's order and made his way to the kitchen as Lisa and Alex emerged with plates of food.

Annie looked at Jay. "You said 'What goes up can also come down.' What do you have in mind?"

"Simple, really," said Jay. "We just have to make sure that they don't get to build their tower. Make sure they never get it high enough. But it's . . . well, it's not going to be very pleasant."

"Go on."

"Look, we've got this far against all the odds. By rights, we should have ended up like all those other poor sods. Dead . . . or living dead. And we've made it by doing what needed to be done. By being hard. We've got to be hard again." He was silent then. Damon emerged from the kitchen with the first of the drinks, handing Jay an opened bottle of beer. Jay thanked him, saw the anxious expression on his face, which somehow gave him a greater resolve. For the first time, it seemed that Damon was truly one of the group. "Some of the kids over there may end up dead, or badly hurt. But that's the way it has to be. We've got to steel ourselves against that. We don't want them over here. They've . . . well they've gone *wild* or something. So, this is what we have to do."

He drank a mouthful of beer and continued.

"I know our petrol reserves are valuable, but we've got to use some to protect ourselves."

"Petrol bombs?" said Alex.

"Right," said Jay. "I know how to do it. Don't ask me why I know how to make them. Just let's say it was one of the skills I had in my previous life."

Jay looked hard at Juliet, his expression softening into a

smile. She didn't know or care what had happened in his previous life. She knew some of it, told in intimacy. But she also knew that there were things he didn't want to remember. It didn't matter. All that mattered now was their new life, in New Edmonville. Her anxieties began to fade, despite the potential hazards that faced them. This was a chance for everyone to start again; a chance for her to forget everything that had happened in her own past and discard all the bad stuff.

"We need lots of empty glass bottles," Jay went on. "Petrol, rags. I know how to make homemade fuses. We load up the dump truck and we head back down there to our friends."

"And we bombard that fucking tower," said Annie. "Burn it to the ground."

"We'll need protection," continued Jay. "So far it's only been stones they've thrown at us. They may have other tricks up their sleeves. But we'll have to make sure that tower burns, and it may mean that some of those kids are also going to get burned. I don't like the idea any more than anyone else. But we've got to be prepared for it happening. It also means that we'll have to set up some kind of base camp down there. Work out a shift system. Burn the tower down, and keep up the bombardment, until they decide they've had enough and move on somewhere else."

"When do we start?" asked Lisa.

"No time like the present," said Juliet.

Jay nodded.

They finished their drinks, ate what they could of the food and set about the tasks ahead of them. Glass bottles were collected from their own trash. They'd got through more bottles of champagne than seemed possible. They looked good for throwing. Rags were easy enough to find. Annie and Lisa siphoned off petrol from their spare supply in the garage; Jay set about his home-made fuses, a process that fascinated Annie from a professional "hardware" point of view.

And throughout, Juliet watched as everyone worked.

They were a community.

They were bound together.

Now they had become an army.

The back of the dump truck was loaded with petrol bombs, carefully stacked and padded in crates for the first journey. The whole process couldn't have taken longer than an hour and a half before they were ready to move. The route would be slightly different because of the truck. Taking a side road past the park which would skirt the rubble of the fallen apartment block, then over rough ground to avoid the shattered flyover. They would have to take a look at the rough ground first; find out whether there'd be any risk of breaking bottles. Alex seemed convinced that they could get to the cliff edge without mishap, but better safe than sorry.

They'd just loaded up and were ready to head off when Robin complained of feeling ill. Jay, Juliet and Alex were up front in the cab. Alex was behind the wheel, and everyone else was in the back, steadying the crates. Lisa asked them to hold on for a moment, while she checked him out.

"It's okay," she said at last. "He's just tired."

Annie looked at her as she took Robin across her lap. Lisa shook her head.

They'd discussed whether Robin should stay at the Rendezvous, not witness what was going to happen at the cliff edge. But that would mean that Lisa would have to remain behind while the others did what had to be done. Annie had suggested that she or one of the others stay and look after him, but Lisa knew that he would be happier with her. And there was the dilemma. Lisa wanted and needed to be a part of what was going to happen. She had no problems about the child-minding part, but the anxieties of waiting at the boarding house, not knowing what was happening out there—it was all simply too much. No, she would go with the others, and so would Robin. But when it came to . . . what had to be done . . . she'd take him away from the edge, maybe beyond the apartment block rubble, so that he wouldn't have to see. Right now, it was vitally important that they all be together.

Annie nodded her understanding and stood up from the dumper to slap the roof of the cab.

"Okay!"

The truck rumbled off down the street towards the park.

In the months during which they'd carved out their lives in New Edmonville, they'd managed to clear most of the main road and the side streets, so that the truck could have easy access to the Rendezvous and beyond. Good, hard work to take everyone's minds off their troubles.

"Bastard!" said Jay, as the dump truck turned in towards the park.

"What?" asked Juliet.

"The microlight. Look at him."

Juliet and Alex strained to look up, and saw the microlight heading away from them, moving in the same direction.

"He's gone on ahead to tell them we're coming," said Juliet.

"Better step on it," said Jay. "Don't want to keep them waiting . . ."

Alex groaned, and leaned forward over the wheel.

Juliet was sitting next to him. Instinctively, she grabbed his shoulder.

"Alex . . . ?"

"Oh, Christ," moaned Alex, and he lolled back in his seat, still hanging onto the wheel. The dump truck slewed to the right.

"Alex!"

Juliet grabbed the wheel, righting it. The truck rumbled on, but now she could see that Alex's face was white and beaded with sweat. His eyes were closed.

"Juliet, I'm . . ."

"Alex!" snapped Jay. "What's wrong?" He began to rise.

Juliet tried to jam a leg down past Alex's own, trying to find the brake. It was no use; she couldn't reach.

"Hang on!" she shouted, yanking at the handbrake.

They hadn't been travelling fast, no more than twenty miles an hour. But the truck still skidded on the grass that fringed the park and jerked to a halt. In the back, there were cries of pain and a rattling of bottles. Alex slumped forward across the wheel, unconscious.

Quickly, Jay jumped out and ran around to the driver's door.

"What's wrong?" called Annie, leaning over the side.

"Something's wrong with Alex."

Jay yanked open the driver's door, jumping up in alarm when Alex pitched sideways and almost fell out of the cab. Juliet grabbed his sleeve, preventing him from falling. Between them, they lowered him down from the cab and onto the grass. Juliet jumped down and began to unfasten his collar.

"What is it?" asked Jay.

"I don't know," said Juliet. "He's just . . . well, he's completely out of it. Unconscious."

"Jay!" It was Annie's voice, from the dumper. And by the tone of it, something was also very wrong up there. Jay moved quickly, jumping up on the side of the truck to look over into the dumper.

Something was very, very wrong.

Robin was fast asleep, sprawled on Lisa's lap. But Lisa was lying back against the side of the truck as Annie shook her by the shoulders, trying to bring her round. She was semi-conscious, moaning. Her face was the same chalk-white colour as Alex's—the same beads of sweat on her forehead and cheeks.

"What the hell is going *on*?" Jay began to climb over into the dump truck.

Just as Gordon took a step forward from where he had been leaning against the cab roof and fell headlong across the crates of petrol bombs.

"*Christ!*" Jay grabbed for him, but missed.

Gordon sprawled, unconscious.

430

"Jay!" said Annie. "I think . . ."

"Gordon! What's wrong, man? Come on . . ."

"Jay, I'm not feeling too good . . . I think I'm going to . . ."

Juliet heard the commotion up on the truck and stood up quickly to see if she could help. Was standing up too quickly the reason for her dizziness? She took two tottering steps and came to a stop, her hand against the side of the truck.

"Jay . . . ?"

Juliet took a deep breath and tried to climb up.

The next moment she was sitting on the grass, not understanding how she'd got there or what was going on. She tried to stand, but now she had rolled over, the grey sky above tilting and filling her vision.

Someone was standing over her.

"Jay, is that you?"

"No, it's fucking not," said Damon, as he moved out of her sightline.

Juliet rolled, and saw him walk to the back of the dump truck. Slowly and methodically, he began to unfasten the flap at the back of the dumper, pulling back the bolts. When it clattered open, he lifted the metal flap and leaned inside. Juliet tried to crawl towards him, but she felt terribly nauseous and there was something wrong with her vision. It was blurring as she watched him leaning into the dumper, struggling to grab something. She tried to call out to him, but now even her voice had gone. Good Christ, was she *dying*?

And then Damon stood quickly back, yanking a body out of the dumper by its jacket collar. The body fell heavily to the grass.

It was Jay.

Moaning, Juliet clutched at the grass, trying to drag herself forward as Damon moved forward again, seized Jay once again by the collar and dragged him several feet from the dumper. Jay began to moan now, just like her; trying to turn, feebly clutching at the grass.

"What's the matter?" asked Damon. "Not feeling too well, Jay?"

"Damon," mumbled Jay, trying to get on all fours. "Help . . ."

"Help?" asked Damon. "You mean the way you all helped Wayne?"

"What?"

Damon knelt down and seized Jay's hair, dragging his head up until they were face to face.

"Thought I'd forgotten, didn't you? Thought I'd forgotten all about Wayne. The way you let him die."

"Damon . . ."

"Shut the fuck *up*, O'Connor!" hissed Damon, and spat in his face. "You thought I was so fucking stupid, didn't you? Well, you're the stupid bastard, Mr. *Leader*. Because Wayne isn't dead, after all. Not dead the way we used to know it. He's been coming to me, in dreams. Telling me things. About him, and about the Vorla, and about the people who are coming."

Juliet tried to call out to Gordon. Was he still up there on the dump truck? Was he still conscious? Nothing would come.

"You thought the Vorla had just gone away, didn't you? You stupid fucking utter *twat*!" Damon smacked Jay hard across the face. Jay couldn't react. Juliet grabbed two handfuls of grass, trying to drag herself across. She didn't move an inch. "All the time you've been playing Happy Families here, the Vorla has been making its own plans. Finding its own people. I just have to pass the Test, and I can be one of its people, just like Wayne. Then we'll see who bosses who around, eh, Jay?"

Jay groaned.

"Oh dear, still feeling a little unwell? What a shame. Want to know *why* you're feeling like shit? Do you?"

Jay's head sagged. He lay still, face down on the grass.

"*Do you?*" yelled Damon, dragging him up by the hair again. "Well, I'll tell you. All the time you and your friends were reading up in your library books, trying to learn how to be fucking farmers, I was reading books as well. Same fucking library, different fucking books. And do you know what I found out? Do you? I found out just what I needed to get from that chemist's shop at the end of Wady Street. They had *lots* of the stuff I needed in there. Can you believe it? No one asked me for a prescription. So when you were all knocking back your drinks at the Rendezvous, you were also knocking back my homemade knock-out pills. All crushed up and ready for use. What do you think of that, then, O'Connor?"

Juliet's vision was so blurred that she couldn't see Jay or Damon anymore. But she couldn't pass out now; she had to get up to the dump truck and warn the others.

Damon began to laugh then; long and loud.

"Come on, then, O'Connor! Do something!"

Damon, Juliet tried to say. But the ground beneath her was tilting. Christ, were they all falling into the Chasm?

"Someone's *coming,*" laughed Damon.

They were the last words Juliet heard before everything fell into the pit.

CHAPTER NINE | BETRAYAL

DAMON STOOD ON THE CLIFF EDGE AND waited for the Big Man to make his appearance. The kids had started whooping and yelling again as he'd strode down from the rubble and right up to the edge. He was careful, just in case the "no stone-throwing" order hadn't been given. Perhaps they didn't yet know what a great part he'd played, how much he was to be respected. Only the Big Man would know.

Damon didn't have long to wait.

The Big Man soon emerged from the ruined house he'd been using as a base while the tower was being built. In the short time since Damon had last seen it with the others, it had already grown another thirty feet, but the Big Man didn't give it a passing glance as he strode towards his side of the ledge, pushing through the kids. They parted, and he stood silently looking across the gulf at Damon.

Watch out for the Big Man, Wayne had said in another dream.

Big Man? How will I know him when he comes?

Oh, you'll know him all right.

And here he was, just as Wayne had said he would be.

The Big Man smiled.

Damon smiled back, and knew that he had passed the Test.

The Big Man held wide his hands, making a broad gesture that suggested he was trying to look over Damon's shoulders. The meaning of the gesture was unmistakable: *Where are the others?*

"Back at the house. I took care of them. Knocked them out."

The Big Man smiled again.

"They're waiting for you. Just what the Vorla wants."

The Big Man threw his hands back in the gesture that Damon remembered from earlier that day. He howled at the sky again, and the kids all around him burst into frenzied activity. Screaming, yelling, and with the kids up on the tower banging on the framework. When the Big Man whirled away, jabbing one arm up at the tower, that command too was unmistakable. Work began again on the tower, but this time the activity was frenzied as ragged figures clambered all over it. The Big Man vanished back into the house.

Damon moved back from the cliff edge, found a boulder to sit on, and watched.

And remembered.

It would have been an easy matter to throw Jay and Juliet back in the dump truck and drive on down here; show the Big Man what he'd done. But there was greater satisfaction to be had. First, he dragged Jay back to the truck and heaved him inside again. Then he moved to Juliet.

"Romeo not up to much now, is he?" He looked down to where she lay, and began to tremble.

"Romeo and Juliet."

Damon began to unzip his flies.

He wiped a trembling hand across his mouth.

This wouldn't take very long. Just a little piece of what Jay had been getting.

He dropped to his knees, flipped Juliet over, and began to pull at the belt of her jeans.

And then he remembered Wayne from his last dream.

Take the one called Candy. Give her what she thinks she wants.

It'll be like twisting a knife in her husband. And that's what we want, Damon. We want them to suffer. And you can enjoy yourself a little in the process.

"I'll enjoy it . . ."

Damon pushed Juliet's legs apart and positioned himself.

But don't touch any of the other women, Damon. The Vorla has something special planned for them.

" . . . enjoy . . ."

Don't touch any of the other women, Damon. Don't fail the Test, if you want to be one of us.

Moaning, Damon moved off. Right at the last moment, he mustn't fail.

"Just the once, Wayne. Just once . . ."

Don't fail the Test.

Moaning again, Damon turned away and masturbated on the grass. When he'd finished, he stood with his back to Juliet, as if she were conscious and he didn't want her to see what he'd done, or to hear him zipping up again. He stood for a long while, looking out across the parkland to the ragged trees. Beyond the trees was his new future.

"I won't fail the Test."

Turning quickly then, he grabbed Juliet's legs and dragged her to the rear of the dump truck. Angrily, he flung her up there on top of Jay, banging her head against the gate in the process. Alex was next, heavier than Juliet. It made him angrier still, but he finally managed to get him up there too. Swinging himself into the cab, he revved the engine furiously, then remembered the crates of petrol bombs. Calming himself, he drove carefully back to the Rendezvous.

He reckoned they'd be out for several hours at least.

So he had lots of time to do what he had to do.

With the solemn grace of a ritual, he laid Jay and Juliet on the sofa in the communal room. Gordon and the kid on chairs facing each other. The dykes on their own bed in their own room. He heaved Alex up the stairs and laid him on the

436

bed in their room. Returning, he carried Candy up and placed her next to him. He placed their hands over their chests, as if they'd been laid out for a funeral.

He stood over them, remembering.

Then, taking off his own clothes, he raped Candy.

That was okay. It was allowed.

He stared into Alex's face throughout, until he'd finished.

Afterwards, he left them there, driving the dump truck out into the park. He stopped next to the charred remains of the bonfire, remembering the nights they'd spent there while the Vorla flowed all around them. How could he have known that the thing he'd feared so much was going to be the thing that would release him from all his fears, show him a New Life? He had to do something else; something that hadn't been requested of him. Just to show that he really was worthy.

Unlocking the gate, Damon had taken one of the petrol bombs, lit the rag fuse and pitched it hard into one of the crates. The fire had taken hold quickly. He backed off, laughing in glee as the fire engulfed the dump truck. Minutes later, when it exploded in a great fireball, he whooped with delight. Liquid fire dropped to the grass all around.

This was good.

Turning then, he'd made his way to the cliff edge, and to the newcomers.

Sitting on the boulder, he watched in awe as the tower grew.

He was elated, knowing that he'd passed the Test.

He couldn't wait until the newcomers reached this side.

He trembled with excitement, wondering what they'd do to the others back at the Rendezvous. Whatever it was, he knew they'd let him join in.

And then he really would have got his own back on Jay fucking O'Connor.

CHAPTER TEN	GORDON DREAMS

S OMETHING WAS WRONG.

Gordon had found a really safe place; a comfortable, warm sleeping place. It was like nothing he'd ever experienced before. In this place there was no New Edmonville, no Vorla, no dead people and no pain. He would stay here forever, with those things remaining on the outside where they couldn't touch him.

But something was trying to drag him out of the safe place; trying to bring him back to the nightmares.

"No . . ." Gordon tried to raise an arm in protest. It felt as heavy as iron.

But there they were again. Small hands on his arm, on his shirt-front, tugging at his trouser legs.

"Leave . . . alone . . . just . . . sleep . . ."

Something hissed angrily in his face, so close that he could feel the breath on his cheek. He didn't care. He wanted only to sleep.

Something shook him again, so that his head flopped back and forth in the chair. It didn't matter. None of this had anything to do with him. There was an angry chittering sound in the room; like agitated birds. Was that it? Were there somehow birds in the room? Gordon tried to slap out again, but couldn't raise his arm.

Something had that arm; even now he was being pulled from his chair.

"Stop it . . ."

Gordon was pulled to the floor. He rolled on the carpet, arms flopping. Now both his arms were being held by small, sharp fingers that pinched his flesh. There was pain there, but too remote and distant to have anything to do with him. He tried to raise his head, and saw a curious thing.

He could see Juliet and Jay, sprawled on the sofa. And he was floating away from them on his back, across the carpet. His heels caught in the rug; he began to drag it along with him. Again came the angry chittering sound. Now he was being pulled to the side, as if the carpet were impeding his progress and whoever was dragging him out of the communal room were trying to free his feet. Something off to his right and out of sight gave off a jangling sound. His guitar.

"What . . . what's . . . ?"

Gordon bumped against another chair, then was pulled around it. Hanging over the arm of the chair, he could see the head and shoulders of the boy, Robin. Like Jay and Juliet, he was asleep; his pink face scrunched up against the arm of the chair, his curled hair flat against the sweat of his forehead. His head moved. Was he waking up? No, his eyes were half-open, the way that kids in deep sleep sometimes looked. Was he going to fall off the chair? No, because now, as Robin's head slumped out of sight, Gordon could hear the chittering sound again; like birds discussing what they were going to do next.

The same somethings that were pulling Gordon out of the communal room were also pulling Robin out of his chair. There was a thump as the boy fell to the carpet out of sight. Now Gordon was pulled around the chair and into the corridor that led to the front door. He watched the walls on either side slide by.

This was okay. It had nothing to do with him. It was a dream in a dream.

439

Gordon's guitar gave another jangle as it was dragged along somewhere behind him. He heard another bump as Robin was pulled along after him.

Was the safe sleeping place that Gordon had found the same safe place where Robin had been for all that time? If it was, he didn't mind staying here for a *long* time.

"Okay," said Gordon. "That's okay . . ."

The chittering came again as he was dragged out through the front door and into the garden. Now all he could see was the great grey sky overhead.

"Good . . ."

And then there was only the grey, and the safety of this place without bad dreams.

CHAPTER ELEVEN | THE CROSSING

DAMON WATCHED THE TOWER RISE, WATCHED the ragged figures crawling and swinging all over the structure as detritus from the ruins was methodically carried to the base. He sat on his boulder and watched as ironwork, railings and wood spars were bound and tied, then heaved up by ropes to the top of the structure and secured there.

He was hypnotised by the organisation of it all.

All the effort was being put into building the tower, and no one was fucking about. He scrutinised the kids' faces as they worked, in the hope that he might recognise someone. But the stuff they'd painted on their cheeks and foreheads made it impossible. He reckoned that the oldest among them were about his own age. Why no adults, apart from the Big Man? No doubt there would be time for answers.

Suddenly he realised that the sky was darkening.

He stood up, agitated.

He moved to the cliff edge and looked down. It was usually possible to see down several hundred feet before everything disappeared into darkness. But now the shadows were almost at his feet. This was the time when the Vorla usually made its appearance, and in the past he'd always been indoors with the others, protected by the light.

Surely he didn't need any protection now? He'd done what Wayne had said, what the Vorla wanted. He'd stopped them from trying to destroy the tower, had laid them all out there back at the Rendezvous just ready to be taken. And he hadn't touched the women—apart from Candy, that was. And that was okay, he knew. So there was no need for him to be agitated, was there? Even if the Vorla came up from the Chasm, he'd be okay. It wouldn't touch him. Would it?

Damon began to pace nervously along the cliff edge.

Beyond and above, the tribe continued its feverish work on the tower. They appeared to have forgotten that he existed over here, and the darkening of the sky made no difference to them. Damon kept glancing from them to the sky to the Chasm. They'd worked right through the night, hadn't they? They'd had no problems with the Vorla. How could they, when they had been sent by the Vorla?

Damon was on their side now.

Wasn't he?

"I'm . . ." Damon tried to shout over, but his voice dried. He paced again.

"Look, I'm . . . I'm just going back! Back to the Rendezvous again!"

The tribe continued its work, climbing and hammering and strapping.

Damon looked down into the darkness of the Chasm, and began slowly to back away. "I'm just going back, okay? I'll . . . I'll wait for you over there. You know where it is. The guy in the microlight, he knows where it is, doesn't he?"

There was no response from the other side. Now the shadows were lying all around Damon.

"So . . . I'll just go . . . and I'll see you all there. Okay?"

Damon didn't avert his gaze from them as he continued to back away.

"Okay," he said finally. He turned and began hurrying for the rubble mound.

"*Stay where you are!*" commanded a booming voice from the other side.

Damon froze.

Slowly, he turned back to look.

The Big Man had reappeared on the far cliff edge, and was staring intently in his direction. All work on the tower had stopped at the sound of his voice.

"*Come HERE!*"

Damon sheepishly made his way back to the cliff edge. He wanted to say something, anything. But nothing would come out. A great terror of the cliff edge on his side and of the Chasm below had overcome him. Night had fallen impossibly fast. Twenty feet from the edge, he stopped.

"Closer," said the Big Man.

"I did everything I was asked to do," moaned Damon. "And more. I burned the dump truck."

"Closer."

Damon reached the edge, and could not look down.

"Look at me."

Damon tried to regain his cool. Somehow, he just couldn't find it when faced by the cold, unblinking stare of the man on the other side.

"If I told you to jump off the edge," said the Big Man, "then you'd do it. Wouldn't you?"

"I did *everything* . . . "

"You would jump off. Wouldn't you?"

"Wayne told me what the Vorla wanted. I did it all . . . "

"*Wouldn't you?*"

"Oh Christ . . . "

"What if I told you that it was the last part of the Test? What if I told you that even if you *had* done everything you've been told, there was still that last thing to do? All you'd have to do would be to step over. The Vorla wouldn't let you fall. It would rise up to meet you, would cushion your fall. Bring you right back up again. Safe and sound, all in one piece."

443

"Oh, Jesus Christ . . ."

"Step to the edge."

"Oh, Jesus *Christ* . . ."

Damon collapsed to his knees on the cliff edge, hung his head and began to sob.

The Big Man burst into laughter, throwing back his head.

At the sound of his voice, the tribe all around him burst into mocking laughter too.

Wretched and terrified, Damon listened to it go on forever.

And then the Big Man turned away, waved his arms in the air, and work recommenced on the tower, even more feverishly than before.

One hour later, sitting on the same boulder, Damon turned his attention from the cliff edge to the tower. He had remained there with anxiety gnawing at his guts as darkness had fallen, waiting for the Vorla to come flowing up over the rim towards him in a glinting black flood. But there had been no sign of it, and the tribe had continued with its work uninterrupted.

But then Damon had heard excited laughter and shouting from the figures working on the tower. Something was going on. Those figures hanging on the frame were beginning to climb down. Others at the base were hurrying out of sight into the rubble. It was now so dark that he could see no details of the figures, only silhouettes. When the silhouette of the Big Man appeared over them, and strode out to the tower's base, Damon knew that their work was completed.

The tower stood at least two hundred feet tall.

The Big Man walked around it, looking up, as if surveying their handiwork. He moved to the edge, looked down, then across to where Damon was sitting. Damon stood up quickly, to attention. The Big Man stood looking at him. Terror over-whelmed Damon again lest he should be told to walk back to the cliff edge. It was impossible to see any expression on the Big Man's face in the darkness.

Then the Big Man moved to one of the cables by the cliff edge. He grabbed it, and looked up at the tower once more. Walking to the other nearside cable, he repeated the action. The same with the two cables at the rear.

If he said something to the tribe, Damon didn't hear it. But he must have.

Because the next moment the whooping and yelling began again all around him as he strode through a milling throng and vanished from sight into the darkened ruins behind.

Damon backed off involuntarily as the figures swarmed around the base of the tower and the cables. He struggled to see what the frenzied activity on the nearside of the tower could be, but there was too much darkness, too many squirming silhouettes.

Something clanged at the base of the tower. Figures were suddenly dodging aside, running and scampering in the darkness as Damon heard something slither and slice invisibly through the air. It sounded like the cable on a suspension bridge snapping. He ducked instinctively, and saw one of the nearside cables that had been holding the tower aloft whiplash madly around the tower itself, severed from its moorings.

Now Damon knew that there were going to be no last-minute checks. No tests. No final measurements. The work was done.

The patchwork tower was coming over.

Damon stumbled further back into the darkness as there was another resounding clang followed by the whiplash slithering sound. The tribe were yelling and shouting and cheering as they ran from the tower frontage. Damon saw more squirming activity, felt his heart beating in his chest and didn't know now whether he was terrified or elated as the rear cables were also severed from their moorings in the ground. Something else seemed to have been built behind the tower, out of sight from where Damon had been sitting or standing. The silhouettes were crowding behind the tower, and now Damon heard their yells of effort as whatever makeshift pulley-and-lever system they'd built there was put into use at last.

That groaning of human voices gradually became the groaning of stretching wood and stressed metalwork.

Damon couldn't take his eyes off the tower.

Something inside it screeched; a hollow, nerve-jangling sound.

Wood splintered and cracked.

The groaning became the sounds of a giant oak tree being felled in a forest.

Screeching, roaring; the rushing of branches crashing towards earth.

The tower began to topple forward, across the abyss.

Damon was well out of danger, but he turned and ran anyway as the great rending and crashing enveloped him. It sounded like the grumbling roar of an approaching avalanche.

He whirled back to look.

Just as the tower smashed down onto the cliff edge at his side.

Damon felt the impact in the ground beneath his feet. He saw wooden struts shatter and explode; heard and saw the rending of metal scaffolding as a great chunk was gouged out of the cliff side. It shuddered and crumbled where he had once been standing. But the tower was at least twenty feet higher than the fissure was wide. It embedded itself in the earth, tilted and rolled . . . and stuck fast.

The tower had become a bridge.

On the other side, the tribe yelled and whooped, danced and ran.

The Big Man did not appear.

Nor did the tribe seem to need an order to begin the crossing. Damon could only stand and watch in awe as the first of the youngsters began to scramble out across the patchwork tower bridge, using the ragged frames and criss-cross scaffolding for handholds as they moved on all fours. There was no time taken to test the safety of their craftsmanship. In an instant, they were scrambling over the abyss.

Damon hesitated.

Should he run to the edge and cheer them on? Show them that he was one of them? Had the Big Man told them all that he was on their side? That last thing, about stepping off the cliff edge, that was surely just to show Damon who was the boss. Wasn't it?

A silhouette that looked the size and shape of a twelve-year-old boy missed his handhold. He struggled to grab something else. But the wooden frame that he fastened on was not secure. It snapped, and he fell sideways from the tower, screaming. Damon froze in horror as the twisting figure vanished from sight.

But the others came on, unheeding and uncaring of their companion's fate. It was as if it had never happened.

Damon walked forward then, hesitantly. He was trying to find something to say as the first of the figures began to near his side. At last, he hurried forward and held onto the tower's top frame; just to show them that he was working to keep the tower in place and help them come over. Anxiously, he scanned the other cliff side, but there was still no sign of the Big Man.

The first figure jumped down onto the edge. A girl? Sixteen, seventeen years old? Then another teenager. A boy? Now they were clambering and yelling wordless sounds as they clambered down all around Damon. He clung tight to the frame, and began yelling the same sounds as more and more of the tribe made it over to his side.

The whooping and yelling were all around him.

The crossing seemed to take forever.

How many of them were there?

Damon turned back once, aware of the gathering crowd

that seethed and jostled and bumped behind him in their triumphant conquerors' dance.

One of the silhouettes stepped towards him, holding out a hand. Was that figure a teenage boy or a girl? Was he or she smiling? It was impossible to tell, in the darkness. Grinning, trying to keep anxiety at bay, Damon let go of the frame and took the welcoming hand.

The figure jerked him roughly forward.

Sparks exploded behind his eyes when the figure head-butted him. Damon fell, pole-axed.

Whooping, the wild figures fell on him.

CHAPTER TWELVE | THE JOURNAL OF JAY O'CONNOR: CAPTURED

THE FIRST THING I REMEMBER WAS THE SCREAMING.

Initially, I felt as if everything had done some kind of back-flip, and I was in bed with Juliet back at the Rendezvous. We were in some kind of crazy action replay, and were waking yet again to the sounds of what had once been Trevor Blake, locked out back in the boarding-house extension. But this voice wasn't screaming that it was "too late," and as I came out of this confusing blur I realised that it wasn't Trevor's voice at all. This was someone else. Was it someone I knew? Whoever, that person was in real pain, and now he was begging someone not to hurt him again. Him? Yes, it was a him.

My eyes wouldn't focus; everything was confused, just a jumble of colours that didn't make any sense. And when I tried to move, my hands and feet were yanked up above me. I felt as if I were hanging in midair, could feel gravity pulling at me. The screaming faded to a horrible, low gurgling. And then a voice I didn't know said: "Where are the other two?"

"I don't know . . . " Now I knew who had been screaming, knew who was in so much pain. It was Damon.

"Where are they?" The other voice was a man's voice—harsh and guttural. I didn't recognise it.

"They should be there," babbled Damon. "I left them there. Both of them. On chairs, inside the boarding house. I swear to God . . ."

"Swearing to *God* won't do you any fucking good *here*!" snarled the other man's voice. Damon began screaming again then, and I knew that the owner of this new voice must have been doing something pretty damn horrible for him to make a sound like that. It was barely a human sound.

"Maybe they just came around," said another, younger voice. This was someone else I didn't recognise. It sounded like a teenage girl, but I couldn't be sure. "Came out of it, and ran away."

"They could be hiding out there," said another voice. A teenage boy? "Somewhere in the ruins."

The man didn't say anything. Damon had begun to weep.

"Want us to search?" asked the girl.

There was another long silence.

At last, the man said: "No, we haven't got time. We've spent the whole night here, and that's too long. We have to get back. We'll send others to look later."

My eyes were beginning to focus at last. I twisted my head round, trying to make sense of what was happening.

"Burn the house," said the man.

Blurred figures were running into sight now. I tried to fix on them, but before I could make out their shapes properly they had vanished from my line of vision.

I turned to look up.

My vision cleared.

Now I knew what was happening.

I'd been tied to some kind of pole by my hands and feet. One ragged figure was holding one end of the pole, another figure at the other end. And I was hanging between them like a freshly killed deer.

"Well, hello," said the face that suddenly thrust itself grinning into my sightline. There was a red sweatband belt tied across his forehead. His eyes were a deep blue, his cheeks heavily pockmarked. This was the first time I'd seen him up close, but I knew straight away who I was looking at.

It was the Big Man, the leader of the tribe.

I couldn't make any sense of it; struggled to remember what had happened, tried to put together in my mind what *was* happening.

"Want to see something?" leered the face.

I cried out in pain when a big, scarred hand grabbed me by the hair and twisted my head so that I was looking away.

I recognised where we were.

In the street, outside the Rendezvous, looking back at the boarding house. The front windows had all been broken from the inside. Glass littered the front garden. Deep inside the house, something crashed. The hand held my hair tight and forced me to keep watching. Suddenly, a billowing cloud of fire licked out of one of the front windows; the curtains catching alight and flapping smoke and sparks. The next instant flames gushed out of the other windows, one after the other.

Ragged figures dashed from the front door as the flames leaped from the windows, blackening the brickwork. I had a glimpse of wild, painted faces as they ran past me.

"Know what I call that?" asked the Big Man, twisting my head around so that we were face to face. "I call that a housewarming."

"And I call you an ugly-looking bastard," I said.

It came out without my thinking of the consequences. The old anger response.

I like to think that I got one up on him by fainting away again before he could say or do anything else. But the bruise and the lump that I found later under my right eye seemed to suggest otherwise.

Something was jerking and swaying me around.

I woke up again, and felt the raw pain in my wrists and ankles. I was still hanging from the pole, but now we were on the move. The weight of my swinging body was rubbing my skin raw where the rough ropes had been tied tight. The motion was making me nauseous. I tilted my head back and tried to get my bearings. There were others behind us, a crowd of kids plodding on and nobody speaking. Then a body swung out from that crowd, and I recognised Alex. They had him strung up on a pole too. I tried to look ahead. More kids crowded together. And was that Lisa I could see strung up on yet another pole? This was like some bloody safari, where the big game was us.

My stomach heaved and I retched.

Surprise, surprise. No one came running to see if I was all right.

When the cramps had gone, something else replaced the sick feeling inside. Where was Juliet, and was she all right?

"Where . . . where the hell are you taking us?"

Something cracked me over the head from behind. The pain was agonising.

"Shut the fuck up," said a young voice. I decided to shut the fuck up.

And then everything started to come back to me. Everyone keeling over at the dump truck. And then Damon gloating over me when whatever he'd spiked our drinks with started to take effect. A lot of what he had said was still confused, but I think I'd managed to get the gist of it. He'd knocked us all out with whatever he'd put in the drink, and had made it easy for our newcomers to get over here and take us. Obviously, the tower-bridge strategy had worked. But what the hell did Damon expect to get out of it? I remembered something about Damon saying that he'd seen Wayne in his dreams, but that part of it didn't make a lot of sense. Whatever Damon thought he was going to get out of betraying us hadn't worked to his advantage, after all. Not according to the screams of pain I'd heard.

Where are *the other two?* the Big Man had asked him. Did that mean that two of us had managed to get away? I prayed to God that one of them was Juliet.

The swaying and jostling came to a halt. I twisted around to try to get a better view of where we were, and hissed in pain when the bastard behind me grabbed my hair and yanked hard. I'd managed to see a glimpse of cliff edge, but we could be anywhere.

"Right," said a guttural voice from somewhere. The Big Man? "Lift!"

Nothing happened, but I could hear the sounds of effort from up ahead. Then I could hear rustling noises, groans of effort, the scratching of wood on wood, metal on metal.

"Again," said the same voice. "Lift."

And this time I was hoisted up, feet first, as whoever was carrying my pole at the bottom end began climbing up some kind of tangled barrier. The blood rushed to my head, and I felt as if I might throw up again. Someone's thigh smacked into my head. The guy who was carrying the front end of my pole? Now I was being hauled up. I could hear the kids above me as they grunted and groaned, could smell their stale breath on my face. What the hell were they doing, and where were they hauling me?

After a lot of sweating and straining, we evened out again so that I was on the straight. I could still feel the blood beating in my ears, but the nausea had gone. I carefully looked to one side as we bounced and jostled on ahead.

I wished I hadn't.

I wished that I was still unconscious.

Because now I knew where we were, and I swear that just the sight of it brought sweat streaming out of my body like the taps had been turned on.

We were on the tower bridge over the Chasm.

Beneath, nothing but the mind-numbing cliff-side drop into darkness. A Grand Canyon right down into Hell. Above and around us, the blank and empty grey. There was a familiar buzzing sound right then, and if I'd been struck dumb with the terror of the drop beneath us, what happened next made my head pulse.

The microlight suddenly swerved into view. Not in the sky above us, but *below* in the Chasm. I saw it swooping along the crevasse, about two hundred feet below the cliff edge, casting its shadow on the far cliff face as it came skimming along like some motorised bat. Droning, it passed below us and out of sight.

Someone up front bumped and jostled. The pole slewed across the edge of the "bridge" and suddenly I was hanging sideways on the edge, while everyone struggled to regain their balance. No one yelled or cursed or spoke. There was just the silent struggle to get me back again, while the Chasm yawned beneath me and I could feel the sheer bloody depth of it dragging at my body. It was as if gravity had suddenly come alive, had suddenly decided that I was ten times heavier than I should be . . . and wanted to drag me right over the edge.

I heard feet slithering; heard the scrabbling sounds of hands gripping wood and metal. I slid again.

I was too heavy for them.

I was going over.

Leaders don't pass out, and they don't piss themselves.

I did both.

When I came to again, I was in even greater pain than before. My neck was badly cricked and each movement caused me agony. My wrists and heels were on fire. But we weren't on the tower bridge anymore. I wondered if I had fallen into the Chasm and this was just another nightmare within a nightmare. Maybe that was what this was all about. The worst shit in the world happening, then the possibility that you were going to get out of it alive. Then even *worse* shit happening, when you never *ever* thought you were going to get out of it alive; then everything coming right for a while, maybe even falling in love with someone, and believing that you could make a go of it even in a worst-case scenario—and then the worst shit *ever* coming down on you.

Get angry, Jay, said this little voice again. *Get angry if you're going to come through it.*

I tried. By Christ, I really tried. Maybe it was the stuff that Damon had put in our drinks still in my system, and still lique-fying any guts I had left. Or maybe it was just that I just didn't have any hope left, and this was one time too many. Part of me knew that once upon a time even the *thought* that I'd been gotten the better of would have brought anger flaring to the surface. Anger that I could use. Sometimes, back in Edmon-ville, for the wrong reason at the wrong moment on the wrong person. For some strange reason, here in New Edmonville it had worked right most of the time. Deep down, I knew that it was to do with Juliet.

For the first time in my life, I really *cared* about someone.

And the possibility that something bad had happened to her, and that there was nothing I could do, filled me with real despair.

We were moving down the middle of a ruined street. There were shattered storefront windows on either side of me, and I tried to read the signs on the stores to get my bearings. Clearly, we were on the other plateau, and I struggled to remember what I could about what had been over here before the quake. I wasn't having much luck; like I said, my geography was pretty bad. There were electrical stores, hi-fi dealers, a building where a double-decker bus had run straight into the front wall and demolished it. You could still see the rear end of the bus sticking out of the wall, the rest of it smothered by an ava-lanche of bricks. This was some kind of high street. I closed my eyes to help me think. When I opened them again, I saw a war memorial on a side street; an angel holding up her arms to the sky. One of the arms had snapped off and was lying in fragments in the rubble all around her, and she was tilted at a dangerous angle, but at last I knew where we were. This was the west end of Edmonville. There should be a traffic round-about up ahead . . . and sure enough, there it was.

If I'd had anything of a sense of humour left, the next thing that happened might have seemed funny. You see, the roundabout was just a simple grassed area, with four main roads connecting to it. Common sense would suggest that the quickest and easiest way forward would be straight ahead, straight on over the roundabout. But no, our safari veered left and went *around* the roundabout before carrying straight on. Right then I could have sweated blood before I found any-thing to laugh at.

Past the roundabout, I could see that the buildings on either side of the main road had collapsed into huge mounds of rubble. We kept right on down the centre of the road, and as I was swayed and jostled along the ruins reminded me of photographs I'd seen back at school. It was like ruins you saw from the Second World War, after the bombings. Christ, it even seemed that everything here was in black and white, just like those photographs.

We had reached the edge of this plateau. I saw the familiar peaks and crags ahead of us, even before we reached the edge. The same bizarre pillars of stone. The same crazy towers with those hundred-yard flattened-off tops; some of them with ruined buildings on them, others with houses intact. One with only a single house and its front garden. And a car parked in the driveway, ten feet from the cliff edge, neat as you please.

We kept right on ahead, following the white line in the middle of the road. And something came to me then, some-thing that seemed very real, and it made me panic.

They were going to march right down the centre of this road, following this white line . . . right over the edge, and into the Chasm.

"All right," I said. "That's enough joking."

No one answered me.

I swayed from side to side as we moved. I'd lost all feeling in my hands and feet.

"Stop."

I could see the crumbled tarmac at the cliff edge.

"That's enough, you bastards. Stop!"

The anger was coming back. At last.

"Will you *stop*!"

I saw the new tower bridge just a second before someone grabbed my hair from behind again. The same ragged, primitive construction. The same makeshift scaffolding of scrap iron and wooden beams, all lashed together with whatever they'd been able to get their hands on from the ruins. Just before my head was slammed hard again, I saw that it was connecting this plateau to the next. Except that the flattened top of the furthest pinnacle looked to be no more than a few hundred feet wide.

Just when my anger was flaring, the bastard behind me put it all out like pouring a bucket of cold water on a flame.

Maybe he or she did me a favour.

By knocking me out again, they spared me another of the nightmare crossings.

After that, there was no way of telling how many other crossings we made or how far we travelled.

But when I woke up again, it was in a place that our captors called home. A place where these other survivors had also carved out space to survive. The Vorla had come to us, and tried to take us. When it couldn't do that, it had tormented us mentally and physically. It had told us that we were in Hell, had even used its own . . . its own *substance* . . . to create those Four Horsemen to convince us that the world had ended and everything was going from bad to worse for us. And then— under torture (and there's no other fucking word for it)—it had told us the Truth. But before all of this, it had said:

457

If there wasn't a Hell before, then there is now.

On that score, it hadn't been lying.

Because when we had driven the Black Stuff away, when Annie and Lisa had kept it at bay with the light, it had explored the other peaks and crags of Edmonville. It had found other survivors, others who had chosen a different way of surviving to ours. Other ways that had pleased it. Pleased it so much that it had allowed them to live; had even encouraged them and helped them and given the poor bastards a new religion in the process. Eventually, it had told them about us and showed them where we were. It had *sent* them for us.

Now they had us.

And when I woke, it was in a place that had been created for us.

I awoke in the ultimate Hell of the Vorla's own making.

| **THE NURSERY**

GORDON WAS SUDDENLY AWARE OF THE light.

There was no gradual awakening, and yet no sudden reali-sation that he was awake. There was only the light, filling his vision. It did not dazzle him, did not hurt his eyes. There was something curiously comforting about it. He did not have to avert his gaze, but was able to look at it continuously. There were very subtle, shifting patterns in there; sometimes like waves gently lapping at a shoreline. Was that the reason for the curious, barely audible hushing sound? Gordon had no idea how long he'd been staring into the light before he became aware of his body. Carefully, he moved his head from side to side, but there was no end to the light. He brought his hands up to his face, and in the process realised that he was lying on his back. Yes, he could see his hands, and wondered at how the light made the flesh of his fingertips look translucent. He struggled into a sitting position and realised that he was sitting on something firm but not uncomfortable. To his fingertips, it felt like perfect white marble.

"Are you all right?" asked a familiar voice.

And when Gordon turned to look, it was as if someone somewhere had turned a dimmer switch. The light was now no longer suffusing everything in his line of sight, although it still remained around him in a bathing glow. Sitting beside him was Robin. His hair was mussed, his eyes sparkling.

"Yeah . . . where . . . ?"

"It's wonderful," said Robin. He looked like any ordinary child on Christmas morning, full of expectation and wonder; ready to dash downstairs and find the presents under the Christmas tree. "It's *wonderful*, Gordon."

Gordon shifted, and tried to get a better view of where they were. It seemed that the light was willing to oblige; as if it were sentient, anticipating his curiosity. It swept away like a curtain, still hanging overhead and on both sides and behaving in a way that light shouldn't behave at all. For a while Gordon could only gawp at the light, wondering at its strange behaviour . . . before he saw what the light had unveiled.

He was looking at what seemed to be an underground cave wall. Fissured clay, funnelled and striated stone dripping with moisture. A stalactite hung from above, water dripping from its tip with an echoing plop.

But his attention was riveted on the figure that crouched on a rock outcropping at ground level, like a slightly raised shelf. It seemed to have been waiting for him to recover consciousness.

It was one of the Cherubim.

A naked girl, perhaps three or four years old. The same tightly curled blonde hair. The same sparkling, impossibly blue eyes. She smiled as she held what seemed to be some kind of dish beneath the dripping stalactite, gathering the liquid as it dropped.

Gordon shuffled uneasily, looking back at Robin. But Robin was smiling too. He seemed not only unworried by the other figure's presence, but almost enraptured by it.

The girl stepped down from the shelf with the beautiful grace that Gordon remembered so well. It was as if the normal laws of gravity did not apply to these creatures. They could move through the air as if weightless, so quickly and gracefully that they might almost be floating underwater. Still smiling, so that Gordon could see the sharp white points of her teeth, the girl sidled up to him and held out the dish.

Except that this was not a dish. It was the hubcap from a BMW.

Gordon looked at it, unsure. It was filled with clear water.

He looked back at the girl, who nodded and held it closer, encouraging him to take it. Hesitantly, he did so, looking back at Robin.

"It's okay," said Robin. "It tastes really good."

Still unsure, but with the little girl watching him intently, Gordon sipped the liquid. Robin was right. It *did* taste wonderful. And he hadn't realised just how thirsty he'd been before he started to drink. Greedily now, Gordon drank it all. Robin began to laugh, and the Cherub was laughing too. It was the sound that Gordon remembered from the past; an excited chittering sound. It seemed to echo, whereas Robin's voice made no echo at all. Where had he heard that sound before?

Gordon watched her in wonder; saw the wide mouth and the pointed teeth, the eyes squinting in pleasure as she took delight in his own enjoyment. Eventually, the Cherub held out her hand and Gordon returned the hubcap.

A flurry of cool air on his face.

And the Cherub was gone.

"That's cool," said Robin. "I wish I could do that."

"Where . . . ?"

"Where are we? Is that what you were going to say? I don't know. But it's . . . it's *fabulous*. I woke up before you. Don't know how long. But the things I've *seen*. Watch this . . ."

Robin held up a hand and waved it as if he were performing some kind of conjuror's trick. The light around them retreated with the familiar hushing sound. It swept away like a living thing, revealing the details of the enormous chamber in which they found themselves. Gordon's heart began to hammer, his senses reeling at the vast space that was being revealed to them. Robin seemed unaffected, but Gordon clutched at the marble floor, suddenly and irrationally afraid that he might be swept from the ground and up into the air; hurtling through space to where the gigantic stalactites descended from above. The light had pooled up there on the "ceiling" from which the stalactites hung; an upside-down, living and iridescent sea.

Gordon struggled to control his equilibrium and looked around.

At first he thought that they were in a cathedral.

Stalactites descending from above and stalagmites rising to meet them on all sides gave the impression of huge Gothic arches, some of them uncompleted, others still in the process of being built. The stalagmites that he could see reminded Gordon uncomfortably of the peaks and crags that had replaced Edmonville. On all sides, the vast walls of some underground cave. Canyon walls of rock, granite and clay. They were sitting on a clear white space that stretched ahead of them like a cathedral floor, narrowing to form an aisle. On either side of the aisle there were pews. Ranks and ranks of them leading down to the altar. Were they pews? If so, they weren't made from wood, like normal church seats. These were curious stone constructions, the same colour as the clay and the rock. And there were what seemed to be glass cases where each individual seat should be; curiously flattened, oblong cases, glowing with the same iridescence that Gordon could see flowing and rippling on the vast cathedral roof, amidst the stalactites. There must be hundreds of them.

Gordon stood up.

Something curious about the movement made him freeze. He had been expecting his shoes to scuff on the marble floor, making the same kind of echoes he'd expect to hear in a church or a cathedral. But there was no noise. He looked down, raised and lowered one foot. The floor looked like marble, but clearly it was some other kind of material. Solid and clean; but he might as well be putting his foot on a mattress or a feather quilt. He looked at Robin. Smiling, the boy jumped up and ran to take his hand.

"Come on."

The next moment Gordon was allowing himself to be led across the white floor to where the pews began. He tried to make sense of the altar that lay ahead, at the bottom of the cathedral. But now he could see that he was mistaken. There was no altar. It was just a curious outgrowth of stone and criss-cross framework of stalactites and stalagmites that made it look like an altar. Wasn't it?

Gordon looked to the side, before they drew level with the back row.

What he saw there made him jerk to a halt with a sharp hissing of breath.

Beneath rough arches of stone and wet rock, there was another chamber; just like the one they were in, if not even larger. The vastness of the space made his mind reel, so that for a moment he had to look down at his feet. There were other pews in the incredibly vast cavern; all of the same design, all containing the same glowing, white flattened boxes. But there were thousands and *thousands* of them, stretching away to an impossible distance.

"It's all right," said Robin, tugging at his hand. "Really. There's nothing to be afraid of. They've already showed me, Gordon. Don't be scared."

Gordon looked up, and became aware that there was yet another vast space beneath arches over on his right. He couldn't bring himself to look, but he knew that the mind-numbingly vast space would be filled with the same pews and the same boxes of glowing light. He remembered something then. Something he'd seen on television about the space probes to Mars, and the vast canyons they'd found there. Canyons so vast that the Grand Canyon could be dropped into one of them and lost forever. The idea of such sheer enormity had made him feel ill just thinking about it. He felt that way now, sensing the enormous vastness on either side of him as he realised that this gigantic cave-cathedral was only a small part of some enormous whole. He'd had the same feeling about the Chasm when they'd been up top. Was *this* where they'd been brought? Somewhere beneath the ruins of New Edmonville? But surely that couldn't be the case. Only the Vorla existed in the Chasm.

Gordon let himself be led to the rear pew. Gingerly, he placed a hand on the ridged black stone for balance. It should have been cold, but it was warm. Nothing here made sense. Gordon closed his eyes, aware of Robin's impatience to show him something.

At last, he remembered what had happened before he'd blacked out.

They were on their way to deal with the newcomers. He remembered travelling in the back of the dump truck, and then feeling nauseous. He'd tried to ask for help, but suddenly was unable to move. The next thing he remembered was being in the communal room back at the Rendezvous. Had that part been a dream? He remembered being dragged out of the room; remembered seeing Robin being dragged across the floor too. By the Cherubim? Was this another dream? Which part was real, and which part was he imagining? Gordon reeled, feeling his sense of reality slipping away again. He screwed his eyes shut, clutched tight to the "pew"; felt Robin hanging on tight to his other hand. When he opened his eyes again, maybe everything would have sorted itself out.

Robin laughed; a conspiratorial sound, as if someone somewhere had just enacted a practical joke that had yet to be discovered. Gordon opened his eyes.

Instinctively, he recoiled.

Robin laughed again.

They were surrounded by the Cherubim.

Silently, and as if materialising out of thin air, they were suddenly on all sides. Two, perhaps three dozen of the same naked children that Gordon had seen that night back at the

Rendezvous. Crouching, kneeling, standing; all in a circle around them. Curled blond hair; bright blue eyes. The faces of feral angels. But now there was a difference. There were several black kids here. Strangely, all of them had the same blond hair as the others, when it should have been black or brown. It made for a startling contrast. Eyes a sparkling brown, not blue. But the same feral grace, the same bony ridges just behind the shoulders.

"They won't hurt you," said Robin, and Gordon looked down to see him smiling up at him. He was right. They were alert, but there was none of the potential defensive threat that Gordon had seen during that strange night. "Come on, Gordon. Come and see . . . " Robin pulled him into the centre aisle, so that he could get a better look at the back row of luminous glass cases. Carefully, not wanting to make any sudden moves, Gordon allowed himself to be led. The Cherubim parted around his legs, moving gracefully on either side. Several of them hopped up onto the pew. Gordon could feel himself trembling when he saw that each and every face was fixed on him expectantly. What was he being shown? What should he expect?

"Look," said Robin, and he let go of his hand as he stepped up to the glass case nearest to them. Except that Gordon could see now that it wasn't made of glass. Robin wiped his hand across the opaque surface, as easily and simply as if he were cleaning a space on a car windscreen. Was it made of ice? No, there was no coldness, no moisture. Plastic? Cellophane? Robin looked back at him, beckoning.

Gordon carefully stepped forward, flinched when one of the Cherubim brushed past his leg. He felt sharp nails when it hung onto the fabric of his jeans; just like a child clinging to its parent. He looked down. It was a boy, perhaps two years old. But its . . . his . . . attention was riveted on the case, not on him. Gordon moved carefully forward again, and looked down into the case where Robin had cleared a space.

There was a baby in there.

465

Cocooned in a cradle of the same white light that coruscated on the ceiling above them. Newborn, by the look of it, with the remains of the umbilical cord still in its navel. It was a little girl; small, perfectly formed hands up beneath its chin as if praying. Eyes moving beneath closed eyelids. What possible dreams could a newborn child have? Gordon looked up at Robin, who had moved to the next case and was busy wiping the opaque surface so that he could see inside. A boy, but this time just under six months old. Tufts of blond hair beginning to grow, just like the Cherubim. The same white light inside, but with no source that Gordon could see.

And as Gordon was led to each of the cases by Robin, the Cherubim clustered around, looking from the face of each child to Gordon's face, as if they were expecting some kind of reaction from him. They got a reaction when Gordon looked into one of the cases and saw something that defied logic. Because the child in there was barely formed. Tiny, the size of a dormouse, its head still not fully shaped, its eyes ink-black dots in a translucent pink lump, its limbs barely evident. This child could surely not be alive. But it was; enveloped by the life-giving light and receiving some kind of otherworldly nourishment from it.

When the Cherubim saw Gordon's expression, they began to laugh.

The same chittering sound that he had heard back at the Rendezvous.

"How many . . . ?" began Gordon.

"Thousands," said Robin in delight. "Thousands and thousands and thousands."

"It's . . . " Gordon struggled with the word. "A . . . *nursery*. But . . . why? I mean . . . how?"

One of the Cherubim swung up onto the back pew with lithe grace. A girl, perhaps three years old. What she carried clunked against the pew. It was his guitar. Balancing on the edge, the girl handed it to him.

466

"They want you to play," said Robin. "It's a long time since they heard it, and some of them have never heard it before."

"Don't understand . . ."

"They'll tell you everything, if you play. They've told me already."

Gordon just looked at him.

"They don't speak," he went on. "Some of them never have. Some of them never had the chance to be taught. And the ones that used to be able to speak . . . well, they just can't do it here anymore."

"Robin . . . what . . . ?"

"They don't have to speak. They can tell you things just by *thinking* at you."

Gordon didn't know what to say or do.

"Play for them," said Robin quietly.

Gordon opened his mouth to say something else.

But then the girl who had handed him the guitar leaned forward from the top of the pew. She held out a beautifully formed hand with razor-sharp nails. Gordon didn't flinch as she stroked his cheek. She smiled then; the most beautiful expression that Gordon had ever seen in his life.

And then, with one finger, she gently touched his lips.

Something was happening.

Gordon couldn't understand it, but he could feel the changes that were taking place inside him. He could feel something coming into him from that one gentle touch; could feel it in his lips, and now in his face, spreading to suffuse his entire body.

He looked at Robin again, wondering.

"Play," said Robin, smiling.

All the faces around him were smiling in expectation.

Wondering, Gordon hoisted the guitar strap over his shoulder, looked around once more at this incredible place with its incredible inhabitants.

And began to play.

CHAPTER FOURTEEN

**THE JOURNAL OF
JAY O'CONNOR:
THE CAFFNEYS**

"WAKE UP, FOR CHRIST'S SAKE. WILL YOU
wake *up?*"

Someone was slapping my face. Instinctively, I raised my
hands to protect myself, and knew that I was in a different
nightmare. I wasn't strung up on that bloody pole anymore.
Now someone had me by my shoulders and was shaking
me. I tried to move and was still constricted, so I shoved my
shoulder out hard at the owner of the voice and I suppose I
must have caught him off-balance because I heard him curse
as he fell away from me. I rolled and felt as if every muscle,
every joint, every square inch of me was hurting. My wrists
and ankles were still tied, and the skin felt like it was on fire.

My eyes cleared.

Wherever I was, it was dark.

There was a man I'd never seen before me, crouching on all
fours where I'd knocked him. Jeans, checked shirt. Straight
black hair. He made a move, as if he were going to grab hold
of me again. I swung around, feeling my head banging like a
drum, bringing my feet up to kick him away.

"Okay," he said, holding out a hand. Looking nervously
behind him, he sat back and ran a hand through his thick
black hair. I guess he was about twenty, twenty-two.

I glanced around, and could make no sense of where I'd been brought.

We were in an office of some kind. In the gloom, I could see desks and chairs; some of them overturned, but others standing neat and tidy as if they were waiting for whoever worked here to come back from their lunch break. Strip lights overhead; calendars on the wall. A noticeboard with names and times on them. "John" would be back at 12:45. Jerry and Kate were on holiday until the 25th. I could see filing cabinets against one wall. Windows and window blinds, still somehow miraculously intact after the quake. Beneath me, some heavy-duty office carpet. This was all bloody bizarre. The last thing I remembered was being carried through the ruins.

"Don't make a sound," said the stranger. He was keeping his voice low and constantly glancing over his shoulder towards a main entrance door. "They might hear."

"Who the hell are you?"

"Simon. What's your name?"

"Jay O'Connor. Where are my friends? Have you seen them?"

"They've got them. Down below."

"Are they safe?"

The stranger gave a rueful laugh and moved to one of the windows, keeping low. "As safe as anyone can be here. For the time being."

"What does that mean? Where the hell am I?"

"You're in Edmonville Town Hall. And you're a 'guest' of the Caffneys."

"The who?"

"The Caffneys. They moved in here, just after the quake. This is where they live." Simon carefully parted the struts of a Venetian blind and looked out. "This is where they bring their prisoners when they're first caught. Until they decide what they're going to do with them."

"What are *you* doing here?"

"Like I said, I'm a 'guest.' Just like you, and the others. Except I managed to get away . . . get *us* away. Now we have to move fast if we're going to get out of here alive."

"Wait . . . wait until I get my head round this . . ."

"If we only knew what happened to those other two friends of yours."

"What do you mean? Which other two?" There was something there; a memory from being carried through the ruins. The Big Man, torturing Damon, demanding to know where the other two had gone.

"There's you and . . ." Simon looked back, closing his eyes to aid his concentration. " . . . and the older guy, Alex. His wife. The good-looking blonde . . ."

"Juliet's *alive*?" Something lurched in my chest.

"Juliet, yeah. That's her. She's alive, she's fine. For the time being. Then there's that kid, Damon whatsisname. And the two women, Annie and Lisa. But the other two are gone."

"Gordon and Robin?"

"That's them. The dummy and the kid. If we only knew where they were . . ."

"They were with us when Damon put that stuff into our drink. Gordon keeled over on the dump truck. The last time I saw Robin he was asleep in Lisa's lap . . ."

"And you don't know what happened to them? Don't know where they've gone?"

Something was wrong here.

Simon was staring back out of the window, but he wasn't looking at anything. He was pretending to be looking, but really he was tuned in to me and was waiting to hear what I was going to say. He was just too keen to hear my answer.

"Who the fuck are you?" I asked.

"I told you, I'm a prisoner . . ."

"Like hell you are."

Simon turned from the window to look at me. His face had hardened. And there was something about his expression, something about the coal-black eyes, that made me think I did know him, after all. No, I didn't know him—but I'd seen someone recently with a very similar expression.

"You're related to him," I said. "Aren't you?"

Simon stood up slowly, no longer apparently worried about being seen from the window. He straightened, and he just looked down at me with that blank face.

"The Big Man who was in charge of those kids," I went on. "The one who brought us here. He's your father, or your brother."

"You're a clever bastard, aren't you?" He smiled then, showing a mouth full of bad teeth that I hadn't noticed before. Then, raising his voice, he shouted: "You can come in now, Daddie-Paul! It's all over."

The main entrance door juddered open, and suddenly we weren't alone anymore.

The first one through was our old friend, the Big Man. Still wearing the same clothes, the same red belt sweatband—and the same expression as Simon, if that was this guy's name. There was another man behind him; about the same age, naked to the waist. The family resemblance was remarkable. I didn't like what he was holding in one hand. It was a gun—an automatic by the looks of it; the first firearm I'd seen since this nightmare had begun. I didn't like the implications. He held the doors open while "Daddie-Paul" came into the room.

He was an old man; perhaps eighty years old. A shock of white hair; a face like yellowed, wrinkled paper. Eyes shut, blanket over his lap. Pushing his wheelchair were two young women. Both with long black hair, and about seventeen years old. Twins? When the chair was through the door, the girls manoeuvred it up to me. Smiling, "Simon" moved to meet them all, looking back at me and gloating.

"Did he tell you?" asked the old man.

"He doesn't know. It's the same story as the others. No one knows where they've gone."

"Except our friend Damon," said the Big Man. He had a voice like grinding glass. He smiled at some recent memory. The expression didn't seem to fit his heavily pockmarked face.

"Maybe it's like the kids said." The man with the gun came up from behind. His naked torso was well muscled but white, as if it had never seen the sun. There were deep scars on his forearms and chest which looked self-inflicted. One of them was carved like a crescent moon, just above his navel. He held the gun up so that I could see it. Grinning, he began to finger the barrel. "They could have woken up and got away into the ruins."

Eyes still shut, the old man shook his head. When he spoke, it was with a strength that didn't seem to fit his frail body.

"Damon did something with them. Something he wasn't supposed to do. He's just too frightened to tell us."

The Big Man laughed again. "Shall I *ask* him some more?"

"At the burning place," said the old man. "He's failed the Test."

The old man winced then, one hand grasping at his chest. The others were instantly silent, and I could sense the tension. Was he about to have a heart attack? The pain on his face eased and his hand dropped once more to his lap. The old man chuckled then; as if laughing at some private joke. What the hell was going on here?

"Where are the others?" I asked. My voice didn't come out as strong or as confident as I wanted it. There was something about this bunch of newcomers. I'd seen traces of it before, in my previous life. When I'd first seen the Big Man on the other side of the Chasm, I'd felt it then; really strong. But now, in the presence of what was obviously a family group—the resemblances were too strong for them to be anything else—I could feel it coming in waves. These people were *bad*. They'd stamp my head flat as soon as look at me.

"You worried about them?" asked one of the girls from

behind the wheelchair. She was chewing gum, and pulled out a long pink strand. "You should be."

"The blonde one," said Simon. "Juliet. She your girlfriend?"

I didn't answer. It seemed to me that anything else I said was only going to make everything worse.

"I think she is," Simon went on. He began to laugh. "Hope you're not the jealous type. What do you think, Henry?"

The Big Man just looked at him and smiled.

Simon looked back down at me. "If you are, there's some heartache coming your way. Right, Henry?"

The girl with the gum laughed.

"He means that him and Henry and Patrick and Don-Paul like *blonde* girls some of the time." She stroked her own long black hair and looked at them with disdain. The other girl remained silent and sullen. "So they're going to fuck your girlfriend to death. If they can get it up, that is."

"It's up already," said Simon, rubbing his crotch.

"Shut up," said the old man. Instantly, Simon was silent. The girl who had been talking made a pop with her bubble gum and was suddenly rigid with fear. Hastily, she gathered up the strands of gum and stuffed them back in her mouth. Was that a muscle twitching in Henry's cheek? No doubt about it, they were all terrified of this apparently frail old man.

There was a long, long silence.

Finally, the old man said: "Leave us alone." He grimaced again, as if the pain were returning. A yellowed hand played around his throat. "I said . . . leave us alone."

The men looked at each other; the girls didn't know where to look. It was as if he'd asked them to grow wings and fly.

"I said leave me with our new guest!"

Instantly, they were heading back to the main reception door. Henry, the Big Man, roughly pushed it open while the others filed out. He seemed unsure about whether he should go or stay. As the black-haired girls shoved past him, I could see that the one who had been speaking was heavily pregnant.

"I'll be right outside if you need . . . " said Henry.

"Out!" shouted the old man, in a voice that deafened me. The main doors clattered shut. They were gone.

Now it was just me and the old man.

I wriggled around to get a better look at him.

"Hello again." He smiled . . . and opened his eyes.

It was dark in the office, but I could still see the glittering black liquid that filled his eye sockets. It swirled there, like black water going down into two miniature drains. He grinned at me, and all at once it was like being back in the boarding-house extension with Trevor Blake. The stuff in this old man's eyes—it was the Black Stuff, the Vorla.

I thought I'd be sick with fear.

"Anything that even the smallest part of us knows," said the old man, "is known by the Whole. Does that make sense to you?"

I couldn't speak. I knew that the old man could taste my fear.

"What happened to Trevor Blake. Our conversation. The death of that small part of us. We know it all." The old man closed his eyes again, hiding the two swirling pools from sight. But just like the shell that had been Trevor Blake, he knew where I was, as if he could see through those eyelids. "But did you really think that you'd chased the Vorla away forever? Just by stringing up a few lights?"

I looked around, tried to see if there was a way out. The old man grimaced once more; this time I could see that the pain was intense. No matter what I was being told by the Vorla, it was still in the body of an eighty-year-old man with serious health problems. Was there a way I could overpower him? The grimace faded, and the old man smiled again, as if he knew just what I was thinking.

"Don't let this frail old shell fool you, Jay," said Daddie-Paul, the grin spreading wider. "He died months ago. There's a small part of him in here now, with the rest of the Vorla. But what

474

you see . . . " He raised veined and wrinkled hands from his lap. " . . . is most definitely *not* what you'd get if you tried to escape. If I wanted to, I could tear you to pieces. I mean that quite literally. It's been known to happen, you know. I keep the wheelchair because the others in my inherited 'family' seem to feel safer from me if I have to use it."

I stopped squirming.

"We know all about you, Jay. All about you and the others. We remember all the times you resisted. Remember all the parts of us that were destroyed. That was mainly down to you. We haven't forgotten that. And all the time you thought you'd driven us away, we were working to create another little family, on the other side of what's left of Edmonville. Are you a religious man, Jay?"

"You fucking bastard."

"We'll take that as a no, then."

"What have you done to the others?"

"They're safe for a time. But we're pleased that you're concerned about them. Have you all grown close in your time here? Do you all *care* about each other now? We do so hope that you do. Because you can't imagine the fear and the terror and the utter, utter *pain* that we have in mind for you. You're going to despair, Jay. You and your friends are going to suffer such agonies that you're all going to beg for death."

"What are you trying to do now? Talk me to death?"

The old man laughed—and there it was again. That hideous multitude of voices all coming out of one mouth. Just like Trevor Blake, just like the times when the Vorla had flowed in a black flood across the ruins of Edmonville.

"We're going to enjoy you, Jay. My, how we're going to *enjoy* you."

"Who are those others?"

"They're my family. The Caffneys. What you see here . . . " The old man raised his hands to his chest. " . . . used to be Daddie-Paul Caffney. Head of the clan. Fifty of his eighty years spent in various prisons for a very creative range of criminal activities. These past ten years confined to his wheelchair, until the earthquake. Henry and Simon are his sons. Simon is the pilot of the microlight. More of that later. There are two other sons, Patrick and Don-Paul. A fifth son, Ronald, isn't with us. He's in prison, back in what you might call the 'real world.' The daughters are twins, Tracey and Luanne. Their hobbies include incest, as you might have gathered. The mother committed suicide shortly after Daddie-Paul took to his chair. Years of worry about the boys coming and going from prison. Not so much the going into prison as the coming home. Daddie-Paul encouraged the boys' sexual appetites not only towards his daughters, but also towards his wife."

"Nice."

"As you say."

"So why are you giving me the family history?"

"We want you to know everything that's happened here. Want you to know what lies ahead. When you and your friends . . . rejected our advances, we turned our attention to the other survivors in Edmonville. Finding the Caffneys in the shattered remains of a council housing estate was very pleasing to us. We visited the old man, showed the other family members what a wonderful thing had happened when he was filled with the Vorla. Oh, the miracles we've shown them. The wonderful things we've done since then. You and your companions rejected us, Jay. The Caffneys embraced us."

"Because they're mad, sick bastards."

"And how could we ask for better qualifications? We gave the Caffneys our Great Plan. To hunt through the ruins, to find the survivors. To kill everyone over the age of sixteen, to save the children so that they could become part of our new family. We're creating a new society, Jay. New rules for a new world."

I was still scared to death, but something about the sheer enjoyment of the thing that sat before me filled me with that slow-burning anger. The Vorla was everything evil about mankind, the essence of real Evil, and here sat a small part of it, taking nothing but delight from the horror and the misery that it inflicted.

"You see, Jay, until the earthquake we were all alone here in this 'No-Place'. Nothing but ourselves to feed on. You'll appreciate, I'm sure, that I'm trying to keep this all very simple for you. The philosophical ramifications of the situation you find yourselves in are immense."

"You're very considerate."

"Thank you. Can you imagine the joy? The very beings who created us . . . who continue to create us . . . are suddenly and wondrously transported here by means which even the Vorla doesn't understand. Here! To the 'No-Place'! Now wouldn't it be foolish to destroy them all? Wouldn't it be foolish to simply enjoy brief moments of torture and slaughter and pain and misery? When they're all gone, we might never see another human again. How much better to keep some of them alive; how much better to create a new society with the Vorla as their God."

"You mean breed them like cattle. Keep the pain and the misery alive."

"Precisely."

"I don't think you can ever understand how much I hate you."

"That's good. We like that. We like that very much . . . "

The old man coughed, one yellowed hand moving to his throat again. Suddenly, he didn't seem to be giving off the same evil power. Something was happening here. Something different. The Vorla was telling me that it was in control, but I could see pain on that face. It said that it could tear me to pieces if it wanted to, but this was surely a frail old man. Did I stand a chance, after all? Had it—they—been lying about that part?

"You're a fucking liar, aren't you?" said Daddie-Paul Caffney.

477

There *was* something different happening here. That voice, for a start. That last statement didn't fit with anything that had gone before, but it was more than that. It was as if there had been a change in the old man's voice. It was the same voice, but there was a definite rise in pitch. And there was great pain there. I could see some kind of struggle taking place.

"I'm still here, you bastards," Daddie-Paul went on. He laughed. This time it dissolved into painful, racking coughs. They subsided and settled. He opened his eyes.

The Black Stuff I'd seen in his eye sockets had gone.

There were no swirling black pools.

I was looking into the yellowed, rheumy eyes of an old man; not some shell filled with everything evil on earth.

"They told you I'm dead," he said. "They're lying. I'm not dead yet. They don't fucking like it—but I'm not dead yet."

I tried to speak, but couldn't. The Vorla had completely possessed Trevor Blake, but it still hadn't been able to take Daddie-Paul Caffney over completely. Not yet. Was there a real chance of getting away, after all? Was there real hope?

The old man laughed again.

"I can read your mind. You going to appeal to my better nature, boy?"

"Listen, let's talk about . . . "

"You stupid little *cunt*! What makes you think that I don't want what the Vorla wants?" Daddie-Paul's face was a mask of rage. I could see the insanity and the cruelty there, and I could feel all my hope draining away. "But what's mine is *mine*!" hissed the old man. "And the Vorla wants it too soon! They can't bide their time. But I'm the head of the fucking family, and when the time's right . . . when the time's right . . . "

I could sense the war that was taking place inside the shell of that old man. Daddie-Paul Caffney was just as evil as any part of the seething black mass inside his body. So evil and so strong that he was still able to put up some kind of fight against what had invaded and possessed him. A fight that

478

Trevor Blake, mad and evil though he was, could never have put up. As the old man's voice faded into silence, I knew what was going to happen next.

I saw the Black Stuff fill his eyes again; saw it swirl and bubble up in his eye sockets until I couldn't see the old man's eyes anymore. His face had gone blank while the Vorla reclaimed its hold over his body. It couldn't have been more than a few seconds but, as I'd come to learn, time had a way of standing still in this hellish place. When it was done, the old man closed his eyelids—and smiled again. When he spoke once more, it was with the voice of the Vorla, as if nothing had happened at all.

"The arrival of a microlight pilot was a great bonus in our plan to spread and connect with the other isolated and fragmented mini-communities. He was so overjoyed to find us, so completely miserable when he discovered our Great Plan. Simon forced him to teach him how to fly. He's a quick learner. We allowed him to torture the pilot to death when he'd finished. Something for which he was very grateful. And so . . . we have breached the Chasm on all sides using the tower-bridge technique where possible. Spreading the Word. Making the family grow. There has been much death, much torture, and a great deal of despair."

"And now you've got us."

"The jewel in the crown, Jay. You resisted so well. Now that's all over."

"If it hadn't been for Damon, you'd never have done it."

"Everyone has innate abilities. We were able to bring them out in Damon . . . which updates you very well, and brings us to the matters at hand."

The old man braced his hands on the armrests of the wheelchair and raised his head. The audience was over.

"*Henry!*"

The main entrance doors banged open, and the Big Man lunged in as if expecting trouble.

"It's time," said the Vorla. "Get the others. Take him to the Council Chamber."

The Big Man strode across the floor as one of the daughters followed him in. As the dark-haired girl pushed Daddie-Paul out of the room, Henry seized me by the collar and dragged me after them like a sack of coal. He began to beat me as he yanked me along.

The Vorla wanted us to despair.

It was doing a good job.

CHAPTER FIFTEEN | JUDGMENT DAY

J ULIET HAD BEEN TO THE TOWN HALL ONLY once before in her life.

It had been for a civic function, hosted by the then Lord Mayor of Edmonville. The town was officially "twinned" with a French town called Pibeau, and a delegation of that town's civic dignitaries had been over for a week's visit. Since Juliet's company had been responsible for the travel arrangements, a half-dozen tickets had been made available for employees. There had been wine, vol-au-vents and long speeches by local councillors on the need for international harmony. It seemed barely possible that this was the same building.

Her recollections of arriving here for a second visit were hazy. Kids screaming and shouting, a great deal of jostling about. Her wrists and ankles were red and weeping from where ropes had abraded the skin. She'd been the first to really come round, to find that the men had been separated from the women. Night was drawing close.

Annie, Lisa, Candy and herself had been thrown into an office filled with overturned filing cabinets and scattered paperwork. When she'd groggily tested the main doors, a girl with long black hair had lunged at her with a carving knife. Juliet recoiled, the door had slammed shut and she hadn't tried again. When the others came round, everyone was suffering from the same painful nausea. It seemed worse for Candy, who was also suffering withdrawal symptoms from the alcohol.

And then Juliet remembered those last moments by the dump truck, when Damon had stood astride Jay and taunted him with what he'd done. She'd sat for a long time, putting the pieces together while the others slowly recovered.

"Why have they separated us?" asked Lisa at last.

No one had an answer. Moving to one of the cracked windows, Juliet could see that they were on the third floor of an annexe to the town hall. The administration offices to the west had collapsed into rubble. There were giant cracks in the wall here, and only God knew how safe this building was. Two hundred yards to the east was a cliff edge. Beyond that, more of the plateaux, peaks and crags to which they had grown accustomed. Juliet looked in awe at the ramshackle towers that had been built and toppled to form a criss-cross connection between these plateaux. None of them had been able to see the extent of the devastation from such a viewpoint before.

A mile or so beyond the stone pillars and peaks that contained the remaining ruins of Edmonville there was nothing but the blank and utterly empty greyness. Juliet looked to right and left, following the ragged outline of the devastation that formed New Edmonville's horizon. Beyond it all, only the greyness and the utter despair that knowledge brought: the Vorla had not been lying. Edmonville had been uprooted and somehow brought down into this empty void. Forever. Juliet turned away; she could look out there no longer.

"Oh God, Annie," said Lisa. "Do you think Robin's all right?"

There could be no answer to that question.

"They'll be dead," said Candy, with hollowness in her voice. "They're bound to be dead."

"Don't say that!" snapped Annie. "We don't know that."

"Don't kid yourself," said Candy, sitting with her back to

the wall and hugging herself tight as if she couldn't get warm. "Alex is dead. They're all dead."

"Shut up, Candy," said Juliet.

"Jay, Damon, the boy. All dead."

"Will you shut up?"

"Don't you see? Every time it looks like we might be going to make it, something else bad happens. We're all going to die here. We're never going to get away. Whoever's brought us here—they're going to kill us." She began to weep.

And then the door banged open, and a man who they'd never seen before strode into the room. He was in his mid-twenties, with dark hair and wearing a brown leather jacket that looked brand new, straight from the peg. He had huge gold rings on each finger, and he was holding a shotgun. He looked anxious to use it. At first, Juliet took him to be the Big Man they'd seen on the other side of the Chasm. But up close she could see that this wasn't him at all. There was a sound from somewhere behind him, previously muffled by the doors. It was the sound of a crowd somewhere else in the building; singing, shouting, yelling. The voices sounded young. No one had any doubt that this must be the "tribe" they had seen with the Big Man on the other side of the Chasm.

"Everybody move," he commanded, his voice slurring. Was he high on drugs or booze? He waved the shotgun at them.

Annie helped Lisa to rise. Candy remained snuffling on the floor.

"I said *everybody!*" yelled the dark-haired man. He looked on the verge of completely losing control, and raised the butt of the shotgun as if he might use it on Candy like a club. Juliet lunged across the room and grabbed her arm, hauling her upright before anything further could develop. The man smiled, but his eyes seemed far away. "My name's Patrick Caffney." He nodded his head then, as if this were the answer to some great puzzle they'd been trying to solve. "The handsome brother. That's me."

They stood looking at him, waiting for something else to happen.

"Oh yes," he said at last, as if returning from his faraway place to what he'd come for. "Follow me." He waved the shotgun at the door and bowed.

They moved quickly past him, expecting him to suddenly "turn" again and bring the shotgun barrel down on someone's head. When the door banged shut they all recoiled instinctively. Patrick Caffney began to laugh, the sound echoing. They were standing on a marble landing which Juliet remembered from her previous visit. There used to be council offices down the corridors to right and left. One of the doors leading to a corridor had been jammed open, and she could see that a ceiling had come down in there, blocking it with debris. Ahead was an elaborate balcony with metal scrollwork which looked down into a stairwell and the main reception area of the town hall. The stairwell was filled with the echoes of young people yelling, singing and screeching.

Caffney waved the gun at the staircase.

"The boy," said Lisa. "What's happened to him?"

"You had better shut your fucking mouth, lady," said Caffney. "And just speak when you're spoken to." His eyes were wild and staring.

Without a further word they descended, the noises of the tribe growing louder as they got nearer.

Below, the glass doors to the reception area had been shattered. To Juliet, it seemed that it had been done deliberately rather than by the earth tremor. Furniture had been dragged from the offices at ground-floor level and smashed against the walls. They picked their way carefully over the broken wood and glass as Caffney urged them on with the shotgun. The walls had been spray-painted with obscenities.

Juliet knew now where they were being taken.

The Council Chamber lay just ahead.

"Stay here!" commanded Caffney when they had reached

the padded double doors. He shoved past them and shouldered open one of the doors. Immediately the sounds of wild voices were amplified, filling the entrance area. Caffney snapped something at someone. There was a brief silence, and then a great roar.

They were expected.

Caffney lunged out, grabbed Juliet by the shoulder and shoved her inside.

For a moment she stood rigidly, unable to move.

The Council Chamber was filled with people. Up front was a raised platform where the Lord Mayor, chief officers and officials would sit. On either side of the aisle in which Juliet now found herself were ranks of well-upholstered seats sweeping in curves to each wall, microphones dangling from overhead rails for the use of individual councillors who would use this room for council meetings.

Except that there were no councillors or local government officers present at this wild and raucous meeting. Each seat contained a young boy or girl. Not one any older than sixteen; all of them ragged and painted in the manner that Juliet remembered from their encounter with the tribe on the edge of the Chasm. Papers from torn council agendas were being flung all around her, like some form of bizarre ticker-tape greeting. Kids screeched and howled, leaping in their seats. Caffney jabbed Juliet between the shoulder blades with the shotgun, forcing her on down the aisle. She turned only briefly to see that the others were being made to follow her.

Something hit her on the shoulder and she recoiled. One of the kids had lobbed some kind of missile at her. Juliet hurried on ahead through the flurry of paper, protecting her eyes.

At last she could see that two figures were sitting at the centre table up on the stage. Another figure was standing guard behind them.

One of the seated figures was a middle-aged woman, grey hair askew. There was a horribly fixed smile on her white face. She was nodding enthusiastically as the kids jumped and shrieked in their seats, in a kind of anxious and terrified approval. One of her eyes had been blacked. But Juliet's attention quickly moved to the second figure seated at the table.

It was Alex.

Like the woman, he had been tied to one of the chairs, and by the way his head was bowed it looked as if he had been badly beaten. Standing behind him was a teenager with a marked resemblance to Patrick Caffney. Juliet looked back through the hail of paper and other debris being thrown at her and saw Caffney wave her on. Reaching the foot of the platform, she could see half a dozen stairs leading up. As she climbed, something else hit her across the shoulders. Juliet whirled then, anger flaring.

A sea of young, painted faces lay before her. But in that blizzard of paper and the torrent of yelling and screeching, she could see something else that at once puzzled and horrified her.

There was no exultation on these faces. There was no cruel happiness or joy there.

She scanned the faces and saw only fear.

"Go on!" snapped Caffney, and Juliet staggered to the table.

Another man grabbed her arm and yanked her down into one of the seats. Candy pushed past her, making straight for Alex. The second man didn't intervene when she pulled back his head and saw the bruises beneath his eyes, the cuts and scratches on his cheeks. A clump of his hair seemed to have been singed off. Candy cradled his head, sobbing. But Juliet couldn't be sure whether she was crying for him or for herself. As Patrick Caffney flung Annie and Lisa into seats, he crossed behind them and seized Candy's hair. She shrieked, and Juliet made to rise; Caffney jammed the shotgun barrel under her chin and pulled Candy into the seat beside Alex.

Throughout, the middle-aged woman at the end of the table nodded her head and smiled at each development. But her eyes were glazed in terror.

There was a clattering noise somewhere behind them all.

Instantly, the two men were alert.

Patrick held his arms up in the air.

The whooping and jeering died away.

Now there was only the soft, pattering flutter of torn paper falling like giant snowflakes all over the Council Chamber.

The two men looked apprehensively behind them.

"Alex," whispered Lisa. "Where's Robin? Is he all right . . . ?"

The second man stepped back and smacked Lisa across the head. Annie pulled her close and looked as if she might launch herself at him. But now the second man's attention was returning to whatever was clattering and banging at the rear of the stage.

An old man in a wheelchair was being pushed in through a rear door by a teenage girl with long black hair. The other Caffneys followed close behind. A great hush lay over the Council Chamber, broken only by the squeaking of the wheelchair as the old man was pushed to the centre table. Another clatter, scuffling footsteps . . . and suddenly Jay was flung out onto the stage. He fell heavily, and as Henry Caffney followed close behind, he delivered a kick to Jay's side that sent him sprawling again.

"Jay!" Juliet lunged from her seat.

She'd tried not to think about what might have happened to him. The fear was too great, and she had struggled to contain her despair at the prospect that perhaps he and the others had been killed. Now that she could see he was alive, hope flared inside her, and any thought of immediate danger was forgotten. Patrick Caffney caught her by the arm and hit her hard across the face. Stunned, Juliet fell to her knees.

"See?" said Simon, pointing to her and smiling. "He *is* her boyfriend."

"You scum . . . " said Juliet, as the wheelchair was pushed right up to her.

The young girl manoeuvred it to the centre of the table. The old man leaned to one side and looked down to where Juliet knelt. Before she could react, a gnarled hand had fastened in her hair and dragged her up close as he lowered his face to meet her.

"I can feel your hope," said the old man, opening his eyes. "It will make your ultimate despair all the sweeter."

Juliet saw the swirling black water in his eye sockets—and knew.

The sight of the Vorla seemed to suck everything good out of her soul.

The old man laughed and let her fall.

Unable to control her trembling, she crawled away from him as he continued to laugh. Someone tried to grab her again, but she dragged herself away. The next moment she was holding Jay. He embraced her as they lay there, and Juliet tried not to weep; did not want to give any of these evil bastards the satisfaction of hearing it.

"Juliet, thank Christ you're all right."

"Jay . . . oh Jay . . . "

"What is my name?" asked the old man.

And the kids in the Council Chamber began to chant. It was a low, hushed and awed sound, filling the chamber.

"Vor-la, Vor-la, Vor-la . . . "

"These people are our enemies," continued Daddie-Paul. "They belong to the Old Ways."

"Vor-la, *Vor-la, Vor-la* . . . "

Annie and Lisa looked out in horror at the naked terror on the faces of the painted savages who had once been the youth of Edmonville. Alex's head sagged to Lisa's shoulder. She held him.

The middle-aged woman just kept nodding her head and smiling her crazed, fixed smile.

"Lisa," whispered Alex, keeping his voice low to avoid further punishment from the Caffney clan standing all around them, "Robin and Gordon got away. They weren't captured.

They thought I might know where they'd gone, so they tried to beat it out of me. But they got away . . . "

"Oh, thank Christ," sobbed Lisa.

Patrick Caffney smacked her across the head again, yanking Alex back by the hair.

"One among them," said Daddie-Paul. "One among them wished to join us, but failed the Test. Bring him out, Don-Paul."

The teenager who had been standing at the top table when Juliet and the others entered the Council Chamber whirled back to the rear of the platform, vanishing around a curtain. A door banged.

"What do we do with the Old Ones?" asked Daddie-Paul.

"*Blood,*" murmured the crowd.

The middle-aged woman nodded and smiled.

"*Pain,*" the crowd went on. "*Death.*"

"Blood and pain and death," said the old man. "Old ways for dealing with the Old Ones. What is my name?"

"Vor-la, Vor-la, *Vor-la* . . ."

A door banged again.

Someone was weeping behind the curtain. A clattering of feet on the bare boards of the platform. A scuffle and a thump as a body was hurled down. The weeping became a frenzied, horrifying plea. Juliet felt a coldness, as if emanating from something very, very bad. The curtain was pulled aside, and Don-Paul re-emerged, dragging someone by the hair right out onto the platform; someone who screamed and thrashed and pleaded.

Someone who was instantly familiar.

Don-Paul let him go, stepping over him to stride back to the table.

Damon groped at the platform, fumbling with bloodied fingers as if he were searching for a lost contact lens. His whole body was shaking, as if he were racked by agonising pain. Juliet and Jay lay only ten feet from him. Sobbing, with great effort, Damon raised his head.

"Oh, good *Christ* . . . " moaned Juliet when she saw his face. They had torn out his eyes.

Damon's eye sockets were ragged holes, filled with congealed black blood and suppurating matter. For an instant, Juliet saw Trevor Blake's ragged and empty eye socket; saw Trevor's face superimposed on Damon's. "Oh, my God, *no.*"

Moaning, Damon groped feebly forward.

"Juliet? Is that you? Are you there, Jay?"

"You filthy, fucking *animals!*" Annie was up and out of her chair, seizing Don-Paul Caffney around the neck from behind. Don-Paul's eyes popped as Annie's forearm choked the air from his throat. He sagged to his knees, clawing at her arm. The next moment Patrick Caffney stepped forward to deliver a vicious, jabbing blow to the side of Annie's head with the shotgun butt. She went down immediately, unconscious. Lisa grabbed for her, knocking her chair over.

The old man in the wheelchair was unperturbed.

"What is the punishment for failing the Test?" he asked, smiling.

"Please, Jay," begged Damon, feeling his way towards them. "Please, Juliet. Tell them I don't know what happened to Gordon and Robin. Please tell them . . . "

"*Blood, pain, death,*" chanted the young crowd. "*Blood, pain, death.*"

The old man nodded.

The middle-aged woman nodded even harder.

"The woman has already been judged. She tried to hide from us in the ruins. For a year, she denied us. Like the others, she spoke in an Old Voice. She spoke of the Old Ways." Daddie-Paul took something from his cardigan pocket and held it up. "Now, she speaks no more." He threw the object down onto the table and the crowd of kids began to yell at the top of their voices.

It was a bloodied human tongue.

The woman looked at it, smiled and began nodding her head again.

The old man's head bowed. Was he in pain? The yelling went on and on. His daughters looked back at their brothers in agitation, as if they should do something. Henry Caffney shook his head.

And then the old man's head rose again. Slowly, he held up his hands and the kids were silent. When he spoke once more, it was in the real voice of Daddie-Paul Caffney. It didn't seem to matter to the kids filling the Council Chamber.

"We leave for the burning place," said the old man.

The crowd began to yell again. Voices cheering and shouting, faces small masks of painted terror.

"Jay!" shrieked Damon. "Don't let them hurt me again! Please God, don't let them hurt me *again* . . ."

But his voice was drowned in the tumult.

And then they were being dragged from the platform and down into the howling crowd of youngsters.

CHAPTER SIXTEEN

THE JOURNAL OF JAY O'CONNOR: HELL ON EARTH

W E WERE DRAGGED OUT OF THE TOWN hall by the Caffney brothers, through a mob of screaming kids. Juliet was torn away from me by the one called Don-Paul, the youngest brother, I guess. He looked ready to explode after what Annie had done to him. For a moment, I thought I was just going to go wild myself. Thinking that I'd lost Juliet forever, then to find her again . . . only to have her dragged away once more. I don't know how to describe it; except that the anger was blood-red behind my eyes, and I was ready to kill one of this insane family. But the extra beating I'd taken from Henry Caffney, and especially the kick he'd given me when he threw me out onto the stage, had done more than wind me. It had robbed me of all my strength.

Two teenage kids grabbed me by my tied hands, and the next thing I knew I was being dragged down the stairs and into the Council Chamber, face first. At the bottom of the stairs, through a tangle of legs, I saw Simon lunge down towards me. He laughed when I recoiled from the carving knife he held up to my face. He stooped and cut the ropes that tied my ankles, and then my hands. I was jerked to my feet. That's when I saw Juliet again; up ahead, being dragged through the screaming crowd by Don-Paul.

Everything was a confused blur after that. The kids began throwing things, jumping up and down in their seats as we were led through them. I tried to look back to see if the others were also being dragged out, but could see only a jumble of twisting bodies.

They dragged me out through the main reception area and down the stone stairs into the street. I didn't know what they had in mind for us all, but I knew it couldn't be good. I tried to concentrate on my breathing as they kept me on my knees while the others caught up. Tried to pull myself together. Patrick Caffney took me by the hair and made me look up at his face. He was waiting for the others to get themselves organised as they poured out onto the streets, occasionally giving a wild yell of encouragement and waving the shotgun in the air with his other hand. Finally I was jerked to my feet. I was taller than Patrick, and he didn't like that one little bit.

Hastily, I looked around for Juliet.

She was holding Lisa, trying to give her comfort and support. It looked as if Annie couldn't be roused after Patrick had clobbered her, so they'd strung her up again beneath one of those rough wooden poles that we'd been brought in on. The two big kids at either end had drug-blank faces and drug-blank eyes. Lisa tried to touch Annie, tried to make her wake up. Henry shoved Juliet and Lisa to one side, barking an order.

Patrick pushed me ahead. The kids parted as I blundered into them, and there was Alex kneeling amidst them, his hands still tied. Candy was kneeling next to him, holding his head and sobbing. Like mine, Alex's legs and feet had been freed. But if I thought that I was in a pretty bad state, Alex was in a worse condition. Up close, I could see that he had been savagely beaten. He looked up at me with dull eyes when I was shoved towards him. Candy was juddering with fear and withdrawal symptoms.

"Help him!" barked Patrick.

493

"Come on, you two," I said. "Don't let the bastards get you down."

I hauled Alex up, and threw one of his arms over my shoulder. Candy did the same, but to little effect. I felt like I was carrying them both.

That's when I saw Damon, being dragged down the town hall steps by a rope leash around his neck. Simon Caffney was holding the other end, laughing like a fucking maniac. Damon groped in front of him, staggered and fell at the halfway point, bouncing and rolling down the stairs. Simon marched on through the crowd of ragged kids, the rope over his shoulder, pulling Damon along the ground effortlessly behind him. The middle-aged woman suddenly appeared in a huddle of kids, all hanging onto her as she was dragged down the steps. Still smiling that same insane smile. Blood had leaked from her mouth down her chin. For her own sake, I hoped that her mind had completely gone. Daddie-Paul Caffney appeared on a concrete ramp beside the stairs, the dark-haired twin girls pushing him. Even in the darkness, I could see the bastard smiling like some indulgent, kindly old grandfather. Which was he now? Daddie-Paul or the Vorla, or some hellish combination of both?

The crowd waited until he reached the street and had been pushed ahead, into the lead. When he waved his hand, they followed. Even though I was moving, Patrick kept jabbing me in the back with the shotgun, urging me on. I fought to control my temper. If it blew now, it wasn't going to do anyone any good, and would only get me another beating or worse.

Slowly, we trudged on along this ruined street. Rubble and detritus had been cleared from our path. But other things had been left on either side.

To give us a hellish floor show as we marched.

The Caffneys had been busy in this part of the city; putting their mark on it.

Bodies hung from crooked streetlamps. Men and women,

some still wearing the rags of their clothes; others naked and tortured beforehand. Some had been simply hanged, their hands tied behind their backs. Most of them seemed to have been up there for a long time. You couldn't look at the terrible, rotting faces for very long. The smell was hellish. Others had been strung up with wire, and then burned.

Every once in a while, Patrick would jab at me and point to something at the side of the street, grinning.

The remains of a man, tied in a sitting position with his back against the burned-out skeleton of a car. A fire had been built between his legs while he was still alive. The pavement was blackened in a great patch around his crotch. His skeletal face was frozen in a silent scream.

Another jab, more grinning.

A naked woman, hanging from a store frontage. Her hands had been tied behind her back and she had been hauled up in that position by her wrists so that her shoulder joints had first dislocated and then snapped completely. It was a grotesque and horrifying sight as she twirled slowly in the air.

Another jab, another grin.

A stained and ragged pile of what at first looked like old clothes. As we passed them, I saw that they were a pile of severed arms and legs; still in shirt or jacket sleeves; still in trouser legs.

On either side now, a line of hastily improvised wooden crosses, X-shaped, the bottom resting in the rubble on the pavements. Men and women had been crucified there.

All adults. No children.

I wondered how many of them were related to this tribe of kids. How many brothers and sisters had been slaughtered and laid out on display? How many fathers and mothers of the kids here had been tortured and crucified? I looked at the wild and painted faces all around me. They looked crazed. Was it just plain fear of the Caffneys, or had some of them actually begun to enjoy this new lifestyle? Christ, we had only been stranded here for a year or so. Did it take so little time for everything to degenerate like this? I supposed that in the Vorla they'd had a hell of a teacher.

I lost track of how long we marched. The sights all around us seemed to do something to time. We were in a Hell of the Vorla's own making, and it seemed that time had no meaning here. I couldn't make out whether we were marching in a circle or straight ahead. Wasn't Hell supposed to be like this? Pain and death and torment forever and ever, amen?

When the old man raised his hand again, the two girls stopped pushing his wheelchair. The crowd behind came to a halt, Patrick grabbing my shoulder and pulling me to a stop, like I was dead keen to go on and find out where we were being taken or something. There were still ruined buildings on either side of the street, but there was a clear space up ahead. I could see the remains of a wire-mesh fence and a security gate. It had all been torn down. Beyond, I could see the silhouettes of what seemed to be huge tanks and cylinders. Massive oil drums and criss-cross connecting pipes, hundreds of feet long and as thick as a man was tall. Was this some kind of petrol plant or refinery?

Was something wrong with Old Man Caffney? His head seemed to be sagging and his two daughters were fussing around him. I strained to look, and Patrick hissed something at me. I took the hint and stayed still. Was the internal war between Daddie-Paul and the Vorla taking place again?

The old man waved once more, and we moved on.

When we reached the fence and the gate, I could see that the quake hadn't been responsible for it all being torn down. This had been done by human hands, to gain access to what was on the other side. A sign lay on the road as we passed: Petro-Ammyln Inc.

We had just passed through the remains of the torn fence when we halted again. From behind, Henry began to shout some kids' names. About a dozen or so ran forward to the old man's wheelchair and positioned themselves around him. They moved on ahead, in a knot of bodies. Patrick jabbed me with the shotgun again, and we were on the move once more.

Now I could see what lay ahead of us.

A crevasse had opened up in the road ahead, zigzagging through shattered tarmac just inside where the gates had once been. There was a familiar ragged cliff edge before us, stretching off into the darkness on our right and left. Whatever lay beyond was separated by a gap about fifty feet wide. Could it be that the remains of this petrol plant, or whatever, were stranded on a plateau? Or was this just a bloody great crack in the ground? Was this refinery where we were headed, or was it something beyond? There was no way of telling at the moment. I strained to see how we were going to get over the abyss, wondered if there was a way round—then saw that the Caffney clan had been busy once again.

Another of the familiar tower bridges had been built on this side, and then toppled over the Chasm to the other cliff edge. Had we all been carried over this one on our way to the town hall "council meeting"? Or was this just a side bridge? Again, no way of telling. But it seemed to me that a great deal more care had been taken here than over the other, bigger bridges. For a start, this one had a flattened level surface, with something that might have been a handrail or barrier on either side.

This was an important place.

Because this bridge had been carefully constructed so that Daddie-Paul Caffney's wheelchair could be pushed easily over the Chasm to the other side.

Sure enough, he was being wheeled over there now, with his dozen little helpers all clustered around to make sure that he would be safe.

"Safety first, eh?" I said to Patrick Caffney.

He grinned and jabbed me with the shotgun.

I slapped it away.

For a moment I thought I'd lost it and gone a step too far.

Caffney's eyes hardened into that manic stare. But almost immediately the look was gone. He grinned back at me.

"I'm going to enjoy hurting you," he said simply.

He gestured ahead with the gun; this time like he was being really polite.

Carrying Alex, Candy and I moved on ahead.

Compared to the other crossings of the Chasm I'd had to endure, this one wasn't so bad. It felt pretty solid beneath my feet; iron spars and wood hammered and tied together into one compacted and seamless mass. Imagine a clapped-out car shoved into a junkyard compressor, then turned into a solid metal cube. The surface beneath us was just like the surface of one of those cubes; impacted, crushed and smooth. Christ knows how they'd done it—but they'd done it.

Behind Daddie-Paul Caffney, I saw Juliet and Lisa trying to keep Annie from being swung all over the place beneath the pole. Don-Paul thought it was a fucking great joke. I kept wishing that he'd miss his footing and go over the edge. Somewhere behind us, I heard Damon howl in pain. Simon Caffney laughed again. I wondered what living next door to the Caffneys had been like on that council housing estate, before the "psychic earthquake" hit Edmonville. I supposed they'd made it hell for their neighbours. Now they were doing it quite literally. To most of the survivors, New Edmonville was a nightmare place, a real Hell. To the Caffneys, it must have seemed like all their dreams had come true. No police to control them; no more social mores to observe. Just do what you like, when you like. A paradise for sadists and monsters.

As we crossed, I could see that the cliff edge we were heading for curved away on our left, making it wider there than at the crossing. And there was some sort of strange construction right on the cliff edge that we'd just left, maybe a hundred feet away. At first I thought it was some kind of plant or metal wreckage left dangling over the side by the quake. But as we moved, I could see that it had the same "homemade" quality as the tower bridge we were walking on. Now it was clear that it was some kind of wooden platform, built right on the cliff edge and jutting out maybe twenty feet or so over the Chasm. I could see two wooden struts at a forty-five-degree angle beneath the rectangle of wood, keeping it anchored against the rough cliff wall. Whoever had built this strange construction obviously had no fear of heights, since they'd have had to climb down beneath the platform to anchor it like that. I remembered the kids who had built the first tower bridge we'd seen. They'd seemed unafraid of the drop into the Chasm then. Or had it been that they'd been goaded to that frenzy of construction by the greater fear of what the Caffneys and the Vorla might do if they didn't get the job done in time? What had the Caffney clan been up to over there? Why rig up a platform like that if they had built a bridge as well? I could see some kind of rope piled up on the platform. Patrick caught me looking, and jabbed me hard. I faced front and continued on.

The platform, or whatever, was lost from sight when we reached the other side.

Daddie-Paul Caffney was trundled on ahead through the maze of pipes and the shadows of great steel canisters on either side. Some of the plant and pipework in here had collapsed and burst in the quake, and the ground crackled underfoot as we walked. There had been fires here at one time, and it looked like one of the fifty-foot-high canisters had ruptured and burned. But the fire must have been dampened down, otherwise there wouldn't have been anything left standing here.

There was another pause while the daughters crowded around Daddie-Paul in his wheelchair. Another "turn" perhaps? It didn't last long this time, and we continued on.

I still couldn't see past the silhouettes of giant tanks and pipes ahead, to work out whether this was a separate plateau or not. But when we were a couple of hundred yards "inland", Daddie-Paul Caffney called a halt and had his wheelchair turned around to face us all. In the darkness and the shadows of the containers, it wasn't possible to see any faces. But I saw the pole-carriers suddenly dump Annie on the ground. Lisa cried out and moved to her. Juliet tried to help, and was flung back against one of the pipes at ground level by Don-Paul.

"You touch her again and I'll . . . " I lunged forward instinctively. Patrick held the shotgun to my face, and Don-Paul stepped in my direction.

"Don-Paul!" commanded Old Man Caffney, stopping him in his tracks. He shuffled uneasily, looking back at his father.

"He's asking for it."

"And he'll get it," said Daddie-Paul. "Just be patient."

The crowd following finally bunched up around us. They shuffled and coughed, and it brought back a crazy memory to me. This was like the time back in Burleigh High, when the kids gathered at assembly before the classes began. They shuffled and coughed, just like this, waiting for the head teacher to make the usual announcements and get the day under way. These were *kids*, for Christ's sake. The same kids I'd seen when I'd been cleaning the school windows, or washing the toilet floors. It was truly bizarre.

There was a flurry of activity within the shadowed figures. Someone was shoving through. They parted, and Damon's wretched form was flung to the ground in the centre of the crowd. As he moaned and gibbered, it seemed barely possible that this was the Damon we remembered. They had reduced him to some pitiable thing that was barely human anymore. Simon Caffney stepped over his body, seized the rope leash and dragged him to the wheelchair.

Damon gibbered and pleaded at the old man's feet.

"Last chance, Damon," said the old man.

"I don't know! I swear to *Christ*, I don't *know*!"

Another gesture with his hand, and Daddie-Paul was being pushed away from us, back the way he'd come. I watched him go and began to wonder. Quite apart from the fact that something pretty bad had been planned for us, something about the old man's behaviour didn't scan. Not just the bizarre shifting between Daddie-Paul and the Vorla, but something else. Something that ate at me. A little voice was frantically whispering in my ear, but I was either too exhausted or too afraid to understand what it was saying. Something about the old man . . . something about the internal battle that was taking place . . . something about the place we'd been brought to . . .

Damon screamed, snapping my attention back to him.

Don-Paul and Simon had seized him by the hands and were dragging him through the crowd to one side. The crowd parted silently, and Damon was suddenly flung back against what seemed to be a wire-mesh fence. He begged and pleaded with them as they held his hands up and strapped his forearms to the mesh above his head. But no one could understand what he was gibbering. It was a hideous, sickening sound. And there was nothing that anyone could do about it. There seemed to be broken, angular pipes and shattered machinery all around his feet. Strange, angular frames; like some kind of mini-junk pile. But it was too difficult to tell in the darkness.

Henry Caffney motioned to his brothers.

Don-Paul moved quickly to Juliet and dragged her into the clearing that had been made in front of Damon. That was it. I lunged forward. Candy cried out as Alex sagged against her. But Patrick had me by the neck from behind before I could take more than two steps. Bracing a foot in the small of my back, he kicked hard and I staggered out into the clearing, falling to my knees. Then Candy, Alex and Lisa were dragged out by a bunch of kids until we were all kneeling together. Only the mad middle-aged woman remained standing, surrounded by kids, all hanging onto her arms while she smiled and nodded, smiled and nodded.

We were going to be made to watch something.

Henry nodded his satisfaction, and that's when I saw that he'd picked something up in the darkness. It was a bucket. Holding it behind him, he said: "Fill it."

A kid ran out of the shadows and grabbed the bucket. It was hard to tell whether it was a boy or a girl. I twisted around to watch the figure run to one of the shadowed pipes at ground level. I could see a valve wheel there. The bucket clattered on the ground, and the next moment that small shape was grunting and straining as it twisted the wheel. Henry Caffney just stared at Damon as he hung there, his head down on his chest, sobbing. The other brothers kept their eyes on us.

I looked back when I heard liquid running into the bucket.

The valve was turned off, and the small figure ran back.

The smell of petrol, or diesel oil, filled the air.

Henry Caffney couldn't be going to do what I thought he was going to do.

He took the bucket from the kid and stepped forward towards Damon.

I could see that Damon could smell the fuel. He stopped moaning and looked up. His face was a terrible eyeless mask. I heard Juliet moan, but there was nothing I could do.

Henry threw the bucket of fuel over Damon's body. One, two, three quick actions with the bucket. The fuel glinted black like the Vorla itself as it splashed in the air, soaking him. Some of it went into Damon's mouth. He coughed and gagged and began pleading again.

"I know you can't see this, Damon," said Henry, standing back. "But you can smell it, can't you?"

Damon could only moan in fear.

"And can you feel this?" asked Henry. He took something from his pocket.

I knew what it was going to be.

Patrick must have sensed that I was going to say something. The shotgun barrel passed quickly in front of my eyes, and before I could react he pulled it back hard across my throat from behind. I gripped his forearms. They felt as cold and as hard as the barrel itself.

Henry struck a match.

Shadows fluttered and danced. Dozens of painted faces were revealed in that one small glare. Smiling, his face like a demon, Henry moved forward once more and held the match up close to Damon's face. Damon felt the heat, and began to scream.

Laughing, Henry stood back. The match continued to burn as his laughter died away, and his face became a blank mask once more.

"Now, for the last time. Where are the other two?"

Damon began to babble. "I hid them. I took them away. The dummy's a queer. Like me. We wanted the boy. We made a deal. I hid them both."

Henry nodded, no expression on his face.

"Shall we send someone to get them?" said Patrick from behind me.

Henry shook his head, still thinking.

There was a long, long silence.

Then Henry said: "He doesn't know where they are."

He dropped the match into the bucket. Instantly, it flared up into a great yellow cloud, sending shadows dancing and leaping into the crowd. The metal tanks and canisters seemed to sway and lurch, the criss-cross framework of pipes swinging wildly all around. Waxwork-mask faces leered and grinned.

And then Henry casually threw the blazing bucket at Damon's feet.

Damon shrieked. He must have known what was happening even though he couldn't see. He began to kick and lash with his feet. But the effect was instantaneous; his trouser legs erupted in flame, lighting up the tangled wreckage around him, surging greedily upwards to engulf his lower body. The flaring light around his legs and feet showed the kind of wreckage he was standing in. It wasn't bent, angular pipework and tangled machinery as I'd first thought in the darkness. It was *human* wreckage. What I had thought were rusted metal frames were charred and blackened ribcages. What I had thought were tangles of bent pipework were human bones; what had seemed to be clumps of discarded batteries and shattered engine blocks were human skulls.

There had been more than one barbecue up against this wire-mesh fence.

Again, Patrick must have anticipated what I might do. His full weight was suddenly on my back, pinning me to the ground. His fist gripped my hair tight as he slid the shotgun barrel away. Then I felt it jammed against the back of my skull. I tried to brace my hands to throw him off, but I couldn't move. I couldn't do a thing. Juliet tried to run forward and was hauled back by her long blonde hair. Somewhere, Candy began to sob.

Damon had become a thrashing human fireball. His shrieking had diminished to a muffled, faraway groaning deep within the flaming mass. We had seen the living dead burn, and that had been a deeply horrifying thing; something we'd had to do, and something we'd had to get our heads around by remembering that they *were* dead and no longer human. But this was a living, breathing person. This was someone, despite our differences and the fact that he had been prepared to betray us, that we *knew*; someone we'd spent time with and who had survived the quake despite everything.

This was the most horrifying thing that I've seen in our new world of horrors.

I found myself praying that he would die quickly.

The mad, blazing puppet thrashed at the wire-mesh fence; no longer human, but a fiery mass that was only shaped like a man.

I tried to yell my fury and my horror. Nothing would come out.

Out of the corner of my eye, I saw Juliet kneeling; her head hanging low, her hair sweeping down to the ground.

The burning puppet sagged against the fence. It ceased to

thrash, its legs moving feebly now in a shroud of blue-yellow fire.

They made us watch, until the fire guttered and died out. Then there was only the darkness, and smoke, and a smell of roasting flesh that made my stomach heave. Somewhere, someone was sick. One of us, I guessed, not one of the tribe.

I thought then that this part of the nightmare was over.

I could never have guessed how much worse it was going to get.

From the darkness, Henry said: "Get ready . . ."

Oh God, I remember thinking. *It's our turn now, and there's nothing I can do.*

"Get set," said Henry. And I realised that he was saying it like a teacher at a school sports day would, working the kids up ready for the big race.

If I'd had only ten seconds, I'd have made for Juliet and killed her. Saved her from what they'd planned for us all up against that wire mesh.

"Go!" shouted Henry.

Suddenly, the darkness was filled with the sounds of rushing feet. The tribe surged forward all around us. I felt someone step on my back, and groaned in pain. The Caffney brothers were laughing their heads off as the kids crowded forward. What the hell was going on? I waited to be yanked to my feet, waited to see that they'd grabbed Juliet or Alex or one of the others. Either I or someone else would end up tied to that bloody fence, standing in the skeletal wreckage of their previous victims.

There was a rattling sound from the mesh. Frenzied and eager. They had to be tearing Damon's corpse down, ready for the next one. And not one of them was yelling or shrieking, or making any kind of noise.

"Have a closer look," said Patrick Caffney, yanking at my hair again.

I saw the fence. Damon had been taken down. But no one else was being strung up there.

The kids were a crowding, clawing mass at the base of the fence.

I saw what they were doing, and refused to believe it.

"Can you see?" asked Patrick Caffney. There was only one way to describe his voice. It was gleeful. "What about that, then? Can you see?"

I groaned in sick horror. I wouldn't accept it.

"Hungry little bastards, aren't they?" said Don-Paul somewhere in the darkness.

The Vorla promised that we'd feel it before we died.

It was living up to its promise.

I despaired.

CHAPTER SEVENTEEN | SACRIFICE

WHEN IT WAS ALL OVER, ALEX ALLOWED himself to be dragged away with the others.

He didn't lift his head to see who was holding his arms, but he guessed that it wasn't Jay. He could hear Candy somewhere beside him as they were hauled through a maze of shadowed pipes and steel canisters . . . and he fought to contain the turmoil of horror and anger that was churning inside him.

He was not as badly injured as he'd made out.

The Caffneys had beaten him when they'd first arrived at the town hall, wanting to know what had happened to Gordon and Robin. Afterwards Old Man Caffney had left the brothers to their own devices; one of the bastards had even held a cigarette lighter to his face, until the flesh was scorched and his hair frizzled. When he'd tried to fight back, even with his hands tied, the big one called Henry had knocked him out. Everything after that was confused. He remembered leering faces, asking the same question: *Where are the other two?* After a while, they'd given up on him. Now he knew that they'd tried other methods on Jay, turning their attentions finally back to Damon when they couldn't get what they wanted there either.

Damon . . . that poor bastard Damon.

Candy was sobbing now as they were dragged on. Was she

mourning her lover? Could he have done something to save him? Or had he held back and allowed the Caffneys to mutilate and murder him?

No, Alex! You know that you couldn't have done anything.

But now Damon was out of the way. Candy's teenage lover was dead. Maybe there was a chance for them to really begin rebuilding their relationship, even in this Hell on earth . . .

No! What chance? You didn't want Damon dead, and certainly not like . . . like that. You couldn't do anything. That Caffney bastard had the shotgun to the back of Jay's head. He would have blown it off if I'd tried anything. Maybe just blown me away instead if I'd made any kind of move. The other one had a carving knife at Juliet's throat.

Even though he was pretty sure that he was capable of walking unaided, Alex had allowed Jay and Candy to carry him from the town hall and through the streets to the petrol plant, or oil refinery, or whatever. He had waited for the chance to whisper to Jay; to tell him that he was okay, that he was faking it, and that if any chance came to make a move, he was ready. But Patrick Caffney had been there all the time, with the shotgun levelled at Jay's back, and the opportunity had never arisen. He'd taken one chance back at the town hall, to let Lisa know that Robin and Gordon seemed to have escaped, to ease the grief he knew she must be feeling—and he'd nearly given the game away then. He couldn't afford to slip up again. Not until he had a chance to do something to help them all.

Helplessly, he'd knelt with the others and watched Damon's terrible death. It was crucifying him inside, mentally and emotionally. Had he really been unable to act, or was inaction some way of paying the bastard back for screwing his wife?

No, God help me, no! I couldn't do a bloody thing. Other than get one or more of us killed.

A great hatred overcame him, like some kind of inner tidal wave. It swamped his other conflicting emotions. He hadn't killed Damon. If he'd wanted to do it, there were dozens of times he could have done so back at the Rendezvous. Hadn't he told Lisa that very thing? No, Damon had been tortured and killed by these murdering bastards, and now it was up to him to do something about it and to prevent what was going to happen to them. He had to use this anger the way he'd seen Jay use it. But when and how?

Bide your time, Alex. Wait for your moment . . .

He lost track of how long they'd been moving through the darkness, but suddenly they were crossing the bridge again, back across the Chasm to the other side. Lifting his head carefully, he could see that there was a great crowd of kids waiting for them on the other side. Clearly, only a privileged few had been allowed to cross and to participate in Damon's death. Alex felt his stomach roll. So this was what the Vorla had done in only one year in New Edmonville. Out of the hatred and the fear and the hunger, it had managed to inflict even further degradation while creating its new young society—cannibalism. Alex hung his head again, deliberately sagging against whoever was carrying him. Eventually he felt and saw cracked tarmac beneath his feet and knew that they had reached the other side. But they weren't heading straight on, back the way they'd come. They were turning to the right, and following the cliff edge. The tribe remained silent. There was only the rustling of the crowd as it moved.

Suddenly, he was flung forward onto rough ground. He lay still for a while, hearing and feeling the bodies crowding around him, some of them stepping on him as they passed. Someone began to lift him, this time gently. He recognised the touch immediately. It was Candy. He saw the shadowed outlines of her face, tears glinting on her cheeks in the darkness. Her hair was awry, and he could feel the desperation exuding from her as she held his head to her breast and moaned. He allowed himself to be held, and felt the hate for the Caffneys and the Vorla burning deep inside. He loved her furiously, and he wasn't going to let anything happen to her.

"Are you despairing yet?" asked a familiar and despised voice.

Alex turned only slightly, still feigning weakness, to see that they had moved along the cliff about a hundred feet or so from the bridge. Old Man Caffney had reappeared again in his wheelchair, both daughters positioned behind him and waiting for the others to finish crowding around. And what Alex at first assumed to be some kind of wreckage just behind the old man, balanced right on the cliff edge itself, he could now see was some kind of wooden platform. It jutted out about twenty feet over the abyss. There was a wooden winch at the halfway point, somehow fastened to the cliff edge, with a great coil of rope piled up there. Good Christ! Did they intend to haul something up out of the Chasm?

"Henry!" called Daddie-Paul.

The Big Man strode out to meet him.

"Did he confess?"

"He didn't know where they were," said Henry. "He made up some lies. But I could smell that he was lying."

"You're sure?"

"He knew he was going to die. If he'd known, he would have told me."

"When we're finished here, I want you and Simon to go back with some of the others. Find them and bring them back here. We must lay the Vorla's hand upon them, and they must be punished for their rejection. Do you understand?"

"You promised us some . . . fun. With the women."

"Yes, you can have all that. But there's something else that we have to attend to first."

Alex prepared himself.

Suddenly, he was dragged out of Candy's embrace. She hung onto him, crying out loud. Someone hit her across the face and Alex fought to stop himself reacting. He was torn away and Candy pushed aside. He had to bide his time . . .

But when, Alex? When, for Christ's sake? They could kill any or all of us any moment now!

He was dragged forward and dumped on the ground again.

Carefully turning his head, he could see that Jay had been pulled forward too, and was kneeling beside him.

"Turn me," commanded Daddie-Paul, and the twins shunted his wheelchair to the side so that he had a clear view of the wooden platform on the cliff edge. For a long time the old man just looked at it. Then his body began to spasm and judder.

Was he having a heart attack? He was having these convulsions with increasing frequency. Alex suppressed the urge to leap to his feet and yell: *Go on, then, you bastard! Go ahead and DIE!*

The convulsions ceased.

Daddie-Paul turned his head in their direction.

"I robbed this place when I was a young man. Petro-Ammlyn Inc. Me and my two brothers. You there, the oldest: Alex. You probably read about it in the papers when you were a kid. Well before anyone else's time . . . well before . . . before . . ." The old man gasped, and his teenage daughters were quickly at his side again.

"What's the matter, Daddie-Paul?" asked the pregnant daughter. "The old pain? You want something for it?"

"I want . . . want . . ."

The old man opened his mouth wide and the two girls recoiled.

Out of his mouth came a great hissing; an echo of the many voices of the Vorla.

The old man lowered his head and began to convulse again.

Henry Caffney took a step forward.

The old man's head suddenly snapped up.

Everyone flinched, captured and captor alike.

"You fuck," said the old man, and he began to laugh. "You *fuck*! You want me to die, so you can have all of me. Don't you?"

"No, Daddie-Paul," said Henry. For the first time, the Big Man sounded afraid. "We don't want that. We don't want that, at all. Do we, Simon . . . ?"

"Shut up, Henry!" snapped Old Man Caffney. "I'm not talking to you."

"Then who . . . ?"

"*Shut up!*"

Henry was silent.

"Like I said," Daddie-Paul continued, as if nothing had happened, "we robbed this place, and we were armed. That was in the days when big companies like this paid out cash every month to most of their employees. Long before cheques and plastic cards. But someone—I never found out who—tipped off the police. They surrounded the place we were using then. Both my brothers were killed. I was shot in the legs, spent six months in prison hospital. Another ten years inside. So I never got to spend any of that fucking money, and these boys lost two uncles. Look at me now." Caffney waved his hands at the plant. "I'm the king of this castle, aren't I?"

"*King,*" chanted the crowd. "King, *king, king!*"

"And you!" screamed Old Man Caffney, stabbing a finger at the Chasm. The crowd was silent instantly. "You get what I *want* you to have! And not before!"

There was confusion in the crowd of children now. They didn't know what or who he was talking to; didn't know how they were supposed to react. Caffney was silent for a long while, arm still outstretched, finger pointing, while his tribe waited.

"Bring the woman out," he said at last. "The one with . . ." And now he began to laugh; a low, liquid chuckling in his lungs. " . . . with nothing else to say."

Do something now, Alex. Carefully, Alex looked across at Jay, trying to attract his attention. But Jay's face was turned to where a bunch of children were leading the tongueless woman towards Daddie-Paul. She still had the same indulgent smile on her mask-white face. It was as if this were some kind of school outing or picnic, and she was enjoying every moment of it. Her mad, glittering eyes filled Alex with horror. He leaned forward slowly, ready to whisper to Jay. But Jay suddenly began to rise, and in the next moment the shotgun barrel was jammed into his cheek. He froze.

"I won't kill you outright if you try anything," said Patrick. "But I will blow half your face off."

Alex willed Jay to glance at him so that he could give him some kind of sign, but Jay turned slowly to look up at Patrick; the barrel denting his flesh, his eyes riveted in hatred on the man with the gun. Patrick laughed.

"Now it's time to fulfil your destiny," said Daddie-Paul Caffney, or was it the Vorla speaking this time? The woman stood before him, a dozen children holding onto her arms and hands. She smiled down at the man in the wheelchair. Caffney grinned up at her. "Do you have any last words?"

"You sick *bastard* . . ." It was Annie, somewhere behind them. There was a grunt of effort, followed by a cry of pain. Annie had obviously been punished for speaking out.

"No?" asked Daddie-Paul.

The woman continued to smile.

"Take her out onto the platform and prepare her."

The children led the woman carefully out onto the platform, over the abyss. Alex watched them begin unravelling the rope, watched as two children began tying the end around both feet, securing it there with heavy-duty multi-coloured rubber bands of some kind. At last he knew what they were about to do. They weren't going to haul something out of the Chasm. They were going to drop something in.

"Ever seen a bungee jump?" laughed Patrick. Alex turned carefully to see that Jay was still glaring up at the man with the gun, that he even seemed to be pressing his face defiantly against the shotgun barrel that was jammed into his cheek. "Believe me, you've never seen a bungee jump like this before.

More like deep-sea fishing. And you should see the way the sharks down there take the bait . . . "

Alex recoiled when Jay suddenly grabbed the gun barrel and shoved it aside. Then Jay was yelling and on his feet, seizing Patrick Caffney by the throat. The next few seconds were a jumbled blur to Alex. Jay was either knocked or fell over his body in the struggle. The impact slammed him to the ground, knocking the breath out of his lungs. Then Jay was dragged away from him, and he could see blood on his forehead. His eyes were open, but they were rolling like a drunk man's. Patrick, or one of the others, had stunned him. He lay, hands groping feebly in the air. A woman screamed as she was held back from running to assist. Juliet?

Now, Alex! For Christ's sake, do something NOW!

"Bring them to the edge," commanded Daddie-Paul Caffney.

Hands seized Alex's hair and his shoulder. He tried to fight back, but he had been badly winded. Was this how it would end? Were they all going to be thrown over the cliff edge, down to the Vorla? He tried to shout for Candy, but nothing would come out as he was dragged through the mud with the others.

And there was the woman, standing on the edge of the wooden platform with her backs to them all. Her arms had been tied to her sides. Alex couldn't see her face, but he knew that she would be smiling. The kids carefully retreated from the platform, and she was standing there alone. There was a bizarre flash in Alex's mind now as he was dragged to the edge. He'd seen a painting or a mural when he was a kid: Joan of Arc, at the stake. The woman at the edge of the platform looked like that now.

"Vorla!" shouted Daddie-Paul Caffney.

"*Vor-la,*" chanted the children. "*Vor-la, Vor-la.*"

"Pain, death, misery," cried the old man.

"*Pain, death, misery,*" repeated the crowd.

514

Alex was on the edge; whoever was holding his hair was forcing him to look down into the Chasm. Fear and horror robbed him of strength. The awesome, bottomless drop made his senses reel; the ragged cliff face opposite swooped down in gigantic carved ridges before vanishing into utter darkness. The platform cast a shadow on the far wall, the woman's silhouette on the edge.

"Give . . ." said Daddie-Paul Caffney, and then his voice changed again, becoming the hideous thousand voices of the Vorla itself. "*Give her to us!*"

Alex heard a brisk clattering of footsteps on the platform, then out of the corner of his eye saw Don-Paul striding across it. His shadow loomed behind the silhouette of the woman on the far cliff wall.

Don-Paul shoved her hard between the shoulder blades.

Silently, the woman fell from the platform, plummeting head first into the depths of the Chasm. Her figure remained still and composed, apparently without fear. As she dropped, the rope twisted and spiralled behind her, slithering and rattling over the edge of the platform. Alex felt as if his heart had stopped. The rope slithered on and on, looping and spiralling as the woman became smaller and smaller, falling seemingly forever.

The crowd of children was silent.

Suddenly, the falling figure was enveloped in the utter darkness.

The rope continued to twist and spiral, the slithering and rattling from the platform becoming louder and louder.

And then the rope snapped taut with a reverberating twang. It sounded like a steel hawser snapping. The entire platform groaned and cracked. The winch at the centre point stretched and creaked; soil pattered over the edge, where the platform had been anchored. For a moment, it seemed that the entire structure would be dragged from its moorings. The tension on the rope eased. The platform creaked again as the strain was taken away. The rope tensed once more as the weight on the other end bounced up and fell, bounced and fell, the platform creaking and groaning like the timbers of an old ship at sea. Finally, it was still.

Alex tried to look away, numb with horror. But his captors held him fast. He was made to look down into the Chasm. The ritual wasn't over yet.

Now there was only silence.

Alex could feel the expectation.

He'd had a chance to do something, to somehow take them unawares. But now that chance was gone. Both he and Jay were going to be thrown into the Chasm. They had other horrifying plans for the women.

The rope suddenly snapped taut again with the same loud reverberation.

The platform screeched as the rope began to vibrate.

Something had taken the bait.

"Vorla!" screeched Daddie-Paul, and it was impossible to tell this time whether it was his own voice or the voices of the evil and madness below.

"*Vor-la, Vor-la, Vor-la!*" There was no exultation in the young crowd. They were expected to perform, and they were performing. Alex could hear the fear.

The rope stretched and vibrated.

The platform groaned and screeched.

"Vorla!"

"*Vor-la, Vor-la, Vor-la!*"

Something on the platform shuddered and snapped. Wood splintered and cracked. Surely this time it would be dragged over the edge?

From below came an echoing sound; like grumbling thunder or the eager voices of some insane and maddened crowd. Now a sound like a pistol shot; a sharp, brittle crack. The tension on the rope was gone. Down in the Chasm, it began to loop and twist as it rose rebounding from the depths.

The rope had snapped, the bait had been taken.

"Vorla!" yelled Daddie-Paul again.

"*Vor-la, Vor-la, Vor-la!*"

Don-Paul was back on the platform, carefully edging towards the winch. He tested each step, then began to turn the handle at the side. The rope began to wind up from the darkness, spooling on the platform at his feet.

You had a chance to do something, Alex.

"Pain, death, misery," said Daddie-Paul Caffney.

"*Pain, death, misery,*" repeated the children.

Now it's too late.

"Vorla!" screeched the old man.

"*Vor-la, Vor-la, Vor-la!*"

Good Christ, you've blown it, Alex. After everything we've been through, you didn't take the chance . . . and now it's all over.

"*Vor-la! Vor-la!*" chanted the children in fear-tainted voices. "*Vor-la! Vor-la!*"

Patrick Caffney dragged Jay to the platform.

CHAPTER EIGHTEEN | THE JOURNAL OF JAY O'CONNOR: A THOUSAND-THOUSAND DEATHS

IT WAS THE GUN IN MY FACE THAT DID IT.

That and the fact that everything seemed so hopeless. When I knew what they were going to do with the woman, what the Caffneys had in mind for Juliet and the others, the anger just exploded inside me. Maybe if I could cause enough confusion it would give the others some kind of chance to act. But I'd blown it. Patrick, or maybe one of the others, brought me down, and the next few moments were blurred. I heard the kids chanting, wood groaning and splintering—and I knew that the poor mad woman had been thrown into the Chasm. Then hands were under my armpits and I was being dragged. Was this the end? They were going to chuck me over the side after her. But no. Suddenly I could see rough wooden boards beneath my feet. Somewhere I could hear Juliet shouting my name. There was real terror in her voice, and it was this that helped me to pull myself together. When my vision focused again, I could see where I'd been dragged.

I was out on the wooden platform, over the Chasm.

There were kids all around me. Wild, painted faces.

"See this?" said a man's voice below me.

Don-Paul was kneeling at my feet, leering up at me. He was holding the frayed end of the rope up to my face. "It took the rubber grip and the brace and everything this time. Just snapped the rope altogether." He looked wild with joy, eyes glittering. Feverishly, he began to wind the rope around my lower legs.

"Never know, Jay. You might get lucky. Without the support and the brace, the drop might just pull your legs off. Then it'll be all over really quickly."

"Jay!" screamed Juliet from the cliff edge.

Henry had her by the hair. Grinning, he made her kneel and looked straight out at me. He began thrusting his pelvis at her face, watching for my reaction.

I don't know how or why it happened. But that's when everything came together in my head. Everything that had been bugging me about Daddie-Paul Caffney and the constant struggle that he was having with the Vorla. It had become worse on our journey here, Daddie-Paul and the Vorla coming and going inside his body. It was so bloody obvious, but perhaps the fear and the horror had been clouding my mind. I saw the community centre that had exploded into flame that night, remembered the screaming and knew that it had been the screaming of the Vorla, not the people inside. I saw the Black Stuff exploding out of the dead every time fire came near; saw the black sea of it rippling back from the light cast by our bonfire. The Vorla was Darkness, and it hated the Light. But more than that, much more than that—it hated fire. Before I knew what I was going to say, it was somehow out of my mouth.

"The Vorla is afraid, Daddie-Paul."

"You're going to die a thousand-thousand agonising deaths down there," said the old man.

"The Vorla is terrified." I raised my voice, turning to look at the kids who were crowding at the edge. "Terrified of what we know. Terrified of *us*."

"Shall I do it now?" asked Don-Paul. He was holding my legs while the kids started back across the platform to the edge. I could feel him trembling with excitement.

"Listen to me, kids!" I shouted. "See that petrol plant back there? Ask yourself why Daddie-Paul didn't stay to watch the burning. It's because the Vorla inside him is *terrified* of the place. It doesn't want him to be here, doesn't want *you* to be here! Don't listen to what you've been told."

Someone was fumbling at my back, perhaps tightening the rope that bound my hands there.

"The Vorla is all-powerful!" shouted Old Man Caffney. "Pain, death . . ."

"The Vorla *isn't* all-powerful!" I yelled. "It *can* be destroyed! Caffney brings you all here because he knows that the Vorla is afraid of this place! It's in him, fighting for control. But he doesn't want it to take control. He wants to stay in charge. That's why he brings it—and you—here. Because he *wants* to terrify it. Show it who's boss. You can feel it now, can't you, old man? You can feel it squirming inside. You can feel its fear. It hates the light, and it hates fire! You kids—don't listen to what these mad bastards say. Fire destroys the Vorla. And who knows how safe those canisters over there are? Haven't you all noticed that Daddie-Paul is never around when there's fire? It's because the Vorla inside him can't stand it. Isn't that right? Well, isn't it?"

"Pain, death, misery!" yelled the old man. At his urging, the two girls pushed the wheelchair right up to the edge so that he could have a clear view of me.

"*Pain,*" began the crowd. "*Death!*"

"It doesn't have to be this way. The Vorla hates us because we rejected it. Hates us and fears us. You can reject it too . . ."

My hands were loose.

Someone was stuffing something into the back of my belt.

"You talk too fucking much," said Don-Paul, rising. He planted a hand squarely on my chest.

"*FEED HIM TO US!*" screamed the thousand voices of the Vorla from Daddie-Paul's mouth.

And then Alex lunged forward and hit the wheelchair hard.

Grabbing one armrest with both hands, he heaved it over. The girls shrieked and fell back as Daddie-Paul clawed for balance. Alex sprawled over the wheelchair, Daddie-Paul fell out of it, arms clawing and pin-wheeling . . . and over the edge of the cliff.

Suddenly, everyone was screaming.

I caught Don-Paul's wrist, saw the look of paralysed horror on his face as he realised what had happened to his father. One of the girls cried "*Daddieee-Paul!*" as the twisting figure dropped screaming from sight.

And when I sidestepped to look at who was behind me, the face of the child I saw there paralysed *me*. He had cut me free, had shoved something into my belt. And even though his face was painted with the same wild streaks as those of the other kids in this tribe, there was no mistaking him.

It was the Crying Kid.

The kid I'd found in the school ruins. The kid that Damon and Wayne had chased away by throwing rocks at him. The face that had somehow haunted me ever since this nightmare started.

He stared up at me with this stark look of hope.

I fumbled for what he'd thrust into my belt.

The shotgun discharged like a roar of thunder, and the kids were running every which way.

Then Don-Paul snapped free of my grasp—and shoved me hard.

I think I heard Juliet scream my name again, but I couldn't be sure.

Maybe it was me screaming.

Because the next instant I fell from the platform, dropping like a stone.

I saw the platform flying away from me, felt wind rushing all around me. I saw the rope coiling and twisting madly as I fell, saw the Crying Kid standing there frozen in horror; getting smaller . . . smaller . . . smaller . . .

I knew that there were a thousand-thousand deaths waiting for me.

Then the Darkness took me.

CHAPTER NINETEEN | STAND-OFF

EVERYONE REACTED IN SHOCK TO ALEX'S sudden move.

Ever since they'd been "judged" back at the town hall, it seemed that the Caffneys had beaten out of him any fight that he had left. But this sudden, violent lunge at Daddie-Paul momentarily paralysed everyone on the cliff edge, captor and captive alike. The wheelchair tipped awkwardly, Alex fell over it, and the next moment Old Man Caffney had gone over the edge. That was when his daughters started to scream and the kids followed suit in blind panic, yelling and running in all directions.

And Henry Caffney let go of Juliet's hair, forgetting that she was there. He stood rooted to the spot, like a statue. He seemed hypnotised by the slowly spinning wheel of the wheelchair as Alex clambered back to his feet. Daddie-Paul's dwindling scream was drowned in the shouts of the running crowd. Juliet lunged past him and fought her way through the milling children to get to the platform. Something was happening there. Somehow, Jay's hands were free and he was struggling with Don-Paul right on the edge.

And then Lisa lunged forward to seize Patrick Caffney's hair from behind, yanking down with all her strength. His head snapped back, his face contorted in agony. Annie seized the shotgun with both hands and tried to wrest it from his grip. But even though Lisa managed to drag him to his knees, he still fought to hold on with one hand while he clutched at his scalp with the other lest Lisa rip it from his skull. Simon Caffney burst through the crowd of kids, running to reach them. From nowhere, Candy lunged out of the crowd and tried to claw at his face. She caught his sleeve as he ran and he dragged her down in his headlong flight. She clung on tight, tearing his shirt. Yelling, Simon turned and kicked her hard. Candy's grip was broken as Simon seized her own hair, ready to smash her face to pulp with his fists.

Roaring like a bull, Alex leapt over the overturned wheel-chair. Eyes wild, fuelled by hatred, he bore down on Simon, who heard and saw him coming. He pulled free from Candy and braced himself, swatting a little girl out of his way as she ran into him, screaming.

"They killed our Daddie!" screeched Luanne, hugging her pregnant torso as if even the baby inside were screaming in distress. "They killed our *Daddieee!*" She tottered towards Henry, looking for protection. Henry still couldn't move; still couldn't take his eyes from the overturned wheelchair and its slowly spinning wheel.

Annie wrenched the shotgun free and it discharged with a shocking roar.

Luanne's face disintegrated in a bloody spray.

Now the children were running screaming from the cliff edge, back the way they'd come.

Luanne tottered forward, three more steps towards Henry. Then her body crumpled to its knees. Still hugging her torso, she sprawled forward into the mud.

Henry sagged and went down on his own knees, now no longer staring at the wheelchair; all his attention centred on his sister's body.

Alex halted in mid-charge, no more than ten feet from Simon, who was now also staring in horror at his dead sister.

Annie swung the shotgun round to cover everyone as Lisa pulled away from Patrick. He remained kneeling, hugging his head; like someone trying to keep their wig on in a heavy wind. Blood was seeping down from his scalp and between his fingers.

"Jay!"

Alex had reached Candy and was dragging her away from Simon when Juliet's agonised cry came from the cliff edge. He looked back to see that Don-Paul was running back from the platform, keeping well out of the way. There was a young boy there too, also running hard, taking a different route from Don-Paul and following the other members of the tribe as they disappeared into the ruins.

But there was no sign of Jay on the edge of the platform.

Juliet clambered desperately out, right to the edge.

"Oh Christ . . . " said Alex. "Jay's gone."

Annie kept the shotgun levelled as everyone headed for the platform.

The Caffneys seemed frozen, staring at Luanne's still body.

Throughout, the other Caffney sister had stood on the cliff edge, hands to her mouth. Now Tracey staggered towards Luanne's body. Hands still to her face, she looked from the body to the others, who retreated to the wooden platform. Suddenly, she whirled away from her family and ran towards them.

"Stop there!" snapped Annie, swinging the shotgun on her.

Tracey halted.

Fearfully, she looked over her shoulder towards her family; then back at Annie.

"Take me with you." It was the first words she'd spoken since their arrival at the Caffney's Hell on earth. Her voice was high-pitched and tremulous, a child's voice in a young woman's body. "Please don't leave me here with them. Take me with you . . . "

"Help me!" shouted Juliet. She was balanced precariously on the edge of the platform, trying in vain to pull the rope up.

"*Please!*" screeched Tracey. "Don't leave me with *them!*"

Lisa had reached the platform first. She rushed out to join Juliet. Annie kept swinging the shotgun from Tracey to the others, who were still apparently too shocked by what had happened to their father and sister to act yet.

The wooden platform juddered and cracked.

Juliet cried out and almost fell. Lisa grabbed her by the shoulder and pulled her back. There was a grinding sound from the Chasm.

"Oh *Christ!*" screamed Juliet. "It's *got* him!"

The wooden supports groaned. Soil began to crumble and patter all around the frame of the platform at the cliff edge.

"Lisa!" yelled Alex, starting out over the shivering boards. "Get her back here!"

"Jay!" yelled Juliet down into the darkness. "*Jay!*"

The rope stretched and vibrated. The platform began to bow downwards into the abyss.

"Juliet!" Lisa grabbed her hard, and began dragging her back towards the cliff edge as Alex finally reached them. He grabbed her other arm, but now Juliet was fighting back, trying to reach the edge of the platform again. "We can't do anything! It's too late!"

"It can't be too late! This can't happen! Not now, not after everything we've been through!"

A wooden support beneath the platform shattered and split. The platform tilted to the right. Lisa and Alex were already holding a rail on the left. Juliet's feet swung into empty space as they clung onto her, now dragging her back to the cliff side as boards on the platform itself began to crack and splinter loose.

"*JAY!*"

"We can't do anything!" yelled Alex. "Juliet, we can't *do* anything for Jay now!"

They fell back onto the cliff edge, stumbling together as the platform suddenly disintegrated. The rope did not snap this time. The demonic force on the other end dragged the winch from its moorings. In the process, the entire structure of the platform fell apart. The winch hurtled down into the darkness, followed by the tumbling, shattered wreckage of the platform itself. The supports that had anchored it to the cliff side followed, huge chunks of earth cascading down into the depths. Everyone recoiled from the cliff edge in case a section of it should also be dragged down into the Chasm. Alex and Lisa hung on tight to Juliet as she strained to return to the edge. She didn't seem to care whether she went over with the wreckage of the platform or not.

The roaring descent of the platform dwindled to a shuddering echo as the last of the wreckage vanished into the darkness.

A gunshot sounded behind them.

Annie recoiled instinctively, looking at the shotgun. But it hadn't gone off in her hands. Tracey was suddenly right beside her, long dark hair flying in panic as she looked back at her sister's body.

The Caffney brothers had vanished in the darkness.

Another shot split the air, ricocheting wildly.

Annie swung the shotgun around, but could see no one.

"Everyone," shouted Alex. "Run!"

And suddenly they were all racing along the cliff side, away from where the platform had been dragged down into the Chasm and back towards the rough-hewn bridge leading across the abyss to the petrol plant.

"Where are they?" yelled Candy. "Where *are* they?"

"Please!" yelled Tracey, running with them. "Don't let them kill me. Please God, don't let them *kill* me!"

Another shot, and this time a furrow of earth erupted right next to Alex's foot.

"The bridge!" yelled Alex. "It's the only way to go!" Juliet looked back at the ragged cliff edge where the platform had vanished.

"Jay . . ."

"Come on, Juliet!" yelled Lisa. "He's gone, and there's nothing we can do!"

"Oh God, Jay . . ."

"Come *on*!"

Another shot sang past their heads.

They ran.

| **THE JOURNAL OF JAY O'CONNOR: IN THE CHASM**

*T**HE DROP MIGHT JUST PULL YOUR LEGS OFF*, Patrick Caffney had said to me.

Was that what had happened?

I'd fallen into darkness, my entire body frozen rigid. I'd stopped breathing. There'd been only the wind whipping past me and the certain terrible knowledge that I was about to die. Then something had hit me hard. I was flung around, whirling and spinning. This was it. I was dead. My legs had been torn from my body and this whirling dizziness and the absolute darkness was Death.

But if I was dead, why was I hurting so much? Why couldn't I get my breath?

Something hit me again, sending me spinning once more. I could feel gravity sucking at me, could feel the blood running to my head. At last, I remembered what had happened to me. I'd been thrown into the Chasm. I panicked, thrashing and lashing out all around me in the darkness.

Another great dragging at my body, another whirling blow—this time much weaker than the others. Now I knew what was happening. I was bouncing and rebounding on the end of that fucking rope. I'd dropped as far as it stretched, hundreds of feet down, and without the brace and supports for my legs. By some miracle, maybe the angle at which I'd gone off the wooden platform, the fall hadn't torn me in two. But any second now I would surely smash into the cliff wall as the rope swung wildly in the darkness. I covered my head with my arms and waited for worse pain to come.

Another bounce, this time nowhere near as bad as the others.

I tried to yell, but nothing would come out. My lungs were hurting, and I was hyperventilating.

Something brushed my legs in the dark. I recoiled. Now I could hear soil pattering in the darkness. I bounced and spun. My legs brushed against something solid again. Was it the cliff wall?

Then I heard the noise from below.

At first it sounded like surf breaking on a beach. A low and distant rumbling sound. It began to grow louder as I spun in the darkness. Now it was a wind, blowing up from this bottomless canyon. The wind was a whisper, now it was many voices, all whispering. There was hatred in that sound. Hatred and anger. It was growing and swelling. Now it was a familiar and horrifying sound. It was the many whispering voices of the Vorla. It was surging up from the Chasm, ready to take its next human bait.

I thrashed and spun desperately, feeling it draw close.

Somewhere far below, I seemed to see something glint, like tar or oil.

The Black Stuff was rising; surging up the sides of the canyon. Hungry and eager to give me a thousand-thousand deaths.

My legs brushed against that solid something again. I lashed out, felt the cliff side, and spun away again on the rope, fists full of stones and soil. The Chasm was filling with the grumbling roar of the voices now; like some terrible express train on its way up from a hellish underground tunnel. Arching my back, I grabbed for my legs. Not far enough, and I was still too winded after the fall. I spun again, out of control.

Was the rock face vibrating beside me? How soon before the Vorla snatched me and dragged me from the rope?

I arched again. This time one hand connected with my jeans, at the knee. I hauled myself up; painful grab by painful grab, spinning and swaying in the utter blackness. My stomach was hurting, my lungs were on fire. Whatever the Crying Kid had stuck in the back of my belt was only making it more difficult for me to right myself. But my fear of what was surging up from below spurred me on. I was sobbing with effort when my hands finally reached the rope tied around my shins and I managed slowly to haul myself upright. The effort had almost exhausted me. What the hell could I do now? I was upright, hanging on the rope. But the Vorla was surely only moments away.

I don't know how or why, but suddenly I'd dragged the thing from the back of my belt, hanging onto the rope with one hand. Some kind of weapon to deal with Don-Paul up top? It didn't feel like a gun or a knife. It felt hard and rubbery, some kind of small cylinder. There were notches and buttons on it.

The Vorla roared in its million voices, just below my feet.

I could sense it opening beneath me, like some gigantic black mouth. It was surging and swelling on all sides around me, ready to swallow me whole and take me to the real Hell that it had promised. It stank of Death and Madness and Hate. When it closed over me, I'd be in the belly of this hideous thing; swallowed whole, my soul to be ripped, shredded and tortured forever.

My hand gripped the rubber cylinder hard in terror.

I felt the indentations, the circular buttons. I squeezed it hard and waited for the Horror to drag me from the rope.

And suddenly there was light.

It glared in my face, lighting up the top of my body. It reflected on the shiny, hideously rippling black mass all around me. My body spun on the rope, the light spinning with me.

531

The Crying Kid had shoved a torch into my belt.

I felt the Vorla shrinking from me as I swayed and spun.

Heart pounding, I knew what to do.

Holding the torch out, I shone the beam directly into the mass. As I slowly spun, the beam moved across its immense black, formless shape.

And it was like a laser beam cutting through cancerous cells.

The Vorla shrieked in its multitude of voices. It deafened and terrified me. As if it were a black curtain being ripped and gashed, the light beam cut through it on all sides. There was a crash like surf again as the Black Stuff splashed back from me, splattering the cliff walls. I saw black waves flowing quickly downwards over the ragged stone walls and if I could have yelled then I would have. But I still couldn't find my voice, and my lungs were still burning. I stabbed the beam downwards into the Chasm. There was a great hissing, like water on hot coals. I could sense its pain and its hatred. It simmered and boiled down there out of sight, waiting for the moment when it could surge up again and take me.

I glanced up.

How far had I fallen? Several hundred feet by the look of it. I could see the platform up there now. A tiny thing on the cliff edge. Was there something moving up there? I tried to shout; again, nothing would come.

I would have to climb the rope.

It was the only way, if I was going to get out of this alive.

I sensed movement beneath me, and on the cliff wall.

I swung the torch out.

The Vorla retreated on all sides from the beam, hissing its hatred.

Christ, if I dropped the bloody torch . . . ?

I started to climb.

I'd managed about two feet or so and had to stop. This was fucking impossible—holding the torch with one hand, trying to climb with the other. I jammed the torch into my belt, at the front, and tried again. Even before I'd made the effort, I felt the Vorla racing up the cliff wall at my side. Frantically, I pulled the torch out again and swung it around the Chasm. The Black Stuff ripped and parted, some of it dropping from the cliff wall in great splattering globules, like a rain of oil.

How long before the torch batteries ran out?

That's when I felt the strain on the rope.

I could feel it in the very fibres, could hear it stretching. I gripped the rope tight as I swayed there. I could feel a tearing, from higher up. And in that moment I knew what the Vorla had done.

Part of it had managed to race past me, up the cliff wall. Somewhere above, it had reached out its long black tentacles and fastened on the rope. It would snap it there, and drag me down.

I flashed the beam up again, heard the Vorla hiss and screech in pain; saw a black, disintegrating cloud of wetness explode away from the rope and back to the cliff wall where it fled into the crevices and cracks, hiding in the darkness.

Movement below, grumbling and shuddering.

I swung the beam down. The Darkness raced away on all sides from the beam.

Movement above, a slithering and hissing. I swung the beam up. The Vorla retreated from the rope once more and took refuge in the fissures of the cliff face.

I couldn't stay on the rope.

There was only one other thing for it. I was sick with fear at the prospect. But there was no other way.

I began to sway the rope back and forth over the Chasm, gathering momentum. As I did so, I kept the torch beam constantly playing up and down, knowing that the Vorla could come at me from any side, at any moment. I was a pendulum now, swinging faster and faster. I jerked the torch beam to the ragged cliff face. The rope was about fifteen feet from the side. Just a couple more swings and I'd be able to grab one of those

533

rock crevices. But even if I made it, even if I could get off the fucking rope and onto the cliff wall, did I really think there was a way to climb out of this hellhole?

I didn't have a choice. I just had to beat down the fear and do it.

I clawed at the cliff face, got a handful of loose stones, and swung out over the Chasm once more.

The rope strained and stretched. I could feel that the Vorla had seized it again from above. I felt something snap. But I was still swinging out; now swinging back again to the cliff wall. I didn't have much time.

The rope juddered and jerked.

I dropped several inches.

The rope was about to be torn loose.

From above, I could hear groaning sounds. Wood cracking on wood. I could hear the distant sound of splintering timbers and screeching boards. The Vorla was tugging hard at the rope now. It was going to bring the wooden platform down on top of me.

The cliff wall loomed large.

This was my last chance.

Jamming the torch down my shirtfront, I grabbed at a boulder—and found a handgrip.

The rope made a long ripping sound.

This was my one, my last chance.

I yanked hard at the wall, seizing another handgrip and hauling myself on top of the boulder that protruded from the wall. There was a rounded shelf there of perhaps two or three feet. Hardly enough to make use of. But I would have to do it.

Suddenly, the tension on the rope was gone. Up above, the Vorla had either snapped it or the wooden platform was coming down. I felt the rope falling around me, coiling and looping. Before the Black Stuff could seize the dropping loops and drag me from this precarious shelf, I tore my legs free and kicked the rope out into the void. It came away from my legs more easily than I had imagined, and I knew then just how easily my legs could have slipped from their bonds at any time and dropped me into the Chasm.

I fumbled and groped for the torch, twisting around on my haunches.

My hands were trembling so badly that the torch beam wavered all around me.

The last coils of the rope fell past, vanishing into the darkness.

And then the Chasm was filled with a great shuddering roar as the wreckage of the wooden platform and winch exploded and bounced from the cliff walls all around me. I shrank back against the wall, shielding my head. Shattered wooden spars whirled in the air, dust choked me. Rocks, stones and soil cascaded in the darkness. The smallest piece of this wreckage could dislodge me from this boulder, and then the Vorla would have me, after all.

For the first time in my life, even since the nightmare of the Chasm had begun, I prayed.

The shuddering became quieter. Now there were only small stones and soil pattering all around me. I waited for the boulder to suddenly slide out of the cliff wall, but it didn't happen. The dust swirled and was gone.

Somewhere far below, I could hear the distant echoes of the wreckage as it fell and bounced from the cliff sides. Now it was only a faint whispering.

Should I stay quiet? Could I fool the Vorla into thinking that it had cast me down into the Chasm? No, it knew I was here. It knew exactly where I was. Suddenly, I'd found my voice.

"I'm still here, you bastard."

Something hissed in the darkness below and above.

I swung the torch beam up and down, heard the Vorla retreat, hissing in pain—and was filled with a glad anger that I was able to hurt it. It might still get me . . . hell, it was odds on that it *must* get me. But I wasn't finished yet, and I wasn't going to give up without a fucking fight.

Carefully, I stood up on the boulder.

There were distant noises from above. Was it the Vorla? No. These sounded like gunshots. I remembered the others up on the cliff top, and the anger came over me again. Just when I needed it.

I examined the cliff face with the torch beam.

There were lots of ledges, jutting rocks and boulders, lots of handholds—and lots of opportunities for me to go plummeting down into the darkness.

But there was only one way to go.

Slowly, carefully, and with the anger like a slow burn inside, I began to climb.

CHAPTER TWENTY-ONE   **LAST DEFENCE**

"LET ME!" HISSED JULIET, REACHING FOR THE shotgun.

They had taken refuge behind a tangle of pipes on the other side of the bridge. Annie had rested the barrel across an iron rail, pointing back along the bridge to the other side. Her face was white after she'd thrown up. The shock of what had happened to Luanne had robbed her of strength. Even now, an hour after their flight over the bridge, the horror of what had happened was overwhelming. She looked at Juliet, saw the fury and the grief on her face.

"Are you sure . . . ?"

"I'm sure," hissed Juliet. "Let me have it!"

But as Annie moved back and allowed Juliet to slide the weapon over to where she crouched, Lisa's hand suddenly closed on the barrel.

"I know you want to kill one of them," said Lisa. "For what's happened to Jay."

Juliet tried to yank the shotgun back all the way, but Lisa held tight.

"But we've only got one shot left, Juliet. And they know it."

Juliet looked back across the bridge. There was no one to see over there. The children had vanished into the ruins, and the Caffney family—minus two—were nowhere to be seen.

"We can't afford to waste that shot, Juliet."

"All right . . ." said Juliet at last. "All right . . . I'm okay now."

Lisa remained fixed on Juliet's strained, white face. When Juliet nodded and seemed to be more in control, she let go of the barrel. Juliet slid the shotgun over, and pointed it across the Chasm to the other side.

Tracey Caffney was behind them, being carefully watched by Candy. She was sitting miserably, head in hands. She hadn't spoken since their flight across the bridge, back to the petrol plant. And there was something about her utter misery that had stopped them from sending her back. There was no denying her utter terror of her own family.

There was a noise from behind, and they whirled as Alex came back from the depths of the petrol plant with a bucket in either hand. Stooping, he brought the buckets to where they all crouched behind the tangle of pipes and valves at the foot of the petrol tank nearest to the bridge.

"I'm going to need help," he said breathlessly. "We need more containers, more buckets or whatever. I got this stuff from the same valve that they used to kill Damon . . ." He glanced at Candy, but she was looking down into her lap. She shuffled, and began to rise. "No," Alex went on. "Not you, Candy. It's best . . . best that you don't see any more of what's back there."

"I'll help," said Lisa, shuffling carefully towards him on all fours.

"Someone's moving over there," said Juliet tightly, levelling the shotgun.

Lisa glanced back apprehensively, waiting for Juliet's finger to tighten on the trigger and for their last shot to be used uselessly in anger.

They all peered back. There was movement in the ruins, but

now darkness was creeping over New Edmonville, and it was difficult to make out the shapes moving out there.

"The kids," said Alex, at last. "They're rounding up the kids from the ruins. Bringing them back to the edge."

"Why?" asked Candy, her voice breaking. "What are they going to do? What are *we* going to do?"

"I've got a bad feeling in my bones," said Alex, carefully positioning the two buckets. "We need to get as much petrol back here as we can. And we'd better pray that Henry Caffney spilt some matches back there, or we're never going to be able to light any fires."

"We don't need any," said Annie. "I've got a lighter." She swallowed hard. "Just call me Ms. Do-It-Yourself." She was trying hard to shake off the horror of what had happened, and it wasn't working. "What's your bad feeling?" she asked, wiping her mouth. She was struggling hard to reconnect with their present danger again, but her eyes were constantly returning to the small dark shape of Luanne Caffney lying faceless and in a bloody mess on the far side.

"Yeah, they're rounding the kids up all right. See over there?"

"Alex!" snapped Candy. "What's your bad feeling?"

"First," said Alex, wiping his mouth with a trembling hand, "it's getting dark. And we know that the Vorla comes out of the Chasm in the dark. So we'd better make sure that we've got some kind of fire going for protection before that happens. Second, the Caffneys know that we've only got one gun, and one shell left in it. My guess is they're not going to risk one of themselves by rushing the bridge. But if they can get those kids rounded up . . ."

"Then they'll herd them across the bridge," said Juliet tightly. "Use them as a barrier. Get us to use the shot, then just swarm over here and take us again."

"Right," said Alex. "So we're going to have to rig something with that bridge. Soak it in petrol, or something. Make sure we can fire it if we have to. That's all we can do if . . ."

A shot rang out from the far side.

Everyone ducked and the bullet ricocheted, screaming amidst the steel canisters.

"If," said Lisa, "we can get to the bloody thing from here."

"Those mad bastards might just do our work for us," said Alex, shaking his head. "Who knows what a gunshot might do if it punctures one of these canisters?"

"Alex," said Juliet, "you're full of comforting thoughts."

"We've got to do what Jay would have done," said Alex.

Juliet looked intently at him. Her voice was strained when she spoke again.

"What's that?"

Alex stared out across the Chasm as the darkness began to creep swiftly amidst the ruins.

"We've got to get angry . . . and *stay* angry."

No one spoke for a while. Tears were flowing down Juliet's cheeks when she turned back to level the shotgun across the bridge.

"Come on," said Lisa at last. "Let's go, Alex."

Alex nodded, and the next moment they vanished back into the darkness.

The others steeled themselves.

And waited.

| # THE JOURNAL OF JAY O'CONNOR: TO HELL AND BACK

BACK AT THE BEGINNING, I TOLD YOU WHAT it was like in the ruins of that school building just after the quake hit. Trapped and blinded in the absolute darkness and the fallen rubble. Scrabbling through broken masonry, burst pipes and water-filled, stinking pools. The feeling of suffocation, the confused memories of being locked in my mother's wardrobe, and the nightmares it had brought. The sounds of my terrified sobbing bouncing back at me, confirming that I was stuck in this terrible, confined place. Clawing towards the light, like a mad animal. The grumbling sounds of an approaching avalanche. Running on the spot, groping upwards, waiting for everything to cave in all around me.

I said then that something happened to me.

Something went wrong inside.

In a crazy sort of way, the terror *catapulted* me out of my mind for a moment. I was suddenly somehow up in the air, above myself and looking down. And despite the darkness, I could *see* where I was. In a rubble-filled pit, and the mad, clawing, thrashing thing that was beneath me was more like an animal than a human being. From a detached distance, I could see my mad, scrabbling fever to crawl out of that

541

hellhole. Now I wonder if that first nightmare in the ruins of the school building was *also* the nightmare of crawling up out of the Chasm. I know it doesn't make sense, but that feeling of being catapulted was like a flash-forward or a flashback. All I know is the terror was the same, and now I can't distinguish between the two. I can't remember much about the climb up out of the Chasm. Only terrible images of the torch flashing in the darkness, and of the great rippling, hissing Darkness recoiling from me on all sides. Did the fear make me go mad again down in the Chasm, the way it made me go somehow "out of my mind" in the school ruins? I don't know.

All I know is that the nightmare seemed endless, flashing backwards and forwards.

I do remember the faint light above me fading to black as the nightmare went on and on. I remember the torch beam beginning to flicker.

And as I climbed, perhaps a part of me believed that I hadn't been able to get from the rope to the cliff-side. That same part believed that I really was in the hands of the Vorla, as Daddie-Paul Caffney had promised, and that this was the thousand-thousand deaths that he had also promised.

Suddenly, there was flickering light up above. Flames, definitely. Rippling and dancing on the cliff face. I clung there, looking at the light. For a moment, still out of my mind, I felt as if I were climbing down. These had to be the flames of the Vorla's Hell, at the bottom of the Chasm. Christ, I'd been going the wrong way!

But then I could see the ragged cliff edge up above.

The Darkness hissed below me.

I stabbed the flickering torch down, heard the Vorla retreat in anger.

There couldn't be any flames in the Vorla's Hell. It hated fire.

That last twenty feet might have been the most dangerous of all. I'll never know. But I *flew* up the side of that cliff face, clawing and gouging soil all around me. If my fear had guided every careful hand and foothold with a desperate sense of self-survival, that was all forgotten in the mad scramble up that last twenty feet.

When my hand finally gripped the cliff edge, I hung there for a long time, fingers gripped in tufts of grass and clumps of soil. The torch beam flickered and wavered down into the Chasm. I could still hear the grumbling of that black sea, somewhere below.

The torch went out.

I don't remember clawing my way up onto the cliff top.

But the next moment I was lying there, face down and trying to find my breath. My body began to shudder uncontrollably. I didn't know whether this was real or imagined, didn't know whether I was alive or dead.

I could see the rough-hewn bridge that led over to the petrol plant.

Someone had started a fire over there, back in the tangled pipework and canisters. That was the reason for the flickering reflection of flames on the cliff wall as I climbed. Were there people over there? I was overwhelmed by the feeling that, whoever they were, those people were important. There were things I had to do. Urgent, important things. *Desperately* important things. But I was still in my nightmare, and I couldn't think straight, couldn't remember a thing.

A deep grumbling came from the Chasm.

I could feel the ground vibrating beneath me.

The Vorla was coming up.

My torch had gone out, and I might have reached the cliff-top but I still wasn't safe. I was still locked in this hellish nightmare place. I began to slide away from the edge, keeping down low on all fours. There was danger here up top. But I couldn't remember what that danger might be. Only that I had to stay low, had to get away from this place without being discovered.

Fifty feet or so from the edge, I looked back.

Something black and glinting rolled up from the Chasm.

A wave of oil and tar flowed and spread over the edge, surging over the grass towards me.

I lunged to my feet and ran.

Behind me, I heard the roar of the Vorla as it erupted from the pit and gushed after me.

Suddenly, there were people everywhere!

Kids who had been hiding behind tangled fencing or shattered cement blocks were suddenly leaping and running and screaming all around me. A man's voice began to yell, as if trying to calm the kids down. I collided with several of them, throwing them out of my way as I ran, and everything was bloody pandemonium. A gun went off somewhere in the darkness.

Suddenly, there was a car up ahead, slewed sideways onto a pile of rubble.

The dark shape of a man suddenly pushed away from where he had been leaning against it. At first he looked unsure as I flung myself forward over the rubble towards him. Then he began dodging from side to side, ready to grab me, trying to guess which way I might go to avoid him.

He guessed wrong.

I hit him hard, square on.

The impact threw us both over the hood of the car.

I grabbed his legs and heaved him over to the other side of the car, heard him cry in pain when he landed awkwardly on the rubble.

I didn't consider my next move. It was just pure instinct. Maybe there weren't any keys in the dash, maybe the damned thing didn't work. Maybe the car had always been there and I just hadn't seen it before. It might have crashed into this rubble when the quake first hit, the driver long gone.

But the next moment I was in the car.

The keys were there, and when I twisted them the engine roared into life.

And right in front of the windscreen, a great tidal wave of bubbling black ooze was rushing at the car.

There were no people now. No running, screaming kids. No men yelling. No figures trying to bring me down.

Just this gigantic wave of glinting black filth, ready to crash down on the car. It would scoop it up, toss it around, tear open the roof. It would fasten its dripping black tentacles on me, tear me apart, devour me body and soul. It would feast on me with insane, inhuman anger, revenged at last for having been denied once again.

I switched on the headlights.

The Vorla shrieked as the twin beams played on its massive black surface.

It splashed away on all sides, the beams cutting through its hideous bulk and into the night.

I dragged the gear stick into reverse, and the car screeched and bounced away over the rubble. The headlights stabbed through the darkness as I frantically jammed the stick into first. In the rear-view mirror I saw the black tide rising and reforming again behind me. Gushing and bubbling, and shrieking in its thousand-thousand voices.

I put my foot down and the car roared away on the main road down which we had all been brought by the Caffneys. In that moment I suddenly remembered everything.

"Juliet . . ."

The black tidal wave roared and surged in anger.

There was a shotgun on the passenger seat beside me, but it wasn't going to help me against what had come out of the Chasm.

I gunned the engine and raced on into the night.

Shrieking its rage, the Vorla came right after me.

| **THE DEVIL AND
THE DEEP BLACK SEA**

"SOMETHING'S HAPPENING OVER THERE!" hissed Juliet, and instantly everyone was alert.

They'd managed to start a fire between themselves and the bridge, using assorted flammable wreckage that Alex and Lisa had managed to find within the plant, keeping it going with the fuel from the opened valve where Damon had met his horrible end. Night had fallen, and with it came the knowledge that the Vorla could erupt at any moment from the Chasm. The flames would be a defence against the hideous Black Stuff as long as they could keep the fire going, and the flickering of the flames against the far cliff face was some small comfort. But while it illuminated the far side, it also meant that they themselves were much clearer targets for any pot shot from the Caffneys' side. And at any moment, when they'd managed to round up enough terrified kids from the ruins, they might follow through with a plan to rush the bridge.

"The Vorla?" Alex moved close to Juliet, scanning the upper part of the cliff which had been illuminated by the fire.

"No." Juliet edged around, keeping the shotgun barrel levelled. "I think I saw someone running on the edge. Can't be sure in this light, though. For a moment it looked as if someone was trying to lower themselves down or . . . There! Look, there he goes!"

A silhouette was dashing away from the cliff edge.

"Jesus!" Juliet's grip froze on the gun. The others tensed all around her in fear as a great black wave surged up from the Chasm, obliterating the running figure from sight. The reflecting light from the fire glinted on its great oily black surface. Screeching in pain from the light, unable to tolerate the glare any longer, it dissolved to right and left into the darkness, emerging again to ripple up over the cliff edge in the darker areas, away from the fire. Now they could see that children were running and screaming on the other side; silhouettes dodging and weaving, arms flailing. It was chaos, and they couldn't make out what was happening now.

There was the roar of a car engine.

"Get ready," said Lisa. "I think they're going to charge the bridge."

They'd gathered makeshift weapons from the ruined petrol plant, to supplement the one shotgun shell. Twisted pipes, jagged glass. As Tracey huddled back in the darkness, moaning and curling herself into a foetal position, they snatched up the first thing they could lay their hands on and prepared. Grimly, Juliet kept the gun levelled, waited for the surge of kids on the bridge, and prayed that somewhere in there she'd see Henry Caffney.

But the children were not swarming over the bridge.

They had vanished once more into the darkness.

And the screams of fear and terror were continuing.

A churning wave of Darkness, blacker than the night, seemed to spout from the ruins; falling from sight again in the chaotic confusion. The car engine roared again and there was a screech of tyres. Twin headlights stabbed into the sky, swept out over the petrol plant, momentarily blinding them. Then they were gone. There was another screech of tyres and

547

the car engine roared off into the night. They listened to the droning as it dwindled and faded.

Now there was only quiet.

"The Vorla's gone," said Candy. "Thank Christ, it's gone."

"No it hasn't," said Annie.

And when they looked at her white face, they instantly followed her shocked expression back into the depths of the petrol plant behind them.

Where the reflection from their fire finally muted into flickering shadows, something was moving amidst the pipes, the bent fences and the giant containers. Something that flowed and spread, glinting black, its oily tentacles creeping and dripping on the metalwork, testing the barrier between light and darkness, looking for a way in.

The Vorla had flowed up from behind, and to their right and left.

Now there was no way back in that maze of pipes to refill the buckets.

Alex looked down at his feet.

Four buckets. Three filled, one half-empty.

He looked back out across the bridge, started to say something about lasting out the night.

Then a bullet ricocheted from the pipework nearby, screaming like a wild bird of prey. They all ducked instinctively, fear stabbing.

Behind them, they could hear the thousand-thousand voices of the Vorla as it swarmed and flowed, hungry for their souls.

Candy gasped in alarm, grabbing at Alex. She pointed up at the giant container nearest to them, perhaps fifty feet away and a hundred feet tall. A black, scummy tide was dripping and flowing over the top rim down towards them. It met the flickering reflective light of the fire on the canister, hissed angrily, and retreated back up over the rim and out of sight into the darkness where the rest of the Black Stuff had surged and flowed in shadow.

Suddenly, anything Alex had to say about lasting through the night was desperately inadequate.

They crouched together in the flickering light, completely surrounded by the Vorla and with their only possible escape from this island plateau controlled by the Caffneys on the other side of the Chasm.

Tracey began to weep.

And no one had the energy or the inclination to quieten her.

| **THE JOURNAL OF JAY O'CONNOR: FIRE WITH FIRE**

I TOOK THE STREET CORNER AT SIXTY AND struggled to control the car as it slewed up onto its front and rear left-hand wheels. I'd seen the stunt performed by experts on television a lifetime ago, couldn't believe that it was happening to me now . . . and yelled out loud in panic as I wrestled with the wheel. The car wobbled and swerved up onto the pavement, clipping the corner of a building and shearing away the trim in a welter of buzz-saw sparks. I wrenched at the wheel again to prevent the car from being flipped onto its back by the impact, and it slammed back down onto its suspension, cracking the rear window. And now the wheel was spinning madly in my hands as the car swerved all over the road, the headlights flashing over ruined and looted buildings.

I couldn't lose control now.

Not with the Vorla somewhere behind, hurtling through the night after me. I could feel it rushing after the car, could feel my skin crawling, and knew how badly it wanted to get me.

Jesus . . .

A rubbish bin bounced onto the hood, disgorging crap all over the windscreen. I hit the wipers and cleared enough space through rotting vegetables and fruit to see that if I continued on down this street it'd be taking me straight to the edge of the Chasm. Pulling hard over to the right, I took the car around the corner of another burned-out building and finally got the vehicle on the straight. That's when I saw the Vorla in my rear-view mirror, exploding around the last street corner in its hunt for me. The tyres screeched. Hearing the sound, the Vorla gushed across the street in my direction. I slammed my foot down hard on the accelerator and took another corner at speed. I didn't know where the hell I was now. Could I swerve the car round, aim the headlights at the damned thing? But what then? It would vanish into the darkness, maybe surround me. The headlights might keep it at bay for a while, but in the meantime I had no doubt that the Caffney tribe would catch up with me while I was stranded there. I had to keep on and try to outdistance it, abandon the car and attempt to make it on foot.

But it can smell you, Jay. It can smell the scent of your fear. It'll just keep on following that scent.

"Fuck it!"

I screeched past the burned-out front of a grocery store—and then cried out loud again when I saw what was in the street before me.

I slammed on the brakes.

There were two . . . no, three people in the middle of the street, frozen in the headlights. I'd braked instinctively, but it was a bad mistake. These had to be members of the Caffney tribe, left behind in the ruins. I should have ploughed right through them. Too late, I wrenched the wheel hard over and the car swerved and slid, hitting the pavement hard. My hands flew from the wheel to protect my face as the car exploded through the plate-glass windows of a fashion store, bouncing and jerking to a halt with glass exploding on the roof and past the windows. The impact knocked the breath out of me.

One of the headlights had shattered, but the other still glared into the store. And I could see that the Caffneys had caught me again. There were dozens of them in the store, surrounding the car, all reflected in the headlight.

And there was a severed human arm on the hood.

No, not a real human arm. It was the arm of a shop dummy, a department-store mannequin. At last I realised that there were mannequins all around me, some of them smashed to pieces by the car as it came through the window.

Was the arm on the hood somehow smoking?

No, the smoke wasn't coming from the arm. It was coming from under the hood of the car. Something had ruptured there, and now smoke was rising in front of the cracked windscreen and I could smell petrol.

There was a blur of movement in the wing mirror and the car door was suddenly yanked open. At first I thought it was Henry Caffney, and I pulled back to kick the bastard in the face. But now I could see that I was wrong. These were other survivors: two men and a young woman, in rags and with a look of terror on their faces that I knew only too well. They were starved. Since the Caffneys had been killing everyone they'd come across over the age of sixteen or so, I guessed that these poor bastards had somehow been able to hide from them in the ruins ever since the quake. The other, younger man and the woman were clambering around to the other side of the car.

"You're one of *them*, aren't you?" snapped the older man, jabbing at me with a rusted iron railing. "One of those murdering bastards!"

"You've got . . . " I could hardly speak. "You've got . . . to get off the street!" My neck was whiplashed. "It's coming after me . . . "

"We've been hiding here for a year," said the old man angrily, jabbing with the railing again. Up close, I could see that he wasn't old at all. The dirt and the scarring just made him look that way. "Hiding in these ruins for a whole bloody year, while you and your kind have hunted the others down like animals.

Now we've got one of *you,* haven't we? Let's see how you like it, you bastard!"

"I'm not one of them." I slapped out at the iron railing. "And you've got to get off the street. *Now!*"

The woman had reached the passenger door. She looked like she might believe me. "You must have *something* to eat. It doesn't matter what. Anything. We've been hiding all this time. Please, you've got to . . ."

There was a sound from the street. A rumbling murmur. The Vorla was coming.

"Get out of the street!" I yelled. The woman recoiled from me in shock. "Hide!"

"We're *sick* of hiding!" yelled the younger man, suddenly yanking the passenger door open and clawing at me. I grabbed the shotgun lying on the passenger seat, raising it awkwardly in a one-handed grip.

"Back off!"

And then the older man lunged into the car, jabbing with the railing as the younger man tried to yank the shotgun out of my hands.

"We only want food!" screamed the woman.

I kicked out at the older man, tried to jam my elbow back into his blackened face as the younger man finally seized the shotgun barrel. Somewhere beyond, the young woman was screaming.

"You *idiots!*" I yelled.

I didn't pull the trigger deliberately, but suddenly there was a deafening roar and the windscreen blew out. The girl's screaming became hysterical, and the younger man recoiled in shock. I had to move now. Snatching the shotgun back, I jabbed the stock hard into the older man's face. He grunted and slithered away from the door as I scrambled quickly out of the car, kicking him out of the way. Banging the gun barrel down across the car roof, I pointed it directly at the younger man on the other side. He staggered away from the car, eyes wild and holding his hands up in surrender. The woman sobbed uncontrollably, both hands clasped to her face and hopping from shredded foot to shredded foot on the broken glass that shuttered the destroyed storefront. I stood aside as the older man pulled himself up against the side of the car. Clutching his bloodied face, he lurched hand over hand around the vehicle to join the others. Now the smell of petrol was making me gag. They began heading back into the street.

"Not that way!" I hissed. Christ, I was hurting badly all over. I looked around at the jumble of fashion dummies lying scattered over the store carpet. It looked like a bloodless slaughter had taken place. "There must be another way out of here," I began. "Follow me . . ."

But when I turned back they had fled back into the street, out of sight.

I started after them.

And then I heard the familiar, sickening sound.

Like the sound of a crowd mumbling; or the underground rumbling of some poisonous river. The sound that was like a million whispering voices.

Moments later, the two men and their woman companion began to scream in terror and agony. The sound made me feel ill, and I thought I might vomit. Swallowing hard, I backed carefully away from the car, trying to avoid standing on glass and giving away my presence. The sounds continued, rising in agony. But the street outside was still empty. Whatever was happening was taking place just out of sight, and I was grateful for that. I'd tried to warn the poor bastards.

Something ignited under the hood of the car with a soft *whump*. The hood jarred open an inch and smoke began to gush into the department store. Blue fire was surging and roaring in the engine. I saw drops of liquid blue dropping to the floor beneath the car, igniting a spreading lake of burning petrol.

Frantically, I looked around for a way out, and could find none.

Should I run back out onto the street and take my chances?

I heard the thousand-thousand whispering, hungry voices out there as the Vorla fed eagerly, taking its insane pleasure from the torment it was inflicting on its latest victims. The voices were still racked in agony, but somehow muted and further away—as if they had been lifted, and absorbed.

Christ, no! Not back out there!

Or should I stay here in the store, take shelter, and hope that I wouldn't be burned alive?

Flames began to leap around the car as I sprinted across the store, leaping over the jumbled dummies. I could feel the pounding of my heart in my chest and my throat when I saw the Exit door sign on the other side of the store. Still clutching the shotgun, I ran to it.

Please God, after everything that's happened. Let that door be open. Let it be OPEN!

Part of me refused to believe it when the door did swing open.

Flames from behind illuminated the small alleyway outside, my shadow leaping gigantically ahead of me. There was only the sound of surging flame behind me now, the noises of feeding and torment drowned out. I swung the door shut.

And in the same instant the car exploded with a shuddering roar. Off to my left, a store window cascaded into the darkness around me, raining fire and a shower of broken glass.

Something beyond the store began to scream.

Something that was not human.

The Vorla, reacting to the sudden fire—just as it had reacted that night in the community centre.

I ran down the alley as smoke began to drift behind me. There were double gates ahead in the gloom, but I wouldn't have to climb them. The bolts were easily withdrawn, and the next moment I was out on a side street and running as fast as I could.

The sounds of screaming faded behind me.

The whispering, obscene voices were gone.

With any luck, the fire had chased the Vorla away.

But the danger was far from over.

I had to find somewhere to rest, somewhere to orientate myself. Somewhere I could work out in my mind the implications of everything that had happened since the nightmare of Day One, and just what the hell I was going to do to help the others back there at the petrol plant.

I'd no idea how far I'd run, knew that I could only go so far in any one direction before I reached the brink of the Chasm again. When I saw the unbroken frontage of an electrical shop, and could also see that the door was open, I knew that I could run no further. The poor bastards back there had probably ended up saving my life and buying me some time. Not to mention the burning car. I staggered through the doorway, pausing only to look back to make sure that the horde of voices and the darkness were not sweeping up the street after me. There was no relief in the desolate quiet of the empty street. It could come anytime, anywhere. Without warning.

Deep inside the shop, surrounded by shelves of silent televisions, video recorders and music centres, I slumped to the floor and dropped the shotgun by my side. I sat for a long time, just getting my ragged breathing back to normal again, feeling the blood pounding in my head and my ears. Letting it all settle down.

But the deep, icy knot of anxiety would not go away.

And then I saw the dictation machines on the shelf beside me. Leaning over, I picked one up.

There were batteries inside, and a tape. When I looked more carefully, I could see other packets of batteries; other boxes of blank tapes.

Why not?

"Jay O'Connor," I said in a cracked voice. I looked at the dictation machine in my hand for a long time, weighing up. "This Is Your Life."

I pressed the Record button.

And began to speak.

And that was two days ago.

Now, here I am, on the fourth floor of this semi-demolished building, looking down on the fallen masonry and shattered brickwork that leads up to the Caffneys' rough-hewn homemade bridge across to the petrol plant. Down there in the ruins, there are about a hundred—maybe a hundred and fifty—ragged kids. They're all crouching in the ruins, hiding behind fallen walls, tangled debris or burned-out cars. And I've been watching the Caffney brothers as they drag more of the kids out of hiding. When the Vorla exploded out of the Chasm and I managed to escape in the car, the kids must have scattered in terror all over the place. And clearly the Vorla left them alone and concentrated on me. But the kids can't have run far, because it looks as if the Caffneys have managed to find most of them again. I thought that maybe what I'd yelled at them, just before I took the plunge into the Chasm, might have had some effect. Maybe made them think. But it looks as if their terror of the Vorla, and the Caffneys, is greater than anything I might have had to say.

Some of the kids are getting merciless beatings as Henry, Patrick and the others drag them back and position them. I think one of them, a boy, is dead. He's lying where Don-Paul threw him and he hasn't moved since then. No sign of the other son, Simon, so God only knows what he's up to. The death of Daddie-Paul must have shocked the whole mad family so much that it gave us an edge, allowing me to get away in the car, the others to escape across the bridge to the petrol plant. But now it looks as if they've got over that. If they were savages beforehand, then they're worse than that now. Just watching them from up here has been enough to convince me. They're perfect servants for the Vorla. Evil, brutal and utterly psychotic. No sign of Luanne's body down there, so I guess they must have moved her. Come to think of it, no sign of the other sister either.

The fire is still burning on the other side of the bridge.

About fifteen minutes ago I caught sight of Alex.

He was running back through the maze of pipes, keeping low, carrying something. No more than a silhouette, but I could tell that it was him from up here. So at least he made it. And there are others crouched down there, taking cover behind pipework and debris, but I can't see who they are. I don't want any of them to be dead, but please God let Juliet be alive.

Now I think I know what the Caffneys are up to.

The fire that Alex and the others have managed to light must be keeping the Vorla at bay—just like our first nights in the park, by the bonfire. But that wouldn't stop the Caffney tribe, so there must be a reason why they haven't just rushed over there already and tried to take everyone. One of the Rendezvous club must have got their hands on a gun. From the way Henry and his brothers are marshalling the kids in the ruins, I guess they're preparing them to make a mad dash at the bridge, try to overcome them by sheer numbers. If that's what they've planned, it can't be long now.

It's getting darker and . . . *Christ!*

The Vorla is out there, in the petrol plant itself.

I just saw something in the shadows of one of the canister drums. At first I thought it was the shadow of someone running. But when I looked closer, when I look closer now . . . yes, it's the Vorla. I recognise the rippling waves, the sickening black flood as it surges and flows in the darkness. It's come up on the other side of the crag that they're stranded on, keeping to the dark places and the shadows. They're completely surrounded by the Black Stuff. If that fire goes out, then they've had it . . .

The fire.

If the fire goes out . . . ?

That's it.

By God, that's *it*!

The lorry that ploughed into the front of this building was carrying oil drums of some kind. They're all over the road. I used some of them as cover to get into this place. Chances are there's still petrol in the lorry's tank. Maybe the contents of those drums are flammable. The whole tribe is concentrating on the petrol plant; no one's taking any notice of anything that's going on behind. And now I remember something that Trevor Blake said about the Vorla, about the "whole" knowing what even the smallest part knows. Back there in the department store, when the Vorla was chasing me and the car crashed—I bet the reason that it stopped hunting for me was that it thinks I'm dead. While it was killing the three poor bastards who stopped me, the petrol tank in the car blew up, filling the place with the thing the Vorla hates most—fire! When it retreated from that place, retreated from the flames and the light, I bet the Vorla thought I was still in the car and that I died in the flames. That's why I've been safe these past two days. It doesn't think I'm here, and isn't expecting any kind of defence or attack so far as I'm concerned.

If I can start a fire down below, behind the Caffney tribe, it's going to cause confusion that Alex and the others might be able to take advantage of, and the Vorla isn't going to like that one bit either. So all I have to do is get down there, siphon off some petrol, open some of the drums without any of the tribe hearing or seeing me and . . .

What the hell is *that*?

Someone's shouting down there.

Sounds like Henry Caffney.

Yeah, it's him all right.

He's yelling across to the petrol plant. Trying to put the fear of the Vorla into them. Maybe using one of Daddie-Paul's New Religion speeches.

Well, make it a good speech, Henry. Keep everyone's attention fixed on the petrol plant, because I'm on my way downstairs.

And I might have my own revivalist speech, to put the fear of God into *you*.

On the other hand, I might be pissing into the wind. One thing's for sure—I haven't gone through all of this, haven't found my way back here, just for nothing.

Juliet may be out there. And she's my life now.

Now I'm angry.

Been that way lots of times.

But never like this before.

I'm cold, and controlled.

And I'm coming . . .

CHAPTER TWENTY-FIVE | FLAMES OF HELL

"**Y**OU CAN'T STAY THERE FOREVER!"
The voice echoed across the Chasm from the ruins on the other side.

Juliet swung the shotgun round, trying to get a bearing.

"It's Henry," said Lisa.

Alex knelt beside them, trying to get his breath back. He'd found something back there in the petrol plant, had just managed to return before the Vorla had surged up around the canisters and the pipes again. He'd found two metal cylinders, braced by some kind of harness. They looked like something a scuba diver might use, but much too cumbersome. For most of the previous day, after the Vorla had vanished back into the Chasm on the far side, he had been scavenging in there; hunting for fuel, trying to find something to help them. Now the night was returning, and the Vorla was already flowing up into the shadows for a second assault. He'd managed to retrieve four cans and two buckets of fuel from the valve where Damon had died, before it ran dry. God knew how long that would last them. Annie moved forward to him, looking at the cylinders. Alex pointed, still unable to speak; but Annie couldn't work out what he'd found, or why he thought it would help them.

"Do you hear me?" came the voice again.

There was a scuffling movement out there somewhere, in the ruins. Juliet swung the shotgun again, but there were no moving targets.

"You can't stay there forever," shouted Henry.

Juliet could contain her rage no longer.

"You going to make us an *offer*, Henry?"

Lisa moved quickly forward to place a hand on her arm, afraid that she might fire the last shot off in anger. Fierce and determined, Juliet looked quickly down at her, shook her head and yelled back at Henry: "You mean you'll let us all *go*?" It was a taunt. They all knew that the Caffneys had no intention of letting them get out of this alive.

"Oxy . . ." breathed Alex into Annie's questioning face. "Oxy . . ." He pointed at the cylinders, then stabbed a finger furiously at the nearest petrol container, towering a hundred feet behind them. Was the Vorla already swarming up the back of that canister in the darkness, waiting for the fire to dim so that it could flood down upon them? "Oxy . . ."

"No!" shouted the invisible Henry Caffney. "We won't let you go, and you can't get away."

"So fuck *off* then!" shouted Lisa.

"But we'll kill you quick." Henry was trying to get something like real empathy into his voice, as if he were giving them a really worthwhile alternative. "We won't burn you, like Damon. We won't torture you."

"You're all heart!" Juliet swung the shotgun continually, praying that she'd get a sight of Henry's head, looking at them over a chunk of concrete or a fallen wall. "I suppose you won't rape anyone to death, either?"

"Not if you don't want us to," said Patrick Caffney from the darkness.

"You *shits* . . ." Juliet stood erect, ready to fire into the night.

"Juliet!" Lisa seized her with both arms around the thighs, throwing her weight against her body. Struggling, Juliet fell awkwardly.

At the same moment, a bullet ricocheted from the pipework where she had been standing, screaming into the darkness.

"Oops!" said a voice from the other side. The Caffney brothers began to laugh. Lisa lay on top of Juliet, preventing her from rising as she squirmed and thrashed beneath her.

"Juliet, no! Let go of the gun! Please, darling. Let go of the gun . . . "

"They . . . they killed him, Lisa. They killed Jay."

"I know, my darling. I know they did."

Both women began to weep, holding each other and letting the grief out.

Annie was suddenly over them, sliding the shotgun from Juliet's grip and taking up position to cover the bridge.

Alex was still fighting to regain his breath.

"Oxy . . . " he began.

"Oxy-acetylene," finished Annie, nodding.

Alex pointed again at the hundred-foot petrol canister behind them, then back at the two cylinders he'd retrieved from somewhere in the plant. He didn't have to say anything more.

"You thick bastards know what oxy-acetylene is?" shouted Annie.

The Caffney brothers were still laughing, but now it was forced; as if the joke were long over, but they had to keep it going to make sure that everyone on the other side knew they were being mocked.

"Oxy-acetylene!" shouted Annie. "See it?" She looked down at Alex, hissing: "Hold it up. Just for a moment, then down again. In case anyone tries to take a shot."

Breathing heavily, Alex did as he was told.

"See that?" shouted Annie.

No answer.

"See it? That's two cylinders of oxy-acetylene. Highly flammable. Now listen to this, you lunatics. Alex is putting those cylinders up against the nearest petrol canister. He's doing that . . . " Annie nodded at him, and Alex seized the cylinders, took some deep breaths and scurried to the canister. Warily, he scanned the top of the container, remembering how the Vorla had swarmed over it the previous night. " . . . he's doing that *now!*"

Annie swung the shotgun back out over the Chasm.

Nothing moved over there on the other side.

And the Caffney brothers had stopped laughing.

"Do you know what would happen if I fired this shotgun into those cylinders?"

Silence.

"Do you?"

Nothing moved, and the darkness was deepening just as it always deepened in New Edmonville. Just as if someone somewhere were operating a dimmer switch.

"Well, let me tell you," Annie continued. "The cylinders will explode. And they'll blow a great big bloody hole in the canister. And then—surprise, surprise—there'll be about ten tons of burning petrol all over the place."

Alex scurried back to where they were all huddling.

Candy put a hand on his arm.

Alex looked at her with real astonishment.

For most of the time since they had been stranded over here, she had been huddled with Tracey. Had it been because Tracey was the outsider? Did Candy feel that from the beginning she had always been the real outsider in this ramshackle group of survivors, and that this somehow made her closer to Tracey, no matter what her mad family had done? Alex looked at the hand on his arm, saw Candy's face in the darkness and felt something there that brought a fire into his heart. In the same moment, Tracey's head slumped down onto Candy's shoulder; an expression of deep weariness, fear . . . and utter trust. Something had happened between them in these last couple of days. Unspoken, but very real. And somehow Candy was different.

Alex clasped her hand fiercely, then ran to join Annie.

"You're not laughing anymore, Henry!" shouted Annie. "Come on, let's hear you all laughing! Let's hear the Vorla laughing when I pull the trigger and the thing it hates most starts gushing down into the Chasm. Let me hear you *laughing*!"

Alex looked at Annie. She was doing what Jay would have done, using the anger to conquer the fear. God, he wished that Jay were still alive; that he were here with them now.

"If you do . . ." Henry's voice was filled with rage. "If you do—then *you'll* burn!"

"It'll be worth it!" yelled Annie.

There was silence again from the other side.

The flames from their makeshift fire cast guttering shadows across the ramshackle bridge and the ruins beyond the Chasm, creating false movement over there.

And then the whispering began.

First like a wind, building gradually in strength. Now a deep and trembling shudder that they could feel in the ground beneath their feet. Now it was the sickeningly familiar sound of the thousand-thousand voices.

They looked back into the petrol plant, expecting to see the familiar black flood surging through the pipework, dripping from the canisters. But although they had no doubt that it was back there in the darkness, they could see no sign of it. The whispering became a thundering, like a tidal wave bearing down upon their isolated crag; to sweep them away in a churning frenzy of Black Death.

"The Chasm," said Juliet, and everyone faced front again. Shadow and light danced and crawled on the far cliff face. Was there movement down there, or was it just the reflection from the flames? The thundering sound was like a storm now; but there was no wind, and the air remained deathly still. "The Vorla," she went on. "It's rising . . ."

Alex seized a bucket of fuel, and broke cover from behind

the pipework to position himself behind the fire. If the Vorla was going to risk showing itself in the flames, then he'd give it something to think about when he threw the entire contents of the fuel onto the fire.

"Oh God," said Candy, cradling Tracey in her arms. "*Look . . .*"

Just below the rim of the cliff edge, on the border between darkness and the flickering reflection of their fire, a black sea had risen to fill the entire Chasm on all sides. It roiled and churned there, hating the light, feeling the painful and searing touch of the light on its surface as it rose and fell . . . rose and fell . . . They could feel its hatred radiating from the abyss. They had thwarted it so many times and, even when in the clutches of the Caffney tribe—the first of its "new society"—they had somehow managed to thwart it again. That hatred, that rage and frustration, had finally driven it to an action that would cause it hideous pain—to show itself in the light.

The Vorla surged up out of the Chasm, into the flickering light, filling the abyss to the very edge, where it churned and boiled in a black, hissing frenzy.

There was another sound now, almost drowned by the frenzy of the Vorla. It was a droning sound, rising and fading, somehow also familiar.

"You want some of this?" yelled Alex, pulling back the bucket of fuel, ready to throw it on the fire. "You *want* some of this . . . ?"

The droning sound rose in pitch, like some gigantic gnat up there in the darkness somewhere. There was no doubt now; it was the sound of an engine.

A shot rang out.

Alex spun, the bucket flying from his hands, fuel splashing down over his legs.

"Alex!" Candy scrambled to him as he fell heavily, the bucket rattling away.

Annie pointed the shotgun at the cylinders, anxiously looking down as Candy turned Alex over.

"Oh God, *Alex* . . ."

Blood was pumping from his shoulder. Candy grabbed at the site of the wound, a crimson flood drenching her hands. Alex moaned and tried to rise.

The droning came again—and there was another shot, this time impacting on the pipework nearby.

"Christ," said Juliet, scanning the darkness above them. "It's the microlight! Simon Caffney's up there somewhere with a gun."

"He can't be!" snapped Lisa, also searching the darkness. "He's flying blind . . ."

"And we're perfect targets for him right here by the fire."

Its surface boiling and blistering, the Vorla shuddered and roared—and a huge black waterspout erupted fifty feet from the ramshackle bridge. That fountain froze in midair, a suspended marble-black column fifty feet tall, while at its churning base the Vorla twisted and roiled in a boiling frenzy.

There was a human figure at the top of the fifty-foot spout, with his back to them. Arms held wide, he was being borne up by the black immensity of the Vorla—all for the benefit of the Caffney tribe, crouching until now in the ruins. Still terrified, still needing the extra stimulus to action that the Caffney brothers had so far been unable to beat into them, the members of its tribe cowered when they saw who was riding the immense black wave, and looking down upon them like a fiend from Hell.

It was Daddie-Paul Caffney.

Cast down into the Chasm, he had risen again from the dead. Borne up by the Vorla, to take command once more, and to bring this maddening stand-off to an end.

"*Blood!*" roared the dripping black figure from above. "*Pain! Death!*"

Another shot roared from the darkness above.

Candy screamed as Alex spasmed in her arms, blood spraying her face from where the bullet had punched a hole clean through his thigh. In agony, Alex's eyes rolled up, his face a contorted mask of pain.

"Do it!" yelled Juliet to Annie.

Annie glanced from the cylinders to where Alex clutched Candy tightly. In a matter of seconds they were both covered in his blood. She looked back to the oxy-acetylene. Tracey was cowering, covering her head with her hands and moaning.

Annie and Lisa's eyes met.

"*Do* it!" shouted Juliet.

"*Rise up, my children!*" howled the Vorla from Old Man Caffney's mouth. It was the voice of the thousand-thousand, Daddie-Paul now absorbed into the hideous, vast, evil bulk of the black sea. "*Rise up and take them! Show them that you're worthy! Destroy them and begin again!*"

"We can hear you, Daddie-Paul!" screamed Henry, suddenly standing up in clear sight. "We *hear* YOU!"

"Annie!" shouted Juliet. "You've *got* to!"

Annie cocked the hammer on the shotgun, pointed it at the cylinders.

And the fuel that had spilled from Alex's fallen bucket and which had trickled in a stream to the fire by the bridge suddenly ignited. A rippling wave of flame raced back across the open ground to where Alex and Candy lay.

"Christ!" snapped Lisa. "Look out . . ."

Suddenly the wave of flame was on them. Alex's trouser legs burst into flame as the fuel engulfed his lower torso. Candy began beating at the flames, and now her hands were on fire as she swatted and clawed. Lisa tore her jacket off, dived onto Alex's legs and began to smother the flames.

"*Rise up!*" screamed Daddie-Paul. "*Rise up, RISE UP!*"

And suddenly, with the Caffney brothers shrieking like wild animals and urging them on, the terrified tribe of children burst from the ruins. Clambering and sliding, yelling and screaming, one hundred and fifty children of all ages erupted from the ruins into the flickering firelight. Whooping, fire and terror reflecting in their eyes, they ran wildly at the bridge. Somewhere in the mad, headlong dash the Caffney brothers were running too; stooping, keeping low amidst the kids. In moments they would be on the bridge.

"*Annie!*" yelled Juliet.

Candy and Lisa had extinguished the flames on Alex's legs. Now they were both pulling him back into the shadows.

The first of the tribe had reached the bridge.

"Dear God," said Annie, and pulled the trigger.

The blast flung the cylinders back against the canister with a ringing clatter.

But there was no explosion.

And no fire.

Annie and Juliet stared at the cylinders.

Nothing.

"Oh Christ . . ." Juliet stood up to face the bridge, hefting a chunk of pipe.

Annie turned the shotgun around, so that she was holding it by the barrel like a club.

Somewhere above, the microlight droned as it circled the petrol plant in the darkness, ready to make another pass.

On top of the black-marble column, shimmering and blistering in the reflected light of their fire, Daddie-Paul Caffney swirled around to face the petrol plant—arms held wide like some biblical Anti-Christ. Like some obscene parody of Moses, presiding over the parting of a Black Sea, he howled in the thousand-thousand voices of the damned; exultant in the knowledge that in moments those who had denied the Vorla would be torn to pieces, or worse.

This was the way it would end, after all.

And then something exploded in the darkness on the other side.

A mushroom cloud of billowing black and orange erupted

from the ruins. Curling and blossoming, it lit up the shattered brickwork and the crumbling façade of the ruined buildings with stark light. Then another explosion. Another and another—one after the other, creating a billowing wall of fire behind the Caffney tribe. A blazing drum whooshed into the air as if it had been fired from ground level like a rocket, cascading liquid fire into the night sky which rained down on all sides.

On the petrol-plant side, the survivors staggered when the ground shivered under the impact of the next detonation. The bridge shifted in its moorings as a gigantic explosion lit up the ruins, bright as day.

Suddenly, the tribe were scattering from the cliff edge once more, running and screaming. The Caffney brothers were left standing alone, still crouched, not knowing what was happening or what to do.

Daddie-Paul, atop the Vorla, whirled back to face the ruins.

The department store behind them had begun to burn, the bottom two storeys suddenly engulfed in flame. Lakes of burning petrol were spreading and devouring the base of the building. Deep within the roaring shrouds of flame, in the middle of the street, was the faint outline of a blazing petrol truck. Its cargo of unrefined fuel had just left the plant a year ago when the quake hit; and the lorry had ploughed into the building, scattering the drums all over the street, where they had lain until this day. The drums were still detonating, one at a time.

Shrieking, arms covering his black and steaming head, Daddie-Paul began to melt atop the bubbling black column.

And Jay O'Connor walked out of the inferno, straight towards him.

"Oh my God," said Juliet. "Oh my God, Annie. *Look* . . ."

He was no more than a silhouette against the blazing inferno behind him.

But there was no mistaking the way he walked, the way he held himself.

He was holding a shotgun in one hand as he came, its barrel pointed at the ground.

Like Daddie-Paul, he had been raised from the dead; raised from the Chasm.

The Caffney brothers had cowered from the sight of their father screaming atop the black wave. Now they followed Daddie-Paul's agonised gaze to the figure who was emerging from the flames. Suddenly, there was no more screaming. The kids in the ruins were no longer running or hiding. They were frozen like the others, watching mesmerised as the figure walked calmly from the flames towards them.

"The Vorla isn't all-powerful," said Jay, his voice carrying above the raging furnace behind him. The blazing building began to crumble and disintegrate, falling in upon itself. "It's been lying to you from the very start. You saw what happened. They threw me into the Chasm—but I'm back. And I'm telling you this: the Vorla is Evil. That's what it is and what it does. We denied it, and so can you!"

"Daddie-*Paul*!" screamed Henry Caffney, on the verge of insanity. Patrick and Don-Paul flinched from him as he stared back up at the dripping black figure of his father.

With fire in front and now behind, the Vorla was in a torment of agony. Hissing and thundering, it boiled and thrashed in the Chasm. Henry watched his father's face melt and dissolve, saw his body come apart in flowing black rivulets. The column sagged and began to fall back. Now Daddie-Paul was a shapeless black lump of tar. The column vanished beneath the cliff edge, the head of the Caffney clan now completely reabsorbed into the hideous black mass.

Henry looked back into the flames.

Jay was still coming on.

Henry raised the automatic pistol that he had been using to

snap shots off at the survivors by the petrol plant, and pointed it directly at him.

Jay was still coming. As he walked, he swung the shotgun up and pointed it directly at Henry.

Sweating, his face contorted, Henry's gun hand wavered.

"Go on, then, Henry," said Jay. "Try it."

Trembling, Henry pulled the trigger.

His gun was empty.

Moaning, he dropped it to the ground. Unable to confront this dead man from the fire, crazed by the apparent second death and defeat of his father and the loss of the sister who was bearing his child, Henry whirled in the other direction. Shrieking, he directed all his insane hatred at the figures who were standing by their own pitiful fire on the other side of the bridge, flinging the empty gun at them. It dropped out of sight into the Chasm, where the Vorla had once more taken refuge, just below the flickering fire-line, seething and boiling in black torment.

Shrieking again, Henry charged across the bridge.

Patrick and Don-Paul were swept along in their elder brother's blood rage. Echoing his cries of savagery, they followed, intent on tearing the others limb from limb.

Now Jay was running after them. Unable to use the shotgun for fear of hitting the others, he hurtled across the rubble-strewn ground as Henry reached the other side of the Chasm. Patrick stumbled and fell on the bridge as Don-Paul jumped over him. Suddenly, there was a flailing jumble of confusion as the brothers reached the other side. Jay saw Henry lunging at Annie as she reared from the shadows, holding the shotgun like a club. He heard the stock of the gun connect with Henry's shoulder, heard him scream again as they both fell, clawing and thrashing. There was a flurry of blonde hair as Patrick seized one of the figures and they both went down.

"*Juliet!*" yelled Jay, and now he was sprinting over the bridge.

Below him, tentacles of stinking black ooze flopped and

writhed from the surface of the Vorla, whiplashing at his legs as he ran. But the light was too much; the tentacles hissed, steamed and fell back into the blackness as Jay leapt from the bridge.

He was *back*!

Juliet was *alive*!

With an anger that was at once fierce and vengeful but also controlled with an ice-like determination, Jay ran at Patrick Caffney. He'd pinned Juliet to the ground, dashing the steel pipe from her hands. His hands were fastened in her hair as he beat her head against the ground. Jay brought all the impetus from his leap off the bridge into a kick which caught Patrick in his midriff, snapping two ribs and hurling him away from Juliet. He rolled in agony, clutching his side as Juliet struggled to her feet. Whirling, Jay cracked the shotgun butt down against the side of Henry Caffney's head. It didn't stop him. He was strangling Annie. Lisa had him by the hair, yanking back hard. Jay positioned himself, brought the butt down squarely in his face. Grunting, blood spraying from his nostrils, Henry fell back.

In a paroxysm of fury, two dozen black tendrils snaked out of the Chasm and fastened on the bridge. Already weakened in its moorings, it shuddered as the others whirled back to look. With a grinding crash, black tendrils already dissolving and steaming in the light, the bridge was wrenched from the cliff edge on both sides. It disintegrated as it fell into the darkness. Now they were trapped on this crag.

Don-Paul Caffney flew through the air, taking Jay by the shoulders.

The shotgun flew from his hands as he went down under Don-Paul's weight. They rolled on the ground, gouging and clawing. Juliet stumbled to her feet, ran to help, and the next moment Henry Caffney had seized her leg and dragged her down.

Somewhere, Tracey Caffney was screaming.

And another shot from the microlight kicked up a showering clod of earth as Patrick joined the fight once more, seizing Lisa by the throat. Suddenly, the remaining buckets of fuel that Alex had retrieved from the plant were clattering over in the struggle, dark-glinting pools of fuel were flowing towards the fire, and everyone was covered in the stuff.

Candy had dragged Alex away from the fighting. His legs were smoking. Now she began to shake him with fuel-blistered hands, trying to wake him.

The microlight buzzed overhead, momentarily visible in the flames.

Another shot screaming in the night.

Alex could not be woken.

"Oh, Alex . . . oh God, Alex. Please don't be dead."

When she touched his face, he was cold.

Henry Caffney screamed as he pulled Juliet on top of him. Quickly she found his eyes, was digging her thumbs into the sockets, her blonde hair shrouding his face as he fought to throw her off. Patrick was groaning and clutching his face where Lisa had kicked him as she managed to pull away from his grasp. Jay and Don-Paul were still rolling in the fuel, trying to reach the fallen shotgun.

Candy stroked Alex's hair gently, as if she had all the time in the world. Somewhere in the darkness, the microlight buzzed and whined as it completed another turn. Simon Caffney was ready to make another pass.

The spilled fuel reached the fire.

Several trails were ignited at once, all flaring and racing to where the figures struggled in the shadows. Lisa saw what was happening, kicked herself free of Patrick once more when he lunged at her, and seized Juliet round the middle, dragging her from Henry Caffney. But it was as if Juliet had the blood rage too; she did not want to be separated from this madman. She wanted to blind him; wanted to punish him for the terror and the misery that he had inflicted. Then

Jay found his feet under Don-Paul and kicked out hard. The impact flung him to his feet. Arms pin-wheeling, he tottered away from him.

Just as two of the converging fuel trails reached his feet.

Time back-flipped again for Jay. Because now he was surely back at the beginning of the nightmare, still in the meat mart with the living dead, watching as they were transformed into staggering human torches.

Instantly, his body covered in the fuel, Don-Paul Caffney became a blundering mass of flames. He shrieked only once before the fire invaded his throat and burned out his vocal cords. His arms flailed and beat at his body as a lake of fire erupted all around him.

Lisa pulled Juliet free and they staggered away as Henry got to his feet.

Jay followed them, dodging quickly aside as Don-Paul blundered blindly in his direction, arms held wide. Pools of fuel erupted around him with every step. Suddenly, fire was surging and leaping all around them. Jay leaped over a burning stream—and there was Juliet at last.

They clung together as if they never wanted to let go again.

They had felt it first out on that dislodged radio station mast. Two strangers in terrible danger, clinging together with an intimacy that defied any rational explanation. The reality of that intimacy constantly tested by the hideous dangers in which they had been placed; pushed to the limit by their separation and the near certainty that they had been separated forever by death. But both were alive, and together again, and in worse danger than ever before. In that brief moment, clinging together, they felt that first surge of wild love again and knew instinctively that they couldn't get out of *this* situation alive. But they were together again. And if they had to die, then at least it would be together.

They turned to watch in horror as Don-Paul Caffney blundered straight into the petrol canister. He pounded and thrashed at the base of the container, as if his blazing arms could somehow beat a hole in the steel and extinguish his agony. But now he was falling to his knees; his body crumpling, sagging and finally sprawling . . . over the oxy-acetylene cylinders. Suddenly, as the fire ravaged and consumed his body, something began to hiss beneath him as he twitched feebly. Already peppered and punctured by Annie's shotgun blast, the cylinders were slow-leaking. At any moment now, they would ignite.

Henry and Patrick were immobilised once more, staring at the blazing mass that had once been Don-Paul. Lakes of fire were burning all around them. Jay looked for the shotgun, saw it lying in a burning pool and knew that it was no good to them now.

"Where's Alex . . . ?" He looked around for him, and saw Candy cradling his smoking shape as they both huddled in the darkness. They hurried over to them, Lisa dragging Tracey, who could only stare back at her immobilised brothers in shock and awe.

And they knew that Alex was dead before they reached him.

Candy looked up at them, her face streaked with tears and smoke.

"We've got to get away from here, Jay!" gasped Annie. "Those cylinders . . ."

No sooner had the words passed her lips than there was a shattering roar. Light flared bright as the cylinders finally exploded. Flames spewed high, gobbling up the side of the petrol canister; a jagged shrapnel of metal hissed and clattered around them.

"Run!" yelled Jay.

"But where?" gasped Lisa. "The bridge has gone."

"Then we'll just have to . . ." But Jay got no further as a horrifying sound began to issue from the burning canister. There was a noise of rending metal and of great pressurised forces about to erupt. The canister must split at any moment, releasing its entire contents. "Come on!" Jay leaned down and grabbed Candy.

"I can't leave him here! I *can't!*"

"Candy," implored Annie. "We've got to move . . ."

"Come on!" Juliet leaned down and seized one of Alex's arms. Jay grabbed the other, a feeling of profound sorrow engulfing him. At first he'd despised the man; had later come to respect and admire his guts and his determination. But he'd arrived too late to help him. Between them, Jay and Juliet hoisted Alex's lifeless body, an arm over each of their shoulders, and began to drag him away from the canister and deeper into the plant. Something ruptured on the other side of the canister with a ripping crack.

Shadows leaped in the pipework and on steel containers ahead of them.

Might a part of the Vorla still be in there, swarming and dripping on the pipes, hiding in the darkness? Waiting to drop down on them from its hiding place in a horrifying and smothering embrace?

There was no time to think about it. They had to get away.

Henry and Patrick Caffney were gone somewhere behind them, apparently engulfed in the flames that leapt from the cylinders and the rupturing canister as they ran on through the maze of pipes and containers. But where the hell could they run *to?* They were stranded on this crag, with no way off.

The ground beneath their feet had lost its solidity.

Suddenly, they were all pitching forward, reeling against the steel pipes and sprawling to the ground as a wave of heat hit their backs. Jay and Juliet struggled to prevent Alex from falling as, with a thundering roar, the canister finally exploded behind them. They whirled to look back, and through a maze of steel saw the hundred-foot canister erupt into a gigantic fireball as tons of burning fuel spewed out . . . and down, out of sight, into the Chasm.

On the night of the community centre fire and explosion,

they had heard a similar screaming. They had heard it when they'd thrown blazing torches into the Black Stuff as they'd stood by the protection of the bonfire. And they had heard it tonight when Jay had somehow managed to create the raging inferno in the ruins.

But nothing could have prepared them for the hideous shrieking agony of the Vorla as tons of burning fuel spewed from the shattered canister and over the cliff edge down on to the black sea. They listened and watched in shock and awe as a towering riot of exploding flame obliterated every detail of where they had struggled only moments before. Something like a gigantic black cloud was rearing behind the inferno, but this wasn't smoke. It was a rearing mass of the Vorla itself, gushing skywards from the Chasm in a futile bid to free itself from the ocean of liquid fire that was pouring down into it. The black cloud disintegrated when it reached the peak of its desperate bid for freedom; its spiralling mass now igniting as the fuel that soaked it finally erupted like some immense firework display, filling the sky with a flaming web of liquid fire. As they watched, the screaming mass of fire was falling back into the Chasm as the canister continued to empty its contents.

The canister next to it also exploded, then another . . . and another.

A sea of fire surged in their direction.

"Run!" yelled Jay, and knew again that there was nowhere to go.

The Vorla might not get them, the black sea might not claim them. But this fiery red sea must either engulf them or force them off the other edge of this crag.

Blindly and instinctively, they ran.

The way ahead was brightly lit by the volcano behind. From all around came the shuddering roar of giant canisters as they began to rupture and split in a hellish chain reaction.

Something droned in the sky ahead of them.

Something that flew erratically, looping and swooping.

Something that was burning, its wings engulfed in a fire cloud from an exploding canister as it hunted for prey below.

"Good!" shouted Candy as they ran, her voice breaking. "*Good!*"

If Simon Caffney was screaming as he tried to control his blazing microlight, the sound was lost in the thunderous roar of the inferno. Suddenly, the entire aircraft was engulfed in flame as the petrol tank exploded, that sound also dwarfed by the eruptions all around them.

The microlight plummeted down behind the silhouetted roof of a ruined administration building, perched right on the far cliff edge. For a moment it was gone from sight. But then it was swooping up again into plain view, trailing a blazing arc of fire as it ascended vertically. Was it, like the Vorla, reaching for the sky in a vain attempt to avoid the flames of its Hell on earth?

It paused, silhouetted for a breath-taking moment against the utter nothingness of New Edmonville's sky. And then it curved and fell, heading straight back to the petrol plant in a shapeless, blazing fireball.

For a moment they hesitated. Aware of the blazing tidal wave that roared behind them, engulfing everything in its path. Now aware of the burning microlight as it headed their way.

Did it make a difference now, how they were going to die?

The fireball swooped down out of sight.

Its impact on the fractured fuel container next to the administration block was instantaneous. The canister exploded like a miniature atom bomb, triggering the containers on either side. The darkness beyond the far edge of the crag was obliterated. Until now, there had been no sun in New Edmonville. Now everything was lit up with the power of a dozen suns as the canisters exploded, disgorging their flaming contents on all sides. Another tidal wave of liquid fire engulfed the elaborate network of pipes and fences ahead as it surged in their direction. In moments the sea of fire on all sides would engulf them.

They staggered to a halt, looking all around at the blazing inferno of which they were the centre.

Death was seconds away.

Jay and Juliet lowered Alex to the ground. Candy said: "Thank you," and cradled his lifeless body in her arms again as she knelt on the tarmac. Such a civilised thank you, as if someone had passed the sugar, or moved a coat so that someone could take up a vacant seat. And because of that, so heart-rending.

Annie and Lisa embraced, Lisa still holding onto Tracey's hand—as if she were one of the other children she had lost, her own two sons and Robin. Tracey weaved from side to side as she clung to her hand, an eighteen-year-old woman acting like a four-year-old who needed the toilet. Her eyes remained fixed on the ground. Had a lifetime in the Caffney household, her new life in the Vorla's New World and the violence and terror of the past two days finally turned her mind?

Jay and Juliet turned from the sight of the burning tidal wave, holding each other close as it engulfed the place where Damon had met his terrible end. They waited for their own end to come.

"Surprise," said a familiar, hated voice.

Henry Caffney limped from around a tangle of pipes, and brought the shotgun to bear on them.

One side of his face had been burned raw; his jacket was still smouldering. His one remaining eye gleamed with insanity. The shotgun itself looked as if it had been dipped in acid, smoke curling from around the barrel and the stock. Henry had plucked it from the burning pool and, despite the damage, it still looked in dangerous working order. Patrick Caffney was behind him, clutching his broken ribs as he stepped out into full view. Unlike his brother, he was fully aware of the flood of burning fuel bearing down upon them. Somehow they had escaped the wall of flame behind.

"I've reloaded," said Henry, grinning. "Two shells in here now. Not one. Got lots more in my pocket."

"It's over, Henry," said Jay. "Leave it."

The ground shuddered beneath them as another canister exploded somewhere on the disintegrating crag.

"I don't think so," said Henry simply, and pulled the trigger.

The sound of the detonation was drowned in the roar of another exploding canister.

Annie and Lisa fell to the ground.

"*No!*" Juliet instinctively pulled away, wanting to run to them. Jay held her close again when Henry swung the smoking barrel in their direction.

"You're mine," grinned Henry. "Nothing's going to take you away from me."

Jay saw the tidal wave of fuel all around, about to engulf them. Maybe this was a better way. He pulled Juliet close.

Henry grinned again, and cocked the hammer on the shotgun.

And then Patrick blundered into him, staggering forward with his eyes bulging. He was clutching his throat. There was a blurring flash of undefined movement, and now Patrick was spinning on his heels. He staggered again, tried to right himself . . . and fell to his knees.

"Patrick . . . ?" Henry still had the shotgun on Jay and Juliet, but was moving quickly forward to see what was wrong. Patrick turned to look up at him, eyes still bulging. Blood suddenly began to seep through his fingers where he was clutching his throat. He tried to speak, but blood flowed out of his mouth in a gargling cough, flowing down over his chin.

Something flurried in the air, whipping Patrick's coat. As if someone had given him a quick blast with a high-pressure air hose. His hair flew as his head snapped back. Now everyone could see what had happened. Patrick's throat had been torn out. Still gargling, he fell backwards and lay still.

Henry whirled, swinging the shotgun.

There was a clattering from the tangle of pipes from where Henry and his brother had emerged.

A naked two-year-old boy with curled blond hair was hanging from one of the pipes. His eyes were gleaming in the light of the inferno, his beautiful face fixed in a ferocious snarl. There was a spot of blood on his chin. As Henry gawped, bringing the shotgun up to bear on the bizarre figure, the child wiped the blood from his chin with the back of one hand—and was suddenly gone in a blur of motion.

Henry whirled again.

"What are you doing?" he screamed at Jay. "What are you *doing?*"

Jay couldn't believe what he was seeing. "The Cherubim," he said in awe.

From somewhere behind, Candy said: "Oh *Jesus* . . ."

And then something blurred through the air, hitting Henry in the small of his back.

He fell to his knees, still gripping the shotgun tight. Jay and Juliet dropped to their knees, Juliet scrambling away to where Annie and Lisa were rolling in pain on the ground. The shotgun blast had hit them in the legs, peppering their calves.

Another flash, the sound of ripping cloth, and suddenly Henry was blundering to his feet. A naked three-year-old girl, same blonde hair, same ferocious blue eyes, was fastened on his shoulders. Henry spun and shrieked as the girl worried at his neck, sharp teeth champing through his collar and into the flesh. He tore her free, tried to get a grip. But the girl kicked off from his shoulders and vanished.

Something flashed by his face. Henry screamed, and suddenly there was a bleeding gash across his forehead.

Another flash, and blood was pouring from his cheek.

"Kill him!" shouted Candy. "*Kill HIM!*"

582

The shotgun discharged into the air and fell at Henry's feet.

Suddenly, there were small naked children all over him, the weight of their frenzied, clawing mass making him drop to his knees once more. Cloth and flesh ripped and tore. Henry continued to scream hoarsely.

And now everything was dissolving into a brilliant white light.

Jay held up a hand to his eyes, scrambling after Juliet. The burning fuel was here. Another second and the tidal wave would fall on them. He had to spend that last moment with Juliet, no matter what. But now he couldn't see anything in the blinding light. He had lost her.

"No . . ." said Jay, in final desperation.

"Yes," said Gordon, stepping out of the light and holding his hand down.

Jay stared up at him, unbelieving.

"Come on, Jay," said Gordon. "Take my hand and follow me into the light."

"Am I dead?" breathed Jay.

"No," said Gordon. "But you will be if you and the others don't come with me now."

"I don't . . ."

"Come *on*, Jay!"

Jay took Gordon's hand. It felt cool and strong.

Gordon yanked him to his feet.

"Juliet!" hissed Gordon. "Quickly! This way. Annie, Lisa . . ."

Jay was standing in the bright light, but now he could see Candy and Alex only feet away.

"Bring them!" hissed Gordon. "*Now*, Jay! *NOW!*"

Jay lunged down and dragged Candy to her feet, pushing her into Gordon's arms. Lunging again, he seized Alex's life-less arm and dragged him. Was this really happening? Juliet was suddenly beside him, helping with Alex's body; Annie and Lisa leaning against each other, Tracey Caffney's eyes wide with fear.

Now there was nothing but the light—and the flash of small, invisible bodies as they returned from exacting Gordon's vengeance on Henry Caffney.

"Follow me," said Gordon.

They followed him into the light.

And then the light was gone.

The tidal wave of fuel crashed down on the lifeless bodies of Henry and Patrick Caffney, finally engulfing the petrol plant and the crag. The last four canisters exploded, fracturing the rock on which the plant had stood. Like a volcano, the crag blew apart, thousands of tons of burning fuel cascading into the Chasm.

From the Vorla there was no sound.

| **THE VORTEX**

"**W**E'RE DEAD, AREN'T WE?" SAID LISA.
She couldn't see Annie, but she could feel her as they clung tightly together. The pain in her legs was appalling.

"It's not supposed to hurt when you're dead," said Annie, hobbling to get a better position. She could feel the blood pooling in her shoes. She too was blinded by the glare and couldn't see the others.

Candy cried out somewhere in the light, and there was a sliding noise, as if something were being dragged away.

Still hanging onto Juliet, Jay reached out in the glare towards her. She cried out when he touched her shoulder. Quickly, she grabbed his hand and he pulled her close.

"Are you all right?" he asked.

"Alex," breathed Candy in fear. "Someone's taken Alex . . . "

"I can't hear it anymore," said Juliet. "The fire and the explosions. It's all gone."

"Was that Gordon?" asked Annie. "Was that really *Gordon?*"

"It was him all right," said Jay. "Are you there? Gordon, where are you?"

There was no answer.

"If he's alive," said Lisa, "then that means that Robin must still be . . . "

"They're all dead," said Tracey Caffney in a dulled voice. "Daddie-Paul and the others. And I'm glad. I'm *glad*!"

Lisa felt down in the glare. Tracey started at the touch. She was kneeling at their feet.

"Is this Heaven?" asked Tracey. "Tell me it's Heaven and not the other place. I don't want to go to the other place, in case they're all there waiting for me."

The glare began to dim.

Breathlessly, they watched as their own shapes became more defined. The brilliant light was fading quickly now. The air was cool and still. No one could speak as they waited in hushed expectancy. There was something about this light, something that didn't make sense. It was *rising* from them, like a great luminous cloud. Now it was roiling in the air above them, undulating and swirling as it rose higher and higher.

They could see themselves now, looked in wonder at their faces and hands which looked somehow translucent in the light. The translucence was fading as their flesh became more solid. They could see that they were standing on what seemed to be a white marble floor.

At last they could see where they had been brought.

They were in a vast cave of some kind.

The light had reached the "ceiling" and was swirling around stalactites. On either side of them, they could see rough-hewn walls of fissured clay, funnelled and striated stone dripping with moisture. No, this wasn't a cave—*couldn't* be a cave. It was more like some kind of cathedral, with stalactites descending from above and stalagmites rising to meet them on all sides to form huge Gothic arches. About fifty feet from where they stood were ranks and ranks of what seemed to be stone pews, divided by an aisle leading down to a distant stone altar. And did the pews have curiously flattened glass cases where each individual seat should be, glowing with the same iridescence that was flowing and rippling on the vast roof, amidst the stalactites? There were hundreds—no, *thousands*—of them.

"Lisa?" said a familiar voice.

Robin was suddenly standing beside her, smiling up.

For a moment, Lisa couldn't speak.

Slowly, carefully, she reached a trembling hand down to touch his face.

He took it, smiling, and pressed it to his cheek.

"Don't worry," he smiled. "You're not dead."

"Oh, *Robin*!" Lisa seized the boy up in an embrace, uncaring of the burning pain in her legs. "Oh, my darling, I thought I'd lost you forever."

"Candy?"

Candy flinched from the voice behind her, turned and refused to believe. This was a cruel trick. She had seen Alex shot twice by Simon Caffney from the microlight. She had seen the wounds, seen the blood; still had his blood all over her clothes. And as she looked at the vision of Alex standing there, she could see the blood on his own clothes, could see the hole in his shirt where the bullet had torn into him. But there was no wound behind the ripped fabric. And although his trouser legs were burned and gashed, she could see unblemished flesh beneath. There was no sign of the terrible gunshot wound in his thigh. Candy shook her head, tears flooding.

"I can't believe it . . . I won't believe it . . . "

Alex stepped forward and took her in his arms as the others watched in equal astonishment.

"I don't know what happened, Candy." Alex's voice was trembling with emotion. "I remember the pain, and the fire. And your face. I wanted to stop you crying, but I couldn't speak. There was fire all around us, but I was so cold. Then there was nothing . . . absolutely nothing . . . "

There could be no denying that this was Alex, somehow miraculously returned from the dead, alive and whole. Candy crushed him close, willing the dream not to fade, praying that she was not imagining all of this.

"They healed him," said another voice.

Gordon was suddenly standing at their side, with his familiar lopsided grin and the guitar slung over his shoulder.

No one could speak.

"It's to do with the light up there," said Gordon, pointing at the ceiling. "And back there, in the nursery." He moved to one side and indicated the rows of pews with a wave of his hand.

Jay moved forward carefully, as if Gordon might suddenly vanish again.

Gordon laughed at his unease.

And then Jay seized him by the arms and shook him, both of them laughing, the laughter echoing and dancing in the "cathedral".

"You're not . . ." began Jay, studying his face. "You're not . . ."

"Stuttering?" asked Gordon. "No, I'm not."

"They touched him," said Robin breathlessly. "On the lips. And they healed him, just like they healed Alex. They're . . . they're really *cool*, Lisa. And this is a wonderful, fantastic place. You should see what I've seen . . ."

"I don't understand," said Jay. "How the hell you got us out of there. What the . . . what the hell the Cherubim are."

"Robin's right," said Gordon. "This is a wonderful place. A place *between* places. We've learned so much and there's so much I could tell you, but we've got very little time." He was anxious now, pulling Jay by the sleeve towards the aisle. "Come on, everyone. Follow me. Quickly."

"The Cherubim *are* real," said Candy. "Then that means that Ricky must still be . . ."

Gordon paused, anxiously wanting to usher them on. But he could see that Alex and Candy's forlorn hope needed an answer.

"All right, listen! There's so much more to it all . . . but I'll try to explain. The children here, the ones you've seen, the ones in those nursery cots. They're dead. All dead."

"Dead?" said Alex. "But we've seen them, we've . . ."

"They're not dead *here*, Alex. But they died in the world we came from. Back home. All the children who've died, who've never had a chance for life . . . they're *here* in this nursery. It's like a 'way station' between worlds. They come here, and they're nurtured. Then, when they get to about three or four years old—by our own world's standards— they move on. To another place, for the next stage of their development."

"But Ricky . . . ?"

"He died, Candy. It was a tragic accident, I know. But he came here, to this in-between place, just like they all do. They leave their bodies behind, but they also have bodies here. Bodies that need to be nurtured and developed. They instinctively know what they have to do for each other. And when they're ready, they leave. Just like Ricky. He was here, he was nurtured, he changed into what he had to become . . . and then he went on. I don't know what the odds are against your ever having seen him here. Maybe something *wanted* you to see him. To make you realise that there's something more than death, that it all goes on . . . Now, come on! We've got to hurry before it's too late."

"But the Vorla told us that this is a No-Place," said Jay as they were led down the aisle, past row after row of glowing glass cases. "The place where mankind's evil is dumped. How the hell does that fit in with . . . with . . . *this*?"

"There's much, *much* more to what Lisa calls the Realm of the Chasm than we ever knew, Jay. Things I've only begun to learn . . . things I don't have time to tell you. But this place is like . . . like . . . an *overlapping* place. There are lots of different realities, all overlapping on each other. Sometimes they connect and there's a pathway between them and . . . No, there's no time! Look, the Cherubim are able to come and go as they please in that No-Place while they're biding their time before moving on. They can slide in and out through . . . through portals I suppose you could call them. That's how they come and go so quickly. That's how we were able to get you away from the petrol plant."

"He asked them," said Robin enthusiastically. "And they did it for him. Rescued you all, I mean."

Something was happening at the bottom of the aisle, down by the stone altar. The same kind of light that shone from the ceiling and the glass cases seemed to be enveloping it. It was glowing brighter and brighter as they moved on.

"Is this a cave or a cathedral or what?" asked Juliet.

"I told you," said Gordon, anxiously hurrying them on. "It's a way station."

"But who made it all, Gordon? Who's *behind* it all?"

"No time," replied Gordon. "We've got to hurry."

"Where are you taking us?" Annie caught sight of something in one of the cases as they hurried; something tiny that surely couldn't be an unborn baby.

"Home," said Gordon.

"*Home?*" Jay halted and stared at him.

Gordon grabbed him and dragged him on again. "The quake wasn't a normal earthquake at all. You know that. It ripped a hole in the fabric of reality, ripped Edmonville right out of the real world and transported it here. To this different reality, where all the rules are different. And I've just told you about overlapping realities. The way the Cherubim can move around. Well, they're using the power that's here to cause another rip in realities."

Up ahead, the stone altar had vanished in the glaring light.

Now there was a spinning whirlpool of iridescence, swirling and filling the cathedral-cave with the sounds of a great waterfall. A wind had suddenly whipped up, tugging at their clothes. The whirlpool was growing brighter, the wind stronger.

"We're going *back?*" asked Juliet in wonder.

"Through a portal between realities." Gordon had to raise his voice now to be heard. "Thanks to the Cherubim. We're not supposed to be here, so we're being sent back."

The whirlpool was an awesome sight now. A gigantic spinning vortex that seemed to suck greedily at them. Instinctively, they held back, fifty feet from the immense churning mass of light, their hair whipping in the wind. Gordon sensed their fear.

"Don't hold back!" he shouted above the wind. "There's not much time before the vortex closes up and the portal vanishes. I don't know if the Cherubim will ever be able to open it again. You've only got seconds, so you've got to move. *Now!*"

"But Ricky . . ." Candy looked back for some sign that these strange and surreal children were hiding in the pews, watching them.

"He's gone *on!*" Gordon shouted. "Now, you've got to go *back*! Before it's too late."

Alex looked hard at Jay.

Jay nodded.

And then Alex strode forward towards the whirlpool, taking Candy with him. Jay watched them enter the light, saw their bloodstained clothes riffling around them, their hair flying in the wind. Alex paused only once, to look back at Jay. And then the light engulfed them.

They were gone.

"Don't be afraid," said Robin, smiling up at Lisa and Annie. "It's going to be okay."

Fiercely determined, bonded by their love, the two women and the boy walked straight across the last fifty feet and into the whirling vortex. Tracey held back, looking at the others, then back into the light. Suddenly deciding, she ran after them—and was gone.

"I'm not sure what to believe," said Jay. "Not sure I understand."

"Don't try," said Gordon. "There's so much *more* going on here that I don't have time to tell you."

"You're different," said Juliet. "Not just the stammering, Gordon. But something's happened to you, hasn't it? Something while you've been here."

"I've learned an awful lot," smiled Gordon. "About an awful lot of things. Now go on, quickly. Before the vortex fades."

Hand in hand, Jay and Juliet walked the last fifty feet.

As the swirling light surrounded them, they looked into each other's eyes.

"Do you believe it?" asked Jay.

"I believe in you," she replied simply.

Jay looked back into the cave-cathedral.

Gordon was still standing back there, not following.

"Come on, Gordon," said Jay. "Let's go."

Gordon didn't reply. He only stood smiling, and watching.

"Gordon," said Juliet. "Quickly, come on."

"I'm not coming," he said.

"What?"

"Like I said, I'm staying here."

"What on earth do you mean?" asked Jay. The wind was sucking at them greedily, pulling them further into the light. The details of the cave-cathedral were fading in the glare.

"There's nothing for me back there, Jay. I've got no one. All I ever had was . . . well, all I ever had *was* my music. No family, no friends, just the music. Just the four walls of a bedroom, and loneliness."

"Don't be stupid, Gordon!" Jay tried to pull forward, but could take only a single step. The vortex had its hold on them both now, and they could not go back. "*We're* there for you now. All of us. Me, Juliet, the others."

"You don't need a sidekick now. You've got to go back and start a new life with Juliet."

"Sidekick, fuck! If you hadn't been there, we'd never have made it. Christ, Gordon. We've been through so much. Don't you know we've all been through Hell and beaten it? We've got to all go back *together!*"

"Go back, Jay. You don't need me. They do."

"You're not making sense. You've *got* to come back with us!"

"They need me here, Jay. The Cherubim. The Chasm's

been damaged by the quake and by our presence. They need a 'grown-up' to help them through to the other side, whatever or wherever that's supposed to be. I didn't tell you that part, but over here I'm *needed*. And I can make a difference."

"We're not leaving you!" shouted Juliet, straining forward with Jay against the wind. "We're not leaving you here!"

Gordon's figure was growing dim, his outline vanishing in the engulfing light.

"I'll miss you both, but I'm glad you found each other."

"Gordon!" yelled Jay. "No!"

"Go back home and make a difference, Jay. Keep what you've found, Juliet. Make it special . . . "

"*Gordon!*"

"Special . . . make it special . . . special . . . "

Gordon vanished in the swirling light.

Clinging together, Jay and Juliet were sucked deep into the spinning mass of the vortex.

Now there was only light, and the roaring of a great wind.

| **GOING HOME**

"**M**Y GOD," SAID ALEX, AS HE STEPPED FOR-ward. "Look at the *sky*."

Candy followed his gaze as they emerged from the light. Annie, Lisa and Robin were ahead of them, standing on grass and also staring upwards.

There were clouds there, something that no one had seen for over a year. The sun was shining. A flock of birds was wheeling overhead.

"Birds," said Lisa. "I never thought I'd ever see them again."

"They're beautiful," said Robin.

Jay and Juliet stepped out of the light behind them.

Before them was a row of terraced houses. Even now, doors were opening and curtains were twitching. Two children on bicycles had stopped on the nearby road, mouths open and gawping at the strange whirling light that had suddenly appeared on the green in front of the terrace; sitting there in their saddles and staring at the strange figures that had suddenly stepped from nowhere out of the light. Passers-by on the other side of the street had also stopped, keeping their distance. In the nearby houses, several 999 calls had been made; not one of them making much sense about what they had seen or what they thought was happening. Did they need the police or the fire brigade? They didn't know. A car pulled up and stopped, the driver climbing out and hanging on his door to watch as the spiralling vortex began to shrink.

"We're back," said Juliet. "Gordon was right. We made it back."

The wind ruffled their clothes; they could still feel the suction on their bodies from the vortex, as if it wanted to pull them back into its whirling centre. But as it began to shrink, the wind and the suction were diminishing as the portal between realities closed.

"Where's Gordon?" asked Alex, looking into the spiral, waiting for him to step out and join them in the real world.

Jay just shook his head, and Alex knew that he shouldn't pursue it further. There would be time for questions and answers later. Now there was only time to look around at the sky, feel the sun on their faces, the breeze on their skins, and see houses that weren't demolished or semi-demolished. They watched the terraced doors open, smiled at the looks of astonishment and bemusement, just felt good that they were in the company of other human beings again. They were back in the Real World, and the nightmare was a long way away in a different reality.

"My legs," said Annie, suddenly looking down.

Lisa followed her stare, realised that she no longer felt any pain.

Their legs were healed, the ripped flesh no longer peppered by gunshot.

"You see?" said Robin. "They made that better, too. Really cool."

"It's all over," said Jay. "We made it."

Juliet turned to the driver who was hanging on his car door, watching them. His radio was blaring out a rock number. "Turn it up!" called Juliet. The driver continued to stare in astonishment at the whirling spiral of light behind them. "The music," laughed Juliet. "Turn it up louder!"

595

"This isn't right," said Tracey Caffney. She had begun to walk forward, veering towards the last terraced house, perhaps a hundred yards from where they stood. "This can't be right."

"What do you mean?" Annie stopped her with a hand on her shoulder. "We're back and we're safe. On the outskirts of Edmonville somewhere, away from the ruins."

"No." Tracey shook her head. "This isn't right at all. Not at all."

Her attention was fixed on the end house. There was a ragged fence there. Parked beside it was a Ford Cortina, raised on bricks, its wheels missing. There was a garden, overgrown with weeds. One of the windows in the front of the house had been broken and cardboard had been Sellotaped over the gap.

"Take it easy," said Lisa. "You're back, and you're safe . . . "

"These houses shouldn't be here," said Tracey in a trembling voice. "When the earthquake hit us, we were lucky to get out alive. That's our council house on the end, there. The roof caved in. All the houses on this side fell apart. There was just a pile of rubble, that's all. There were people all around here. Lying in the street. Hurt and dying. Mrs. Rogers was lying just there. She'd been killed by her own chimney falling. This isn't right at all. These houses haven't been touched. It's like the earthquake never happened . . . "

The door in the end house suddenly opened.

"Oh, good *Christ*," exclaimed Annie, recoiling. She was the first to see who was framed in the door.

"What's wrong?" Jay pushed forward, and halted in alarm.

Henry Caffney was standing in the doorway, stripped to the waist. No red sweatband. But it was the same man.

"What is it?" came another hateful voice from deep inside the house. "*Who* is it?"

"Daddie-Paul Caffney . . . ?" Jay could only stare.

Henry saw Tracey as she pushed forward, and his jaw dropped. He took a step forward, staring at his sister, then looked back in the house.

"You're . . . you're never going to believe this, Tracey," he said to someone inside the house. "You're just not going to fucking *believe* this!"

Horrified, Tracey had frozen, her hands to her mouth.

She took a step back when she heard the next voice coming from inside.

"Stop bothering me, Henry. Whatever's happening, just sort it out. I'm busy."

It was her *own* voice.

"Oh no," said Tracey. "Oh no, no, no . . . "

"Come and see this!" Henry said back into the house. "You got a fucking twin out here."

"What's happening, Jay?" Juliet was suddenly at his side, hand on his shoulder.

Jay could only shake his head and look.

And suddenly Tracey Caffney was standing in that doorway, next to her elder brother, staring out at the Tracey Caffney standing with the strangers who had suddenly appeared from the swirling light in front of their house.

They stared at each other in shock.

"I thought . . . " The Tracey standing beside Jay and the others dropped her hands to her side. "I thought I'd got away." She was talking directly to her twin now, as the other Tracey stepped out of the house, eyes wide. "I thought it was all over, and that I'd never have to live like that again."

Tracey's twin looked back at Henry once. Fear had come into her expression now. Slowly, she began to walk towards her.

"I thought I'd got away!" cried Tracey, suddenly throwing wide her arms and running towards her other half.

There was no sense in it, but now the other Tracey was running from Henry, her own arms held wide to take this strange and frightening twin into her embrace.

The air began to vibrate.

It was as if someone had switched on an enormous generator

nearby. They could feel the vibration in the ground beneath them; could somehow feel the very air stretching.

"Look out!" yelled Jay instinctively, pulling Juliet back as the others cowered.

The two Tracey Caffneys flung themselves into an embrace.

And the resultant detonation blew in all the windows of the terraced houses.

Jay and Juliet whirled back into the others, the blast throwing everyone to the grass. Henry Caffney vanished from the doorway, hurled back into the house. The two boys were flung from their bicycles, one of the bikes spinning and wobbling across the road. The man by the car fell back inside, the door banging against his legs, the entire vehicle rocking on its suspension. Slates began to slither and slide from the roofs. Birds flew in panic from the nearby trees, scattering wildly in the sky. Burglar alarms began going off all over the council estate, a grim reminder of the first days in New Edmonville after the quake had hit.

And when Jay and the others looked back, the two Tracey Caffneys had gone.

There was no evidence that they had ever been there.

Just a blackened, scorched mark on the grass where they had met in that last embrace.

"What happened?" Candy was clinging tight to Alex, still unsure of whether any of this was real; still desperately worried that Alex might vanish like a dream. "What *happened*?"

"What happened, Henry?" echoed Daddie-Paul's hated voice from inside the house. Suddenly, the door slammed shut. Henry had kicked it closed in panic.

"Oh my God," said Annie. "I think I see." She helped Lisa and Robin to stand.

"What do you see?" Jay stared at the blackened patch as if the answers might be written there. "What the *hell* is going on?"

"Positive and negative," said Annie in a dull, flat voice,

thinking aloud. "Different realities, like Gordon said. Oh God, we're not *meant* to be here at all."

"Annie," begged Lisa. "*Please?*"

"Don't you see?" said Annie. "It's like Gordon said. There are different realities all overlapping one another. I've read something about it before. The theory that there are dozens, maybe hundreds or thousands, of different realities, all overlaid on top of each other. Maybe dozens of Edmonvilles, hundreds of Lisas, thousands of Robins. All going off in different directions, depending on the different choices that people make, that circumstances dictate. Gordon just didn't know everything that psychic earthquake did when it hit Edmonville, otherwise he would have told us. He couldn't have *known*!"

"Annie, you've got to make better sense than that," said Alex. "Something bad is happening here, and we need to know."

"We're still here," Annie went on. "We never left. Edmonville is still in one piece. There are no ruins, no dead people. No great big gaping hole in the ground where Edmonville used to be before it was ripped out of the earth and transported to the Vorla's No-Place. It's all still here. Somewhere out there, in Edmonville, *we're* all still here, as if nothing ever happened . . . because nothing *did* happen."

They were silent then, all looking at each other and still not comprehending as the burglar alarms continued to ring all over the council estate. Now people were beginning to emerge in shock from the terraced houses, carefully picking their way over the glass from shattered windows, carefully edging open their doors. Somewhere, a baby was howling.

"Reality was *split*," Annie went on. "Somehow that quake warped two realities. One of those realities was *us*—and Edmonville itself. We were all ripped away, and transported to that other reality, where the Vorla is. But there's an Edmonville that was never hit by a psychic earthquake. That Edmonville is right *here*! And in this Edmonville, the earthquake just never happened! And our other selves are still here, still living our lives the way we used to live. Still going about our business as if nothing ever happened, because here—*now*—nothing has happened. We're not supposed to be here. Tracey coming into contact with her other self in this other reality was like positive meeting negative. Matter meeting antimatter. They *cancelled each other out!*"

"Oh Christ," said Alex, understanding at last.

"We can never go back home," said Alex. "We don't belong here anymore."

"Maybe . . . " Candy was fighting to come to terms with it all. "Maybe . . . we could just move away. Never come into contact with our other selves. Start all over again somewhere else in the country. Maybe somewhere else in the world."

"This isn't our world any longer," said Annie. "Whether we meet our other selves or not, I think we wouldn't survive here. We don't belong. We would all die."

There was no way anyone could be sure that was true. But somehow Annie's words contained a fundamental truth that instinctively no one could deny.

"What are we going to do?" asked Candy hopelessly.

Jay took Juliet's hands and looked back at the whirling vortex. It had shrunk to a portal no bigger than ten feet wide, ten feet tall. The wind that plucked at them no longer had the strength it did before, but the suction was still there. In moments, it would dwindle, shrink and be gone forever.

"What *can* we do?" said Jay simply. "We're going home."

They followed his gaze, into the vortex.

No one had to ask him what he meant.

Juliet squeezed his hand, then held her hand out to Annie.

Annie took it, and held her hand out for Lisa and Robin.

Alex and Candy completed the chain.

Silently, one by one, they stepped back into the shrinking vortex of spinning light.

The kids on the other side of the street, bicycles recovered, stared in awe as the luminous whirlpool shrank to the size of a man's head. The man in the car yanked the gear-stick into reverse and screeched away, back down the street, convinced that there was going to be another explosion.

Within the Caffney house, a hated voice yelled: "Tracey? Where the hell *are* you, girl? Henry, get the fuck off your back and open the door! Henry . . . ?"

The spinning ball of light snapped out of existence.

Overhead, the birds wheeled and circled in the sky, still alarmed at the vibrations in the air. The burglar alarms whined on and on, the baby competing for attention.

On the grass outside the terraced houses, there was only a blackened patch of grass.

And no sign that anyone—anyone at all—had ever been there.

| **THE JOURNAL OF JAY O'CONNOR: EPILOGUE**

I'M SITTING ON THE EDGE OF THE CHASM, NOT so far from the place we called the Rendezvous. It was the place that in due course we all called home after the quake hit; the place where we clung together, and planned together, and defied the Vorla together. It's burned out now courtesy of the Caffneys, and we've spent some time wondering whether we should rebuild it, make it habitable again. There are lots of other places we could find to repair; other places with only minimum structural damage—but the Rendezvous is so special to us, despite the horrors we endured, we're reluctant to abandon it. Alex seems keen to give it a try. I don't know. Maybe we will, maybe we won't. Time will tell.

Time.

That's what we have lots of here.

All the time in the world.

I'm dictating onto the last of a dozen tapes or so, putting these last thoughts down. There's so much to be done.

I'm looking down into the Chasm, and still can't believe that I was down there and that I was able to climb out. Maybe in another reality I didn't. But I won't go into all that, because it can do your head in the more you think about it. All I know is that once the Chasm was a thing to be feared. All of mankind's evil, its hatred, its insanity, was down there. Thousands and thousands of years worth of pure Evil, generated by mankind; the pure evil *energy* of it somehow transported here and dumped into that pit. The sum total of all our Evil, all brewed into that great black sea. It tried to destroy us, and we denied it. More than anything, it wanted us to fear it.

But for now, we needn't fear it. Not for a long, long time anyway.

Because it's gone.

Lisa felt it first.

She brought us to the edge, just here, shortly after we returned. We stood in a line, holding hands, and we knew— just *knew*—that the Vorla had been destroyed. Her parents had drummed religious education into her head when she was a kid; managed to put her off for life. But she still remembers a lot of those verses; knew what the Vorla was trying to do when it made us see its false Four Horsemen of the Apocalypse. She used one of the verses then, as we looked down into the abyss and knew that the Vorla had been destroyed. From Revelations.

"Then I saw what seemed to be a sea of glass mixed with fire. I also saw those who had won victory over the beast and its image. And I saw a new heaven and a new earth: for the first heaven and the first earth were passed away; and there was no more sea."

Hundreds, maybe thousands of tons of burning fuel spewed out from that petrol plant and down into the Chasm. We saw great waves of the Vorla screaming and burning like tar. The liquid fire that gushed down there must have ignited the Black Stuff, burned it out, scoured it from the Chasm. It can't rise out of the abyss again to attack us; can't further its plans to create its obscene New Society; can't torture or maim or inflict agonies on the survivors here.

But that doesn't mean we're free of it forever.

It took thousands, maybe millions of years for the Vorla to grow to that size; took it all that time to form what Lisa calls a hideous "collective consciousness." And the process won't stop now. Somewhere deep down in the Chasm, maybe the first glistening-black pools of it are forming again. With each murder, each rape, each violent crime, another thin trickle of Black Stuff will be dripping in the darkness. With each act of malice, each act of greed, or envy, or ill-will, perhaps those thin streams will be reaching out for each other in the cracks of the cliff face. How many hundreds of years before it begins its task again? How many thousands of years before it regains its first glimmerings of "collective consciousness" once more?

Maybe everyone will have a change of heart in the "real world"?

Maybe they'll all start being kind to each other; maybe there'll be a spiritual revolution and they'll be able to eradicate all evil acts forever; maybe that evil energy will just stop coming over here, and won't be dumped down there in the Chasm anymore?

Big maybe.

Or maybe we'll be the new caretakers of the Vorla. Maybe we'll find a way to stop it growing down there. Maybe . . . just maybe . . . we'll even find a way to send it *back* where it comes from.

In the meantime, we've got the chance of a new beginning here. No threat from the Chasm, and no Caffneys trying to build a new society for the Vorla. The first task is a big one. There are other survivors out there somewhere on the peaks and crags of New Edmonville. If the Caffneys could build bridges between those plateaus, then we can do it as well. I'm hoping that those kids managed to survive the petrol-plant fire. I've a feeling that most of them did, and they're still out there. We've got to find them, show them how wrong the Vorla was; help them make a new start. There's one kid in particular who I've just got to find.

I have to find Paulie, the Crying Kid.

He's been on my mind a lot, from the very beginning. He

saved my life when the Caffneys threw me into the Chasm, and I can still see his face up there on the wooden platform as I fell into the pit; that face getting smaller and smaller as the darkness swallowed me up. I can't get rid of the feeling that he's so like me when I was a kid. Some secret part of me still wonders if the Crying Kid *is* me, when I was younger. I know that doesn't make sense, but I can't get rid of the feeling. I need to find him again; need to make sure he's okay. Just how he ended up on the other side of the city, with the Caffneys, is anybody's guess. Lots of mysteries out there, all waiting to be tied up. It's up to us now to create that new society, our way.

No sign of Gordon since our return.

He must still be in that in-between place, with the Cherubim. Maybe he doesn't know that we're back. Or perhaps he's just biding his time; getting more answers to the great mysteries that are all around us in the Realm of the Chasm. Who knows? Maybe he's finding out the Meaning of Life. One day soon, he'll be back. I know it. When he does, we'll . . .

"Jay?"

"Oh . . . Juliet."

"What are you doing?"

"You mean this? It's a dictating machine. I've been using it these past few weeks, talking to it, getting my head around everything that we've been through."

"Have you got any of the answers?"

"One big answer to my problems. She's standing here with me now, right on the edge of the Chasm. How are the others?"

"They're good. Better than good. I've got great good news."

"There's a fleet of rescue helicopters on the way, after all?"

"Better than that. Candy's pregnant."

"God . . . she's sure?"

"Definite."

"Damon's, or Alex's?"

"She doesn't know."

"How is Alex taking it?"

"He says he doesn't care. I've never seen them like this before, Jay. They look so . . . so damned happy."

"So we're going to have a first-born in New Edmonville? The first real new citizen of our new society."

"We should change the name. This isn't Edmonville, or New Edmonville."

"So what should we call it?"

"Eden."

"Eden? You mean like in the Bible?"

"Yes, except we've already thrown the serpent out of this garden."

"And maybe we can keep it out."

"I'm sorry . . . I interrupted you. With the tape, I mean."

"No you didn't. You're just in time."

"For what?"

"Come here, love. Sit beside me. This is nearly done . . . "

So I'm nearly at the end of this last tape; the batteries are running down.

Since the quake, we've all had our fair share of death and horror and nightmarish things that should have sent us mad. But we've made it through and, as a group, we're closer than family now. We've got a huge task ahead of us. Find the other survivors, find those kids. Begin again, create a new society. Keep a watchful eye on the Chasm. Funny thing. I started out as a caretaker cleaning up other people's mess. Now I'm doing the same sort of thing here. Me and the others; caretaking the Chasm, watching to make sure that mankind's mess doesn't start acting up again. But like I say, we—or whoever comes after us—should worry about that in a thousand years' time or so.

But do you want to know something? I'm glad I'm here. I'm glad that we didn't get back. I'm glad that we've got a chance for this New Beginning, glad for the chance to start again and avoid all the old ways that have been screwing people up ever since we came out of the trees and started living in caves. We don't have to make the same old mistakes here. We've got the chance to make it so much *better*.

There's another reason why I'm glad we're here.

I had a dream last night.

In the dream, I was back in Edmonville. The earthquake had never happened, and I was on my way to work. I was walking down Wady Street, steeling myself for another day under Stafford the head teacher's lash; not much else to look forward to but another night of drunken oblivion with Fritzy and the others in The Fallen Oak. There was a woman on the other side of the street, heading in the opposite direction. Long blonde hair, dark suit. She was the most beautiful woman I'd ever seen. It was Juliet.

She looked at me as we passed, and looked away.

I looked at her, and moved on.

In the sky overhead there was a rumble of thunder.

A little further on, I looked back to watch her figure vanish in the distance. Maybe she had an appointment with Trevor Blake.

I knew then that in that existence we never met and we never fell in love.

We both went on with our lives, following them through to whatever end fate might have in store for us. Something tells me that they wouldn't be happy-ever-afters.

Want to know something else? I don't think that was a dream at all. I think I was seeing something that was really happening in the Edmonville we'd come from.

And that's why I'm glad I'm here.

Because Juliet and I are together.

Because of it, I know I'm a better man than the other Jay O'Connor in that other existence. I've found something here with Juliet that I never could have believed possible in my other life. And each day that passes, I thank my lucky stars for it.

I'm standing now, ready to finish.

Once, I thought I'd keep these tapes as a reminder of how it all began. But we don't need this record to remind ourselves of the pain and the death and the blood that's been spilled here in . . . in Eden. We don't need to remember the old ways. We just need to go on. Find the survivors, heal the wounds, and make our New Beginning. That's why, when I've finished dictating, I'm going to throw this tape machine and my half-dozen tapes into the Chasm.

Juliet's pulling at my sleeve . . . and there's a look of joy on her face. She's pointing, and I'm looking and . . . Christ!

It's Gordon!

He's walking across the grass towards us, that guitar over his shoulder. Playing the harmonica and with a smile on his face that says he's got an *awful* lot to tell us. There are birds overhead. *Birds!* No . . . not birds . . . they've got wings, but they're not birds. God, I can hardly believe it.

So much to do.

But lots of time to do it.

And by God, this time we'll try and get it *right*.

ABOUT THE AUTHOR

Stephen Laws is a full-time novelist, born in Newcastle upon Tyne. He lives and works in his birthplace. The author of eleven novels, numerous short stories and novellas (collected in *The Midnight Man*),he is also a columnist, reviewer, film festival interviewer, pianist, actor and recipient of a number of awards.